Praise for Maeve Binchy's

CHESTNUT STREET

"Maeve Binchy and the short story [are] a perfect match. . . . Witty. . . . Heartbreaking. . . . Remind[s] readers why Maeve Binchy was one of the most beloved writers this country has produced." —*The Irish Times*

"Delightful. . . . Poignant. . . . The more you read, the more you want to read." —*BookPage*

"[An] extraordinary look at ordinary people as they struggle with family relationships, romances gone awry, and the possibility for a better future. . . . One finds here insightful observations about human nature—all with Binchy's thoughtful and loving touch that will be sorely missed." —*Publishers Weekly*

"This set of previously unpublished linked short stories will warm the hearts of fans everywhere." —*Library Journal*

"Binchy was well known for creating realistic characters who interact in ordinary ways, in ordinary places. . . . Her many fans are sure to line up to read this." —*Booklist*

Maeve Binchy

CHESTNUT STREET

Maeve Binchy is the author of *Maeve's Times: In Her Own Words* and many bestselling novels, including *A Week in Winter*, *Minding Frankie*, *Heart and Soul*, *Whitethorn Woods*, *Circle of Friends*, and *Tara Road*, which was an Oprah's Book Club selection. Married to Gordon Snell, she lived in Dalkey, Ireland, until her death in 2012.

www.maevebinchy.com

ALSO BY MAEVE BINCHY

CHESTNUT STREET

Maeve Binchy

ANCHOR BOOKS

A Division of Random House LLC

New York

FIRST ANCHOR BOOKS EDITION, FEBRUARY 2015

Copyright © 2014 by Gordon Snell

All rights reserved. Published in the United States by Anchor Books,
a division of Random House LLC, New York, a Penguin Random House company.
Originally published in hardcover in the United States by Alfred A. Knopf,
a division of Random House LLC, New York, in 2014.

Anchor Books and colophon are registered trademarks of Random House LLC.

Selected stories by Maeve Binchy first published in the following: "Star Sullivan"
as the first chapter of *Star Sullivan*, copyright © 2006 by Maeve Binchy (London:
Orion Books, 1996); "By the Time We Get to Clifden" in *The Return Journey*,
copyright © 1999, 2009 by Maeve Binchy (London: Orion Books, 1998);
"The Builders" as the first three chapters of *The Builders*, copyright © 2002 by
Maeve Binchy (Dublin: New Island Books, 2002); and "Fay's New Uncle" in
The Maeve Binchy Writers' Club, copyright © 2002 by Maeve Binchy
(New York: Anchor Books, 2010).

The Library of Congress has cataloged the Knopf edition as follows:
Binchy, Maeve.
Chestnut Street / Maeve Binchy. — First Edition.
pages cm
1. Families—Fiction.   2. Domestic fiction.   I. Title.
PR6052.I7728C53 2014   823'.914—dc23   2013041009

Anchor Books Trade Paperback ISBN: 978-0-8041-7008-6
eBook ISBN: 978-0-385-35186-7

Book design by Betty Lew

www.anchorbooks.com

Printed in the United States of America
10 9 8 7 6 5 4 3 2 1

CONTENTS

{ CONTENTS }

The places Maeve created in her novels and stories—Knockglen, Castlebay, Mountfern, and so many others—became just as real for her readers as those of the real Ireland. In fact the Irish Tourist Board often had to explain to visitors that they couldn't actually get on a bus or train to go and see them.

Chestnut Street, too, is fictional, but the Dublin portrayed there is very real: a city changing over the years in ways that come vividly to life in these stories of its residents and their families.

Maeve wrote the stories over several decades, reflecting the city and people of the moment—always with the idea of one day making them into a collection with Chestnut Street as its center. I am very pleased with the way her editors have now gathered them together as she intended, to make this delightful new Maeve Binchy book *Chestnut Street*.

Gordon Snell

Dalkey, Ireland

CHESTNUT STREET

DOLLY'S MOTHER

It was all the harder because her mother had been so beautiful. If only Dolly's mother had been a round, bunlike woman, or a small wrinkled person, it might have been easier for Dolly, this business of growing up. But no, there were no consolations on that score. Mother was tall and willowy and had a smile that made other people smile too and a laugh that caused strangers to look up with pleasure. Mother always knew what to say and said it; Mother wore long lilac silk scarves so elegantly they seemed to flow with her when she walked. If Dolly tried to wear a scarf, either it looked like a bandage or else she got mistaken for a football fan. If you were square and solid and without color or grace, it was sometimes easy to hate Mother.

But only for a moment, and not real hate. Nobody could hate Mother, and certainly not the dumpy daughter that Mother treated like a princess. She always spoke of Dolly's fine points. Her lovely deep-green eyes. People will get lost in those eyes, Mother had said. Dolly doubted it—there was precious little sign of anyone looking into them for long enough to realize that they were green, let alone run the risk of sinking hopelessly into their depths. Mother always called on Father to admire Dolly's wonderful texture of hair. "Look," Mother would say excitedly. "Look at how thick it is and how healthy it is; we may well see the shampoo companies begging Doll to do advertisements for them." Father would look obediently and with some mild surprise as if he had been called to see a kingfisher that had just disappeared. He would nod eagerly to please his wife and daughter. Oh, yes, he would agree. A fine shock of hair, all right, no molting there.

Dolly would examine her dull brown hair without pleasure. The only thing to be said in its favor was that there was a lot of it. And that was what Mother had unerringly been able to identify and fasten on in her extravagant compliments.

All the girls at school loved Dolly's mother—she was so friendly they said, so interested in them. She remembered all their names. They loved coming round to the house on Chestnut Street on Saturday afternoons. Dolly's mother used to let them play with her old makeup. Ends of lipsticks, little, nearly empty pots of eye shadow, compacts almost worn away by dabbing. There was a big mirror with a good light where they could practice; all Dolly's mother insisted was that every trace of it be removed with cold cream and tissues before they went home. She managed to make them believe that this was what kept the skin healthy and fresh, and Dolly's friends enjoyed the cleansing almost as much as they had liked the painting of their young faces.

Dolly's friends. Were they really friends, she often wondered, or did they just like her because of Mother? At school they didn't make much of her. After class Dolly often sat alone while others went off arm in arm. She was never the center of any laughing crowd in the playground, nobody chose her to go shopping after school, she was usually one of the last to be picked for any team. Even poor Olive, who was fat and had thick, whirly round spectacles, often got picked before Dolly. If it hadn't been for Mother she might have sunk without trace in that school. She should be very, very grateful that, unlike almost everyone else around her, she had a parent who was universally approved and liked. She should be grateful, and she usually was. She was happiest playing with her cat.

Mother always baked a funny cake for the sale of work, not a big showy one that would embarrass you or a little mean one that would make you feel ashamed, but like the one covered in Smarties, or the one with nasturtium flowers on it and a cutting from a newspaper saying that they were safe to eat. Mother had lent marvelous things for the school play and hadn't complained when they got torn. Mother had asked Miss Power for the knitting pattern of her cardigan, and then had actually gone and knitted the thing, telling Miss Power that she had chosen a different color in case they looked like identical twins. Poor Miss Power, plain as a pikestaff and not willowy and lovely like Mother, had pinked with pleasure and had become nearer to human than any of them had ever seen her.

For Dolly's sixteenth birthday, Mother was making a marvelous production. And every step of the way she consulted her daughter.

"Now, you must tell me what you'd like and what the other girls do. There's nothing so silly as a mother getting it all wrong, and taking you to the pictures and McDonald's when that's far too young for you."

"You'd never get it wrong, Mother," Dolly said in a dead sort of voice.

"But of course I would, darling Doll. I'm a hundred years older than you and all your friends. I have ideas from the last century. That's why I'm relying on you to say what you want."

"You aren't a hundred years older than us." Dolly's tone was level. "You were twenty-three when I was born; you're not forty yet."

"Oh, but soon will be." Mother sighed and looked at her perfect face in the mirror. "Soon a wizened, stooped, eccentric old forty-year-old." She pealed with laughter and Dolly laughed too. The notion was so ridiculous.

"What did you do when you were sixteen?" Dolly asked, trying to put off the moment when she would have to say she didn't know how to stage the celebration, and was dreading it in any form.

"Oh, love, that was so long ago. And it was a Friday, so we all did what everyone did then—we watched *Ready, Steady, Go!* on the television, and we had sausages and a birthday cake and we played all the Beatles on my record player. And then we went to a coffee bar and drank cups of frothy coffee and giggled and everyone went home on the bus."

"It sounds lovely," Dolly said wistfully.

"Well, it was the Dark Ages," Mother admitted ruefully. "Nowadays things are much more advanced. I suppose you'll all want to go to a disco? What did the others do? Jenny's sixteen, Mary must be sixteen, Judy?" Mother looked at her brightly, listing the names of Dolly's friends, alert and interested. Caring that her daughter should not be left out of whatever was the scene.

"I think Jenny just went out to the pictures," Dolly said.

"Of course she had Nick—that's right." Dolly's mother nodded sagely. She was the confidante of all the girls.

"I don't know what Judy did." Dolly was mulish.

"But you must, darling. She's your friend."

"I still don't know."

Mother's face softened visibly. Dolly could see a change of approach. The note was soothing now. "Of course, of course, and let's not forget she may have done nothing at all. Or just had a family gathering. No, there's no reason why you should know."

Dolly felt worse than ever now. She was revealed to Mother as a person whose friends had celebrations without her, but as someone so pathetic that she had to give some kind of cringe-making party herself so as to buy their friendship. Dolly's heart was heavy. She knew her face looked heavy and sad as well. She wished she could smile for this bright and lovely mother who was trying to help her, who had always been there supporting and suggesting and admiring. But the smile wouldn't come to her face.

Mother would have every reason to play the martyr, to feel that her daughter was monstrously ungrateful. But Mother never behaved like that. Judy's mother was constantly saying that daughters were a scourge to the flesh and a torment to the soul. Jenny's mother was like a Special Branch officer, so suspicious was she of even the most innocent activities. Mary's mother looked like a medieval painting of a mourning Madonna; she seemed stooped under the weight of her responsibility for a teenage girl. Only Dolly's mother was full of hope and plans and enthusiasm. Wasn't it bad luck that when the cards were being given out she had been dealt dull old Dolly instead of someone more colorful and lively who could respond.

"Why are you so nice to me, Mother?" Dolly asked seriously. She really and truly wanted to know.

Mother's face showed hardly any surprise at the question. She answered it as cheerfully and with the same kind of smile that greeted almost everything.

"I'm not being nice, darling, I'm being ordinary . . . but it's your sixteenth birthday and that should be a happy day, something you'll remember . . . even if it's silly, like mine was. At least I remember it, and all our idiotic clothes and hairstyles. That's what I want you to have, a happy day."

Dolly thought for a moment. Every single one of the girls who had been to their house had praised Mother. They had all said she was like a marvelous big sister—you could tell her anything, she always understood.

"Mother, don't bother. Honestly. It won't *be* a happy day. There aren't any happy days. Honestly. Days just aren't happy like they were for you, like they are for you. I'm not complaining. It's just the way it is."

She willed her eyes not to fill with tears, she prayed for some understanding to come on her mother's face. What came was a look of great concern, but Dolly knew that it wasn't real understanding. It was just more of the same. Like it had always been.

Mother's words washed over her, reassurance, everyone feeling down when they were fifteen, being neither old nor young, more reassurances, soon everything would look rosy again, Dolly's beautiful green eyes would shine again, her lovely thick, shiny hair would fly about her as she raced off, full of excitement about life and all the adventures it held. . . . Dolly sat there glumly as her mother stroked her hand.

She looked down at Mother's long, thin white fingers with their perfect, long shell-pink nails, she saw Mother's rings, not very huge in themselves but making Mother's little hand seem still frailer by having to bear them. The hand stroked Dolly's square hands, with their bitten nails, their ink stains and the scratches from the blackberry bush.

Dolly knew that the fault was hers, Mother was so good; it was Dolly who was rotten. Rotten and ungiving to her core. Right to the base of her hard, square, unattractive heart.

Father often looked melancholy, Dolly thought, a little stooped and tired as he walked up the hill from the railway station carrying his briefcase, but as soon as he saw Mother he cheered up. She might wave to him from an upstairs window and then run lightly down the stairs to embrace him when he came in the door. She didn't peck at him; she threw both her arms around him and encircled him, briefcase, overcoat, evening paper and all. Or else she might be in the kitchen, where she would drop everything and run to him. Dolly saw how pleased and even slightly surprised he was each time. He was not given to such spontaneous gestures himself, but he responded like a flower opening to the sun. The worried look of the commuter tired after a day's work disappeared. Mother never laid any problems on him the moment he arrived. If there had been a burst pipe he heard about it later. Much later.

And so, as Dolly knew would happen, the subject of the sixteenth birthday was raised as an excitement, not a problem. Mother's eyes shone with the excitement of it. A girl turning sixteen—it was a symbol, a landmark, a milestone. It had to be marked. *What* would they do to make the day marvelous for Dolly?

Dolly saw Father's face become tender. Father too must know of other households where the mothers were not as Mother was here. Where there was strife about children having any kind of party. How blessed he was to have the single exception, to have married the only woman in the world who positively relished a celebration for teenage girls.

"Well, now." He beamed. "You're a lucky girl and there's no doubt about that, Dolly. Well, well, a sixteenth party no less."

"I don't mind if we can't afford it," Dolly began.

"Of course we can afford it. What else do we work for, your mother and I, except to be able to afford the odd little treat like this."

Again, Dolly found herself guiltily wondering, Could this possibly be true? Did Father go out that long journey to the faceless office and come back tired every evening so that he could afford birthday parties? Surely not. And Mother, who went to work mornings in a big florist shop, was it all for a nest egg so that they could have these kinds of treats? Dolly had always thought Mother liked being among the beautiful flowers, and having lunch with her friends there and getting tired flowers to take home, where they often came to life again. She thought that Father went to work because it was what men did. They stayed in the office and dealt with files. She realized she must be very stupid about a lot of things. No wonder she couldn't have these great conversations with people, like Mother did. Only the other day she had heard Mother talking to the postman about happiness. Imagine talking about something as huge as happiness to a man who came to deliver the letters. And he had seemed very interested and said that not enough people ever took those kind of things into consideration.

"Mother, I'm bad at knowing what people like and what they want. You are very good at it. What do *you* think my friends would like?"

Dolly felt about as low as she had ever felt. And who in the world would have an ounce of sympathy for her? A spoiled brat, is what they would say she was. A girl who was being offered everything and could accept nothing. Mother didn't know any of these thoughts. She was too busy being helpful. "What about a lunch?" she said suddenly.

"A Saturday lunch at the Grand Hotel—you could all dress up and you could have one bottle of wine between all of you, if you have lots and lots of mineral water. . . . You could order from the menu . . . choose what you like. . . . How about that?"

It had definite possibilities. It was so utterly different.

"Would you come with us?" Dolly asked.

"Nonsense, darling, your friends wouldn't want an old fogy like me . . ."

"Please, Mother," Dolly begged.

Mother said that since she would be working on Saturday, well she could wear a silly hat and just drop in and join them for a drink . . . or whatever.

Dolly's friends thought it was a great idea. Jenny said she would wear her new outfit and it would make Nick sick as a parrot to know she had been lunching at the Grand. Mary said she'd go and grab a look at the menu so they'd know what to order. Judy said there might be film scouts there or men who ran model agencies. They said Dolly's mother was a genius to have thought of it.

"How is it that your mother is so fabulous?" Jenny asked with interest.

"Meaning that I'm not," Dolly said.

"Oh, don't be so boring, Dolly," Jenny and Mary said together, walking away from her, and Dolly sat in the classroom wishing the world would end. Suddenly and in a big splash of sunset. There seemed to be no point in living in a place where it seemed like a good idea for your parents to pay huge money to take people out to lunch, people who accused you to your face of being boring. Miss Power came in and found her sitting there.

"Stop slouching, Dolly. Go out and get some fresh air, get some color in your cheeks, and, for heavens sake, don't come to school with a torn tunic and a ripped jumper. You can be sure your mother was never like that when she was your age."

"No, I'd say she was perfect then too." Dolly's voice was sour and hurt. The teacher looked after her and shook her head in disappointment.

Mother had arranged a hairdo at Lilian's and a manicure for the Saturday morning of the birthday lunch. Dolly hadn't wanted it, any more than she had wanted the voucher for the new outfit.

"It will be a disappointment, Mother," she had said. "Everything is."

Had Mother's eyes grown a little steely or did she imagine it?

"Shall I choose something for you to wear, then?" Mother had said. And of course she had found a lovely green exactly the color of Dolly's eyes, she had said, and it did fit, and the other girls loved it; they were being polite to her today, of course, because she *was* getting them taken to the Grand Hotel, Dolly realized. But still they did seem to think that she looked well. And her hair was shiny and her nails, though short, were pink and neat, and the girl had given her a thing to paint on that meant you couldn't bite them anymore.

The hotel manager had welcomed them warmly; the booking had been made in Dolly's name.

"And your lovely mother will be joining you later," he had said.

"Yes, she's working, you see," Dolly explained.

"Working?"

"In the flower shop," Dolly explained.

For some reason he found this amusing. He smiled and then quickly reassured her. "Of course she is. Wonderful woman, your mother. We see her from time to time here. Not often enough."

When Mother came in, it did appear as if everyone were admiring her. She seemed so excited by the group of girls that

she was joining . . . you would have thought it was the most glit-
tering gathering in the land, not four ill-at-ease teenagers lost in
a world of too much splendor. Suddenly the lunch looked up; a
very very little wine was allowed to toast the newly sixteen-year-
old. The girls felt grown up, and they felt as if they belonged.
Dolly saw them looking around more confidently now. The day
would be one they would all remember. Would she remember it?
she wondered to herself. Would she be able to recall it years and
years later, like Mother had about records and television programs
and coffee bars?

Mother had said that they should all take a little stroll downtown after lunch, see the musicians and dancers by the fountain.
She had a few things to do later—she'd leave them to their own
devices. Feeling adult and in charge of their own destinies, the
girls got their coats from the cloakroom.

Dolly had no coat, her soft green jacket and skirt was complete in itself. She waited while the others had gone to titivate still
further, and idly pushed open the door to the manager's office,
where Mother had gone to pay the bill personally. She wanted
to thank Mother, and thank her with warmth and say that it had
been great, and that she did like the green outfit. Mother and
the manager were standing very close. He had one arm around
Mother and with the other hand he was stroking Mother's face.
She was smiling at him very warmly.

Dolly managed to get back, but the door still stood open. She
sat down on one of the brocaded sofas in the hall.

In seconds they must have noticed the open door and they
came out, Mother looking flushed, as did the hotel manager.
Their fear of discovery took on a new horror when they saw the
girl sitting solidly on the sofa. At the same time the chattering
schoolmates arrived, so it was goodbyes and thank-yous and off
with Mother downtown for the action. Jenny, Judy and Mary
went ahead. Dolly walked thoughtfully with her mother.

"Why am I called Dolly?" she asked.

"Well, in order to please your father we called you Dorothy after his mother, but I never liked the name, and you were like a little doll." She had answered, as she would every question, simply and without guilt.

"Do you do everything to please other people to make them happy?"

Her mother looked at her for a moment.

"Yes, I think I do. I learned that early on: it makes the journey through life much simpler if you please other people."

"But it's not being honest to how you feel, is it?"

"Not always. No."

Dolly knew if she asked her about the hotel manager she would get an answer. But what would she ask? Do you love him? Are you going to leave Father and live with him? Do other men take you in their arms? Is that what you are going back to, what you meant when you said a few things to do?

And suddenly Dolly knew she would ask no questions. No questions at all. She knew that she would have to think about whether her mother's way was in fact the right way—life was short, why not smile, why not please people . . . people like her old mother-in-law, Dorothy, now long dead; like Miss Power at school, by knitting a cardigan; like Father, by running to the gate to meet him; like her lumpen, surly daughter, by giving her a birthday party.

And, as she linked Mother's arm to walk towards the fountain, Dolly knew with a shock that she would never forget her sixteenth birthday. It would always be there, frozen forever as the day she grew up. The day she realized that there were many ways to go, and Mother's was only one way. Not necessarily the right way, and not at all the wrong way. Just one of the many ways ahead.

IT'S ONLY A DAY

It was great the way they always found something to talk about. Schoolgirls in a small town. The nuns thought they talked about their careers, and plans for living a Christian life. Their parents thought they talked about getting good results in the Leaving Certificate. The boys in the Brothers thought Maura and Deirdre and Mary talked about clothes and records because that's all they ever seemed to be going on about whenever you came across a group of girls in their school uniforms.

But in fact what they talked about was love and marriage. In all their aspects. The love bit would naturally precede marriage. And there were all kinds of love—there was first love to consider, and false love, and love that was untrue, and love that was unreturned, and love that went through difficulties. But then it would all be crowned with marriage.

Maura and her friends Mary and Deirdre didn't talk much about love after marriage because, once you got there, then surely that was it. Then everything else would fall into place. Well, of course you were going to be happy ever after. What was the point of the whole thing if that wasn't the way it would turn out?

And wouldn't it be *great* to be married. Your own home—you

could come home whatever time you liked. And get up whatever time you liked. And eat whatever you liked. You could get chips seven nights a week if you wanted to. And people would be giving you presents; you got new things. Not pillows that generations had slept on, or saucepans that had the bottoms all black. Everything was shiny when you got married. Of course it would be great being married once you had fallen in love and he had fallen in love with you.

They were fourteen when they thought like this. When you thought the best bit would be being able to come home as late as you like.

When they were fifteen, Maura and Mary and Deirdre talked about the kind of people they would fall in love with, and the general view was that the pool wasn't nearly large enough to choose from; in fact, the choice was particularly limited once you looked around you. Few young women had ever been given such a poor field of exploration.

In films there were casts of thousands, in films handsome strangers rode into town. In real life there were the fellows from the Brothers, who would make a jeer and call you names. You couldn't love any of them.

When they were sixteen they got technical. The actual physical business of love, how it was done and the etiquette surrounding it all.

Mainly, they talked about the first night, because the first night of marriage would be the first night of making love also. You couldn't think of one without the other. Even in the modern up-to-date 1950s only a fool would do what poor Orla O'Connor had done. Her fellow had run off to England as soon as he heard the news. And there was Katy, who had to marry the eldest Murphy boy in such a hurry. Katy stayed at home and looked after her enormous baby, the one who was born prematurely after six months of marriage . . . and she never went out anywhere even though her husband drank like a fish until all hours. Well, he had married her, hadn't he? He had done his duty, faced up to it. He could hardly have a word said against him now. Katy wouldn't want to say a word against a husband who had stood by her at the time of her disgrace. No matter if he drank himself senseless from one end of the county to the other.

So these were awful warnings for Maura and her friends Mary and Deirdre. Stronger and more terrifying than a thousand warnings from the pulpit, school or home were the two living examples in their own hometown, the feckless Orla and the grateful, trapped Katy.

For Maura, Mary and Deirdre it was as clear as anything. There was nothing to be gained and everything to be lost by having a first night of sex or love or whatever it was that was separate from the first night of marriage.

As if acting in a play, they went over and over what would happen when they got to the hotel on the first night of the honeymoon. Presumably they would unpack, and maybe kiss a bit and say hadn't it all been a great day?

"Remember, you're married—you don't have to do anything like the unpacking or anything at all," Mary said excitedly.

"Yeah, but you'd need to get your clothes out of the cases; they'd be awful crushed for the honeymoon," said Deirdre, who was the best dressed of them.

"And you wouldn't want him to think that he'd married a slut or anything," said Maura, whose mother went in a lot for what people might say or think.

So they agreed that you would unpack and then change into something smart for dinner and you'd go down to the hotel dining room together and the waiter would call you Mr. and Mrs. And they all giggled at the thought of it, and then because you couldn't make the meal last forever, you'd come back upstairs and . . . and now there were different schools of thought.

Did you go down the corridor to the bathroom first and come

back and wait for the man to do the same, and if so, did you get into bed or did that look too eager? Or did it look stupid sitting on a chair?

Or did you let him go to the bathroom first, so that you could be even fresher and even more nonoffensive when the time arrived? That was a possibility . . . but then they had heard a story once of this couple where the man had been asleep by the time the girl got back from the bathroom, and she didn't know whether to wake him or not and it had all been terrible.

They wondered would it hurt, would it take a long time or a short time, they wondered did you say thank you, or did he say thank you, or maybe you both might say, That was wonderful!

They also speculated at great length about the actual wedding feast itself.

Mary was going to have the menu with the slice of melon and ginger to start instead of soup. It was a shilling dearer than the one with mushroom soup but it was very sophisticated.

Deirdre was going to have the soup because her people would be bound to choke on the ginger and embarrass her, and she was going to have an accordionist who would play during the meal to cover the silences, and then to drown the noisiness when people became somewhat livelier later on.

Maura wanted all the women at her wedding to wear hats. Big hats with brims and flowers and ribbons on them. Not small, close-to-the-head navy or wine-colored velour hats like older women wore at Mass, but big colored ones, straw or silky, dressy like you'd see in a film or a newsreel about a wedding or show-business people or royalty. And she wanted every man in the church to wear a flower in his buttonhole.

Mary said she was daft—who round here would dress up like that? Deirdre said they'd only think she was cracked and trying to ape the British aristocracy. Men would go in their good suits as usual and open the collars of their shirts and take off their ties after the second drink, the way they always had. Women would buy a costume and maybe a small matching hat but probably not, just a mantilla in the church and then nothing on the head. This garden-party thing was the stuff of dreams.

Maura feared it might be so, but she was also quick to criticize the melon and ginger and the permanently playing accordionist as pretty much creatures of fantasy as well.

And then they were seventeen, and they all went their ways, Deirdre to do nursing in Wales, and Mary to the tech to do a course in bookkeeping, and then to work in her parents' shop, and Maura to Dublin, where she did a secretarial course, and enrolled as a night student in UCD.

They all met every summer and they laughed and talked like the old days. Deirdre reported from Wales that everyone was sex-mad and that no one, literally no one, waited until the first night, and they made remarks like:

"Blodwyn's getting married."

"Oh, really—I didn't even know she was pregnant."

Mary and Maura listened in wonder to the tales of such a free and easy society.

Mary said that they could all say what they wanted to about Paudie Ryan, but his spots were gone now and he was a perfectly reasonable fellow.

"Paudie Ryan?" Maura and Deirdre chorused in disbelief. But Mary was unyielding. The other two had gone off to Wales and Dublin and left her. She had to go to the pictures with someone, for heaven's sake. Paudie Ryan's father owned the other grocery shop in the town. Maura and Deirdre sensed a merger might be in the air.

Maura's mother said that a wedding was indeed very much on the cards between Mary and Paudie. She nodded about it a lot with an approval that drove Maura mad.

"Very best thing for both of them. Very sensible of them. The right thing to do for their families, for their futures."

Her head seemed to be going up and down, nodding with pleasure like clockwork. Maura was incensed with rage.

"God Almighty, Mam, you're talking about them as if they were crowned heads of Europe . . ."

"I'm talking about them as two privately owned groceries with the threat of the supermarkets hanging over us all—why wouldn't we all be pleased?"

Maura knew there was little point in talking to her mother about love. It wasn't a subject that had much future in a conversation. In fact it always ended the same way, in a snort. "Ah, love. Love is the cause of many a downfall, let me tell you."

She never told her. And Maura didn't really want to know. It seemed to underline what she had always believed, which was that her own parents tolerated each other and lived in a state of barely contained neutrality, which they saw as their destiny.

Love certainly seemed to have little to do with what had brought them together, which appeared to have been her mother's dowry and her father's ability to run a hardware store. It wasn't anything she could discuss with her family. Maura's elder sister was a nun. Her big brother, as silent as her father, worked in the shop, and her young brother, Brendan, the unspeakable afterthought, twelve years younger than herself, was a nightmare.

As the years went on, Maura felt that her real life was in Dublin. She earned her living by typing people's theses and even manuscripts of their books. She met the kind of people that she would never have met at home. Professors, writers, people who often went into pubs in the middle of the day for hours and stayed up all night to write or study. People who didn't go to Mass; people who had companions rather than wives, friends rather than husbands.

She met people who worked in television and radio, who were actors and politicians, and found that they were all very normal and easy to talk to, and lots of them lived desperately racy lives and didn't go home to their own homes every night.

Maura pretended not to be shocked in the beginning and very soon she didn't have to pretend anymore; it was the sixties, after all, and even Ireland was changing.

She fell in love with a man who was married, but she said she couldn't see him anymore because it would break up his marriage and that wouldn't be fair. Maura noticed with rage that he had a series of other companions after her, and that his wife still appeared on his arm at premieres and cocktail parties. It made nonsense of this love-and-marriage thing. But maybe they had been very childish, she and her friends Mary and Deirdre, back in the awful, old-fashioned fifties.

After what seemed an endless courtship Mary eventually married Paudie Ryan, and Deirdre came home from Wales in a very short skirt that caused a lot of comment, and Paudie Ryan's awful sister, Kitty, was the bridesmaid. Kitty wore a particularly horrible pink, which pleased Maura; at least it meant that Mary had stayed true to some of her principles anyway—like decking out an enemy bridesmaid in the worst gear possible. And there were melon slices instead of soup.

Maura's desperate brother Brendan and his horrific friends kept asking Maura and Deirdre were they on the shelf now and would they like to play a game of Old Maid. That was bad enough but a lot of the older people were just as rude and intrusive.

"Time you two were settling down yourselves now," they would say, wagging their heads in a way that made Maura want to scream.

"Too choosy, that's what they are," said Maura's father gloomily.

"Wouldn't want to wait too long all the same," said Maura's mother.

"Is there any hardware shop in the neighborhood you'd like me to marry into, by any chance?" Maura snapped, and regretted it immediately.

"You could do worse," her mother said, mouth in a hard line.

Later on in the day, Deirdre whispered to Maura that she too might be getting married, but that David's people where Chapel and hated the whole idea of priests and it was all very problematic. They went to Mary's room as she was getting changed into her going-away outfit.

"Well, I'll be the first to know," she said excitedly.

"Know what?"

"About the first night," Mary said, as if it were obvious. It was the middle of the liberated sixties. Even the swinging sixties.

Deirdre, seven years in permissive Wales, looked aghast.

Maura, seven years in bohemian Dublin, with a total of three consummated romances to her record, looked at Mary in disbelief. But it was their friend's wedding day, so they recovered quickly. And they all giggled, as they had done ten years ago.

"Imagine," they said. "Imagine."

Maura found her family particularly trying that weekend of Mary's wedding. Her sister the nun was home from the convent, dying to know every detail of the ceremony, and had Mary promised to Obey. She had—good, good. There was a lot of nonsense talked about that these days, said her sister. The women's liberation people were only doing more harm than good.

Maura snapped at her that just because nuns took a vow of obedience, it didn't mean that half the human race, the female half, should do the same thing. Her sister's eyes looked hurt and pained, but Maura saw their mother making terrible facial gestures and signs behind her. It was as if to say, "Go easy on poor Maura—she's obviously very jealous of Mary getting married."

This annoyed her even more.

"What do all those antics mean, Mam?" she demanded.

"Oh, very touchy, very touchy indeed," said her mother.

Her elder brother said, "That friend of yours Deirdre is a bit of a goer—I'd say she's no better than she should be over in Wales," and Maura wanted to smash him into the ground. He had reached this view after feeling under Deirdre's short skirt and getting a knee in the groin as a response.

Her young brother, Brendan, who normally had a variety of songs to sing tunelessly to his unmusical strumming of a guitar, had only one song, and the chorus was "I'll die an old maid in the garret."

Her father, as usual, said nothing, had no views on any subject, and her mother's face was set in such hard disapproving lines it didn't look like a face anymore, it looked like a diagram.

Maura couldn't wait to get back to Dublin. To Dublin and to Larry. Larry, the *love* of her life. Maura hadn't told them anything at home about Larry, and she told Larry a fairly edited version of things at home. It wasn't that she was being secretive or deliberately trying to live two separate lives, pretending to be different things to different people, it was just that the vocabulary wasn't there. There weren't the words to say to her mother.

"Look, please don't worry about me. I'm not remotely jealous of poor Mary marrying that *ahmadahn* Paudie Ryan. I have a terrific fellow altogether in Dublin, and we're as good as living together, I'm in his flat so much and he's in mine, and it's all great."

She might as well tell her mother that Martians had arrived in the hardware shop with an order for a spaceship.

And even though she could talk about everything to Larry, and they got on so well on every level, she couldn't really explain her inquisitive mother, who automatically counted up to nine on her fingers when she heard of a pregnancy to check that it was all within the correct timescale. How could she tell Larry about her sister, the nun, with the earnest face, saying that the women's movement had a lot to answer for, or about her silent father, or her discontented brother making swipes and gropes at women because he was afraid of them. Or about Brendan, the evil-tempered spoiled brat who got away with pure murder.

The worlds would have to continue to live apart. Maura sighed as she got into her car to drive back to Dublin.

"I wonder would some men think driving a car was a bit fast," her mother said, having given the matter some thought.

"I wonder," Maura said, keeping her temper with difficulty by stamping a nightmarish grin on her face.

"It couldn't be that that's holding the men back," her mother speculated.

"Perhaps I should take the car into the square and burn it symbolically—would that do, do you think?" Maura offered, still smiling idiotically.

"Oh, wait till you end up like your aunt Anna—that'll soften your cough for you," said her mother.

Maura drove back to Dublin wondering had her mother ever even remotely loved the silent man in the hardware shop. Why had they had four children together, one of them at an age when people might have thought they were past that sort of thing. It was a mystery.

Larry cooked dinner for her. He told her that she looked beautiful when she was tired. He said he had another short story accepted. He said they should go to Greece for a holiday. He told her about the beautiful light out on the Greek islands. He told her he loved her. And she fell asleep in his arms.

Maura got the letter from Deirdre a few months later. She and David were getting married. David's father and brother loved fishing; if they could combine it with a week on a riverbank then they'd swallow the Catholic ceremony and come over to Ireland by car. Would Maura be the bridesmaid? She could wear whatever she liked, honestly, none of that caper of dressing her up in puce like Mary had done to poor Paudie's unfortunate sister. Please, would Maura do this for her—it would be just one day out of their lives, then they could go on living as they wanted to live. Forever.

Maura read the letter many times. Something in it had touched her. Deirdre, fast Deirdre, leading a liberated life in Wales, was going to give her parents the day they wanted so desperately, the day that would mark them out as respectable people in their community; they would marry off a daughter in the parish church in the local hotel, everyone would come and listen to them make their vows. Deirdre didn't need it; she had been living with David for two years, she would not be living back in her hometown afterwards, it wasn't as if she sought the neighbors' approval.

And this Welsh David was agreeing to it all, even if disguising it as a fishing holiday. Maura felt a pang. She felt very disloyal even allowing the thought to seep into her heart. She and Larry had been of the same mind since the start. Love did not need chains. Ceremony and ritual were in fact fences and padlocks. They were like saying to society, All right, we've promised in front of you all and now there's no getting out. You've seen us make the bargain so if one of us cheats on it, then the full force of public disapproval can come down.

Making public marriage vows with all the dead old words and the meaningless ritual was reducing love to a series of charadelike phrases.

Larry and Maura loved each other—of course they were forsaking all others, of course it was for richer and poorer and sickness and health. Larry had paid for the holiday in Greece out of his new contract; Maura hadn't left him when he got pneumonia—she had sat beside him until he got better.

Love wasn't a contract with small print entered into by two suspicious parties who each thought the other was going to rat on the deal.

Marriage made little of love.

Larry and Maura knew too many married people who lived according to the letter of the thing rather than the spirit of it. Their love would not be brought down like that.

So, because this was undoubtedly true, Maura felt guilty when she wondered why they couldn't give her mother and father the day, just one day, out of their lives. And her sister could come

down from the convent, and Brendan, well maybe she could bribe
Brendan to behave. But it went against everything they believed
in, so Maura put it firmly out of her head. She wrote to Deirdre
and said she would be honored to be the bridesmaid and would
wear a lemon-colored linen suit and big white hat with lemon
ribbons on it. Deirdre wrote back pleased and said that Maura
had always been a devil for hats even when she was a kid in the
convent.

"I'm dying to see you in the outfit," Larry said.

"I'll do a fashion parade for you before I go."

"Am I not coming with you?" he asked.

This startled Maura. Life had never been better for the two
of them. They lived almost entirely in Larry's flat on Chestnut
Street; since they had come back from Greece it seemed foolish
to be apart. Little by little she had moved in her clothes, her pictures, her books. They were getting to the point of subletting her
flat to someone else.

Everything Larry wrote was being published, and Maura's own
typing business had gone so well that she now had an office and
employed someone to help her.

Things were on an even keel—why did he upset them by
wanting to come to her hometown?

"You wouldn't like it. Too much ritual, feudal," she said.

"Well, you have to go through it for your friend; I'll come and
hold your hand."

He really didn't get it. He didn't realize what expectations his
visit would cause, what speculation, how he would be inquired
about, his motives questioned, his whereabouts checked and his
name brought into conversation forevermore.

It was different for him. Larry's mother was long dead, his
brothers and sisters scattered, his father a vague, reclusive man
who seemed mildly pleased to see his son, but never to worry
about him. How would he know the frenzied interest that his visit
would create.

But he was adamant.

"I love you, I want to see you up there at the top of the church all dressed in lemon and a big hat and everyone admiring you. Let me be there. I'll be so proud."

She looked at him in frustration. If he would be proud of her in lemon, why not in ivory in the real starring role; it was only a day, one day out of their lives.

It would get her mother off her back, the nuns in her sister's convent could cease their novenas, Mary, now the serene Mrs. Paudie Ryan, would stop telling her about some very nice commercial traveler who was about to settle down, her brother Brendan would not be able to ask her, as he did now with sickening regularity, whether the family was normal at all, one sister a nun, a brother a confirmed bachelor, the other sister an old maid.

She would ask him. She would propose to Larry. There and then. All he could say was no.

"Would we get married ourselves, do you think?" Maura heard herself say, through the roaring sound in her ears.

He didn't look shocked, he didn't look guilty or reproachful. He wasn't even slightly apologetic. He was just interested.

"What for?" he said.

"To tidy things up, sort of," she said lamely.

"Are you serious?"

"Half serious, yes."

"But I love you, you love me—what would we need it for?"

His much-loved face was honest and open. He was genuinely puzzled.

"There's a way," Maura began slowly, "that if you really loved me, and I believe you do, then you wouldn't mind going through one day of ritual and vows and rubbish, as we may see it, just to make other people contented."

"But it's our life!" cried Larry. "We've always said, believed that the world is the way it is because people did a whole lot of things without even thinking what they meant in order to please other people. That's what makes love lose its meaning."

"I know." She spoke from the heart.

She did know and she agreed with him. Real love had nothing to do with Deirdre pretending to David's family that it was all a fishing holiday, just so that Deirdre's family could sleep easy in their beds.

The next weekend she went home, she told her mother that she would be bringing a friend to stay for Deirdre's wedding.

"She'll have to share your room," Maura's mother said. "Your sister will be home for the weekend; you know how she loves a wedding."

"It's a man friend," Maura said and had the pleasure of watching her mother's face change color.

"Well, why in the Lord's name didn't you say so earlier, and we could have booked the hotel? Now it's full with all those Welsh people coming for the wedding."

"Can't the holy nun share with me? It's only a night."

"Maura, I'll thank you not to make fun of your sister and the vows she took—you know she can't share a room, not since she went into that nun's cell."

"God, Mam, it doesn't matter where he sleeps. He can sleep in the dining room, can't he?"

"He cannot. And tell me is he by way of being a boyfriend?"

"Mam, I'm twenty-five going on twenty-six—you don't call it that nowadays."

"What do you call it, might I ask?"

"A friend, like I said . . . Larry's a friend."

"It doesn't do getting your name up with a man like this and just telling people that he is a friend, and really I don't know what your father will say."

"I don't know what that expression means, 'getting your name up' with someone, and you and I know very well what my father will say; he will say nothing, as he has said for the past thirty and more years."

"You're a very difficult young woman, Maura. I'm not surprised that no man has seen fit to take you on."

"Mam, Larry is coming to Deirdre's wedding. I don't care whether he sleeps with you or with me or with the nun, but could we drop the lectures."

And later Larry said, "I'm looking forward to it all. And if there's anything I can do to help, you must let me know."

It was too late to say that the most helpful thing would be to stay in Dublin, so Maura smiled wanly.

"Entertain the Welsh," she said. "That might be the best help."

Maura and Larry drove down together. There was barely time for introductions before Maura left for Deirdre's house to get ready. Deirdre was very over–made up, her white lace dress a little loose around the waistline to hide the very good news that had been confirmed a couple of months ago.

"I hear you brought a fellow," she said as she put on her eye shadow.

"A sort of a fellow," Maura admitted, not daring to think about the conversations now taking place between her mother and Larry. "You look lovely, Deirdre."

But the bride had little time for compliments.

"Just pray that David's family stay good humored," she said. "You've never seen them when they glower; it's a terrible thing to see."

Deirdre had hired an accordionist, as she had planned to do all those years ago. He was a man with a very, very red face, and there was some doubt expressed about his staying power.

"Don't worry about him," Maura said to Deirdre. "He'll be fine when the time comes."

She didn't think it necessary to tell the bride about to depart for the church that the accordionist was on a high stool in the hotel already getting himself in the mood. His first few squawks were so disastrous that a shuffle of embarrassment began to ripple around the wedding party. Somewhere in the body of the dining room, Larry was quietly asking did anyone have a guitar, and to her horror, from the top table, Maura saw her lover and her poisonous young brother, Brendan, heading out together. No scenario could have been as bad as this. Minutes later, she saw in disbelief, Larry begin to strum and to sing in a very uncertain and shaky voice the first three lines of "Men of Harlech." As if by magic the Welsh chests swelled up and the hotel dining room echoed to the sounds of a male voice choir singing their hearts out. They barely paused to swallow the soup and roast chicken as they thundered through "The Ash Grove" and "We'll Keep a Welcome in the Hillsides." Larry kept "Bread of Heaven" till just before the wedding cake and the speeches. By this time the wedding was such a thundering success that David's family hardly wanted to go off fishing at all; they wanted to spend a week singing in this hotel.

Maura was not a serious drinker, but the strain had been rather a lot for her, and mercifully she was so reached by it all that she did not realize the sleeping arrangements involved Larry, the one and only great love of her life, sharing a room with her brother Brendan, the most smelly and horrible person in Ireland.

Maura slept a drunken, disturbed sleep and woke with an inexplicable thirst and a need for rehydration, unaware that Brendan had been filling Larry in on the situation. He thought Larry was one of the Welsh contingent. He made an attempt to explain Ireland to him. He told about the hardware shop, and how his father didn't speak much at home, but loved talking to farmers about tractors.

He told how his big brother didn't know how to get girls and was always making grabs at them, which they hated. How his eldest sister saw visions up in the convent, and how his other sister had missed the boat. He didn't know what boat, but there was some boat she should have caught somewhere, and then she would have got married like all her friends did, and all her mother's friends used to come to the house and sympathize because Maura had missed the boat.

Brendan said that he was going to be a famous guitarist himself and was very interested in the notion that he might learn a few basic chords and perhaps even read music one day.

Larry and Maura were leaving around lunchtime, Maura with an unaccustomed hangover, Larry with a new understanding about life in a small town.

Maura's mother clucked around the car.

"Will we be seeing you around again? I mean, will you and . . . er . . . Maura be coming back here together?" she asked, eyes darting from one face to the other.

Maura wanted to reach out from the car and, with all the strength that remained in her weak body, deliver a stinging blow to her mother's chin that would knock her senseless.

"He lives in Wales," said Brendan, amazed that people could be so stupid.

"Not all the time," Larry said diplomatically. "And if I were invited, I would love to come back here again and again and get to know you as I hope Maura and I will get to know each other too."

Maura looked at him weakly; this was worse than she had believed possible—now their expectations were really high. Three miles down the road he stopped and asked her to marry him.

"You're doing it out of pity," she said.

"No, I'm doing it because it's right," he said.

"Ask me later when I'm better," she said.

"No. Tell me now."

"It's only a day, one day out of our lives; yesterday wasn't bad."

"If you think that wedding day was good, you ain't seen nothing yet!"

He told her that he wanted the church full of people in big hats like the one she had worn.

It was only one of the many aspects of the dream they both shared.

FAY'S NEW UNCLE

Fay barely knew that she *had* an uncle. He hadn't come to her father's funeral, he never got in touch with her and her brother, Finbarr, about anything at all. He had not been mentioned by anyone in the family.

So it was a total surprise when she got the letter from a district nurse way at the other side of the city asking if Fay could become involved in the matter of her uncle, Mr. J. K. O'Brien of 28 Chestnut Street. Mr. O'Brien was, at present, in hospital and quite frail. He could be released only after a conference with a relative. Her name had been given as his only surviving relation.

At first Fay was about to say it was a mistake. She didn't know anyone in Chestnut Street, but then her name was O'Brien and on her mother and father's wedding certificate the best man's name had been written down as James Kenneth O'Brien. He could be her father's brother. But why get in contact now?

Fay was going to be twenty-five on her next birthday. What could explain the silence, coldness and distance of a quarter of a century? She would ask her own brother, Finbarr, but he was away. He worked as a steward on a liner and was often gone for months at a time.

"Don't get involved, Fay, I beg you," her friend Suzanne advised. "You're too kind, too easygoing. This old guy will want you to clean his house, wash his smalls, do his shopping, all in the name of family. But where was he when you needed him?"

"I didn't need him," Fay said.

"Yes you did, when they came and took the house from under you after your father died . . ."

"To be fair, there were a lot of debts and he hadn't paid the rent for a while," Fay said.

"Yeah, but a couple of hundred from Uncle James Kenneth would have helped."

"He might not have had it." Fay was defensive.

"If he lives in Chestnut Street he has it. Those houses are going up in value every day; remember that before you agree to do every hand's turn for him, Fay."

The girls had been friends since school. They worked side by side in a dry cleaner's and lived on dreams that one day two handsome, rich American men would come in to have their elegant suits pressed. Their eyes would meet the eyes of Fay and Suzanne and the next thing would be dinner, almost the next thing would be marriage and then there would be a life of ecstasy in Malibu.

But these men never turned up, so Suzanne and Fay shared a bed-sitter and saved some money every week to spend on a holiday in Ibiza in case the American movie men had taken their sharp suits there instead.

"I'll go and meet the nurse anyway," Fay said.

Nurse Williams was brisk and to the point. Mr. O'Brien had suffered a mild stroke; they needed to be sure that there was someone to keep an eye on him, to make sure that he took his medication, that he ate sensibly and looked after himself. Often it was a matter of post-stroke depression, and if this were to be avoided they would need to be sure that he wasn't left to wallow around on his own.

"I don't think you understand, Nurse. This isn't a loving extended family. I never saw the man in my life, and he never remembered me or my existence until he needed me."

"He remembered you and agreed that we get in touch only after a lot of probing on our part and a great deal of reassurance that you would not be put out. We told him it would only be a formality."

"And would it? Be only a formality, I mean?" Fay asked.

"No, to be honest, I think it would be more of a commitment, unless of course you could come to some arrangement with his neighbors."

"What are they like?"

"Well, Mr. O'Brien has bad luck in one way. The neighbors on either side are absentee landlords, people who own the property but rent their places, so the cast keeps changing. Some teenager down in Number Eighteen feeds his cat for him. I know that there's a nice, but fairly scatty, hippie girl nearby in Twenty-Six, and a rather earnest couple in Number Twenty-Five, but perhaps you could make further inquiries . . ."

"What do they call him? 'James'? 'Jim'? 'Kenneth'?" Fay asked.

"I'm afraid they call him 'Mr. O'Brien,' even us. It's what he wants," Nurse Williams said apologetically.

"Everyone?"

"Yes, everyone."

"Heigh-ho," said Fay.

"I'm Martin O'Brien's daughter, Fay," she said to the small man in the hospital bed.

"And where did he get a name like that for you?" the man said.

"He and my mother baptized me Mary Faith. I chose Fay."

"Huh," he said.

"And what do people call *you*?" she asked.

"You won't be here long enough for it to matter," the man said.

"Are you normally this charming to everyone or is it only because I am your brother's daughter that you're making a special effort with me?" Fay asked.

"Very droll, very smart arse," he said. "Like your mother."

"She needed to be both to survive without a penny piece from Martin O'Brien. If it had no sense of direction and four weak legs Martin O'Brien put the housekeeping money, the rent and the electricity on it. That was the system." Fay spoke without either bitterness or regret. It was the way things were.

"All I need is for you to sign me out—you can go your own way then."

"I'm sorry, but I have a very great sense of duty. I can't leave you alone to fall over and die."

"I haven't a notion of falling over and dying. I'm still a young man. I'm only seventy-four years of age, I'll have you know."

"You probably had no notion of having a minor stroke either. Can you let me have the keys? I'll go to your house with Nurse Williams and we'll see what has to be done."

"You're not getting your hands on the keys to my house . . ."

"Right, Mr. O'Brien, keep your keys, stay here, die in this hospital, let that child feed your cat till it dies. What do I care? I never gave you a day's thought in my life up to this, or you me. Why should things change now?"

"Are you normally as charming as this to everyone or is it only because I'm your father's brother?" he asked.

There was a hint of a smile on both of their faces. She held her hand out.

"The keys, Mr. O'Brien, then?"

"It's Jim, Mary Faith," he said sheepishly.

"It's Fay, Jim," she said and headed off for Chestnut Street.

———

"You'll have to be prepared for the house to be in a terrible state—sometimes they are." Nurse Williams had seen everything and knew it all.

"What do we do if it is?"

"Sanitation comes in if it's really terrible," Nurse Williams said, putting a handkerchief to her face as they opened the door of Number 28. But the place was fine, bare to the point of being sparse. There were few pictures on the walls, chairs that had never been comfortable and never been smart. A very small television set and a very big old-fashioned radio stood beside each other on a table. Folded newspapers were piled high on a stool. Pale, faded and many times washed tea towels were stretched out on the backs of chairs. There was no smell of food or decay.

A very small fridge held just butter and margarine. A kitchen cupboard held a lot of tins and packets.

J. K. O'Brien of 28 Chestnut Street, no matter how upwardly mobile his address, did not live high off the hog. Fay thought of the near-tenement where her mother had brought her and her brother up. It was very poor compared to this, but there was more life in every floorboard there than there was here.

What *had* the brothers quarreled over? Would Finbarr know? He was older—he might remember some row. Still, she must get down to the problem in hand.

"It's too big for one person, really. Would he be better to sell it and get a flat in sheltered accommodation?" Fay asked.

"Of course he'd be better doing that, but do you think he will?" Nurse Williams knew people held on to places. "No, he'll stay here until he drops."

"Should he live downstairs? He obviously doesn't use that sitting room at all, and he could put a shower in the downstairs cloakroom."

"He'll do nothing, Fay—we have to do it before we let him out."

"But who'd pay for it? He doesn't look as if he's got very much. I've got nothing at all . . ."

"If he let upstairs he'd get plenty, but then who'd come and live with him, a complainer like that?" Nurse Williams tried to work it out.

"What was his job before he retired?"

"He worked in the post office, I think it says on his records."

"He'd have to have a pension from that, so he'd be well able to afford the shower. Can we get someone in your outfit to put the money up for it first and then tell him he has to pay for it?"

"I'd say that would be best. I'll get on to it from my end," Nurse Williams said.

Mr. O'Brien was outraged when he came home and heard that he would have to pay for the shower.

"If you were an ordinary person, Jim, you'd have all that money back in a couple of months just by letting the upstairs as a flat. It would be paid in no time."

"But who would I have upstairs?" He sounded aggrieved and very annoyed.

"Who indeed? I can't think of anyone that would stay there for five minutes," Fay agreed.

Jim O'Brien was confused. "But didn't you and that bossy nurse just tell me that the upstairs could bring in a great income?"

"Yes, indeed it could, but only to someone normal, someone who didn't grizzle about everything as soon as the door opened."

"You've trapped me!" he cried.

"No, you see Nurse Williams and I thought you *were* normal; most people are. That was the mistake."

"Why did you think that?"

"Because we didn't *know* you, Jim, and how you are overinterested in everyone else's life and behavior and oversecretive about your own. You've told me something about every single person in this street, how Kevin and Phyllis across in Number Two were devoted to each other, how Lilian in Number Five supports the whole household, how Miss Mack went blind, how Mitzi in Number Twenty-Two had a romance outside her marriage years and years ago, how Dolly's mother overshadows her daughter over in Number Eighteen . . . ."

"Yes, but all things are true," he blustered.

"The thing is, however, that none of them know anything at all about *you*," Fay said. "They don't know where you came from, what you did as a living, how long you've been here. They didn't know I was a relation; they thought I was a social worker."

"It's none of their business," he grumbled.

"I agree, but I *was* asked in by the hospital to help them work out whether you could live on your own, so I have to do my job and find out for them."

"And what have you found out?" He was anxious even though he was hiding it.

"That you'll be much better off living on one floor, and that I'll leave you my phone number for emergencies and I will call to see you every month. They'll let you stay here, Jim." She gave him a grin.

"You've been very good in ways," he said. "Badly brought up, of course, no manners or anything, but I suppose that was *her* fault. But still you came when you were needed—I'll say that for you."

Fay looked at him for a long moment without saying anything. Then she spoke.

"I don't know what you have against my mother. Finbarr and I have nothing but good memories of her. She loved your brother; she said she knew he was a gambler when she married him so she only had herself to blame. She worked long, hard hours cleaning floors and stairways to keep food on our table and the rent paid."

"She was a vulgar woman who drank great big pints," J. K. O'Brien said, as if that settled it.

Fay looked at him in astonishment. "She worked her hands to the bone cleaning in order to pay for what she called her 'entertainment,' which was to take my father out on a Saturday and buy them two pints each in the local pub. She did that to the week before she died. And he died a year later of a broken heart. Whatever you heard bad of her it wasn't from your brother."

He was silent now.

"So, have we finished with each other now for a month, Jim? My telephone number at work is here on this piece of paper. I don't have a phone at home, nor a mobile."

"Where's home?" he asked suddenly.

The first question he had asked about her during all the days of negotiation about him and his health, his house and his future.

"I share a bed-sitter with my friend Suzanne, who works with me."

"How much does it cost?" he asked.

She told him.

"Is it very smart?" he asked.

"No, it's quite shabby, as it happens."

"So, would you and Suzanne like to come and live here at a cheaper rent?" he offered.

Fay paused. "At no rent at all and it's a deal," she said.

"At *no* rent?"

"We'd keep an eye on you, do your shopping, tidy up the garden and cook you Sunday lunch every week," she offered.

"I could get a fortune for upstairs. You and that bossy nurse as good as said so," he complained.

Fay shrugged. "You *could* get a fortune, if you were normal, Jim."

"Yes, well that's as maybe. And what do you and this Suzanne want to do with your lives? Or do you intend to go on working in this place forever?"

"What place, Jim?"

"The place you work in, a laundry or something, isn't it?"

He had almost remembered.

"A dry cleaner's, but you were near."

"Well?"

"Well, we hope we'll meet some gorgeous fellows who will marry us and take us away from all that steam and checking in dirty garments." Fay managed a cheerful smile as she always did when talking about what had to be endured.

"Where do you go to meet these people?" he asked, interested.

"We don't meet them all that much, Jim. We *think* about meeting them or we meet fellows who fall short of the mark in Ibiza every May."

"And what would you need to meet nice smart fellows?" He seemed genuinely interested.

"I don't know, maybe to be a bit smarter ourselves, brighter, you know, better educated, coming from a nicer kind of background, but since we can't be that, then we have to hope to be lively and knock them out that way!"

"Seriously, would you like to live upstairs?"

"Only if there's no rent, Jim, because if you're not going to be a normal landlord, we can't be normal tenants."

"But the cost of the bathroom downstairs?" he wailed.

"Will add hugely to the value of this house, Jim."

"When can you move in?" he asked.

"Suzanne will have to come and vet you first," she said.

"No, Fay, no. We're going to be clipping his toenails, feeding him porridge. *No!*"

"We have a fantastic flat for free—come and see it."

"Nothing's for free. We know this."

"It's a respectable address; fellows will think we are something if we live in Chestnut Street rather than four flights up over a fast-food place. And we have a room each—think of what that might mean."

"Will you swear you won't let him interfere in our lives or tell us long boring stories about the past?"

"I swear, because it will be easy," Fay said.

They established house rules. The girls could come in and go straight upstairs without having to come in and check with Jim O'Brien each time. They were never going to tell him what time they were going out or coming back. They would make no loud noise upstairs or have parties without permission. They would cook a four-course Sunday lunch for him every week and invite a neighbor or two on each occasion so as to set up a social life for him.

It worked amazingly well.

It meant that Jim O'Brien got invitations out to other houses, which had never happened before. He came home full of tales about the various households he visited.

The girls suggested that they all buy, between the three of them, a washing machine and a dryer, and everyone learned to use it. They bought a clothes rail and took lots of wire hangers from the dry cleaner's.

"Don't iron his shirts," Suzanne pleaded, so Fay taught him how to do them himself.

A couple of months later they bought a freezer between them. Jim liked that and made neat little labels for everything they put in.

He asked them about their lives. He was interested in Fay's brother, Finbarr, the oceangoing steward.

"Have you met him?" he asked Suzanne.

"No, he's never really at home, you see. What a life!" She sighed.

"He'll come home one day; they all do. Home and settle. You might fancy him, you know."

"Why should I?"

"Well, if you're a pal of his sister that means you have something in common—that's how marriages often start."

"If you knew so much, Jim, why didn't you marry?"

"I was stupid, kept thinking I had to have a nest egg, and by the time I did have a proper nest egg, I was old and set in my ways and it was no use to me," he said.

Jim O'Brien had a disconcerting habit of saying something simple and vulnerable when they expected him to be sour and putting people down.

When Finbarr came home next, Jim suggested that he form part of the Sunday lunch.

"Why did we never meet you when we were young, Jim?" Finbarr asked casually as they were doing the washing up.

"I was half cracked and took a dislike to your mother, quite wrongly as it turned out," Jim said.

"Oh, why do you think you did that?" Finbarr asked.

"Young fellas are eejits. Look at you yourself now and that gorgeous girl under your very nose and you don't even notice her," Jim said.

"What gorgeous girl?"

"Suzanne."

Finbarr nodded. "She's a fine girl, all right."

"So what are you drying dishes with me for? Why aren't you asking her out?" Jim wanted to know.

"I'll kill him, your wonderful uncle. Kill him with my bare hands," Suzanne hissed in the next room.

Fay laughed. "Ah, go on, Suzanne—someone has to light a fire under him."

"Yeah, wait until he does something heavy trying to get a fellow for you," Suzanne grumbled.

But she combed her hair and put on a little more lipstick, and when Finbarr suggested a walk along the canal she was ready to show him the way.

"What are you doing for Christmas Day, Fay?" her uncle asked when the others were gone and the two of them sat and had a cup of tea together to end the Sunday ceremony.

She was surprised. "Why do you ask?"

"Well, it's not going to be a Sunday, you see, and I wonder would our arrangement extend to us having a Christmas dinner together? I have enjoyed these Sunday lunches, you know. It's worked out from my point of view very well."

"Sure, of course, Jim."

"And you, do you think the arrangement is working?" He seemed anxious for her approval.

"Certainly I do."

"But you'd like a fellow of your own?" Now he sounded even more anxious.

"Well someday, yes, Jim, not today necessarily."

"But you're not rushing away? Not this minute?"

"No, of course not, now that you've fixed my brother up with Suzanne, I'll sit on with you for a bit."

"Good."

They sat there amicably, and an hour later a man knocked on the door. He was Billy Young, a financial adviser. He seemed delighted to meet Fay. Her uncle had spoken about her a lot, and had said she was a rock of sense.

"You're very pretty for a rock of sense," he said admiringly.

"Thanks, Billy," Fay said.

"Well, I'll get back to being an adviser," Billy said with a grin that broke her heart.

———

She went up to her room and remembered that she had to call Nurse Williams tomorrow for the regular check about whether it had worked out well or not. Had it been a success?

She lay on her bed and looked out over Chestnut Street. It had been a success. How dull that looked when written on an official form.

A PROBLEM OF MY OWN

I was sick to death of those Fifth Form girls confiding in me.

"You're so understanding, miss," they would say in a treacly tone that always won me over. Of course I was understanding, nicer, more liberal than their parents, younger, more interested in them than the other teachers . . . no wonder they loved me. Full of good, hearty advice about everything.

"Well, if he didn't dance with you last night, Susie, perhaps he's got something else on his mind, exams maybe. No? He danced with other girls. I see—well, it could be that he hasn't the courage to ask you; boys can be shy too, you know. He's not shy—he's a bit of a showoff. I see. Well, perhaps that's an extreme form of nervousness. He's a teenager too, and we all show nervousness in different ways. Why don't you pretend that you don't mind at all, and dance with other people happily; if he sees you looking happy and relaxed, he might pluck up courage . . ." And then, weeks later: "I am glad it worked. No, don't thank me—it was only your own common sense . . ." And weeks later: "Well, I suppose boys change their minds the same way as girls do . . . No, Susie, I don't think that your heart is actually cracking; I think it would be very foolish to be a nun just now. I know it would show him, but think of all those years as a nun and the getting up early on cold mornings and the funny clothes you'd have to wear. Much wiser to be an academic—he'd be really pissed off over that."

And the same in the staff room. Never a problem of my own, always somebody else's. "I know, I know, Miss O'Brien, it *is* very hard, of course it is, but you know I get the feeling that Mr. Piazza would be more upset than relieved if you arrived at his house and told his wife everything. Oh, I do see your point about total honesty, but Mr. Piazza might have thought of that one evening as something more . . . well, not so much casual . . . but something lovely just to happen once, to be a beautiful memory. It would change from being a beautiful memory into a problem if you were to tell Mrs. Piazza about his having said he had loved you for years. No, don't cry, Miss O'Brien, please. I'm sure he did and does love you, but there are different degrees of love, especially to an Italian music master. I think his love for you is more the admiring-you-as-you-take-the-girls-out-to-hockey type of love than the leaving-his-wife-and-seven-children-and-renting-a-small-room-with-you sort."

When would I have a problem of my own? Not amongst my friends out of school either; they had too many that had to be dealt with first. There was Lisa, who had this white, drawn look for ages and we all knew she had some dark brooding secret, but while that's all everyone else was ever to know, I was the one who had to hear about the man in the bank who had discovered the foolproof way to transfer money out of other people's accounts into Lisa's, so that they could eventually have a small fortune and run away and live in a white house beside the sea on a Greek island and cook kebabs at night and drink wine and make love on the beach for the rest of their lives. It was a case of "Well, of course it sounds idyllic and we all have a right to happiness, and I know there is hellish inequality in the world and that grabbing what you can is one way of dealing with it, but you know those cases of people who are found out and who go to gaol. Well, certainly he's very clever and brilliant and fired by love and all that, but who exactly is he taking it from? I mean, won't somebody notice that they're being robbed? Oh, Lisa, stop crying. I didn't say he was a robber, I just said it's not without its pitfalls."

And there was my great pal Donal, so good-looking that he had a problem every week trying to disentangle himself from yet another situation and get into a further one. "Donal, of course I agreed with you that she is being unreasonable to want to get engaged after such a short time, but on the other hand you did make her leave her own flat and move into yours. She has to say something to her mother, you know, just some kind of hopeful words. I see, well then you should be very honest, shouldn't you? Remember the last times you were so honest, you were always glad afterwards. I know, I know, but women do get upset about things. No, I know I'm different, but then I'm your friend, I'm not one of your girls, but listen to me. There's no point in telling her you have consumption, and it wouldn't be fair to her; she'll agree to it anyway and swear to stay and nurse you for the rest of her life. You'll have to say it was all a mistake and you're sorry, and you'll have to help her find another flat. No, I don't think she'd find a revolting liver ailment a turnoff either—remember that actress, the one you told that you had gout. She still sends you telegrams at work saying 'ratfink.' Come on, it'll only take a weekend to do it, and then you'll both be free for the rest of your lives."

It seemed to be years of helping other people have pregnancy tests done, abortions arranged, cover stories created, years and years of inviting certain people to parties so that other people could pounce on them, centuries of being asked to go over and distract some girl who was showing too much interest in someone else's man, a lifetime of giving sound middle-of-the-road, unpaid agony column advice.

So one Thursday afternoon at four o'clock when school broke up, I decided that I would get a giant-size problem of my own. I would plunge myself wholeheartedly into a situation that would be so terrible and insoluble that at least half a dozen of my friends would have to hold consultations about it, would have to take me aside for serious conferences, would have to take me out of myself to get me over it. Somebody else was going to have a sleepless night or two over me, and I was going to behave unreasonably throughout the whole thing . . . consistently asking for advice, and then never listening to it, let alone taking it.

It was hard to think of a desperate situation to enter as I was walking down the leafy road from the school with exercise books under my arm. Where did everyone else find them? Often they were a result of some happy drunken gathering, so I supposed I could begin there. But it was a bit early to get drunk, so I went home and planned it out on paper the same way that I would have organized a history teaching schedule for the year. First I made a list of places that I could get drunk in that evening. Selectivity was the problem since pubs there are in plenty. I chose about four where I thought there might be actors, or writers, or artists, or public relations men, which a lifetime of listening had taught me to recognize as problem men.

Then I made another list of the kind of clothes I should wear. Not the gray skirt, gray jumper and white blouse that always seemed fine for school and the gentle evenings out that I was used to. It had better be something problem-creating, so I tried on a blouse that was too small, a skirt that was too tight, jewelry that was too flashy and perfume that was too perfumey, and put all the makeup I had on my face. In honesty I thought I looked very silly indeed but perhaps it was the kind of appearance that would attract some married homosexual who had robbed a bank to put me in a position where I might be expecting twins, about to be arrested and hiding from gangs who were pledged to destroy me.

In the first bar the barman said inexplicably, "Is it raining outside?" This gave me a lot of cause for thought in case it might be a code or something, and what he really meant was the man in the corner would like to make me an offer I couldn't refuse about white slave traffic. What he really meant was that my mascara was running in six black lines down my face and my skirt looked as if it had shrunk in a sudden shower. I cleaned my face, which made me look as if someone had beaten me up, but that was fine too, because at least it looked adventurous and not comfortable. I didn't want to look comfortable, under any circumstances. But nobody came over and lit a cigarette for me and nobody said anything except to ask was the seat beside me taken. So I moved on.

In the next bar there seemed to be a livelier lot. At least there was a great argument going on between some howling drunks about the words of "The Listeners." It seemed ideal as a situation to include myself, and serendipity that I knew the words. Inch by inch I got nearer, as drunkenly they criticized each other's versions, and almost accidentally I seemed to get included in their rounds. The only thing they wouldn't do was let me speak. Each time they ordered they said, "A gin and tonic for the lady," but I never got any words in at all. I filed it away as a useful way of becoming drunk cheaply because nobody asked what I was doing there, but, unflatteringly, nobody seemed to have the slightest interest either. I offered to buy a round, hoping to earn some hearing or at least attention this way. "Never let a woman pay," they all chorused, and I took it as some kind of bonus that they at least realized that a woman I was.

It was getting late and they were buying beer to take home with them. It was going to continue in some flat, so I'd better stay with it, I thought. I bought half a dozen and they were put in a brown paper bag, and I tagged along hopefully with them to the bus stop. There, unfortunately, they hailed a taxi, and as I was getting in too, they shook their heads. "Can't take you with us," they said.

"I've bought my beer and everything," I said tearfully.

"Simon wouldn't like it—must never take another man's woman, first rule," they told me.

"I don't know anyone called Simon." I pleaded that I wasn't Simon's bird—they must be thinking of someone else.

"Well, why were we drinking with you all night if you weren't Simon's bird?" they asked unanswerably and left me on the pavement with all this beer. There was a discotheque nearby, so there I went. The average age of everyone dancing in the strobe lighting was at least ten years younger than mine, and many of the dancers were fifteen years below me. But I'd paid to get in, so, clutching my beer, I stood by the wall. Sudden shouts of recognition and delight. The whole Fifth Form seemed to be there. No wonder they are too weak to retain any history, I thought gloomily. They were ecstatic to see me. Not in the least surprised.

"I brought you some beer," I said helpfully.

Nothing could have been more acceptable. The prices at the disco were very steep; they had run out of drinking money. Their boyfriends were enchanted with me—what a schoolteacher, what a woman; they whistled appreciatively. None of them asked me to dance—you don't dance with someone as old as me. Any thoughts of a hopeless, problem-filled relationship of the *Tea and Sympathy* kind vanished. I said I had to be moving on.

One of my friends had got into dire trouble by being approached by a conference businessman in a big hotel. Maybe that would be the best thing to try now, considering the lateness of the hour. There was no trouble getting into the hotel and no trouble meeting conference businessmen. The only trouble was that they were all whey-faced and lined and eating tranquilizers and talking about output and the product and the recession and looking at clipboards. It had been a bad day, and tomorrow was going to be a worse one. I asked one of them casually had he seen the play *Death of a Salesman*. He looked at me wildly.

"No," he squeaked. "God, were we meant to have seen it?"

Then they all started going off to bed and making big scenes at the desk about being called at 6:30 a.m. and having breakfasts with no cholesterol in them, and would their shoes definitely be cleaned, and had the hotel realized that if it forgot to call them, there would be a high-level investigation and heads would roll. There wasn't a pleasure-loving out-of-towner in the bunch, so I thought I'd better go to the phone and try and raise some excitement that way. Anything to get their haunted, hunted faces and their ulcers out of my mind.

I rang Donal in case he might be having a party. He wasn't. He was making the final and potentially successful advances to an air hostess; my phone call had ruined it, and she was getting her coat. It had given her those few seconds she needed to clear her head. He was less than delighted to hear from me.

I rang Judy, who sits up all night drinking black coffee and having intense conversations with hopeless cases, men she loves passionately. They drain her and she drains them so emotionally that there's a kind of atmosphere of drama and stress hovering around the place like ectoplasm. She was deliriously happy that I had called; she had been hunting for me all night. She had this appalling situation. Sven was out in the kitchen trying to put his head into the oven; he'd been at this for hours. It was all too terrible. I remembered Sven, didn't I? He had been living in the commune because his analyst had said he needed a lot of giving and taking, but really Sven had been doing all the giving and none of the taking. Judy wanted him to come and live with her. Sven said that he was a disappointment to everyone, to the analyst, to the commune, to Judy . . . he could see nothing but the gas oven, really . . . it was all so bleak, Judy said . . . so draining.

I pretended we had been cut off. I kept shouting, "Hallo, hallo!" and then hung up.

The taxi man told me on the way home to Chestnut Street that all women were scum. He had always half believed it deep down, but now he knew it. Scum. And his wife was the cream of the scum. She had been carrying on with a neighbor for months, apparently. He had only just discovered and faced her with it.

Tried to defend herself, she had. Scummy thing that she was. Said she had been lonely, what with his irregular hours. What would make a woman do a thing like that, lady, he asked me, hoping that I would set him straight.

"Scummishness," I said. And we fell silent.

At home there was a letter from a friend whose husband had been behaving oddly. She thought he might be having an affair with someone at the office. He was beginning to look lined and whey-faced and was taking a lot of tranquilizers. I wrote her a quick postcard saying that it was all nonsense. He was only caught up in the rat race like all those businessmen I had seen that night; he couldn't have time for another woman. And then I tore it up. Why was I always consoling my friends and none of them were consoling me?

I had a cup of some drink they say soothes away the cares of the day and gives you healing sleep. I hoped that it might also soothe away all the gin so uselessly downed during the evening, and prevent a hangover. It would be irony indeed to have to face a day of teaching with my head hammering and not a problem to show for it.

And then the phone rang. It was two o'clock; it had to be someone who was pregnant or who wasn't, some voice complaining that yet another disastrous romance was fizzling out on her sofa or in her gas oven. Wearily I answered. It sounded like a very drunk man.

"Yes?" I said, resigning myself.

"I'm very drunk," said the voice, a bit unnecessarily but with a need for definition of terms before we started. "I had to be drunk, otherwise I'd never have had the courage to ring you. I fancy you enormously, I think I love you, actually, I'm not sure about loving you, but I do know that I need you. I'll have to meet you properly, I can't bear all these hypocritical chats we have, talking about things that don't matter like scholarships, and homework, and the need to study. I want to talk about you, yourself, and me, and myself. I want to walk in the country with you. I want to have dinner with you in lovely places, and hold you and look after you."

Well, that all sounded fairly genial of him, I said heartily, but on the other hand did I know him at all?

"No, of course you don't. How could you know me when I have to talk about homework and scholarships with you and the goddamn need to study . . . and I don't know you. When we have been able to get away from all those terrible buildings and corridors, and car parks and parent-teacher meetings, then I'll know you and you'll know me."

It obviously had something to do with school. The mad thought that one of the pupils was a ventriloquist or some kind of male impersonator came to my mind.

"Who is that?" I said crisply.

"Oh, that voice, I love it, I love it, so cool, so unflappable, so unlike any other female voice in the world," he said happily. "I'm Susie's father, of course, and I've been in love with you forever. I'm Simon Scott who loves you, that's who I am."

Mr. Scott, Susie's father? An insignificant sort of man, but then, weren't they all? Tall, sort of middle-aged, middle-size, always talking about scholarships and homework and the need to study. Oh, God, this was something else. But suddenly it came to me in a flash that *he* could be my problem, I could become all emotional and upset over him, and confide to people how terrible the situation was, and why hadn't I met him earlier, and why couldn't he leave his wife for me. And the coincidence about his name being Simon—that was staggering. That was the fictitious man that those drunks in the bar had said I belonged to. Perhaps it was the same Simon.

"Do you have a lot of drunken friends who are trying to remember the words of 'The Listeners,' Mr. Scott?" I asked.

"My darling, my darling, you are psychic—of course I do. They all came around to my house and they're in the other room still trying to remember them. We are made for each other, my love. How else would you know what I am thinking and I am thinking what you are thinking . . ." His voice trailed away, the effort of trying to make a long sentence was very hard.

Very well, Simon would be my problem. Donal and Judy, and Miss O'Brien and Lisa, all of them would have to talk me out of him, make me see sense. I must make sure first that he was a proper problem.

"What about Susie's mother?" I asked. There was no problem about getting involved with a man who was free. I couldn't recall Mrs. Scott from parent-teacher meetings, but then tonight I could hardly recall anyone.

"She never understood me, not from the start; she has no soul. She's away now, coming back tomorrow. She went to see her cousin—that's the limit of her imagination, going to see a cousin. I don't hate her, I'll always be good to her, but you . . . I must have you . . . I need you."

It sounded very promising indeed.

"Would you have to meet secretly?" I asked. "Would you just be able to snatch minutes to come and see me? Would we have to pretend in front of other people that we hardly knew each other? Would it be full of confusion and recriminations, and a misunderstanding twice a week?"

He sounded startled by these questions. Not at all what he had expected, but what he *did* expect was of course impossible to imagine.

"Yes, a bit at the beginning," he said nervously. "But love will find a way. We'll be able to steal precious time together, and we can share real thoughts, not talk about going to see cousins, and not a word about scholarships and the need to study. . . . It will be magical," he finished off a bit unconvincingly.

"Right," I said. "You're on. What will I do now—will I take a taxi to your place immediately so that we can get the value out of it while she is away, or would you prefer to come here? Then tomorrow we could snatch a few precious moments in a pub at lunchtime, and you could pretend to come in to the school to talk about Susie and you and I could pretend to be having a discussion in one of the classrooms and we could steal a few magical embraces there?" I was getting quite pleased by the thought of it all now, and quite looking forward to the adventure.

Mr. Scott said, ". . . er, well."

"Oh, come *on*, Mr. Scott," I said encouragingly. "You've been in love with me forever, you said, you think we're made for each other, I think it's a *great* idea. If we want to share real thoughts, and you want to hold me and look after me, then we shouldn't waste any time getting started. I'm delighted you phoned me and I think it will all work out splendidly. You just give me your address, I'll come along straightaway, and I'll give your drunken friends a poetry book with the words of 'The Listeners' in it, and they'll go home happily, and we'll tidy ourselves away before Susie comes back from the disco. And we'll have a great affair."

A change had come over Mr. Scott. He seemed less drunk. He also seemed less ardent. The walks in the country and the dinners in lovely places seemed to have receded.

"Well," he said. "What I was doing really was telephoning to tell you *one* aspect of my feelings for you. Just one. Of course there are many others, like great respect and admiration. My wife, you . . . er . . . remember my wife . . . she's not here just now, she's visiting her cousin, but she'll be back tomorrow early, or even very possibly tonight. Yes, quite possibly tonight. . . . Well, my wife and I have often said that we think Susie is very lucky to have such a level-headed teacher as you, not a person who does reckless things, not a person who acts hastily. We need you, yes, need you for Susie's education and her scholarships and . . . er . . . everything."

"Oh, very well, Mr. Scott," I said in irritation. "Very well, we won't have an affair then, if that's what you're getting at. I don't mind. I can have an affair later on in the term, or perhaps around

Christmas—that's a good time for a bit of drama and tragedy. . . . No, stop apologizing—it's perfectly all right. Just get rid of those drunks before Susie comes home, and tell Susie that she shouldn't be out so late anyway—she has all those exams to think of. She should keep her dancing for the weekends when she doesn't have school the next day. And in my view you should tidy up all those beer cans. When Mrs. Scott comes back from her cousin's she won't want the place looking like the back room of a pub. . . . Not at all—you're perfectly welcome, Mr. Scott. . . . No, you didn't disturb me at all—I wasn't in bed. I've just come in, actually. I was wandering around the town trying to start an affair with somebody highly unsuitable, but it didn't seem to work. But I can always try again tomorrow, if I don't have too many marking exercises, or if I'm not holding some tragedy queen's hand."

His voice was inarticulate with relief. I could barely hear what he said, but I decided to agree with him.

"Yes, of course I was having my little joke, Mr. Scott—naturally I was. I've got an extraordinarily well-developed sense of humor, and I'm known as a rock of good sense and fund of good advice. Those are the exact phrases, I think. . . . Ask anyone."

ALL THAT MATTERS

Nessa Byrne's aunt Elizabeth knew all about everything and she was never wrong.

She came to visit them in Chestnut Street every June for six days, and because she had high expectations, they cleaned the house and tidied up the garden for about two weeks before her visit.

Aunt Elizabeth's bedroom was emptied of all the clutter that had built up there in the year since her last visit. They touched up the paintwork and lined the nice empty drawers with clean pink paper.

Nessa's mother often said with a weary laugh that if it hadn't been for Elizabeth's annual vacation the whole place would have been a complete tip.

But then Nessa's mother should not have felt guilty; she had neither the time nor the money to spend on house renovations. She worked long hours in a supermarket and supported three children without any help from her husband. Nessa never remembered her father going out to work.

He had a bad back.

Aunt Elizabeth was her father's elder sister. She had immigrated to America when she was eighteen. She worked there as a paralegal. Nessa wasn't quite sure what it was and you never asked Aunt Elizabeth a direct question like that.

Nessa's father smartened himself up when his sister arrived. No sitting in his chair looking at the races on television, and he helped with the dishes too. He always seemed very relieved when Elizabeth left.

"Well, that passed off all right," he would say, as if there had been some hidden danger there that none of them would have been able to avoid.

Aunt Elizabeth would be out all day, visiting places of culture. She would go to art exhibitions, or the Chester Beatty Library, or on a tour of some elegant home.

"All that matters is seeing places of elegance, places with high standards," she would tell Nessa as she trimmed and clipped the brochures to paste them into a scrapbook. Nessa wondered who would see these scrapbooks year after year. But again, it wasn't a question you would ask Aunt Elizabeth.

There was no call for jolly happy family pictures. Certainly not at Nessa's home. And not at a picnic out on Killiney Beach or on Howth Head, where Nessa's mother would have packed hard-boiled eggs and squishy tomatoes to be eaten with doorsteps of bread. Aunt Elizabeth wouldn't want to record this, no matter how much the sun had shone and how heartily they had all laughed during the day.

But on one evening during her yearly visit Aunt Elizabeth would invite the whole family for a drink at whatever she had decided was the new smart place to go in Dublin.

And it *was* a drink, not several drinks, orange for the children, a red vermouth with a cherry in it for Nessa's mother, a small Irish whiskey for her father and the house cocktail for Aunt Elizabeth herself.

They all had to dress up for this outing and a waiter was usually invited to take a snap of them all blinking in whatever unfamiliar background. Presumably, when the picture was developed, it would be inserted in the scrapbook.

"All that matters," Aunt Elizabeth would say, "is that we are in the right place."

Nessa wondered why this was so important. But Aunt Elizabeth looked so smartly dressed and confident. She must be right.

Aunt Elizabeth often went to a big newsagent's shop in O'Connell Street with a small notebook. Nessa sometimes went with her.

"What are you writing down?" she asked once, and then felt guilty and anxious. You didn't ask Aunt Elizabeth direct questions. But, oddly, there seemed to be no problem.

"I'm looking through the magazines and writing down the names of people who go to art gallery openings and first nights. It's amazing how many of the same names turn up over and over."

Nessa was confused. Why should anyone care about who went to what? Even if they lived here? But if they lived three thousand miles away? It was insane. Her face must have shown this because suddenly Aunt Elizabeth spoke to her seriously as if she were a fellow adult.

"I'm going to tell you something very important, so listen well. I know you are only fifteen but it's never too early to know this: all that matters is the image you create of yourself. Do you understand?"

"I think so," Nessa said doubtfully.

"Believe me, it *is* all that matters. For a start you should call yourself by your full name, Vanessa—people will have more respect for you."

"Oh, I couldn't do that—they'd all think I was a gobshite."

"And you should *never* use language like that, about yourself or about anyone. If you are to amount to anything, then you must have a seriously great sense of respect about the way you appear to others."

"Ma says that as long as you're nice to other people that's all that matters." Nessa showed some spirit.

"Yes, Vanessa, and very worthy of her too. But look at your mother, worn out slaving in a supermarket, allowing my brother to spend her earnings as well as his dole money on drink and horses."

Nessa held her head up high. "My dad is terrific."

"I was at school with your mother and father. I was three years older than them, but I look ten years younger. All that matters is giving a good impression of yourself to others. It's like a mirror. If you look well, and people think you look well, then they reflect it back at you."

"Yes, I see."

"So, Vanessa, if you like, I can help you a little, advise you about clothes and posture and the things that matter."

Nessa was torn. Did she accept the advice and become elegant like Aunt Elizabeth? Or did she tell her to get lost, that she was fine as she was with Ma and Da?

She looked for a moment at her aunt, who must be forty-seven. She barely looked thirty. Her hair was short and well cut; she washed it every day with a baby shampoo. She wore a smart dark-green suit that she sponged every night with lemon juice. She had a variety of brightly colored T-shirts, and one really nice brooch on her lapel.

Ma looked so different, never time to wash her long greasy hair, tied back in a rubber band. Ma didn't have highly polished court shoes that she stuffed with newspaper at night, like her sister-in-law. She had big, broken flat shoes that were comfort-able at work and on the long walk home.

Nessa's school friends had always admired her aunt. They had always said that she was lucky she had got away from Chestnut Street and done well for herself in New York. God, they said, any-one could do well in America compared to here.

Yet it looked as if Aunt Elizabeth had reinvented herself somehow and might be able to reinvent Nessa too, if she were given permission.

"What are you thinking about, Vanessa?"

"Why did you go to America, exactly?"

"To escape, Vanessa. If I had stayed living in my mother's house in Chestnut Street there would have been nothing for me here, working at a checkout till somewhere, nothing better."

"Some people in Chestnut Street have great jobs." Nessa was mutinous.

"Now possibly, then no." Her aunt was very definite.

"Could you make me . . . you know . . . a bit in charge . . . I don't know the exact word, but like you are?"

"Yes, Vanessa. The word is *confident,* by the way, and I could. But before I start I want to know if you are serious. Will you call yourself Vanessa, for example?"

"It's not important, surely?"

"It is in a way; it shows that you want to have style."

"Okay, then," said Vanessa Byrne agreeably, hoping there would not be too much flak at home.

"Are you off your skull?" Da asked her when she mentioned her new name.

Her brothers fell about the place laughing.

"What do *you* think, Ma?" she asked, going out to the kitchen, where her mother was peeling potatoes.

"Life is short. Whatever makes you happy," her mother said.

"You don't really mean that, Ma."

"Jesus Christ, Nessa or *Va*-nessa, if that's what you want. You ask me a question, I answer it, then you tell me that I don't mean it. I'll tell you what I mean. I've been sitting with an east wind coming in the doors, which they leave open all day until I have a pain all down my whole left side. I've heard at the supermarket that we may all have less hours' work next month, and what will that mean to this household? Your aunt will be back shortly from some museum or other expecting finger bowls and linen napkins on the table. I don't care if you call yourself Bambi or the Hag of Beara, Vanessa—I have far too much on my mind."

And at that moment Vanessa decided she would be a person of style.

Before Aunt Elizabeth left Chestnut Street to return to America, Vanessa went up to sit in her bedroom and watch her pack.

She noticed that there were no gifts for anyone back in New York. Her aunt always brought the family gifts—big art books. Things about Vermeer or Rembrandt. They would open them and leaf through the colored pictures politely the night she arrived, then the books would go on a shelf beside last year's Monet and the year before's Degas.

"Jaysus, wouldn't you think she'd give the kids something to spend?" Vanessa's father would mutter.

"Shush, isn't it nice that she brings some sort of culture into this house." Ma always tried to see the good side of things but Dad was having none of it.

"She never brought anything but fights and arguments into this house. We were all perfectly happy, five of us in this house, until Lizzie started her act, saying the place was shabby and common and whatever."

"Don't call her Lizzie—she hates it."

"It's her bloody name, and now she's started filling Nessa up with these notions as well."

Vanessa had heard all these conversations. The houses in Chestnut Street were small; there wasn't much you didn't hear.

Aunt Elizabeth had closed the bedroom door and turned her radio to Lyric FM. This way they wouldn't be overheard.

"That's Ravel, Vanessa. All that matters is to recognize good music. You'll be surprised at how quickly it all will become familiar."

"What should I do first, Aunt Elizabeth?" Vanessa asked.

"I think you should give your room a style of your own."

"Like get rid of all my own things in here—is that what you mean?" Vanessa liked the film posters, fashion articles and footballers that decorated her walls.

"Keep only things that are graceful and elegant, Vanessa. Only items that will speak well of you."

Vanessa looked bewildered.

Her aunt explained. "How are people to know what we are like unless we send them messages, child? The way we dress, the way we speak, the way we behave. How else are people to get to know us?"

"I suppose so." Vanessa was doubtful. After all, you knew who you liked and who you didn't like—it hadn't all that much to do with messages.

She watched as the suitcase was neatly packed, transparent bags of underwear, scarves, T-shirts, all immaculately folded. The scrapbooks took the place of the art books she had brought over with her.

Aunt Elizabeth had been born in this house forty-seven years ago, and look at her now. It could happen to Vanessa too. She looked at her reflection, tousled, grubby even, her school shirt torn at the collar, her skirt stained with food and pen marks.

"There's no money for new clothes or anything," Vanessa said as she saw she was being observed. She half hoped that some financial help might be offered, but then Dad always said that Lizzie still had her confirmation money.

"So you'll have to learn to look after what clothes you *do* have, I suppose." Her aunt was vague, as if it had nothing to do with her.

"And my hair?" Vanessa looked despairing.

"Go to Lilian Harris at Number Five."

"Yes, but again, where would I get the money to pay her?"

"Do something for her instead—you know, take her mother for a walk, do the shopping one day a week, then she can give you a proper haircut every month."

It was a possibility, certainly.

"It would be easier if you were here," Vanessa said, looking at her very elegant aunt, who was creaming her long, slim hands carefully. Ma's hands were cracked and red and had never known hand cream.

"You can write to me, Vanessa, telling me your progress."

"And maybe come and see you in New York one day?" Vanessa was daring.

"One day, maybe."

Vanessa had heard warmer invitations in her young life. But she was not going to get moody about it. "Let's go down for supper. Ma's making shepherd's pie as a treat for your last night here and she's inviting Miss Mack and Bucket Maguire."

"That's nice." Aunt Elizabeth made it sound as if some poison were being prepared for them. "Remember, don't eat any of the mashed potato on top, Vanessa, no bread and butter, and try to encourage your mother to have salads in future."

During supper Vanessa Byrne watched her tired mother, her impatient father and her ill-mannered brothers, Eamonn and Sean, gobbling up the shepherd's pie. She never felt more like a traitor than that evening as she nibbled at the meat part of the pie and halved a tomato with her aunt. It was as if she had crossed a line, changed sides.

She wrote for advice three times to Aunt Elizabeth in New York. Always she got a frank and helpful reply. Yes, indeed, Vanessa should take a Saturday job in a restaurant but she must choose a smart place, and insist that they give her a uniform to wear. An entirely fictitious reference was sent from New York to help her get such a job.

No, it would be very foolish and time wasting for Vanessa to try to learn to play the piano. She was too old to start a musical education at fifteen, she would be better to borrow CDs from the library and learn to appreciate music made by others.

And yes, Vanessa would be well advised to go to any poetry readings, book launches or cultural events that she heard of around Dublin. She would meet a lot of interesting people this way.

And Vanessa did. Including Owen, who was twenty-two and couldn't believe that Vanessa was still at school. She was going to write about this to her aunt, but something stopped her. Like the fact that she had never asked Owen back home to Chestnut Street. Like that she didn't want to tell her aunt that she was having sex with Owen.

Aunt Elizabeth came over, as usual, the following summer. She was impressed by Vanessa's bedroom. It was cool and elegant. Vanessa had very few clothes these days but those she had were well cared for. Vanessa's mother confided to her sister-in-law that the girl had become distant and secretive. Her father said that Nessa was a proper pain in the arse. Eamonn and Sean said little except to hint that they were broke to the hilt.

Vanessa was slimmer, and different somehow to last year. Her hair was short and blond and shiny. She brought her aunt to an open-air concert, the launch of a poetry book and an antiques exhibition. Everywhere Vanessa knew people or nodded at them. She was confident and so definitely on her way out of Chestnut Street that it was awe-inspiring.

Once or twice she mentioned Owen. And the fact that his

father was a well-known lawyer. Aunt Elizabeth came in, as if on radar, to know more, but Vanessa was prepared.

"You don't tell me about your private life, you never say who loved you and you loved in return. I thought it was a bit . . . I don't know . . . undignified . . . to talk about things like that."

"You're learning fast, Vanessa," said Elizabeth with a slightly anxious look at her nearly-sixteen-year-old niece.

Three months after her aunt returned to New York Vanessa Byrne discovered that she was pregnant.

She met Owen in a really smart tapas bar and told him. He had just been saying that she had *the* most amazing taste in finding places when she gave him the news.

"Hey, Vanessa . . . this is not for real," he said.

She waited politely for him to say something else. Something like that it was all a bit earlier than they had hoped, but what the hell, they were always going to be together anyway. Owen did not say this. He said, "Jesus, Vanessa, I'm *so* sorry," and suddenly she understood that years and years ago something like this must have happened to her aunt too.

She smiled a cold little smile and said yes, wasn't life really shitty, and got up and left the restaurant.

She lay in her cool, uncluttered bedroom and by the dawn she knew she would go to New York. She worked out the finances. If she sold her record player, her new shoes, her good bracelet, she would have the fare. She had a passport since her sixteenth birthday. Just in case Owen had been going to invite her skiing.

She would turn up at Aunt Elizabeth's and ask her what to do.

Her mother said that she just gave up.

In the middle of the school term Nessa was going to fly to New York. The rest of the family wasn't able to go to the Isle of frigging Man but Nessa was going to New York. Her father said it was history repeating itself. Just like Lizzie, gone in two minutes, then they never saw her, apart from her arriving back every year like some bloody duchess. Eamonn and Sean sat, dumbfounded. Imagine that Aunt Elizabeth had sent for Nessa.

Vanessa decided not to tell her aunt until she got there. She didn't have the work address so she went straight to the address miles out in Queens. She kept checking her address book. This was such a rough area, such a poor building, almost like a slum. Aunt Elizabeth couldn't live here, surely?

Vanessa sat on the steps outside, waiting for her aunt to return. Eventually she did, at 8 p.m. It was 1 a.m. in Dublin. Everyone in Chestnut Street was asleep. She saw Aunt Elizabeth walking up from the corner. She walked straight and tall, yet looked tired. Her face changed when she saw Vanessa sitting on the steps. She did not look greatly pleased.

"What happened?" she asked.

"I needed some advice."

"You could have written." Her aunt's voice was cold.

"It was too important to wait."

"Where are you staying?"

"I thought with you, like you stay with us when you come to Dublin." Vanessa hoped that some spirit shone through her voice. She was deathly tired and frightened but she didn't want it known.

She followed her aunt's trim figure up four flights of stairs and down a long corridor. Children were crying behind doors, and cooking smells filled the building.

The big room was shabby, with peeling walls. An ironing board stood at the ready and a steel clothes rail held all the garments that would be worn to work. Two faded armchairs and a single bed in the corner looked as if nobody had ever visited them. A tiny two-ring burner and a sink formed the kitchen. Not a place where gracious meals were made and served.

Vanessa said nothing, just sat there waiting for her aunt to make coffee.

"I suppose you're pregnant," Elizabeth said.

"Yes."

"And he doesn't want to hear about it?"

"How do you know?" Vanessa was astounded.

"You wouldn't be here otherwise."

"You always know what to do, Elizabeth." Vanessa realized that she had dropped the "Aunt" bit. It didn't seem appropriate somehow now that she had discovered the strange secret life that had been lied about for so long. She remembered so many things that had been said: All that matters is to have fresh flowers, all that matters is to have one piece of really good furniture polished with beeswax. Vanessa looked around her; compared to this place Chestnut Street was like a palace. And to think that poor Ma had been scrubbing and cleaning to make things look right.

"Does anyone else know about this, Vanessa?"

"No, only Owen and, as you say, he doesn't want to hear about it."

"All that matters is that it stays that way. It's quite easy if you realize that. Now, are you having a termination or will you have it adopted?"

It was all so businesslike, so authoritative, so like the old Aunt Elizabeth, that Vanessa almost forgot the strange, unexpected surroundings.

"I haven't decided yet," she said.

"Well, you must decide soon. And then we have a lot of things to consider. If it's a termination he and his people should pay. You have no money, I have no money. If not a termination then we have to think of a cover story and a job for you. Just remember that whatever happens, you can't be allowed to ruin your life staying at home wheeling a pram up and down Chestnut Street, marking yourself out as a loser before your life has properly begun."

It was all so clear and obvious to Elizabeth, yet it didn't seem quite so clear to Vanessa.

"It might be easier to be there rather than anywhere else," she began tentatively.

"Easier than what?"

"Than asking Owen and his family to give me money, than making up some fake existence over here in America." Vanessa looked around her.

"You don't like my home, apparently, so why did you come here, then?"

"I didn't say that—it's just very different from what you made us think."

"I'm not responsible for what you thought."

"Do you really have a big job as a paralegal? Was any of it true? Anything you told us about your life?"

"I work in Manhattan for a legal firm, I meet a lot of cultured people there, I go to lectures and art galleries with them. I spend what I earn in giving a good impression, a good account of myself. Now is there any other intrusive question you would like to ask, you who have turned up pregnant on my doorstep looking for help?"

"Just one more. Were you ever in the same situation as I'm in now?"

There was a long pause. Vanessa wondered whether she would answer at all.

Eventually she said, "Yes I was. Thirty-one years ago. He will be thirty-one at Christmas. Imagine!" She spoke in wonder.

"And where is he?" Vanessa whispered.

"On the West Coast, Seattle, I believe. Of course he may have moved. He tried to find me when he was twenty but I didn't let him. I wrote and said that all that mattered now was that he forged ahead with his own life; his adoptive parents were substantial people, he had a good education. I never heard from him again."

Outside the windows of this lonely, shabby walkup apartment the sounds of traffic and police sirens wailed.

Suddenly it was all very clear to Vanessa that all that mattered was that she get out of this place, far away from this lonely, obsessive woman.

She had to come all this distance to realize that her mother's tired face would eventually light up at the thought of a baby in the home again, and that her father was always great at rocking a pram while he watched the horses line up at the Curragh. Eamonn and Sean would get used to it like everyone got used to everything, except possibly being abandoned thirty-one years ago to substantial people in Seattle.

Vanessa knew she would be called Nessa again and that she would always thank her sad loser of an aunt for showing her the way.

JOYCE AND THE BLIND DATE

Joyce hated Greek food; it all looked like goat's balls to her and the wine people drank with it seemed to taste like paint remover. She didn't know *why* she had agreed to go out with Leonard and Sally, who were sickeningly in love with each other, and nauseatingly enthusiastic about everything, particularly goat's balls and paint remover. It was just one of those times when you couldn't say no. Sally had said, "What night will you come with us to this new place we've found? Name any night, and we'll all go and have a great evening."

When somebody asks you to name any night, it's like a declaration of war not to go. And of course there would be the blind date too. Norman, this guy was called. Norman, who had just come to live on Chestnut Street, round the corner from where Leonard and Sally were always so unreasonably happy and sunny.

The blind dates were never actually described as that. They were never presented as a series of men, one after the other, who might conceivably shack up with Joyce and take her out of herself. Joyce didn't want to be taken out of herself if it meant that she was going to live with some grinning, cheerful man in an utterly tasteless block of utilitarian flats, braying with excitement over some new ethnic food every week.

Joyce wanted to live by herself in her tiny town house with its beautiful furniture and lovely ornaments, and be visited regularly by Charles, who designed the most exquisite clothes in the world. She was a fashion model, and she was like another beautiful ornament in the little house that Charles had given her. She dressed as carefully for his visits as she did for the fashion shows where she wore the clothes he designed. She walked as elegantly to pour him a Campari and soda as she did down the ramps at the big collections. It was cool and understated, and peaceful. Nobody ever threw plates on the ground and shouted and swore eternal love in public to each other in that background. So, it was a bit lonely sometimes, but self-pity was for losers, and Joyce was definitely not a loser.

She dressed for the Greek evening with her usual precision, laying out on the bed a cream dress, but replacing it with a darker one because she remembered how waiters can spill things over you in darkly lit places. Her best handbag, no. Her new shoes, no. Her beautiful locket, yes. Not much could happen to a locket even with Leonard and Sally.

Sighing and hoping that the evening might at any rate yield some horror story that would amuse Charles, she went out the door. Taxis always seemed to appear for Joyce. She got resignedly into the back, discouraged conversation from the driver, who thought she was a pretty bird and asked her was she going out for a night on the town.

"I think I gave you the name of the restaurant," Joyce said coldly.

"Snooty bitch," thought the taxi driver, and the journey took place in silence.

Time and time again she had told herself it was a false kindness to go out with Leonard and Sally. She and Sally had done a secretarial course together years ago, but their lives were so different now. Joyce had money and fame and style, Sally had Leonard and the most awful flat in the world. It's just that they were like friendly puppies—you couldn't kick them. And in a way maybe they got pleasure and even status from all this presenting of ghastly men for her. Maybe they got a kick from saying that they could get their friends a date with a famous model. Perhaps they just liked her along to show that they could rise out of their dreadful life. But that was a bit mean, Joyce told herself; no—that was unfair. Leonard and Sally were so kind, they probably just liked her for herself. You met so many bitchy and cynical people in the fashion business it was hard to realize that not everyone had an angle.

Sally and Leonard were at the table, a bottle of the evil-smelling wine already opened. No sign of the man. Perhaps he couldn't come. Joyce told them some tales of the latest collections, and Leonard and Sally giggled like conspirators, delighted to be let in on the secrets of the rich and the famous.

"Where's Norman, then?" she asked eventually. For once both Leonard and Sally looked a bit embarrassed.

"He'll be a bit late—he's been tied up," said Sally.

"He won't come—he's got a cold," said Leonard.

Everyone laughed, since it was so obvious that stories hadn't been synchronized.

"Oh, all right," said Sally. "Joyce is an old friend—I'll tell her. We went to his flat to collect him, and when Leonard mentioned that you were going to be with us, Norman became all stupid."

"He said models weren't his scene," said Leonard.

"He said he wouldn't know what to say to a beautiful, leggy clotheshorse," said Sally.

"He said that models only talked about themselves," said Leonard. "I told him you were our friend, but he got a bit bolshie, so I said to him that it was his loss, and told him to stuff it."

"And I said to him that he was stupid to make generalizations, so he said he might come," said Sally. "But I think we'll just go ahead and order, and not pander to him."

"And what does this Norman do for a living that he has such strong views on everything?" asked Joyce rather testily.

"He's an actor. He's very good, actually—we've seen him in quite a few things," Sally said, her loyalty overriding her pique about Norman's nonappearance.

"Well, actors are pretty good at talking about themselves, I would have thought," said Joyce cheerfully, and the subject was dropped for a deep discussion about goat's or sheep's balls in sauce.

A huge shadow fell over the table and the fattest man that Joyce had ever seen towered there.

"Am I too late to join you?" he asked, slightly sheepishly. There was a lot of banter, and shouting, and Sally saying that they thought he was so bad-mannered perhaps he should be sent to another table as a punishment, and Leonard saying that Joyce was so broadminded she was going to allow him to sit down. Norman took her hand in his, which was about four times the size of her own.

"I'm sure it will be very nice to know you," he said reassuringly, and then all was babble again about more wine, and whether one large salad with chopped cheese in it would be enough for the four of them or if they should have two.

Joyce wasn't all hard; she could be very kind to old ladies who wanted to cross the road, and she was sentimental about animals or crying children. Immediately she decided that this poor guy had put on a big front about model girls being empty-headed because he was so gross and enormous, he felt that a model girl wouldn't even talk to him. Totally forgiving of his rude remarks as had been reported to her, Joyce decided she would be charming to him and make him feel at ease.

"They tell me you are an actor, Norman," she said, beaming a great ray of interest at him. Her lovely fine-boned face looked even better when she smiled, which was rare. Models usually trained their faces to look well from all angles, and in what might pass for repose. "Where can one see you act?" she continued.

"I'm glad you asked that," he said cheerfully. "Because one can see me tomorrow night on television if one has a telly."

Joyce decided he was nervous, not rude. He couldn't seriously be taking her on for that use of the word "one." She didn't like it herself; she didn't know why she had said it.

"Oh, one has a telly." She laughed. "But one rarely watches it. However, tomorrow is an exception. Is it in an advertisement?"

Sally's and Leonard's forks stopped halfway to their mouths. Norman looked amused.

"Norman's a real actor, you know, Joyce," said Sally. "He's not just in advertisements."

"Lots of real actors are in advertisements" said Joyce, flustered. She had thought he might be playing a fat Italian eating a tin of beans or some funny, clowning window cleaner falling off a ladder to get to his pint of beer. She was annoyed with herself, for her efforts to put this fatso at his ease were rebounding on her in an unexpected way.

Norman rescued her. He actually dared to rescue her. "Of course there are lots of actors in advertising, Joyce," he said consolingly. "Lots of us wouldn't be able to pay the rent without it, but tomorrow night is a play, a very good play, actually, a new one, by a woman. It's her first television play and I think it's going to go down very well."

They all started talking about the woman, a night telephonist who got so bored with having little or no work that she wrote the play between calls.

"I play the guy who gets the girl," said Norman.

"Is it a comedy?" asked Joyce innocently.

"No, it's more of a thriller, really. It's rather thoughtful and what the critics will call 'psychological,'" said Norman. But he looked at Joyce levelly, and she realized with horror that he thought she had asked was it a comedy as some kind of insult.

Since she had been very young Joyce had found it easy to attract men, and to get them interested in her. She knew when to talk, when to listen, how to smile. It had worked over and over. It was still working with Charles. This fat guy was resisting her only through nerves, and she would reassure him as the meal went on. Her smile never faltered as she told him that she would certainly watch the play and was looking forward to it greatly. He smiled easily back at her. She had the oddest feeling that he knew what she was at.

Joyce managed a lot of the salad and as few of the various bits of suspicious meat as she could swallow. Norman suggested that they have a red wine as well as the paint remover, and this was much more to her taste. The early uneasiness past, she relaxed, and so it seemed did everyone else. In fact, it wasn't a bad evening at all, she thought suddenly. There was nothing to tell Charles that would make him laugh delicately. You didn't tell Charles that a poor, foolish, fat guy fancied you pathetically. That would be embarrassing, and it wasn't funny. And in a way it wasn't even true. Norman laughed and joked and was pleasant company. He didn't seem ashamed of his bulk, nor apologetic for his existence. He had got over his nerves about her quite well. She must have been very successful at making him feel accepted.

Would she come back and have more coffee at Leonard and Sally's flat? No, really she couldn't. She had to work next day. The penalty for all this money was that you had to have eight hours' sleep, whether you liked it or not. They did understand? They did grudgingly, but they were all disappointed. It seemed a pity to break up the evening. Joyce was determined to be gracious to the end.

"If I'm going to watch you tomorrow night on telly," she said to Norman playfully, "would you all like to come to watch me on Friday? It's this charity show in Park Lane, and I'll be able to get a few tickets. There'll be Champagne as well, so it won't be all hell."

Leonard and Sally were stunned. They had never been included in the glitter of Joyce's life. They only heard about it secondhand. They weren't to know, of course, that Charles would be away on Friday and that in fact the tickets for the do weren't going at all well. They looked as if they had won the football pools.

Norman looked disappointed. "This Friday? Oh, dear, I can't, I'm afraid," he said. No explanation of what he was doing, just regret.

"Well, we'd simply adore to, anyway," said Sally, almost hugging herself with excitement. "Will it be very smart? Would my black dress do, do you think?"

"Is it dinner jacket?" asked Leonard. "I have a blazer and black trousers. Is that all right if I wear a bow tie as well?"

Joyce was unreasonably infuriated with them. She wanted to scream that it didn't matter whether they came in jeans—a few of the debby types would anyway. She wanted to shout at Norman, "You stupid, ill-mannered thug. I'm being kind to you, I'm making you feel normal, acceptable. Why haven't you the manners and the sensitivity to see that and accept it?" But years of hiding real feelings came to her aid.

"The black dress would be super, darling, and blazers are really the equivalent of dinner jackets, I think they're even nicer, Leonard. I'll get the tickets to you, and I'll meet you after the prancing-around bit and introduce you to people."

Then in a very casual voice to Norman: "Are you sure we can't persuade you to change your mind, Norman? After all, you did change it about coming here tonight, I'm happy to say."

"Not Friday, unfortunately," said Norman. "I'm meeting Grace, who wrote the play. You see, she's thinking of writing a one-man show for me and it's only in the very early stages yet, so we decided we'd have a read-through of the bit she's done, to see how it works."

"Couldn't she do that another day or night?" asked Joyce icily.

"I'm sure she could, but it would be awful to ask her to change it. I wouldn't let her down. She's getting herself geared to have it ready by Friday. You can't say suddenly that you can't make it because you're going to a fashion show. I mean it would be like slapping a friend in the face."

"Of course," tinkled Joyce. "But I'll be loyal to you anyway and watch tomorrow night."

There was the marvelous, graceful goodbyeing and thankyouing that Joyce was just so good at, and at the very minute she wanted a taxi, one appeared, and she was gone with a whiff of the most expensive perfume that money can buy.

Norman let himself into his flat and sat down on the huge swivel chair, which was the only thing he owned in the furnished apartment. He loved this chair; he took it everywhere with him and left it in his brother's house if he was in between flats or off on tour. He could think in this chair, and he wanted to think about the evening.

Yes, he thought, letting the air out of his lungs in a big sigh of relief, yes, it had worked. It had been so hard at the beginning but it had worked. He had nearly blown it by telling Sally and Leonard that he didn't like talking to model girls because they were so self-centered and empty. That was the trouble with Sally and Leonard: they were so nice and undevious you found yourself telling them the truth . . . or nearly the truth, anyway. Thank heavens he had managed to force himself into going. It was another hurdle, another notch, another score, whatever way you counted it. And, actually, she hadn't been bad, that Joyce— she wasn't by any means the worst of her trade, probably. In fact, he had imagined on occasions that *she* had felt a bit unsure of herself, not quite in control of everything and everyone. It had warmed his heart to see that, and he had admired her professionally for the way she got out of it. Grace would be proud of him; he'd tell her all about it tomorrow night when they were watching the play together.

Grace had taken him on as one of her projects. Grace had changed her life. They had met a year ago, when Grace's play had been accepted for television. She was seventy-two, she had a face like a monkey, she had the hardest life that anyone Norman had ever met could have lived. She had nursed a dying mother, a dying father, a dying husband, a dying son. That's why she was a night worker. It was easier to get someone to sit with the dying for a few hours at night than in the daytime. Grace had never known any money, any success and very little happiness. She had never expected any. Her one rage was that she hadn't written a play when she was twenty-one, instead of when she was seventy-one. She had known as much fifty years ago as she knew now.

She and Norman had met at the first rehearsal. Norman had been his old self then, laughing at himself too soon, too loudly, making jokes about being too big for the chair, too heavy for the floor or the stage, telling tales about how he got stuck in a bus seat.

"Why do you go on like that, lad?" Grace had asked him.

"Well, if I say it first, I suppose I think that people will know I realize I'm fat, and then we can all settle down again," said Norman honestly. He had never asked himself about this comedy routine. It just worked—that's all.

"I was settled down already," said Grace.

The director had wanted to play the hero as a buffoon; that's why he had cast Norman. He was going to make Norman into a ludicrous, no-hope guy, which made it whimsical and rather sweet that he got the girl in the end.

"That's not the way I wrote it," said Grace.

Oh, there had been a lot of taking her aside and explaining how important a director was, and how his views were sacred, and how Grace knew nothing about drama. She was adamant.

"He's not a foolish character, he's a strong character," she repeated. "There would be no point in the story if he was a buffoon."

"But," said the director, "that's why I cast Norman. He's a

character actor. If we wanted a straight hero, we'd have got some-one totally different. Not his shape, if you see what I mean."

"Everybody has to be some shape," said Grace unanswerably, and to everyone's amazement she had won.

She also became Norman's best friend.

"Leave where you are, lad," she advised him. "Get a new agent, live somewhere different. You're only twenty-eight years of age. Don't wait until you're seventy before you understand how to win in this old life."

Norman had been sure she was going to be a well-meaning person who was going to put him on a diet and set him jogging. He was doubtful. He didn't listen to her easily. Gradually, like a dripping tap, her words sank in. "Stop apologizing, stop joking, forget being the clown who laughs on the outside and cries under the makeup. Like yourself, lad, like yourself—others will take you at exactly the same value as you put on yourself."

Norman hadn't agreed. He hated people who thought too well of themselves. He always wanted to put down the kind of toffee-nosed person who thought they were God's gift to the human race. Drip, drip of the tap—he believed Grace, and everything she told him seemed to work.

"You're different, lad, you're not like stuck-up people. You're a fine boy—just let people know you are a fine, decent boy. Stop pretending to be some joke roly-poly without a brain in his head."

Week by week he'd worked at it. He gave himself tests. Some-times he failed them; mainly he passed. Go to an audition. Never mention size, shape, weight *once*. Let the other guy tell you that you can't have the part because you're too fat. Go into restaurants, order what you want, no jokes to the waitress about the doctor saying you must build yourself up. Ask people to dance, don't apologize, don't explain. Seven months he had been doing it. It was really working.

And tonight. Tonight. That was really a triumph, the more

you thought of it, a beautiful society-type model, as thin as a whip, asking *him* to a fashion show in Park Lane. No, it wasn't pity. It had been at the beginning, the first ten minutes after she saw him, but not anymore. And she hadn't been a bad girl at all, that Joyce, very bright, really. He was half sorry he had made up that lie about Grace and the read-through of her play. It wasn't Friday at all; it was Thursday. Still, it wasn't an excuse made from fear or inadequacy—it was part of being like an ordinary fellow. It was the kind of thing a lean, handsome young actor might have done, play hard to get. But he hoped he would meet her again with Leonard and Sally; she had been very nice.

And in the little bijou house, Joyce was walking around. She wasn't tired; she couldn't go to bed yet. She wished she had gone back to Leonard and Sally's. He was a funny fellow, that Norman. There was some strength there in him that she didn't understand. She couldn't understand why she had begun the evening pitying him in some way. It was probably because he had been fat. She was very sorry he wasn't coming on Friday. She would have liked to talk with him afterwards. He was very clear-sighted about things. She would like to know what he thought of posh charity do's anyway—were they dishonest, were they a means to an end and therefore justified? She didn't like him having his head together with this Grace person instead of being with the rest of them. Grace was probably a girlfriend of his, she thought, slightly annoyed.

She picked up the television magazines to see what they said about his play. There was a picture of Grace and a little story about it being her first play. Grace looked a hundred. She could be Norman's mother, or his grandmother. For no reason at all, Joyce found herself smiling, and went to bed quite happily.

LIBERTY GREEN

Everyone assumed that Libby Green had been born and christened "Elizabeth." What else could "Libby" be short for? And
when she was growing up, everyone read the Crawfie diaries,
about the little princesses who were called Lilibet and Margaret
Rose. Princess Margaret had not been able to pronounce her elder
sister's name. It was very endearing, and people thought it must
be the same with Libby. Couldn't get her tongue around a big
word like "Elizabeth." Wasn't it sweet.

After a while Libby never bothered trying to explain. It was too
complicated to say that she had been called Liberty. It sounded
like the name of a shop, or one of those funny little bodices you
wore to keep your chest warm and flatten it at the same time. Or
the Liberty Bell in Philadelphia. All in all, it was much easier to
say it was short for "Elizabeth."

And it was not a matter of being unfaithful to her parents'
dreams for her; they talked about little else but freedom and liberty in their house when Libby was growing up. The American
Declaration of Independence was framed in the dining room, the
words of the French national anthem had been stuck on a piece
of cardboard on the back of Libby's door for as long as she could

remember. All over the house the walls were hung with extracts from Paine's *Rights of Man* and the Magna Carta.

In other families during the war, children remembered talking about the Blitz, the blackout, the Morrison shelters, digging for victory and careless talk costing lives. In Libby's house on Chestnut Street they talked about equality and freedom and the Spanish Civil War, and the conscientious objector.

One of her grannies said that the most important thing in the world was having an aired vest and never sleeping in a damp bed. The other granny said that having clean socks and being regular were life's two priorities. Libby knew that this couldn't be right, because Mother and Father thought it was all to do with meetings and posters and standing up for people's rights.

There were always refugees staying during the war, and even after it. People were coming from different lands where they weren't free. Libby knew that this must be the most important thing. Specially since the bathroom was always full of nonfree people, and sometimes she had to share her bedroom with girls or women who came from faraway places where things weren't run properly.

Libby was very bright and hardworking. Miss Jenkins told Mother and Father that she would certainly get a place in the grammar school. They were pleased for her but worried because it was rather faraway; it would mean two bus trips each way, each day.

"Lots of people do that," Libby said, afraid that she might be going to lose an education because they were afraid to let her take two buses.

"It is her key to a whole new world," Miss Jenkins said, astounded that so many parents raised objections when their children were offered the chance of a lifetime. There was always something, like the cost of the school uniform or the fear of their moving into a different class system. She was surprised at the Greens; they were usually such forward-looking people. How strange that they should feel so mother hen–ish about letting their daughter travel what was not a great distance. Surely they, of all people, would realize the freedom that a child would get from a good education. And they should be able to give a bright twelve-year-old the freedom to take a bus, for heaven's sake.

But then Miss Jenkins didn't know what Libby's life was like at home and, out of loyalty to Mother and Father, Libby didn't tell her.

It would be hard to explain that she didn't go out to her friends' houses after school because Mother and Father were so uneasy until she got back. It was often simpler to stay home. She could invite people in, but then it always seemed odd that she couldn't accept their hospitality, so she didn't encourage friendship; it gave her more time to study, of course, but it was all a bit lonely. Not so much fun getting high marks if you didn't have a great friend to giggle with in between, and to rejoice or sympathize with over all the adventures of the world.

But when she got to grammar school, it was different, and Libby met another marvelous teacher, as nice as Miss Jenkins; it was a Mrs. Wilson. She watched out for Libby, ensured that she became part of the debating team, that she was allowed to go to sports events.

"What do they think will happen to you?" Mrs. Wilson snapped once, in exasperation. "You are fifteen."

Libby hung her head.

"It's their way of showing me how fond of me they are, I think," she said in a low voice.

"The greatest way to show people how fond you are of them is to give them some freedom." said Mrs. Wilson.

Libby said nothing; the teacher was immediately ashamed.

"Don't mind me—maybe I'm jealous; no one cared enough for me to watch out on the road until I came home," she said.

But Libby knew that wasn't true: Mrs. Wilson thought her parents were gaolers, and foolishly repressive. At times Libby thought that too, but she hated other people thinking that about them. They were her parents; she could see how much they loved her, and worried about her. She knew all the things they did for her. How her father painted her grazed knee with iodine, how her mother brought her cocoa in bed, how they listened when she told them tales about school. How her father worked long hours as a clerk in a solicitor's office, how her mother took in typing and bookkeeping work to help with the expenses. And she, Libby, caused a lot of the expenses: shoes were always wearing out, and there were school trips to places, and pocket money. She was as protective of them as they were of her, and she loved them.

There was a half-term camp. All the other sixteen-year-olds were going, but Libby's parents said no, truly, they couldn't spend a whole weekend wondering was she all right, had she fallen into a swirling river, had one of the rough boys forced himself on her, had their bus driver got drunk, had their teachers been careless.

Libby gave in without very much of a struggle, and that night, as she was looking sadly out of the garden shed towards the west, where the others had all gone, singing on their bus tour, only a few tears of self-pity came down her face. As she wiped them away she saw a struggling pigeon trying unsuccessfully to launch itself. It had a broken wing, and its round eyes looked anxious, its cooing sound had no confidence. Libby put it in her cardigan and took it indoors. She watched the scene almost as if she were outside. The three of them calmed the pigeon and put it in a box of shavings. Her father made a delicate splint for the wing and her mother helped him, so they could support the broken wing. They got bread and milk for the bird, and a few cornflakes. They put a lid on the box and cut holes in it. Its muffled, rhythmic cooing sounded much less agitated, Libby thought, and she saw her mother reach for a purse.

"Go and get it some birdseed, Libby. We know it would like that."

How could you not love people so good and generous as this just because they wouldn't let you go on the school outing?

For days she stroked the pigeon's head and admired its feathers. She had never really looked at a pigeon close up before. A wonderful white line on the bend of each wing, a bill that was nearly orange, its big chest, which trembled less as the days went on, was purple-brown with underparts of creamy gray.

"Lovely little Columba," she said to it over and over.

"Why do you call it that?" her father wanted to know.

"It's Latin for a dove or a pigeon too, I think," she said.

He looked at her with undisguised admiration. "To think a daughter of mine would know the Latin for things," he said, delighted. "But it's nearly time to let Columba go, I'd say."

"Go?" Libby didn't believe it. This murmuring, cooing bird had got her over the disappointment of half-term, it had brought her back to school without any hard feelings about the parents who had deprived her of a great trip. And now they were going to send it away.

"You can't talk about freedom, Libby, and then not let a wild animal fly away free," her father said.

"There's no use in preaching one thing and practicing another," said her mother.

They went out to the little back garden and stood near the shed where she had found Columba and watched the bird soar away. As she looked up into the sky Libby felt that she grew up. She joined the people who understood things rather than those who just learned things and accepted them.

She knew that her parents would never let her go free because they had no idea she was a prisoner. She watched them shading their eyes in the evening sun and looking on, delighted that their work had restored a bird to the wild, just as they had been happy to look after displaced Europeans immediately after the war; as they had brought tea to old tramps under bridges when neighbors said that the tramps should be taken into care, washed and tidied and minded for their own good; as they took the unpopular position opposing fox hunting; and had written letters to the royal family about shooting parties on their estates, and to film stars about fur coats. Libby's parents had looked happy when they had come back, cold and tired, from their protest marches with their banners, from their committee meetings, from their fund-raising for causes. All of these had been good things. They were just blind to her need to be free.

So in that moment of growing up, Libby decided she would look after her own freedom. She linked arms with them back to the house.

"I wonder what Columba will have for his tea?" she said cheerfully. "Nobody to hand him a plate of birdseed tonight."

They looked pleased, as if they had feared she would make more fuss.

"Come on. I'll make your tea for you anyway—I'll do beans on toast," said Libby. "*And* I'll cut off the crusts."

"Nobody had such a good daughter," her mother said, squeezing Libby's arm.

Libby felt a pang of guilt. Her mother did not know that she had grown up about twenty seconds ago and that nothing would ever be the same again.

At school, she changed. She joined the others after class, she got to know them, to talk to them. She came home on a later bus. She steeled herself to walk in cheerfully and face the reproach and anguish and concern. She was always calm and regretful that they felt such anxiety on her behalf, but this new adult Libby never suggested altering her behavior. She was so nonconfrontational, so willing and eager to help and be part of the family when she was at home, that she eventually broke down a great deal of their resistance. She arranged that she apply for university places far, far from home, and lived her life on campus, writing a long, newsy letter once a week, and making three-minute phone calls and coming home every vacation for a while. Sometimes she invited friends home to stay.

In her last year at university she brought Martin to meet them.

"Is he the one?" her mother asked her.

"I very much hope so," Libby said.

"You won't do anything . . . I mean, you will be very . . ."

"Oh, I won't and I will." Libby laughed, as she helped her mother dry the dishes. Martin was politely talking to her father about his garden shed.

"But what I mean is you're not . . . ?" Her mother couldn't finish the question.

"The answer is yes." Libby tortured her mother for a moment. "Yes, I am most certainly thinking of marrying him."

Her mother was both relieved and startled at the same time. She seemed glad that Libby wasn't saying yes to an open sexual relationship, but amazed that her child was about to marry and start a home of her own.

"Well, you have always been free to make your own decisions," Libby's mother said, sincerely believing this to be true. She hugged her daughter and wished her all the happiness in the world.

Libby and Martin got jobs in schools in London, and a small flat with a garden. Martin came from a big family: he had three brothers and two sisters. Nobody ever had any privacy, any time to themselves.

From the start their married life was happy. They didn't crowd each other out. Libby, so glad not to be questioned about what took her so long on the way home from work, fell into the habit of calling in on the library and bookshops. Martin stayed on and played football with the boys; sometimes he had a pint with the sports master. They shopped together on Saturdays, and took a bag of washing to the launderette. They did twenty minutes' serious housecleaning every morning and kept their place looking fine. They often asked each other why people made such heavy weather out of being married and running a home.

Every second Sunday they visited each other's families. Libby's parents still had causes, petitions and crusades. Martin's parents still lived a crowded communal lifestyle.

"No babies for us to play with on a Sunday?" Martin's mother would say, disappointed, looking at Libby's flat stomach every fortnight as if it might have swelled since the last visit.

"It's your decision—fertility is a matter for people themselves—but will we ever be grandparents?" Libby's mother would inquire.

There was plenty of time. So much to do, so many children to teach, so many projects to set up in the library, and children's corners in the bookshop, and like-minded friends to call round for meals and conversations.

Libby was almost thirty before she began to think of the future, of someone who might be part her and part Martin—who would, therefore, be a wonderful child. So she stopped taking the contraceptive pill. She remembered the day that she got the result of her test; it was the day she discovered that Martin was having an affair.

A great deal had been written about personal freedom. People had to have their own space, make their own choices. We were not the gaolers of other people, even those to whom we might be bound by marriage vows. Perhaps it wasn't an affair, more a whirl, a fling, a *thing*, even. People talked of having a *thing* with other people, nothing to break up a home over.

She waited for a couple of weeks before she told him that they were to be parents.

"Oh, shit," Martin said.

So Libby knew it was more than a whirl or a thing; it was an affair, a love affair.

They hadn't wanted it to happen, Martin explained. He and Janet had not set out looking for something like this. But it just had. There was no denying it, pretending it didn't exist, the huge attraction between them. There was only one life—this was it; it wasn't a rehearsal. He and Janet had to take their happiness.

Libby nodded glumly.

"It's early days, still. The pregnancy thing, I mean, it's not too late—for an abortion?" Martin asked.

"I have no idea," Libby said, and left the house.

She went to the bookshop; they were stocktaking. She helped them until ten o'clock. When she got home there was a note from Martin. "I've gone to Janet's, I assumed you would not want me here when you got back."

She sat and looked out at the stars in the sky for a long time. It was the weekend to visit her parents, so Libby went alone. She told her parents about the baby and they seemed very pleased. She didn't tell them about Martin. It didn't seem right to dim the pleasure.

In the weeks that followed she told them little by little. Always in a matter-of-fact voice. She never let them know of the nights of despair, the plans to kill Janet, the dream sequences where he would come back and she would forgive him the affair, defining it only as a fling. She never told them at school, nor in the library, nor in the bookshop, where she thought that Mr. Jennings knew something was amiss, but he was too much of a gentleman to mention it.

The medical examination showed that the baby was, in fact, going to be two babies. The baby-minding for twins would be more serious. She would not survive on a school salary alone, and she could not ask him to support two children he didn't want. She asked for a paid job in the library, and one in the shop. She told them why.

"I thought you and your husband had the perfect marriage," said the librarian, as she got Libby a few hours. Mr. Jennings said nothing, but wrote to the head office and got Libby a very good part-time job.

The babies were a boy and a girl. There were flowers from

Martin with a note saying he wished her every happiness and he didn't know the etiquette in matters like this, but she would have his eternal admiration and gratitude for giving him his freedom.

She hadn't known it was possible to love as much. Their little faces, their tiny fists, their sheer innocence and the way they depended on her for everything. Her life was fuller and happier than she could have believed possible. At school, where she worked a half-day, people said Libby must be made of stone; she had shown no sense of loss when her husband went off, she was able to leave those babies to a minder. Some women were as tough as nails. In the library they said she was a tragic figure but brave, brave like Joan of Arc. Mr. Jennings said nothing about her, but often brought the catalogs around to Libby's house so that she could read and make her choices of what to order from her own fireside.

Libby's parents came to call. They loved their grandchildren and, as the children grew, they were full of encouragement for them.

"Go ahead, climb that tree!"

"Surely, you'll let them ride bicycles on the main road, Libby—what harm could come to them? You must let them go out with their friends on their own."

It was as if their own restrictions of twenty-five years ago had never existed. And as she listened to them speak, Libby knew that she must listen. She must grow up again as she had grown up the evening her pigeon had flown away.

You couldn't love something and keep it a prisoner. No matter how much her heart would break, she had to give her children the wings that they already wanted. So she lived by this principle. Even though she must have inherited her own parents' anxieties, she showed no trace of them. She lay sleepless, waiting for her sixteen-year-old twins to come back in someone's car from a party. Or, when they were eighteen, for her son to wheel his motorbike into the back garden. Or, when they were nineteen, for her daughter to come home later and later from dates with a leather-jacketed, low-browed man who looked at worst as if he were a serial killer and at best a professional heart-breaker.

She spent longer hours in the bookshop. Mr. Jennings suggested she leave the school and work there full-time. It was a big decision but she was surprised how few people cared. Her son and daughter were too busy being twenty, her parents too tied up in their own concerns, her ex-husband too concerned with serious litigation. Janet apparently had not understood how he and Harriet had become involved, not wishing to hurt anyone but we only had one life—this was not a rehearsal and they had to take their chances at happiness.

When the twins were twenty-one they told her that they were going to Australia, one with a good job, the other with a de facto relationship that would guarantee a visa.

Australia wasn't far, they said. It wasn't forever. They'd come back; she'd come out to visit.

Her heart was like lead, her face a frozen mask as she presided over their departure. Sometimes she overheard them on the phone talking to friends: "No, she doesn't mind at all, glad to get rid of us, I'd say."

Could they really think that? These children whom she'd loved for twenty-one years? Always on her own; Martin had taken no part in their lives. They had never sought him out. Now they would be gone, and on the other side of the earth. They would think that she didn't care, that their leaving was something that probably suited her.

She went, like a robot, to the airport to see them off. She waved until their plane must have been well over France and maybe farther south, over Italy. Her eyes were unseeing as she turned away to go back to her empty flat. She walked towards the exit without seeing the man sitting waiting for her. Mr. Jennings, his eyes full of hope.

"Oh, what are you doing here?" Libby cried, embarrassed to

have been seen so nakedly vulnerable, mourning her children who had flown away.

"Waiting," he said simply.

"But what were you waiting for?" She looked at him with gratitude. It was so good to have him here to take away the empty feeling.

"For freedom, I suppose," Mr. Jennings said thoughtfully. "The freedom for me to ask you and tell you things I have wanted to ask and tell for years, and for you to listen without too much else taking up your heart."

This time Libby Green didn't feel she was growing up. She had grown up long ago; there was no further growing to do. But she did feel she understood more about this freedom thing. By giving it, you got it. She wondered did everyone else know this, or was she the only person in the world who understood?

THE CURE FOR SLEEPLESSNESS

Molly lay there in the dark, watching the hands of the clock move slowly, very slowly onwards.

It *must* be more than 3:17 now; it had been 3:10 ages and ages ago, and much more than seven minutes must have passed. And then hours before that it had been 2:30. What had happened to the clock—possibly it wasn't working?

But it was. Molly ran her hand through her dark, curly hair and twisted to find a more comfortable position. She listened to Gerry's breathing. He had been fast asleep since 11:30 and he would wake with a start when he heard the alarm at a quarter to seven. That was a whole three and a half hours away. Could Molly get any sleep before that?

Sometimes, when she propped herself up with pillows, she dozed a little and got a crick in her neck. Sometimes in the middle of the afternoon she laid her head on the kitchen table and slept uncomfortably for fifteen minutes. But it was never an easy sleep. The children needed her—Billy, who was three, would come and tug at her arm, urging her out to play, and Sean, the baby, in the pram, might feel hungry or just in need of company, and set up a great wail.

Molly had been to the doctor. He had asked was anything wrong, had she worries. Not more than most people, she had thought. She missed work—it had been a lively office, and she missed meeting her friends for lunch and being involved in their lives. She sometimes found that after you had cleaned a house, done the shopping, the cooking, the washing, the ironing, the garden, then washed, fed and entertained two children, you were utterly exhausted and at the same time your mind was curiously empty. She found it hard to concentrate on newspapers, television programs. It was ages since she had read a book. Gerry came home from work late two or three times a week and it was all she could do not to scream at him. This wasn't the way it was meant to be if you were planning a dream lifestyle, but it was the way things were.

And Molly did love Gerry and wanted to be his wife and be with him always. And Molly adored Billy and Sean. They were the children she had dreamed of, real little personalities both of them, adorable, and so funny she hadn't realized they would be such an entertainment.

And there was no way she could continue with her work in a busy advertising agency; she had *wanted* to be at home while the children were growing up—it had been her choice.

So she told the doctor truthfully that she didn't have any anxiety gnawing away at her.

He gave her a mild sleeping tablet, and suggested warm milk at bedtime. It didn't work. The nights were getting longer and more wakeful. Under Molly's big dark eyes there were now big dark shadows. The woman at the cosmetic counter told her about coverup cream that hid the dark circles. She was sympathetic. Molly felt that many women might have come to her for the same cream. When you were wearing full makeup certainly it worked; you looked less tired. But it was not a magic cure.

Molly didn't go on about it to people. Gerry had a complicated journey to work; they lived on Chestnut Street so that they could have a garden for the children. He had his day's work to do—things were more pressured in the company than they used to be, and Molly, Billy and Sean were depending on his salary, so he had to stay on top of his work. He didn't want to be hearing dreary tales about how his wife who had the time of Reilly all day, couldn't sleep at night.

Molly didn't want to tell the two friends who she still saw from work; they would crow and say that she should *never* have left the agency.

She didn't want to tell her neighbors—they would ask about it all the time and it would be added to the list of familiar topics they covered every day in more or less the same order. No point in telephoning her sister far away and telling her. So instead she wrote to her American friend, Erin, who lived in Chicago. She and Molly had been writing to each other for nearly twenty years, having started when they were nine and their convent schools had tried to broaden horizons. Erin had never been to Ireland despite her name; she was married to Gianni, who had never been to Italy despite *his* name.

One day they would come and would stay with Molly and Gerry for three nights before going to look for her roots and then to Italy to find where Gianni's people came from.

This had been talked of for years. It would never happen, any more than Gerry and Molly would ever pack themselves and the two children on a plane to the Midwest of America. Still, it was good to dream.

"We are much too young to be writing each other letters about symptoms and aches and pains," wrote Molly. "I'm only mentioning it because I don't want to be dreary to people round here. You don't count because you are thousands of miles away. And also because you might have a solution. Like you knew what I should wear at Billy's christening and what to cook for Gerry's thirtieth birthday."

Erin wrote back swiftly. "Tell me is it serious, this sleeplessness, because I *do* have a magic cure. But it's not one that should be used lightly, not for just one night here and there. If it's real sleeplessness, then I'll send you the cure."

Molly thought about it: yes, it was real.

"It's serious. Please, please send the cure."

During the long nights she wondered what it might be. An herbal tea? An oil you massaged into your temples? A candle you burned in the bedroom? But when it eventually came, it was a letter. Some old-fashioned, spidery handwriting, real pen and ink, obviously very ancient.

It had belonged to Erin's grandmother, who had come from Ireland, of course. She had given this to some friends and it had always worked. They had come to plant trees for her or give her gifts of thanksgiving. At Grandmother's funeral more than a dozen people said that they had her sleep cure. Erin wrote about it reverently and with awe.

"It should work for you, Molly. It came from Ireland and now it's going back there. I really hope it does."

Molly sat down to read what the old woman had written. Perhaps she had not been old when she wrote it. Maybe it was something that had been passed on to her. If she had left Ireland and gone to make a life for herself in the United States there might have been many a sleepless night involved for her.

Molly read the advice slowly. It was a detailed instruction about how the cure would take three weeks and you had to follow every step of it. First you had to buy a big notebook with at least twenty pages in it, and stick a picture on the cover, something connected with flowers. It could be a field of bluebells or a bunch of roses. Then on the night you couldn't sleep you must get up quietly and dress properly as if you were going out visiting. You had to fix your hair and look your best. Then you made a cup of tea and got out the notebook with the flowers on the cover. In your best handwriting you wrote "My Book of Blessings" on it. That first night you chose just one thing that made you happy. No more than one, and choose it carefully. It could be a love, a baby, a house, a sunset, a friend. And you wrote one page, no more, no less, about the happiness that this particular blessing brought you.

Then you spent a whole hour doing something you had meant to do, like polishing silver, or mending torn curtains, or arranging photographs in an album. No matter how tired you felt, you must finish it, then undress carefully and go back to bed.

Don't worry if sleep doesn't come immediately. There are still nineteen nights more of the cure.

Molly thought the whole thing was idiotic. She felt that Erin's grandmother must be a simple-minded old bat to think that this would work, but she had promised Erin that she would follow the rules.

Night after night she felt ridiculous as she planned new outfits to wear for her small hours' rendezvous with a notebook covered in daffodils. And she thought up little jobs to do.

She dug out the home framing kit and put up pictures of Gerry, Billy and Sean all over the bathroom. She gathered together her recipes and made a Molly's Cookbook. This meant that she found herself cooking new and different things instead of the same old favorite. She listed the books she had meant to read, cut out reviews of them and began to visit the library again when she took the children for a walk. While she was there she borrowed a book on flower arranging and did some spectacular arrangements.

Every night she wrote about a different blessing.

Things like the night Gerry finally told her he loved her, when his face was white and red alternately, in case she might not love him too.

Like the moment after Billy was born when she held him in her arms.

Like her parents' silver wedding anniversary, when they had said that they knew their daughters would be as happy as they were and everyone had cried.

Like that time in the advertising agency when the boss said

that Molly had saved all their jobs by her quick thinking and they had all raised a glass of Champagne to her for winning the account.

The twenty days were up. There were still dozens of blessings that she hadn't written about. She read over what was already there with interest. How strange that there was only one from the office; the others were all about the family.

Her house was brighter, her life more organized, she had learned that she had a real gift for flower arranging and would do some professionally for the local hotel.

Of course she still couldn't sleep. Or could she?

Disappointed that the twenty nights were over, and there was no need to get up and do these night tasks, she prepared for the hours of tossing and turning and, to her surprise, found that it was dawn. She had slept for seven hours.

It must be a fluke, a coincidence.

A silly idea about a book of blessings couldn't really work. Not seriously.

She must write to Erin about it.

One week later she had news from her friend in Chicago.

"Now that you are sleeping again, we must really put our minds to the next project. In a year's time we will be thirty, and we live in an era where people are going to other planets and we haven't worked out how to cross the Atlantic Ocean. If it's only a matter of getting the fare, then we must do it. My old Irish grandmother had some kind of magic about doing that too. After all, she made her own way to the New World all those years ago. I'll see if I can find anything in the papers. Or maybe you had a grandmother somewhere with some magic that we could lean on now when we need it."

And slowly, Molly began to realize that the magic might not have come from the grandmother, that it might have come from the fertile mind of Erin, who could write letters that made you spellbound.

MISS RANGER'S REWARD

Ronnie Ranger had been having a hell of a day. She eyed the gin bottle several times but it was too early. Three o'clock in the afternoon of even a very bad day was too early. And anyway she must keep some wits about her for this evening's scene. So, the gin would give her the courage to say what had to be said, but it would also release the tears, the self-pity, the whines. Another cup of coffee, and maybe an onslaught on the house. You can speak with more confidence from a house that doesn't look as if it's run by a slut.

Gloomily she got out the vacuum cleaner, sulkily she sprayed polish on dusty surfaces with rings of coffee or wine on them. Wearily she emptied wastepaper baskets and pushed a lackluster mop around the kitchen floor. The place looked better, certainly, but she could get no lift from this. How nice it would have been to be a woman who became excited by the results of hard housework, how great to look around a cleaned-up nest and feel a glow of pride. Perhaps Gerry was right—she wasn't the kind of woman to make a home for a man, or for anyone. She should go on being a career girl and live in a modern service flat with a lovely old Cockney dear who would come in and do for her every second day, like her sister Frances.

But what career? At thirty-eight, a washed-up dancer. Too old, too tired and, if the truth had to be faced, too bad a dancer to be a winner, or even to earn a decent living. So it had to be a home . . . well, a home, of sorts. There weren't any alternatives.

Gerry would be home at six, for an hour. He would have a bath, change, take a quick drink and then go out again. There were these clients, you see, they were only in town for a few days, it was very important to see they had a good time. Not all work was done over desks in offices, you know, a lot of it was done on expense accounts in restaurants. He wished he could take her, but Ronnie knew the score . . . they were all incredibly old-fashioned in his setup, they would want to know why he hadn't taken his wife . . . and that would means lots of explanations, Ronnie could understand that surely, couldn't she?

She could. But she didn't like it. Two years ago, when she had moved in with him, there were never client's dinners. A year ago, when the dinners had begun, they were over at eleven and he would rush home; nowadays they often involved his having to stay the night in the hotel with the people because it was simpler.

Ronnie was just like a wife, she thought to herself, but like the worst kind of wife—she had no security, no confidence that he loved her, would stay with her and look after her, no respectability in a world that seemed to care little or nothing about respectability . . . except so far as Gerry's business associates were concerned. There were a hundred ways in which she was beginning to think of herself as a loser, and very few ways where she could see she was winning. It was ironical that she, who had always scorned her friends' settling for compromise marriages, should envy them now. Even Gerry's wife, somewhere out in the green belt with her two children, her two dogs, her generous housekeeping money and her circle of friends, was better off.

Ronnie, earning a pittance by doing the administrative work at a local dancing school, wasn't well off at all. It was only three days' work at the most a week, it wasn't well paid and Gerry expected her to dress well and serve expensive food. He paid for the place on Chestnut Street, and all other bills.

She had given up teaching dancing in schools for this. It hadn't been a great sacrifice giving up the teaching . . . driving around for three hours here, and four hours there. Great unmusical, unrhythmic lumps of girls who didn't really care about what she was teaching, but imagined themselves swaying at some disco. Dealing with headmistresses about fees, filling in income tax returns, knowing that she was never going to make it herself and never seeing a pupil who would either.

Tonight she was going to say something to Gerry about the whole setup. Tonight she was going to sit calmly for the twenty minutes he might allot for a drink and explain that she was getting a very poor share out of everything they were meant to be having together. But she must say it calmly, because if she showed any emotion, he would say that she was behaving like his wife . . . with all the hidden menace that this remark implied . . . like the threat that she too would be abandoned. But Ronnie would be left with no car, no children, no dogs, no allowance. Ronnie, in fact, would be the one who would have to go. This was his house, not hers.

Perhaps she should leave it until they had more time; twenty minutes was not long enough to explain to his handsome, intelligent face all that was wrong, without seeing the flash of impatience and annoyance come across it. But when would they have time? This weekend was his one-a-month back with the family, so that the children wouldn't grow up without knowing their father. If only she had something to do herself, she was sure she would make fewer demands, and indeed feel less need to make them.

The phone rang at that very moment, and she half expected it to be Gerry saying he had decided to change in the office, but it was the hesitant voice of a girl or a woman who sounded a little unsure that she was onto the right number.

"I'm looking for a Miss Ranger, who used to teach dancing at St. Mary's a few years ago. I may not have the right number."

Ronnie was stunned. Nobody ever rang her at Gerry's place. She had never given the number to any of her decreasing circle of friends. They phoned her at the dancing school if they wanted her.

"Yes, but how did you know where to find me?" she asked guiltily. She was afraid that Gerry would come in at that moment and realize that someone had penetrated his own net of secrecy.

"It's very complicated," the voice said. "My name is Marion O'Rourke, and I've often wanted to find you, and just by chance I was having lunch with a man who works with Gerry, and he said, making conversation, you know, that Gerry lived with a woman called Ranger who was a dancer, so I thought I'd give it a go anyway. I'm delighted I found you in."

Ronnie felt outraged that a pupil, someone she had taught, some girl she couldn't remember, should have found her so easily. She felt even more annoyed that one of Gerry's colleagues should mention, "just making conversation," that Gerry lived with a dancing teacher. Where was the secrecy, where was the need to keep everything quiet now?

"I was wondering," Marion went on, oblivious to the effect she was having, "would you like to have a meal with me sometime? I'd love to have a chat with you about old times, and I'm only here for a few days. It would be great to see you again."

Ronnie was even more perplexed. It couldn't be a plot? This wasn't by any awful chance Gerry's wife, wanting some kind of showdown?

"What old times?" she asked ungraciously.

The girl sounded hurt and embarrassed. "I'm sorry, Miss Ranger. I suppose it does sound funny—it's just that . . . well, I owe you a lot, and I wanted to say . . . well, to thank you for teaching us dancing so well and to tell you a bit of what it meant to me—that was all."

Ronnie was guilty at once.

"I'm very sorry . . . er . . . Marion. Of course that would be nice. It's just that I never expected to be thanked or anything by a pupil. There are so many of them, you know, and they usually forget."

Marion laughed, feeling cheered. "That's right—we forget that we aren't just as important to a teacher as the teacher is to us. You probably remember the people who taught you, but have forgotten all about us. Anyway, if you *are* free, in the next day or two I really would like to meet you . . . if you wouldn't be bored."

She sounded nice and straightforward, and easygoing. Ronnie hadn't talked to anyone like that for quite a time. Marion O'Rourke? No, not an idea who she was. Half the girls in that St. Mary's had Irish names anyway, including that bitch who ran the place, Sister Brigid, who had fought her for every penny, and ended up asking Ronnie for a contribution to the church building fund. In a way, it might be nice to meet someone from that life; they could have a few laughs about it.

"I'm free this evening," she said suddenly.

"Great!" Marion was delighted. They made arrangements to meet at a restaurant. Ronnie wondered how they would recognize each other, but Marion assured her that everyone remembered their teachers, so she would do the identifying.

It put off any confrontation with Gerry and it saved her having to think of what to eat that night. She would have to leave now to get to the restaurant by seven, so Gerry could run his own bath and pour his own vodka and tonic.

She left a note. "Gone to have supper with an old friend. See you later on, love darling, Ronnie." She was quite pleased with it. It showed nothing of the tension she had been feeling ten minutes earlier. She put on her cape and a little makeup, and headed out into the cold evening wind.

She looked around the restaurant expectantly. There were four women sitting alone at tables amongst the other mixes of couples and groups. It interested her that women went out alone so much or were prepared to sit in restaurants alone waiting for companions. It wasn't something she thought she would do herself. Perhaps I'm getting terribly old-fashioned and set in my ways, she thought suddenly.

From one table a girl with black curly hair and a black-and-white caftan waved enthusiastically. She had a great grin on her face and a bottle of white wine already opened on the table.

"Miss Ranger, you haven't changed a bit—seven years and you look just the same."

Seven years, thought Ronnie. She must be about twenty-three or twenty-four. Nice open manner—I can't remember her from a crowd of kids in blue uniforms tied around the middle with pure blue sashes. Well, the convent didn't kill her anyway; she escaped from Sister Brigid fairly unscathed.

"Marion, you're going to have to call me Ronnie," she said firmly. "I won't let anyone in this restaurant realize that a grown-up, sophisticated woman like you was once my pupil."

Marion beamed with pleasure. The meal got off to a good start. They talked about the town, the restaurant, the fact that more women ate out alone, the nonsense of having a full menu in English and then "café" instead of "coffee." They talked about making your own wine, growing your own tomatoes, a film that had won awards for no reason, a by-election that had been a surprise. They talked about Marion's job; she was a teacher, apparently.

"Do you teach dancing?" asked Ronnie. Really, this must be the reason the nice, bright girl had sought her out. Either she wanted to get some advice about where else to teach, or she wanted to compare notes about what it was like.

"You can't be serious?" said Marion, startled.

"Well, why not?" said Ronnie. "I mean, I taught dancing for years—it's not like being a lavatory cleaner or an astronaut, it's a job a lot of people do."

"I teach in a primary school," Marion said. "I've been there two years now. We have a half-term—that's why I'm away at the moment. But you can't have thought for a moment that I'd have been able to teach dancing . . . me . . . were you joking?"

Ronnie was a bit confused. "Well, you said on the phone that you remembered and liked the dancing classes, and that you wanted to thank me. . . . I sort of had the idea that maybe you'd followed in my footsteps or something."

Marion looked at her levelly.

"Miss Ranger, Ronnie, I mean, I'm sixteen stone weight. I weigh two hundred and twenty-four pounds with nothing on. That would be some dancer."

"You don't look it, but I don't see that it would have made all that much difference, anyway. Dancing teachers don't have to weigh in like boxers."

Marion laughed. "I don't look it because I wear tents. And I'm sitting down, but the reason I wanted to meet you and thank you was actually to do with my weight. You see, when the dancing classes started, I couldn't bear to join them. Sister Brigid said that it would be six pounds a term for the course . . ."

"She only gave me three pounds a pupil," spluttered Ronnie.

"Oh, the balance probably went to the church building fund," said Marion. "Anyway, my father, who thought I must have everything, insisted. I remember the first day dreading it. I was so fat and ungainly, and even drill classes were a horror, gym was a nightmare, and I thought that dancing would be the worst of all."

Ronnie looked at this calm girl sitting in front of her, but then we were all confused when we were kids.

"So, on the first day of the class I pretended to be ill, and I hid in the cloakroom until the lesson was over, and then I just came home and pretended I'd been. My father was so interested in it all and kept asking me what we had learned. I felt such a shit, thinking of him wasting his hard-earned six pounds on nothing, that the next day I determined to go. We were all lined up and you were teaching us the steps of the samba. I remember it vividly the way you rocked backwards and forwards and the whole group were doing it soon, and then the bit I dreaded came where we had to pick partners and learn to do it as a couple. I knew nobody would ask me, and I'd already worked out that there was an uneven number so I *knew* I'd be the one left out. But before we actually got into twos, you came over and took my hand as your partner and the music started again. You kept shouting over the music, 'Not so stiff, relax, let your bodies move, not just your legs, for God's sake.' They were all a bit stilted like puppets, and as you and I were dancing, we went past other couples and you gave them instructions. All the time you and I were dancing it perfectly. You asked me my name. Then when some of the others were still getting it wrong, you said, 'Let yourself go, girl, for heaven's sake—do it naturally with some rhythm like Marion and I are doing it.' For the first time in my whole life I was there not looking pathetic and foolish. Nobody in the room thought you were pitying me—you had picked me before I was the last one left out.

"Miss Ranger, you have no idea how important that was. And it didn't end there—the next day and the next and the next. You sort of automatically accepted that I was your partner and sometimes when steps were difficult . . . like that side bit in the tango, you would say, 'Marion, for heaven's sake, you go over that side and show one lot, and I'll try and drum it into this lot here.'

"And amazingly everyone accepted that I was a good dancer and they used to ask me to show them the steps in the cloakroom and when we had school dances at the end of term . . . no boys, of course, just ourselves; the music was heathen enough for the nuns without having real live men in the place. But at these dances, people were always asking me to dance with them; I couldn't accept all the girls who wanted to dance with me. And I can actually date all the growing up I did from that point. I used to hide, I used to get red over nothing. Whenever we were reading in class and someone would come across the word *fat* I would be scarlet thinking they were all looking at me. Then I used to dread hearing about Falstaff, or about Caesar saying, 'Let me have men about me that are fat . . . yond Cassius has a lean and hungry look.' I thought the whole class was thinking about me. You really did a lot, so I just thought I'd tell you."

Ronnie looked at her carefully. Yes, Marion had a chubby face, she had more than one chin when she laughed, her hands on the table were round and plump rather than long and tapering. Beneath the folds of that caftan there could well be rolls of flesh. But you'd have to be in a pretty weight-hunting mood to think, 'This is a fatso.' She looked so calm, Ronnie thought for the twentieth time; yes, that was definitely the word that described her. Could she really have undergone all these horrors, and did Ronnie really save her from them, or was it some romanticized tale to describe leaving the normal tortures of adolescence?

As if Marion had read her mind, she said, "You probably think I'm exaggerating all this, and that all convent schoolgirls were wretched and miserable, but it's not like that. Fat girls were rubbish at school; the others may have been insecure too but they took it out on the fat ones. There were only two other fat girls in the school. I can remember their names to this day—one of them was in the dancing class but she was a very sulky girl anyway, and she had a best friend, so the two of them just giggled and didn't really learn, and the others laughed at her attempts to dance when you got us all to do the basic steps of a slow waltz. Nobody, no one person, laughed at me, because you said, 'Right, Marion, off you go; watch her feet, everybody.' And they did—they watched my feet with something like respect for the first time in my life."

Ronnie didn't know what to say. Eventually she said, "I don't know whether this will make you feel better or worse, but I just don't remember you. I suppose that means you can't have *seemed* fat and pathetic to me. I'm not very kind, you know; I couldn't have been doing it out of pity. I probably just found you, the one kid who had a sense of rhythm and used you to help me. You shouldn't really thank me for being kind, because I don't remember being kind. It's not in my nature."

"I know," said Marion frankly. "You weren't very kind or interested in us, really. You weren't like Sister Paul, who always went out of her way to be nice to the less fortunate ones. If you had raging acne or came from a very poor family or were fat, Sister Paul took you under her Christian charity wing. It was patronizing and embarrassing beyond belief. But you were quite indifferent, and a bit hard—that's what made me think, I really might look normal to you, and that's what made all the difference."

Indifferent, and a bit hard. A tough, self-interested, rather sour young woman. That's what I was then, that's what I am now, Ronnie thought. No wonder Gerry expects me to be able to take things the way they are. He probably assumes that when my self-interest takes me elsewhere I'll move off from him, and that he is entitled to act the same way. Even this grateful schoolgirl saw what I was all those years ago.

"How did you know a friend of Gerry's?" Ronnie asked suddenly.

"It's James, you know—he's a junior in Gerry's office. He's often spoken about him. James invited me here for the few days, actually. He and I have known each other for about a year and he was thinking that we might get engaged soon."

"And would you like that?" asked Ronnie.

"Yes and no. I've seen so many people's marriages break up, I don't want to rush into anything just to say, 'I'm married.' When I was sixteen I used to think that it would be lovely to be married; you would have one up on your friends, and that they would all say to each other, 'Imagine that Marion O'Rourke is married!' I don't think like that anymore. I mean it's committing yourself to one person and one way of life; you've got to be pretty sure. James says we can wait a bit—he just wants us to be respectable in front of my father and doesn't give a damn if we live together. Nobody in that office is too excited about relationships; hardly anyone has a conventional marriage."

"No, that's right," said Ronnie grimly.

"So, I come here for the odd weekend and he comes to see me, and in the meantime he has his work and I have mine, and if I could get a nice teaching job here, I'd come here, but I think that it's foolish just to go in and live with someone and expect everything to be marvelous, don't you?"

"Oh, yes," said Ronnie.

"I mean, you still teach dancing and everything, don't you, Miss Ranger . . . Ronnie? It would be a crime if you weren't teaching. Think of all the good you've done everybody all along the way."

And slowly and sadly Ronnie tried to think of all the good that she had done for everybody along the way while Marion's calm, round face looked at her pleasantly and encouragingly.

DECISION IN DUBLIN

❦

He was her only son and she knew that nobody would be good enough for him. Not if one of the royal family were converted and the marriage took place in St. Peter's in Rome. Yet she wanted so much for him to be happy. He had been her whole life. For twenty-two years, since he was a little six-month bundle in her arms and her husband had come in that evening with stars in his eyes and said he was leaving home.

Maureen had been too proud to go back home to Chestnut Street, back to Dublin to the family and friends who would have supported her, sympathized, clucked at the faithlessness of men. There would have been a life, all right, a granny, aunts, uncles, cousins for the baby, Brian. But Maureen had rejected it. Her pride would not let her take the I-told-you-so's, spoken or just hanging in the air. They had warned her about the handsome man she had loved so instantly and passionately. She had refused to hear a word against him. She had flashed the engagement ring at them triumphantly. Now, they had been wrong, hadn't they? He *did* want to marry her and honor her until death did them part. Or, as her mother said caustically, until something marginally more interesting turned up.

Something marginally more interesting had turned up when Brian was six months old. The handsome husband had left. But Maureen knew with grim pleasure that he hadn't stayed long in that nest either. Long enough to father a daughter. After that there were no more children.

He had been an exemplary father, the handsome bounder, he had paid the maintenance, had sent birthday and Christmas presents, had sent postcards and letters, and turned up four times a year for pleasant, cordial visits.

"There's no way I can ever be a father to you, Brian," he had said. "I gave up that right when I abandoned you as a baby. But I would like to be your friend whenever you need me."

He spoke of Maureen with admiration and distant affection as if she had been a faraway cousin, he always praised her, so that she could never, with any sense of fair play, rail against him. She had long stopped loving him, and his compliments only made her smile. A bitter smile, remembering how much she had believed them in the old days, not realizing them to be part of the easy charm that was his stock in trade.

"You should go back to Dublin," he told his son many a time.

"Why?" Brian wanted to know, not unreasonably. He knew it was his mother's hometown, yet they never visited it. Relatives rarely came to see them from that side of the sea.

"It's a great city," Brian's father explained, his handsome face lighting up with the good memories. "I've been back a few times for work. It's got a good feel about it, sort of citylike in some ways, with all those huge buildings and bridges over the river, but still it's like a small town too; you keep meeting people you met yesterday. You'd like it, even as a Londoner I liked it."

Maureen hated the ease that this man could show about her own city. She had made herself an exile because she couldn't face their pity and their protective concern, not even for her father's funeral. But he who had caused it all went back lightly and saw only its good, remembering none of the false promise of the time.

Brian had grown handsome like his father, but she liked to think that he had grown caring and sensible too, qualities he must have inherited from her. He had known that money was always tight, that his mother had worked in a chemist's selling cosmetics not because she loved this but because it paid the mortgage on their house. Brian knew that there wouldn't be holidays in Spain like many of his school friends had, nor expensive leather jackets, and not even the mention of a motorbike.

But he did have a bed-sitting room of his own, where his friends were always welcome, and when he began to go out with girls, they too were warmly received at the house. His mother didn't ask were they Catholics and was it serious. As mothers went, Brian thought, he had been very lucky in his. She was quite glamorous-looking, only twenty years older than he was, nice red-brown hair and freckles. What his father called a Dublin face. He wished his mother had more friends, men friends, even. She couldn't be totally past all that sort of thing in her early forties. Not if you were to believe all you read these days.

And now Brian was in love, really and truly in love . . . this time with Paula. He couldn't believe that she loved him too. She was so beautiful and so sought after. She was playing the lead in the small pub theater where Brian worked as an administrator. People were flocking to see her in this new play. Even the critics from national papers had come to see it. The wall of the pub had a glass case with all the reviews. One review had talked about Paula as a future star and had congratulated Brian by name for his discovery. Brian had a dozen copies of that paper; he carried them everywhere. To have his name and Paula's together in print. To have himself congratulated on discovering her, even though it was not strictly true, was heady stuff.

Brian had a feeling that his mother didn't like Paula.

Nothing had been said, nothing ever would have been said. But he knew his mother well enough to sense a freeze. He couldn't think why. Paula was so polite and courteous every time he brought her home. It wasn't that she was an actress; his mother had met and coped with many actress girlfriends before. It hadn't anything to do with his staying over nights in Paula's place, because since he had been eighteen she had told him he was a grown-up and must consider himself a free agent.

He wished that his mother would settle down to a girlie conversation with Paula. He would leave them alone a bit, and perhaps a friendship would develop.

Paula and Maureen sat at the kitchen table. Brian had made an excuse and left them for an hour.

Paula looked at the attractive woman with the red-brown hair and freckles on her nose. Why had she never married again? It wasn't that she was a religious maniac or anything—she seemed quite normal, nicely dressed too, and well groomed. Of course, she worked in a place where she could get free samples and everything. She was perfectly pleasant, but Paula knew that Maureen didn't want her for Brian.

Maureen looked at the striking girl with the jet-black hair pulled in a spiky frame around the pointed white face. She was a modern beauty, small, graceful and with a confidence that Maureen envied even from a generation away. And she was going to have Brian.

They fought for subjects that would not make them fall into roles. Paula tried not to be the love object and Maureen tried hard not to be the mother watching the only son leave the nest. They did all they could to skirt around it.

Paula talked of her family, who lived in the East End and who all thought it was highly uncertain to be an actress. They'd have liked to see her in a small dress shop, where she could move upwards and become the manageress. Still, they thought it was much more steady, Paula ventured cautiously, now that she had got herself an Irish bloke who had a job in administration. Sounded very safe.

"Do you think of Brian as Irish?" Maureen asked with interest. Her son had never been in her native land.

"Well, of course I do—that's where you're from, and his father hasn't been much part of his life."

"We don't go back to Dublin. We think of ourselves as Londoners, I suppose," Maureen said slowly.

"Wouldn't you like to go to Dublin?" Paula asked. She thought she was on safe ground here; she wasn't prepared for the look of anxiety and pain on the older woman's face.

"Too many ghosts, I suppose, too many explanations," Maureen said.

"Like do they not know that you and Brian's dad split up?" Paula asked, bewildered.

"They know but they don't talk about it. If we went back, then I suppose we'd have to talk about it."

"Well, the longer you leave it, the harder it's going to be." Paula was cheerful, then suddenly a thought struck her. "Hey, why don't we all go together? Then I'd take the spotlight off you—they'd all be so shocked at me, they'd have no time to think of you and divorces a hundred years ago."

With a sudden shock of recognition Maureen saw in this girl some quality she had seen all those years ago in the man she married. A quick enthusiasm that just dismissed all other difficulties. It would be impossible to refuse anything to Paula, as it had been impossible for her to refuse that bright, cheerful man all those years ago. Brian would refuse her nothing. She would break Brian's heart.

There were package weekends to Dublin, and they found themselves booked on one. Brian said it could be considered work for him because he and Paula could go and see whatever fringe plays were showing. Paula said she heard there were some new boutiques she wanted to tour, and Brian said he was definitely going to see the Book of Kells, and Paula said she was going to take a train out ten miles down the coast because there was a James Joyce museum there, and then she was going to a singing pub, and perhaps, if pressed, she might stand up and perform.

They were going to go and eat cockles and mussels in restaurants, they would go to the Guinness brewery and drink the real stuff made with Liffey water. There was the house where Oscar Wilde was born, and the one where George Bernard Shaw lived. The more they talked, the more ridiculous it seemed to Brian that he had never been in this city before. And the more Maureen dreaded their return.

"Will it have changed much, do you think?" Paula asked as they were checking in at the airport.

"It's twenty years since I left. It will have changed utterly," Maureen said, her voice sounding very Irish as she said the words. She sat in silence on the plane, and the young couple didn't try to get her to join their chat. She thought of her mother's voice. Clipped and curt, as it had been over the years on the few occasions she had telephoned. But of course it would be good to see her, and for her to meet her grandson for the first time. Yes, indeed. And was this girl the fiancée. No, nothing so definite. Quite. Quite.

And they would be staying in a hotel to get value from the package deal. Certainly.

And had Maureen any objection to meeting her sisters and brothers after a quarter of a century, almost, or would it be all right to see them?

Maureen had stammered that she didn't want anything special organized. Just if they happened to be around, she would love to see them all, that is, if they wanted to see her.

"Well, you'll see them on Sunday lunchtime," her mother had said.

Apparently after Mass on a Sunday they all still gathered at their mother's home. There was often a match on a Sunday nearby, and there were always fifteen or twenty in for soup and a drink. It had been a tradition and they all enjoyed it, Maureen's mother said crisply. Nothing to do with duty or formality, just a family meeting easily without making demands. Someone brought a salad, someone brought cheese, another brought wine, another a few bottles of beer. Only an hour or two, but pleasant. Still, of course Maureen probably had her own ways beyond in London, and everyone must live according to the way they had decided.

Maureen fumed at that. It was so patronizing; she had not decided to be a deserted wife for twenty-two years. It had been decided for her. Her thoughts were confused and unhappy when they landed in Dublin.

The road around the airport was a highway now; it had been a crowded, windy road when she had left. The signs were in kilometers as well as miles, the petrol was sold in liters, there were big new hotels in their own grounds, there were gaps where old buildings had been taken down. The bushes were still green, the letter boxes were green. But the phone boxes had changed and were mainly blue and white.

The city center had changed since she had left Dublin in her flush of love and hope. She felt gray and empty not being able to explain anything of this place, where she had lived half her life. She was as dull to these bright youngsters beside her as she must have been to Brian's father. The gray stone buildings of her native Dublin made her seem duller than ever.

She sent them off to explore on that Friday; later they would meet at the theater. She wanted to wander alone. She wanted to harden her heart for Sunday lunchtime, when her sisters would look with disapproval at the punkish girl that her son had chosen as his life companion, without any mention of church or chapel to seal it.

She walked down the Liffey quays, where she had run as a schoolgirl, and paused, pleased to see that some of the old second-hand bookshops, with their little outdoor tables for display, were still there. She looked up at the law buildings, and the big dome of the Four Courts, which had always seemed so huge to her but now looked like a properly proportioned building. She even giggled to herself as she passed St. Michan's Church, where they had gone as schoolgirls to shake hands with the skeletons. Down in the vaults, for some reason never satisfactorily explained, some of the mummified bodies had survived intact. Perhaps she should tell Paula and Brian about this place. With a shock she realized that she did indeed think of them as a couple now.

She arrived at O'Connell Bridge. It was sunset. She looked down the Liffey. It wasn't the most beautiful city in the world, but it looked well at sunset on its river, as all cities do. It had grace, and perhaps Brian's father had been right—maybe it was the right size for a city. Not too many to get lost in, not so few that you'd feel suffocated.

She turned away from the red gold on the River Liffey and walked on, almost unthinkingly. She wondered what her life would have been like if she had stayed here. Would she know everyone, as the crowds seemed to do, nodding and waving and greeting one another as they got on and off buses and crossed at busy traffic lights.

Would she have married an Irishman who spent a lot of time at the match or in the pub, like her sister's husbands seemed to do? They came back home in the evenings, of course, and stayed there for life, unlike her own husband. Would she have had a son as good as Brian, a sense of pride that she had brought him up so well and all on her own?

She hadn't needed friends and a social life and a big family and a lot of carry-on like that. She had been fine. She swallowed a little. And she *would* be fine, even when Brian left to go with Paula, which would not be long away now.

She hardly noticed that her steps had taken her to the area where she'd lived. She was now only two streets from her home. She stopped, startled that her journey should have led her here almost accidentally.

Her mother's house was only a couple of hundred yards away. The house where she had been born, where she came back each day after school, and then from the teachers' training college, until the day when she told them she had met this *marvelous* man and was in love. The house where she had refused to finish her training as a teacher, saying she could always take it up again in England if she wanted to.

The house where her mother had told her this marriage would not last and that she was going to wreck her life. The house where she would go on Sunday, with her son raised in a single-parent home and his punk girlfriend, shortly to be his live-in lover. To prove that they had been right.

She walked closer to see the house. No harm could come from looking at it. She supposed it had got shabbier in the years. But no, it looked surprisingly bright, its red brick well pointed as if it had been maintained properly, window boxes neatly kept and brass that shone. The curtains looked smart too. Maureen didn't know whether to be pleased or sorry.

Again, she felt her feet take her across the road. It was something that was outside her own will that made her climb the six steps and knock on the door.

Her mother answered, seventy now, not fifty, lined but not frail. She wore a smart red cardigan and a red checked shirt. She didn't look at all surprised to see Maureen.

"Come on in—you must be tired."

"No, no, not a bit. I think it's the newness of everything . . . or the sameness. Seeing everything again. I must have walked miles."

"Where did you go?" Her mother hadn't kissed her, exclaimed or shown any emotion other than pleased welcome.

Maureen told her the route, and they talked as friends who hadn't met for a long time, which was what they seemed to be.

"You're still on your own?" Maureen looked around.

"So are you all week, I imagine." Her mother was always dry.

"Yes, I go out to work, of course."

Her mother nodded. "Yes, well your father provided well for me; I didn't have to."

There was a small silence, but it wasn't hostile.

"And you see the family on Sundays—that's nice."

"It is nice. It's very nice, and the odd time during the week too. But in a way I owe you that."

Her mother was pouring the boiling water into the teapot. Maureen felt the years slip away. It was the same big brown teapot of her youth, or else one exactly similar. Imagine that teapot having survived when so little else had.

"Why do you owe that to me?"

"I was too sharp with you, I laid down the law too much when you went off with that chancer . . ." She paused as she saw the pain on Maureen's face. Then she continued again. "No, Maureen, it's myself I'm being harsh with now, not you. I was far too definite with my predictions and my laying down the law. If things had been fudged and vague I wouldn't have cut you off from me, lost you forever."

The teapot was brought to the table. It was the same teapot, surely.

"I had too much pride," Maureen offered.

"We all have pride; we're full of pride when we're young. When you left without a backwards glance I thought, I'll lose them all that way unless I soften a little. So I did. I didn't give out about Kathleen's fellow drinking, or about Dermot not going to Mass anymore. I didn't say a word about Geraldine's 'friend' who she goes to dancing class with. After you left me I learned my lesson. That's why they come to me on a Sunday. They think I'm grand nowadays, Maureen; they all have a good word to say for Mam. Dermot put up those window boxes for me, Geraldine's 'friend' digs the garden, Kathleen's fellow puts a tie on him for two hours a week and comes in here and behaves like a normal human being and Kathleen can't thank me enough for it."

Maureen listened, dumbfounded.

"And in a way, child, that's what you'll be doing with this Paula one, isn't it? Pretending."

"It's hard," Maureen said. "Why do we have to do it?"

"Because life is a bargain, I suppose," said her mother. "Because that is what they all meant about give and take. You give your approval whether you mean it or not, and you take their affection."

"But you were right about me," Maureen said. "He didn't love me, he never intended to stay with me forever. . . . You were right."

"He probably did love you at the time, and he did think he would stay. At the time." Her mother's voice had never been so gentle.

"But you were right to have tried to stop me. You could see from the outside that it wouldn't work."

"Was I right? I lost you for all your adult life. That doesn't seem such a clever thing to have done. Still, I suppose I mightn't have kept the others without you. So for that I am always grateful." She stretched out and touched Maureen's hand.

"And what should I do about Paula? Pretend I think she's ideal for Brian?"

"I'm long past telling you what to do."

"No, really, I want to know."

"I think then you should go on as you are. Taking no real view one way or another, but letting him know you'll always love him, whatever he does. I didn't let you know that."

"But she's just dazzling him—she'll leave him like I was left!" Maureen cried.

"Look at it this way," said her mother. "She'll be leaving from a less formal situation than you were. I don't suppose they'll be getting married exactly or anything. Just living together. That's easier to dismantle. I'd encourage that if I were you."

The sound of church bells for evening devotions rang out as they had rung all the years of Maureen's childhood. She had thought of them as just one more set of rules. Like school bells, like bells in teachers' college, like telling you what you should do and where you should be. Tonight they sounded different, a gentle, mellow sound, telling you that there was something there for you if you needed it.

She kissed her mother on the cheek and held her to her for what seemed like a long time because it was an embrace between two women who had never held each other like that before. Then she left the house saying nothing else, and walked with a light step to meet her son and his girlfriend at the theater. And afterwards she would walk through Dublin with them, knowing that this Paula probably did love Brian at the moment, just as Brian's father had once loved her.

THE WRONG CAPTION

Nora had once worked on a newspaper where they printed a picture of a couple's golden wedding anniversary with the caption DON'T KNOW WHY THIS *MUST* GET IN, APPARENTLY HE'S A BIG PARTY SUPPORTER. That particular issue became a collector's item, heads had rolled and nobody ever wrote down any instruction that could not be printed as it stood.

The next paper she worked for believed wrongly that its editor was a charismatic, and so the front pages were filled with pictures of arm-waving congregations. It was only when the editor was heard to say that the best caption for the twentieth such picture should be GOD—NOT AGAIN that people realized they had misinterpreted his allegiances. But not soon enough to alert those who thought that GOD—NOT AGAIN was exactly the three-word snappy line they needed under the picture and printed it.

So by the time she had made it to a national daily, Nora was only too well aware of the dangers of the wrong caption. She was almost paranoid about scraps of paper with any misleading information on them being left around the place. The others laughed at her. They tried to tell her that she was in the big time now, not in a Mickey Mouse weekly paper. But Nora said that mistakes could happen anywhere, and that if you had lived through the misery of that couple whose golden wedding was destroyed by the reference to their political clout, you too would be careful. If you had been part of the team that dealt with the hurt telephone calls and letters over the seemingly blasphemous caption to a picture of innocent worshippers, then you would regard caution as your watchword.

Nora had other watchwords too. She was uncompromisingly honest. Her weekly expenses could never have been criticized by the harshest of auditors, nor referred to as splendid fiction like so many of other journalists might have been.

Whenever she was sent to cover a rally or demonstration, Nora made a huge and concentrated effort to count the number who turned up rather than accept the word of authorities, who usually said there was a trickle of protest, and the organizers, who said it was a seething multitude.

She would not write glowing pieces about the magical quality of some free cosmetic, she never praised a hotel that gave her a free lunch and hinted at a free weekend. She didn't butter up those in high places who might have the power to give her a better job, a brighter window to sit at, a bigger byline. Everyone on the paper liked Nora. They accepted her obsession with getting the right caption as a kind of nervous tic, like the way some people had to have an undrunk cup of coffee growing cold on their desk before they could begin to type a story, and others who kept saying, "You know what I mean," after every sentence.

And as the years went by, men being men said to one another that it was strange Nora hadn't married, she was quite a nice-looking girl. Not bad at all, they would say with some surprise and shake their heads. Their only criterion for getting married was being nice-looking so if Nora had passed that test wasn't it odd that she hadn't gone the distance?

And women being women used to say that Nora kept her private life to herself unless you asked her and if you did ask her she said, like everyone else, that all the good men were long gone and had usually been nailed down by an appalling vixen.

When Nora went home to Chestnut Street, she started mentioning Dan a bit.

Dan was a teacher she'd met when she was doing an educational story. She had gone to his school with a photographer, and Dan had been impressed that Nora had checked the names of those posing for the group photograph herself. She had her notebook out and confirmed their names, left to right, writing everything down.

"I thought the photographer did that," Dan said.

"On normal markings we do." The photographer was easygoing and resigned. He explained that in the office, they were all used to Nora. She was a cross to bear but in all other ways she was normal. Everyone was allowed one obsession.

Dan thought she was delightful, the way she blew her hair out of her eyes and her pencil flew across her notebook in the hieroglyphics of shorthand.

"I didn't think people still used that," he said as they walked in easy conversation through the school grounds.

"Only ancient ones like myself do," Nora confessed. "It's from the era of belted raincoats, and hold the front page. You wouldn't remember that."

"I'm as old as you are," Dan said, stung.

"I'm nearly forty," Nora said.

"I'm thirty-six and a half," said Dan.

It was the real thing. More real than anyone in the office had ever known. Nora began to lose weight and talk to the youngsters about how many calories there were in so-called low-fat yogurt. She took serious advice on hair color and opted for highlights. She examined her clothes critically; she said she didn't want to be palmed off with useless comforting things like fashion being what you chose to wear, what you felt comfortable in. She said she didn't give a damn about comfort—she wanted to be stylish and fast. She was certainly reading informative literature about cosmetic surgery, if perhaps falling short of the final commitment. But she said these were desperate times; she was going to meet Dan's mother and didn't want to look older than her.

"She could hardly have conceived at the age of two or three," Nora's friend Annie said, but Nora took no notice whatsoever of Annie, who had married, unwisely, as it turned out, but at the age of twenty-one and had no need for rejuvenation in the high passion of her courting.

At Dan's mother's house Nora made thirty-seven ageist jokes, putting herself down. She mentioned cradle snatching seven times and said she had never really got used to the talkies, and she found more peace in black-and-white movies because Technicolor hurt her eyes. To Dan's bewildered mother, Nora pretended that she had done her early reporting during the First World War and had cut her teeth on the suffragette movement.

On the way home, Dan stopped the car and asked her to marry him.

"You're too young—you don't know your own mind," Nora said.

"In the forty or fifty good years we may have ahead of us, it would be a huge relief to me if you didn't have to keep this up the whole time," Dan said.

"Will they be good years?" Nora hardly dared to believe it.

"I think they will if we could drop the geriatric patter." Dan was thoughtful. "I can see you interrupting my speech on our wedding day with a few references to weddings you remember with the czars or maybe if it's a bad day you might go back to the Brehon laws."

"Wedding?" Nora cried. "You mean a wedding with people looking at us?"

"No, no," Dan reassured her, "there will be nothing like that. There will be instructions on the invitation that they are to arrive blindfolded."

They fixed on a day only two months ahead. Nora opened her mouth to say that at her age every minute counted if you were to beat the sell-by date, but she remembered what Dan had said, so she didn't say it.

Nora gave herself only one hour a day to talk about her wedding plans; she was worried that her work was suffering because she thought so much about Dan with love and hope, and about the wedding day with dread.

Annie was mystified. "It's only a day, for God's sake. You look great—what on earth is worrying you?"

"If you could point me to a shop that says 'Everything for the Aging Bride' then maybe I'd calm down." Nora's face looked tragic. The girls in the office directed Nora to the trendy boutiques. They told her to shut up or they wouldn't organize an office collection for her. She had to sneak time off to tour the boutiques. They were all staffed by eleven-year-olds. She found herself apologizing and backing out.

"Only having a look," she would squeak, acting like a shoplifter.

Eventually she realized she would have to come to some decision. The day was drawing nearer and she had reached no conclusion, since she had had no conversations, let alone fittings, in these frightening places.

"I'm looking for something for a wedding," she said eventually in a high, shrill voice unlike her own.

The young assistant seemed to look at her as if it was a very gross suggestion.

"A wedding?" she repeated doubtfully.

Nora had promised to stop wisecracking about age only to Dan. There had been no agreement that she had to stop making such pleasantries when she was not in his company.

"Not strictly a mother-of-the-bride outfit, but I do have a key role so it needs to be smart," she said.

"Friend of your daughter's, is it?" The eighteen-year-old was trying to be helpful. Nora's heart was like lead.

It was, of course, a nightmare—they kept asking her what the bride was wearing. She kept saying she didn't know. She had now announced that she was going to be matron of honor, and the bride was her dearest friend.

"Why don't you ask her what she's wearing?" asked the increasingly confused assistants.

"I don't like to ask," said poor Nora piteously.

They wanted to know if the bride would be wearing white. Nora had poured scorn on that one.

"It's a pity," said the boutique manager. "If she were wearing white, you could have worn anything."

"I think she'll wear white if I ask her to," Nora said desperately.

They found this a truly confusing wedding, but they kitted her out incredibly well, considering they had been given absolutely no information and a dozen contradictory signals. The dress and hat were stunning.

"I think you'll outshine the bride entirely," said the boutique manager.

"Ah, to hell with the bride," said Nora and saw that they took rather a long time to verify her credit card. She didn't blame them for assuming she was barking mad. It would have been the only reasonable explanation.

She collected the dress and the hat and the shoes the day before the wedding. They all stood around admiring her.

"What kind of a bag will you have?" they asked.

Nora had forgotten the bloody bag; she couldn't carry her huge office shoulder bag, and any evening bags she had at home would be wrong. There was nothing in the shop that suited. Then, one of the assistants lent hers.

"You can drop it in the day after," she said generously.

Nora opened her mouth to say she would be on her honeymoon and then closed it. Anyway, Annie could bring it back for her.

The day was a blur. Dan's mother, who had been keeping her distance a bit after the first startling meeting, was full of praise.

"You look absolutely lovely," she said.

Nora had a remark ready about the picture of Dorian Gray in her attic but bit it back. Her colleagues praised her to the hilt; they had even arranged to have a wedding picture in tomorrow's paper. Nora was about to help the photographer set it up.

"I can do it, Nora," he said. "There's only two of you—I can write the caption."

And as she looked at the way Dan was watching her, she smiled, her first real smile of the day. It was going to be great, forty or fifty years, maybe; it was something she never thought would happen to her. She sighed a deep sigh of happiness.

Annie took the bag back to the boutique the next day. They were agog in the shop. They had seen the photo in the paper.

"She married him herself!" said the boutique manager in outrage. "I knew there was something fishy about it all. She said 'to hell with the bride'—nobody with any feeling would have said that." Annie hadn't an idea what they were talking about, but she could trust Nora to have got mixed up in a shop where everyone was mad.

"Was there a scene in the church, you know, like *Jane Eyre*?" asked the girl who looked as if she should still have been at school. Annie was dying to be out of the place; she had a hangover and a nineteen-year-old unsatisfactory marriage to worry about.

"No, no scenes," she said tersely.

"Didn't they have to read new banns or anything?" These assistants were beginning to doubt that the institution of marriage could survive with people like Nora around.

Thinking that her head was worse than she suspected, Annie started to leave the shop.

"Is that why she didn't come back herself—she's actually gone off with him?" they asked.

"Of course she's gone off with him, on her honeymoon."

The baby-faced manager was a liberated woman—she said she always liked to see women be assertive—but this was ridiculous. "You should not be assertive at the expense of a sister," she said. "My one hope when I saw the picture was that they had written the wrong caption."

Annie knew that she now needed both a cure and an appointment with an analyst. With all the strength she could muster she said, "It was not the wrong caption. Whatever mistakes Nora made in her life, and she made many, including choosing this place to buy her wedding outfit, she was never responsible for a wrong caption in her life."

She left unsteadily, watched by the staff of the boutique.

"Do you think *she* was the one who was meant to be the bride?" one of them said as they saw Annie teetering away.

STAR SULLIVAN

Molly Sullivan said that the new baby was a little star. She was no trouble at all and she was always smiling.

Shay Sullivan said the new baby was a star picker of winners; it pointed its little fist at the horse on the list that was going to win.

So she became known as Star and everyone forgot that her real name was Oona. Star forgot it herself. At school when they read out the roll call they always said, "Star Sullivan?" On the street where she lived, people would shout over to her, "Star, would you do us a favor and mind the baby for me?" or run to the corner shop, or help to fold a big tablecloth, or find a puppy that had gone missing. Star Sullivan had a head of shiny copper hair, a ready smile and a good nature, and she did everything that she was asked to.

There were three older than Star in the family and none of them had her easy, happy ways. There was Kevin, the eldest. He said he was going to work in a gym, eventually own his own sports club, and he fought with his father about everything.

There was Lilly, who was going to be a model one day and had no interest in anyone except herself.

There was Michael, who spent more time in the head teacher's office than he did in the classroom. He was always in trouble over something.

And then there was Star.

Often Star asked her mother, would there be another baby coming? Someone she could push in a pram up and down Chestnut Street. But her mother said no, definitely not. The angel who brought babies had brought enough to Number 24. It would be greedy to ask for more.

So Star pushed other people's babies and played with their cats. On her own.

Chestnut Street was a lovely place to play because it was shaped like a horseshoe and there was a big bit of grass in the middle beside some chestnut trees.

Some of the people who lived there went to great trouble to keep it looking nice. Others just sat there at night and drank lager and left the cans.

There were other children around but Star was shy. She was afraid to go up to a group playing in case they told her to go away. Everyone else looked as if they were having a good time already, so she hung about on the edges and never joined them.

Molly Sullivan was glad that her youngest child was so little trouble. There was too much else to think about. Like Shay's gambling, for instance. He said he was doing it for them all, for the family. He was going to have a big win and take them all on a holiday. Foolish, decent Shay, who worked in the kitchens of a big hotel and dreamed of becoming the kind of man who could stay there as a guest. As if any of them except little Star would ever want to go on a family holiday, were he ever to afford it!

And Molly Sullivan worried about her work. She worked shifts in a supermarket where they were very busy and she was run off her feet. She had to keep a big smile on her face and be very quick, lest they think she was too old and let her go.

She worried about Kevin. He was grumbling because he was

still picking up towels and taking the bookings at the sports club. He thought he should have been made a trainee manager by now.

Molly worried about Lilly too. She worked far too hard, endless hours at a telesales center, so that she could pay for further model-training courses. She was thinner than ever and ate practically nothing at home. Of course she said they had *huge* lunches in the office, which was odd, as Molly didn't think they had a kitchen there. But then Lilly wouldn't say it unless it was true.

And as for Michael! Well, he was a worry from dawn till dusk. His teachers said that he would barely be able to read by the time he left school. He had no interest in any subject. His future looked very bleak indeed.

So it was always consoling to think about little Star, with her eager face. Star, who had never caused any trouble to anyone. Star wore Lilly's old clothes with pleasure, and even the T-shirts of the two boys. She didn't ask for anything new.

At school they said she didn't find the work easy and was always very anxious if asked to read or recite a poem. She was a kind child, they said, and if anyone else fell in the playground or got sick, Star Sullivan was always there to help. Maybe she might be a nurse one day, suggested Miss Casey, one of the teachers. Molly was pleased. It would be lovely to have a nurse in the family after the two dreamers who thought they were going to run a sports club or parade down a catwalk, and Michael, who might well end up in gaol.

Shay said that Star would make some man a terrific wife; she was so interested in things instead of just sighing and shrugging her shoulders like the rest of the family. He would explain the odds to her and the difference it made if the going was hard or soft, and the weights the jockeys had added, and how to do an Accumulator or a Yankee. She would ask bright questions too, and once or twice had prevented him from doing something foolish.

"Only once or twice?" Molly had said wearily.

"That's what I mean," Shay said. "She doesn't make bitter,

harsh remarks like you do, like everyone else does. She's a little treasure, Star is."

And Kevin never said a word against her. She helped him clean his shoes and asked all about the people who came to use the fitness machines in the gym. And she never took any of Lilly's things, just admired them. She never told her mother that Lilly stuffed uneaten food in the back of the dressing-table drawers in the room they shared.

Even Michael had a soft spot for Star. She didn't carry horrible news back from school about him. In fact, she told her parents that he was getting on much better than he actually was and sometimes she tried to help him with his homework, even though she was two years younger.

So Star got to the grown-up age of thirteen full of hope and dreams and sure that the world could be all right if you just believed that it was. They didn't realize at home that this was the way she felt, because 24 Chestnut Street was not a house where there was time for people to sit and think about the Meaning of Life.

And there was always a drama, like when Molly had the money saved for a new washing machine, and Shay put it all on a greyhound that was still hopping on three legs around Shelbourne Park.

Or the time when Lilly had fainted at her telesales office and had been sent home with advice from a doctor that she take greater care of herself, as she was starting to show signs of an eating disorder.

Or Kevin's latest row with his father about not having had enough money to send him to a proper private school, where he could have learned physical education. And Michael was suspended from school for a whole term and was taken back only because Molly went to the head teacher and pleaded with him.

At Star's school they were just relieved that Star had a smile instead of the constant sulk and sneer that so many of the girls wore all day. Star did not have a pierced nose or lip, saving endless hours of argument. If someone was needed to help clean up the classroom, or put out the chairs, or change the water in the flower vases, Star would do it without a seven-minute protest, which the teachers would get from the rest of the class.

When Molly came in on the parent-teacher days they told her that Star was a great girl, no trouble at all, which Molly knew already. Star wanted to be a nurse, and the teachers would say, Sure, she would be a wonderful nurse, and with a little extra help there was no reason why she couldn't do that. Was there a chance she could have private teaching? Sadly, Molly shook her head. Not a chance in the world; the money they had barely covered things as they were.

Could the older children help, possibly? Miss Casey wondered. Molly thought glumly about the three older children and said, Not really, to be honest.

Miss Casey didn't even go down the path of asking if the parents would help. A neighbor, maybe? They all led very busy lives, of course, but there *was* a nice neighbor called Miss Mack in Chestnut Street. She was blind—people did go to visit her and read to her, and it was said that she helped and encouraged them, so maybe it might work for Star.

"Tell Star she'd be doing the old lady a kindness—that will make her go to see her," Miss Casey said.

Star found that Miss Mack was very interested in Star's schoolbooks.

"Could you read me again the bit about the French Revolution that you read last week? It's very exciting, isn't it?"

"Is it, Miss Mack?"

"Oh, yes, we have to think about why those lords and ladies around the court of the king were so stupid that they didn't see what was going on in the country and how poor the great mass of the people were. Or *did* they see and not care? That's what I want to know."

"I think they were just blind, Miss Mack," Star said, trying to excuse people, as usual.

Then she realized what she had said. "I mean . . . I'm so sorry, Miss Mack."

"Child, it doesn't matter at all. I *am* blind. I wasn't always blind—it's only a word—and in my case it has to do with muscles and things in my eyes wearing out. I recall perfectly what you looked like when you were a little baby. But in the case of the nobles, that was a different kind of blindness, where they wouldn't see what would disturb them."

Star was so relieved that her blunder had not caused a scene or an upset that she rushed to speak. "I suppose we all do that, Miss Mack—try not to think about bad things, don't we? You know, try to stop fights and rows and things. I mean, if I had been alive at the French Revolution, I'd have tried to stop them fighting, I wouldn't have let them have the thing that chopped people's heads off. And the heads falling into baskets."

"The guillotine, Star. Say it now, say it slowly several times and you'll never forget it."

Star said it obediently.

"Did you want to stop people fighting, Miss Mack?"

"Yes, I did, but I learned that people only do what they want to do. In the end that's how it is. I think we are stronger if we sort of accept that. It lets us get on with our own lives."

"But aren't other people our own lives, Miss Mack?"

"They are, child. They are, of course."

Miss Mack sighed. Star didn't have to tell her of all the problems there were at Number 24. Everyone knew. Shay, who would gamble his last cent on anything that was offered. Molly, who was worn out from working and saving. Young Kevin, moody and unhappy, kicking stones around the road. Lilly, who had starved herself to become a model and now had an eating disorder. Michael, who was as near to a criminal as a fifteen-year-old could be. Thoughtful little Star, with the pensive eyes and the long shiny hair, who worried about them all from morning to night.

It was Star's fourteenth birthday and a lot of things happened that day. The Hale family moved in next door into Number 23. It had been empty for six months because the Kelly family, who had never visited poor old Mr. Kelly, who used to live there, had fought over what should be done about it. In the end they sold it quickly to the Hales. Star watched them arrive as the removal van was being unpacked, hoping there might be a girl her age. She didn't have many friends at school, as the other girls thought she was a bit boring.

But no sign of a schoolgirl. A man, his wife, who looked a lot younger than him, a greyhound and finally, last out of the van, a boy—well, a man, nearly . . . someone about eighteen or nineteen. Star watched in amazement as he took out of the van a guitar and a racing bike. She saw how he pushed his damp hair away from his face. She saw the sweat on his dark gray T-shirt as he helped to carry in the furniture. Could he be part of the removal company or was he part of the family? As the minutes went by she found herself hoping that he was part of the family. Imagine having a boy next door. A boy who looked like that!

Soon she could bear it no longer and went down to stand at her front door.

"Hallo," she said as he passed by, carrying a table.

"Hallo there." He had a great smile.

"I'm Star Sullivan," she said. Her heart was beating fast. Never had she found the courage to talk to a good-looking boy like this. Somehow this was different.

"Well, hallo, Star Sullivan. I'm Laddy Hale," he said.

Laddy Hale. She said the words with wonder. It was such a great name. She had better go now before she said something stupid and made him lose that big smile.

Star was in love.

TAXI MEN ARE INVISIBLE

A lot of the lads on the taxi rank went to Italy during the World Cup. But not Kevin. He couldn't be out of the house. Who would get the early morning tea for Phyllis, help her out of the bed to the shower, dry her back and sit her down at the knitting machine, where she worked all day, with the kettle and little grill near to hand?

The children would have come in, of course, if Kevin had put it to them that he hadn't taken a holiday in twenty-two years. But every day for three weeks?

And Phyllis would not have liked her sons or their wives dragging her poor body into a shower and out. And anyway it would have been so selfish to spend all that money just drinking and laughing with the lads. Kevin considered it only for five minutes before putting it out of his mind.

He'd go to the pub and watch it there. A lot of people said that would be just as good, same crack as being there without all the money and the foreign food.

On June 21, 1990, when Ireland played Holland and drew one-all, Kevin met the couple for the first time. He was just about to knock off and go down to Flynn's when he saw the couple running towards the rank, where he was the only car. All the other taxi men were either abroad or already installed in good positions in Flynn's.

They were in their forties—although the man might even have been as much as fifty—and well dressed. They had come out of one of the red-brick houses with the gardens, in the road that led down to the rank.

He could see them looking at each other with huge relief to have found a taxi as they ran across to him.

"I'm afraid . . ." he began to say.

And he saw the woman's eyes fill with tears.

"Oh, please don't say you can't take us. The car won't start and we're late already. We're going to see the match at my in-laws' house—please take us." She mentioned where it was, a good fare, but half an hour there and half an hour back to Flynn's.

"Look, I know you were going to see the match, but there'll be no traffic on the road and I'll give you twice what's on the meter."

The man was nice too. He wasn't at all patronizing, just doing a deal.

It would be a good few quid extra. Kevin thought he might take Phyllis shopping tomorrow in the wheelchair—she'd like that.

"Get in," he said, opening the door.

They had little to worry about, this couple. A big solid house where the roof wasn't a permanent anxiety. They had the use of all their limbs, both of them. The woman didn't have to bend over a knitting machine and the man didn't have to work long hours in a taxi that he shared with another fellow.

Kevin wasn't normally envious of the passengers that traveled in the back of his cab, but there was something about this pair that got to him. They seemed relaxed with their money and good clothes, and their ability to get a taxi and cross Dublin to go to a big party in a house where no one would ever have supported football a few months back. They didn't nag each other about the car that hadn't started, about one making the other late.

He called her Lorraine. Kevin wondered about names. No one in his street was called Lorraine or Felicity or Alicia. They were Mary or Orla or Phyllis.

Lorraine: it suited her somehow. Gentle, calm—and she seemed happy too.

They spoke with the easy confidence of good friends. He wondered how long they'd been married. Maybe twenty-three years, like he and Phyllis were. It would have been a different kind of wedding.

They gave him the extra money with an easy grace, and they left him with huge wishes and hopes for Ireland's victory.

Kevin tuned in the car radio. They would be just in time for the match; he would be thirty minutes late in Flynn's.

It was only four days later, on Monday, June 25, the day that Ireland played Romania and won on a penalty shootout, that Lorraine's husband met a girl with big, dark eyes. A lot of them had gone from work straight to a bar, and there had been great excitement. The girl had come in from her office nearby, and somehow they had all got together in the celebration, and then, of course, nothing would do but they all had to have a meal. They could get taxis home afterwards; nobody had brought a car.

Kevin had cheered the match to the echo in Flynn's but he had been drinking red lemonade. He could get in a great couple of hours on a night like this. The other fellow who shared the taxi wouldn't want to be driving, even though it was officially his night. Kevin might take in thirty quid if he got a few good fares.

Half of Dublin seemed to be wandering round the streets looking for taxis.

He recognized the man and assumed that the woman was Lorraine. He was about to say wasn't it a small world, but he stopped himself.

"First we want to go . . ." The man was checking with the girl.

There was a lot of giggling and then whispering and the man said, "Actually, that's all—we'll both get out here," and then there was the sound of nuzzling and kissing. The man looked Kevin straight in the eye as he paid the fare, plus a tip. He didn't even recognize him. Taxi men are invisible.

Lorraine came to the rank next morning. She recognized Kevin.

"You're the man who drove us when the car broke down," she said.

She had nice eyes, trusting eyes.

"And did it break down again?" Kevin asked.

"No, but Ronan's office was celebrating the match and they obviously all got drunk so they decided to stay in a hotel, the lot of them," she said. "So I need the car to go up to the school and I'm going to pick it up from outside his office."

Kevin grunted. It was as if he had sent out a signal of disapproval.

Lorraine sounded defensive. "Much better to have done that than drive home drunk," she said.

"Much," said Kevin.

"And there wasn't a taxi to be found anywhere on the street," Lorraine said.

"Never is when you need one," said Kevin.

Dublin is small, no matter what people say. There are over half a million people in it, but it is very small.

Kevin picked up a girl at Heuston Station. She was with her mother, who was coming to Dublin for an operation.

The older woman was nervous and bad-tempered.

"Most other women of your age, Maggie, would have a car

of their own instead of throwing away money on taxis," she grumbled.

"Mam, don't I live in walking distance of work and isn't it healthier to walk?" Maggie said. She was about thirty, Kevin decided, long, dark, curly hair.

"If you had a car you could come home for the weekends."

"I come home every month on the train," Maggie said.

"Any other woman of thirty-five would have three children of her own and a house where I could stay instead of a one-room flat."

"You're sleeping in the bed, Mam. I'm sleeping on the sofa."

"That's as may be. But it still doesn't mean that you shouldn't settle down one day."

"I will, one day," Maggie said with a sigh.

"Oh, yes," her mother said.

Ronan got Kevin's taxi from the rank when he was going to the airport. Kevin saw Lorraine waving from the garden. A boy and a girl were also waving—they looked about fifteen and sixteen.

"Nice to have children," Kevin said as they pulled out into the traffic.

"Yeah," Ronan said absently. "Of course, they're not children anymore, lives of their own; they don't really care about home at that age."

"They might, you know, without actually showing it," Kevin said.

Ronan didn't answer; he was rooting in his briefcase. He was a man who didn't want to chat all the way to the airport.

When they got to the set-down at Departures, Kevin got out to take the case from the boot of the car.

He turned in time to see Maggie running into Ronan's arms. Ronan took the case and they went hand in hand into check-in.

———

Kevin always worked Christmas Eve. He drove Maggie and Ronan to Heuston Station. Maggie was crying. "I can't bear it—four days," she kept saying.

"Shush shush shush, you'll soon be back."

"But they're such special days, and I want to be with you," she said, weeping.

"Sweetheart, they're just days. They'll pass. Don't fret."

"All that Christmassy lovey-dovey stuff," she wailed inconsolably.

"You know there's no lovey-dovey stuff," Ronan said.

He went into the station to put Maggie on the train, then he asked Kevin to drive him to a florist and a supermarket. In both places he had orders ready, a huge flower arrangement in one, a food hamper from the other.

Then he went home. The door of the big red-brick house opened and from his car Kevin saw Lorraine and the children running to greet him. In the cold night he heard Ronan calling out, "Happy Christmas!"

Ireland lost to Italy and the dream was over. But life went on.

After Christmas, Phyllis had to stop working the knitting machine because her hands got too misshapen.

There were two new grandchildren that spring, and the babies were often brought around to Chestnut Street for Phyllis and Kevin to mind while the parents had a night out or day off. They sat there and looked into the two prams.

"Life didn't quite turn out as we thought it would," Phyllis said to Kevin one evening.

"It doesn't for anyone, Phyllis," said Kevin. "Let me tell you that from my experience of the world."

That day he had taken four suitcases from the red-brick house and a box of papers and books. He had driven them with Ronan to the block of flats where Maggie lived. It was a different flat, a bigger one, one that would have room for them both.

Ronan had left the car behind at the red-brick house.

He was in walking distance of work; he was now a member of the serious taxi-taking community. So it was only natural that in the month ahead Kevin, as a taxi man, should come across him occasionally.

As on the day when Kevin transported the suitcases, he never entered into the man's life. Ronan didn't invite it and, although always courteous and pleasant with small talk, he gave no evidence of ever having seen Kevin the taxi man before.

Also Kevin wanted to punch him hard in the chest for having left that nice woman with the kind eyes.

Kevin looked up at her house often. The garden had become neglected, a fence was falling down. The paint was peeling off the front door.

In his own house, Kevin had done a few improvements. His sons had helped him repair the roof. They came up every Saturday until it was done. Then they put a coat of paint on the place. He bought them a lot of pints in Flynn's to thank them for their work.

Over the months he saw his own property improve while Lorraine's house went downwards. He was interested in her life because he had seen her so happy before it all fell apart. He wondered whether the children were a help to her. He knew that they went out with their father on Saturdays. Kevin saw them getting the bus. Their mother would wave goodbye from the house, but it wasn't a jaunty wave.

He knew that's where they were going because one time the bus had been full and they had taken his taxi instead.

They had talked at the back of the cab.

"Please God he won't bring Lady Margaret again this time," the girl said.

The boy was more tolerant. "She's okay, just a bag of nerves, and she always says the wrong thing."

"She can't keep her hands off him. She's always stroking his sleeves and things. It would make you throw up," the girl said with disgust.

"Well, she has to do something—he won't let her smoke in front of us, because it's a bad example," said Ronan's son.

"He's quite mad in a lot of ways, isn't he?" Ronan's daughter said in a conversational and casual tone.

Kevin watched the next World Cup, not in Florida but in Flynn's.

Most of the fellows on the rank were deep in debt when it was all over. Some of them got sunburned, and had red, scaly heads as well. From time to time, Kevin thought of the sunny day he had driven Lorraine and Ronan across Dublin, before Maggie had come into their lives and changed them forever.

Kevin still worked long hours. It had become a habit with him. He couldn't stop. He was tired and depressed on the cold February evening in 1995 when the hooligan element that came to Dublin for the Ireland-England match wrecked Lansdowne Road. There seemed no point in a game of football when a minority of thugs could take it over. He sat glumly by the fire.

Phyllis asked Kevin not to work so hard.

"You're only doing it for me, and, honestly, we have enough. We got the roof mended way back, the house can't fall down. The kids have all got jobs. What I'd really love is if you spent a bit more time at home, and maybe we could go out to the new cinema complex once a week and maybe go for a pint afterwards. I had someone check it out, and it's all on the level, no steps any-where. Wouldn't it be a great outing?"

Kevin thought how true it was that life doesn't turn out as you think. Five years back he would have thought there was nothing

good ahead of them, but they had fine times. He knew they were
luckier than a lot of people.

He saw Ronan and Maggie from time to time. They were like
man and wife. Even more so when their baby was born. A little girl who was baptized Elizabeth. Kevin had driven Maggie's
mother and sister from the christening.

Maggie's mother had not improved in temper.

"Well, I'd say the Blessed Virgin is delighted to have that scrap
called after her own first cousin."

"Aw, Mam, will you stop? Didn't they have it christened to
please you—isn't that good enough for you?"

"It is not good enough," Maggie's mother said. "All this talk
of partners and union and everything, with everyone there in the
church knowing that he's a married man and that our Maggie
deliberately set out to have a child out of wedlock."

"Shush, Mam, the taxi driver will hear our business."

"Hasn't he his eyes and mind on the road, or he should have,"
she said and closed her mouth with a snap. Just in case.

Lorraine didn't seem to mind Ronan calling in to his former family home. Sometimes Kevin took him back from there to the flat
where he lived with Maggie and Elizabeth. It was all very difficult. Kevin could tell that Ronan found the old family house
restful.

His children were not always free on Saturday nowadays; there
was a match or a project or a date.

They said that Daddy shouldn't be so doctrinaire. Even if
he lived at home he wouldn't be seeing them on a Saturday—
nobody's parents saw people on a Saturday.

So Ronan did a few of those little jobs around the house,

propped up the garden fence, painted the window frames and the front door.

Kevin thought he seemed loath to go when the time was up. The flat was festooned with baby clothes, and he didn't get all that much sleep, probably.

Kevin didn't believe they would get back together, but things were definitely less hard for Lorraine with the kind eyes than they had been in the days and weeks when Ronan had first left the nest.

Kevin drove Maggie and the baby one day.

It was on a trip to examine a new baby-minding facility—apparently the first two had not been satisfactory.

Maggie lit up a cigarette.

"Don't tell me it's a no-smoking taxi or I'll jump into the Liffey," she said.

"I don't mind, but is it good for the baby?" Kevin said.

"Of course it's not good for the baby," Maggie snapped at him. "Any more than living in a flat in the center of the city is, or the belching fumes of diesel or her mother having to go out to work every day."

"So what does your husband think about it all—is he a smoker?"

"No, you must be psychic. He hates it, and he says I'm damaging her little lungs at one remove, and that it's a bad example, and I'm not allowed to smoke in front of his two great louts of children. Not that he cares about her little lungs when she's bawling with them at three o'clock in the morning. He even goes to sleep in a different room because he has to work. There's nothing said about me having to work."

"Well, could you give up work?" Kevin was interested and caring.

"No, because he's not my husband, he's my partner, and when you live with a partner you go out to work. It's the wife who sits at home and collects the money. That's reality. That's the way things are."

Her face was angry and upset. Was it five long years since he had seen her first? He had been annoyed with her then, a home wrecker, selfish. Yet here she was, a forty-year-old with a baby, and very little security.

"Roll on November," she said, and inhaled her cigarette down to her toes.

"November?" asked Kevin innocently.

"The referendum—the divorce referendum, twenty-fourth of November," she said, and looked out at the traffic.

In Kevin's house there was a bit of aggravation about which way to vote.

Phyllis was voting yes. She wanted people to have the right to start again if they made a mistake. She didn't want to punish them.

Kevin wasn't so sure. If you made things too easy, fellows upped and went. He was going to vote no.

"Women could up and go just as soon as men," Phyllis said with spirit, Phyllis, who would never get up and go from her wheelchair and would never want to be a day without Kevin.

"I've seen a lot of unhappiness as a result of divorce and people leaving their homes," Kevin said, shaking his head.

"Well, if you have, you haven't seen it in Ireland because there isn't any divorce here yet." Phyllis spoke with authority.

They debated not going out to vote at all, since one would cancel out the other, but neither of them wanted that.

"My side needs it more than yours," Phyllis said.

"I'm not totally convinced that you're right," Kevin said. He had been listening a lot in his taxi and thought that a no vote was much less than certain.

On the day of the referendum he had Phyllis tucked in the front of the taxi.

They saw a woman holding a baby.

She hailed them and seemed disappointed when she saw the taxi was engaged.

"I know where she's going. I think I'll stop for her," Kevin said.

Maggie and her daughter, Elizabeth, fell gratefully into the back of the cab.

Phyllis talked to everyone whom she met, and Maggie was no exception. By the time they got to the apartment block Phyllis had discovered more about Maggie's life than Kevin would have discovered in a decade—Maggie's mother had her heart scalded; her boss was getting cross about time off to mind the baby; she had hardly any friends left and had just voted yes, and if the referendum passed, her life would change for the better.

"Good luck to you," Phyllis said. "That man's marriage is well dead by now and he can start again properly instead of just messing about."

"Yes, that's what I say. I suppose it will take a year or so, but then the world will settle down."

"I expect the two of you are planning it already?" Phyllis said eagerly.

"He hasn't said anything, but I expect he's thinking about it." Maggie bit her lip.

"Well, of course he is," Phyllis said. "Of course, what kind of a man wouldn't want to look after you and the little girl properly?"

Maggie's face was rather troubled.

Kevin suddenly agreed. "Ah, yes, of course he'll marry you. What else would he be living with you for and having a child with you, if he weren't going to marry you?"

Phyllis looked at him with surprise. You never knew what way Kevin would turn.

"And why isn't he voting with you?" Kevin asked.

"He has to see his big dreary children today," said Maggie. "He probably won't be home, with me, until late tonight."

From his vantage point at the rank, Kevin saw Ronan going into Lorraine's house. He had a tray of winter pansies. She brought him out a mug of something as he worked. They laughed together as old friends. There were no signs of the big dreary children that he was meant to be visiting. Kevin smiled to himself.

He would work late tonight. Phyllis would watch endless television discussions on the referendum and then, as far as tomorrow was concerned, he would be glued to the results nonstop.

He thought about Maggie alone with Elizabeth in her flat.

He thought about how life never turns out like you think and hope it will.

On November 25 Kevin saw Ronan coming out of his office.

By now Ronan sort of recognized Kevin and would say, "There you are again," to show that he was aware they had met.

"It's going to be close," Kevin said.

"Too damn close," Ronan said.

Kevin looked puzzled. "Well," Ronan went on, "it would be better if the whole country was one way or the other. This way it's divisive."

"That's true. Anyway I expect even if it does pass, most people won't bother getting divorces at all, most people have their own arrangements made by now, perfectly adequate arrangements." Kevin could sense Ronan eager to agree.

"It's interesting that you should say that—it's my own view precisely. If it ain't broke why fix it, that's what I say, or am going to say if the matter is brought up."

Kevin paused for a moment to think. What he said now could be quite important. It might even make a big difference. He could come down in favor of fair play for the wife or the partner, but not both.

He nodded sagely. "Of course, if you're in a proper relationship it doesn't need bits of paper, and registry office marriages and amendments to the Constitution. Any reasonable woman would understand that, surely."

Ronan leaned forward, listening.

"Could you say that again? I'm going to have a bit of an ear-bending tonight."

Kevin said it again and added more.

There was a lot of celebration in the kitchen. Phyllis and her friends were raising a glass to the new Ireland.

But Kevin wasn't thinking about it; he was thinking of the people who traveled in his car.

He knew that he must not be foolish about all this. Ronan would not return to the red-brick house where he had planted the winter pansies, but he would visit often and easily.

And Lorraine, the woman with the kind eyes, would not have her husband back to live. But there would surely be a little unworthy feeling of satisfaction that there was no second wedding day, no second wife, even though the law of the land had changed to say that there could be a second.

And Kevin smiled to himself, thinking of the small but not insignificant part he had played in bringing more peace to the troubled gray eyes of Lorraine.

He decided not to think at all about the dark, anxious eyes of Maggie. He wasn't God. He couldn't solve everything.

A CARD FOR FATHER'S DAY

Lisa had paused in the big store and watched the people buying cards for Father's Day. Every year she did this, and often went up real close to listen to what they were saying.

"I think he'd like this one—there's a lovely poem," a girl might say.

"He doesn't ever read the verse," her sister would reply.

Or she might see women in their sixties buying them. Was this to send to an old man far away in a nursing home? Or for their own husbands, maybe? She had never bought a Father's Day card because she never had a father. Well, she had, of course, twenty-five years back. But he had not been interested enough to want to know anything at all about her. She had long stopped asking her mother.

It was only a question that made Sara, her mother, sad.

"He never fell out with you, Lisa, he never saw you; it was me he fell out with."

Over the years Lisa had learned that he had been a student, and his family was wealthy, and ambitious for him. They would not have wanted him to have married Sara, a seventeen-year-old girl from Chestnut Street who worked in a factory. They wanted him far away from the relationship, so they even left the country. They were not to know what a determined young woman Sara was, strong enough to raise a child alone and to become manager of a firm of contract cleaners.

So somewhere in America she had a dad, a man who would be forty-four now, maybe a big businessman living in a white wooden house with children of his own who would send him cards on Father's Day.

Would he ever think of the child who had been born a quarter of a century ago, a child who longed to meet him just once. Once would do and for him to say that she had turned out so well.

For Lisa *had* turned out well. She was the personal assistant to a very senior executive who also happened to be a good and kind man. Mr. Kent, who respected her enormously and gave her more and more responsibility at work. He urged her to take more courses and saw that she got credit for everything she did.

"Always trust your instinct," he would advise. "Listen to the first thing that comes into your head—it's often the right thing."

"I think he fancies you," the other girls said.

But Lisa knew this wasn't so. Mr. Kent was a widower who was now very happily married to his job. He spent long hours in his office, and had never given her the slightest indication that he was interested in her. Which was just as well, really, because he was very old; he might even have been over fifty. He often asked her if she had fallen in love yet or if she would leave the company to marry and bring up babies. Lisa would always laugh easily and tell him that she had never truly loved anyone at all more than herself.

"Too set in my ways, really. I love my own flat, my own freedom. I was brought up to be independent; you should blame my mother."

Mr. Kent knew Lisa's mother, Sara; her company had the contract to clean their offices. Mr. Kent had put more business her mother's way. He was a thorough gentleman.

He was not a man who would understand how she felt mistrustful of young men and their promises of commitment. It was as if the disappearance of her own father at the very moment he knew of her future existence had made her unwilling to trust any men at all.

There was a very pleasant young man called James around at the moment but she knew she was frightening him away by her refusal to believe that he could be sincere. She couldn't be full of suspicions and misgivings forever, James had warned her. What a terrible, terrible waste that would be. But Lisa would not tell this to her kind boss, Mr. Kent; instead she would jokily blame her mother.

"Sara was wondering if she might have brought you up to be too independent," Mr. Kent said.

Lisa was surprised. Her mother rarely spoke of her private life at all to any customers. Least of all, she would have thought, to Mr. Kent.

He saw that she was startled and hurried to explain.

"We often talk together at the end of a long busy day. She often comes in to supervise the cleaning team then. She is even more proud of you than I am."

"Well, she did a great job," Lisa said. "And you completed it. I wouldn't have got half this distance without your encouragement."

"Perhaps I pushed you too hard. Maybe I made you concentrate too hard on work, so much so that you forgot to consider all the young men around you?"

He sounded genuinely anxious.

"And, Lisa, I had another reason for caring that neither your mother nor I are putting too much pressure on you."

"You had?" She was very confused. His voice sounded entirely different now. This wasn't a normal office conversation.

"I didn't mean to tell you but I see you've guessed."

"Guessed?"

"I've asked your mother to marry me, and she said yes. We were to tell you tonight."

He looked at her, his face all lit up with the pleasure of it.

"What do you think, Lisa—what is the first thought that comes into your head?"

She went to embrace him.

"I think that from now on I'll always have someone to buy a Father's Day card for," she said.

THE GIFT OF DIGNITY

Everyone knew that David Jones was having an affair. David's boss, Mike, at the picture framer's, knew and he couldn't understand it.

David's wife, Anna, was such a star. Small, dark, eager and enthusiastic. She was always laughing and cheerful no matter how many gloomy days the company had been through.

Her kitchen was their meeting place as they sorted out their problems and organized rescue missions for the firm.

Anna was there, elbows on the table, dreaming up new schemes, new promotions, ways of cutting costs.

She would serve them hot lentil soup, assuring them that it cost three pence a mug and no profits were being frittered.

David's twin sister, Emily, knew, and it broke her heart. She had been so close to David for thirty-five years—they shared everything, and she really did have this twin thing of knowing when he was happy or when he was upset. But she had not felt any intuition about the affair; she discovered it by accident when she was at a wedding and overheard someone pointing out a blond woman as Rita, who was having a steamy affair with that guy David, who worked in the picture framer's.

Emily had to sit down with shock. And as she watched with a heavy heart during the rest of the wedding she saw her twin brother close at Rita's side, touching her arm, smiling at her with a special smile. And Emily knew it was true.

Anna's father, Martin, knew about the affair, because he had been staying in a hotel on the south coast on business and seen in the register that a Mr. and Mrs. David Jones with their address had also checked in. What a wonderful coincidence! he thought. We can have dinner together. And how odd they didn't tell us last Sunday. He was not at all suspicious until he rang his wife, and mentioned the fact.

"Don't be ridiculous, Martin. Anna was here with me this afternoon—she's only just gone. It must be some other David Jones."

"Yes, of course," Anna's father said in a hollow voice, because he had seen the address and knew that it was not. Anna's father stayed in his room and had a plate of sandwiches served to him lest he meet his son-in-law and risk a confrontation.

Anna's friends all knew that David was having an affair because he certainly didn't go to any trouble to hide it. They saw him with Rita at the golf club, in wine bars and nuzzling in a car outside the railway station.

It wasn't something they ever mentioned to Anna. At first because they thought she didn't know and they did not want to be the one who brought the bad news. Then later, when they assumed that she *must* know, they didn't mention it because it was up to her to bring the subject up if she wanted to.

And when she *did* bring it up they could be sympathetic, shruggy or whatever was called for. And obviously she knew about it.

David was making no secret of Rita; there was no way that he was under any kind of cover.

Anna's best friend, Marigold, knew, and she wondered how on earth Anna could bear it. Yet Anna went along with her life quite normally. She walked the children to school, two little boys, seven and six, and then she went to work until it was time to collect the children again. She always had a welcome in the house for everyone and her smile was just as bright as before Rita had come on the scene.

Rita, with her threatening behavior. Ice cool and haughty, driving poor, stupid David mad by playing hard to get when he least expected it.

Marigold would never forgive Rita for demanding that David leave Anna's birthday party to go and see her. Marigold had been standing nearby when the call came.

"I have to go," David had said, his face grim.

"Nothing wrong?" Anna looked worried.

"No, a work thing, has to be sorted out," he said and he was out the door and into his car.

Marigold had wanted to run after him and beat him with her fists. How dare he leave his wife's birthday party. How dare he pretend it was work. Mike, his boss, was there in the room with them. Everyone would know that it could have nothing to do with work. David was not even giving Anna the dignity of lying to her properly.

Marigold had helped Anna to wash up that day.

"Pity David had to leave," she ventured.

"I know, but he puts everything into that company," Anna said, eager and full of support. "You noticed Mike was happy to stay on drinking wine, but David went to cope with whatever it was."

She sounded admiring about it all.

Oh, well, Marigold thought, if that's how she's going to play it, fine—everyone must make a personal decision about these things. Friends must not barge in and force them to take a different attitude.

Marigold sighed at the faithlessness of men. Something she had known many years ago, before her own bitter divorce. Would it have been an option at that time to pretend that she was blind to what was going on? Would her husband's affair have fizzled out if she had been able to ignore it?

No, not for her it wouldn't have been, but for others it might be, so she resolved not to tackle Anna about it all.

It never crossed anyone's mind that Anna actually didn't know. They all assumed that this was her way of coping. So when it was known that Anna's great friend Sally from school days long back was going to come for a visit, everyone sighed with relief. Anna would be able to talk to Sally about it. The weight was now off their minds. Sally would cope.

Sally was one of those amazingly organized women whom everyone should have hated from pure jealousy, but, in fact, everyone loved her.

She was in her late thirties, looked in her twenties, had short fair hair that looked just as well after a rainstorm or a swim as it did when she came out of the hairdressing salon. She had a job as a columnist on a big London newspaper, she was often on television talk shows, she had a handsome husband, Johnny, who adored her, two teenage children who were proud of her and who did not take drugs, run with a gang or fill the house with terrible people.

Sally had time for her friends, and every year she came to stay with Anna for a long weekend. Sally admired everything, remembered everyone's names, brought silly gifts for their children and organized a great Chinese meal out just for the girls.

They all knew that if anyone could sort it out, then it would be Sally.

Emily came to lunch just before Sally's visit.

"Can I take the kids for a bit when Sally's here—you and she will have lots to talk about."

Anna's face was all smiles.

"Oh, Em, you're so good, such a sister-in-law there never was. No, I don't need you, as it happens, because Mike and his wife have said the very same thing. They're going to take them to the ice skating, would you believe, and Marigold next door has offered to take them to a computer show, and everyone has been so marvelous."

Emily's face was grim. She knew why everyone was busy taking the two little boys away. They all hoped that if Sally had time and space she would sort out Anna's problems. Sally could tell Anna to face the facts. She must give David an ultimatum: either he gives up Rita or he leaves home.

Emily felt sure that her twin brother would give up this strange, pale girl.

Perhaps it was only a fling; he might not have felt appreciated enough. He might only have done it to prove that he could. Once he saw how much Anna cared, Rita would be given her marching orders, the reconciliation would be tearful and sweet. It might make the marriage even better. Stronger.

Emily wondered why she had such misgivings about it all. She found herself alone with her twin brother for a few minutes.

"Anything wrong, Em?" he asked.

"You know what's wrong." she said.

He looked up, surprised. "I don't."

"Then you're an even greater fool than I thought," Emily said, near tears, and left him looking bewildered.

Why hadn't she said it straight out there and then? Because she was afraid that Anna or one of the boys would come back and join them. And she didn't want to wreck it when she knew that Sally would do it much better.

Anna was taking four days off from work for Sally's visit. She did her shopping to fill the freezer with treats. She had got nice new pillowcases and matching towels for the guest room. It was wonderful to have a friend like Sally, unchanged since the days when they sat in school tunics and planned for the future. And it didn't matter that Anna worked in an office and Sally was a regular guest on *Any Questions?*; they were still the same people.

Sally had brought exactly the right video games for Frank and Harry. She never exclaimed on how big they had got or tried to kiss them, but gave manful handshakes instead. She told them that when they were ten and nine they could come to London and stay with her and she would give them a weekend to remember— they must start writing down now all the things they wanted to do in three years' time.

Sally admired the house, the gorgeous colors in the bedroom, the window boxes, all the fresh air. No one would have known the splendor of Sally's own house in London. She spread such delight and enthusiasm all around her no one remembered she was a celebrity whose home was often featured in big color spreads in magazines.

She listened to Anna's story of the picture framing business and how it had survived a crisis yet again. And how her job was very tiring but they were very good to her and gave her staggered hours, and how David had to do a lot of traveling these days for the company and was away from home at least one night a week, sometimes two.

"That's hard," Sally said sympathetically. "Is he buying wood for frames or meeting possible new clients or what?"

Anna was vague. "I don't know. A little of both, I imagine. Anyway, there it is. It has to be done."

Her smile was as bright as ever.

Sally went walking with her friend Anna and admired the countryside. She was so *lucky* to live in this lovely part of the world. Unlike so many people who came up from the south and said the north was grim, Sally always praised it to the skies. No wonder she had so many friends. And they couldn't wait to see her. They were all begging her to come for coffee, to drop in for a drink, to admire the new baby, the new pergola in the garden. It didn't take Sally long to realize that something was up; they wanted to see her without Anna.

Sally thought it all through.

It couldn't be a matter of Anna's health—she had never looked better, she had described her recent checkup, they both went for routine screenings and examinations. There was nothing wrong with the boys. The business was staggering and lurching on as it had always done.

It had to be David.

David, who now went on vague business trips.

They were going to tell her that David was straying from home and that Anna had no idea about it. Would Sally act as some kind of go-between. And Sally made a decision that she would do nothing of the sort. If Anna asked her advice, she would give it, but she would listen to no confidences from friends.

So she refused all offers of tête-à-têtes, saying that she was rushed off her feet. Instead she went everywhere with Anna, waiting for her to open up, if this was what she had in mind. But there was no expected confidence.

If there was anything going on, Anna certainly knew nothing of it. Sally and Anna had told each other everything from the day of their first period to the first groping experiments to betrayals by boyfriends, to their anxieties and doubts about marriage. If Anna thought that David had another woman she would have told Sally.

David, on the other hand, *did* look different, and edgy and ill at ease. He seemed fearful of being alone with Sally in case she brought the subject up. He asked her a great deal about her own work and told her little of the business.

"Anna tells me you travel a lot now. That must be nice. Or is it just tiring? Where do you go?" Sally's voice was clear and straightforward as it was in television, no fuzziness or leaving room for vague answers.

David looked rattled. He immediately went on the defensive. "Well, it's easy to say it's all fun and games but it has to be done, in a business like ours. It has to grow, expand, be open to new ideas, see what's going on. It's not all drinking cocktails in hotel bars, you know." He glowered at them both.

Anna was stung. "I never said for a moment that it was. I said it was tiring for you, that's all." She looked hurt and very put out.

And he hastened to reassure her. "Sorry, I got the wrong end of the stick—I thought you were telling Sally that I was always swanning off to places."

"Lord, David, why would you think that?" Sally asked, her blue eyes clear and unfaltering in their look.

David shrugged and turned away. "I don't know."

Then he recovered and turned his famous smile on them both. "Just executive stress, and sheer bad temper and bad manners. Am I forgiven?"

Anna rushed to give him a hug; Sally gave a broad smile.

"What's to forgive, David? Simple misunderstanding," she said.

On the night of the Chinese dinner, Anna said that she was going to get her hair done. It had been a gift from the rest of the girls, a voucher so that she would look terrific in the photographs that they took every time Sally came to town. It was the late-opening night in the salon. Marigold had made the appointment for her at Lilian's place.

"Perhaps I'll come and get my hair done with you?" Sally suggested. She knew she had been hijacked by the girls.

"No, no, they want you to themselves for a bit. I'll join you later." Anna was proud that her friends all liked Sally so much. It would openly cause a scene now if Sally were to refuse. Grimly she walked into the Chinese restaurant and explained to the waiter that she was paying for the wine, which should come now, and that the food, which would be Menu C, should wait for a while.

"Right," she said looking around the eight faces, "we have three quarters of an hour. Tell me about it as quickly and as clearly as you can without wasting a single second."

There was a pause. *Nobody* was direct like Sally was direct. Then the story came out.

A sorry tale of deception and this odd, pale, unlikable girl, Rita. A photographer who had sadly come to choose frames for an exhibition and had fallen for David. She was thought to have had a man up to that time, but the man had been sent away. She lived in a big studio flat not far away. David was spending more and more time there, parking the van outside in the afternoons. At any gathering where Rita was present, David stood by her side, grinning sheepishly and smiling proudly. They all wanted to smack the smile off his face.

"Maybe he loves her," Sally said simply.

This silenced them all.

Love wasn't a word they expected to hear mentioned. Betrayal, yes, or cheating, adultery, unfaithful, total liar. Not love.

"He has no business loving her," said Emily, David's sister.

"He doesn't know how to love," sniffed Marigold. The others shook their heads and thought that whatever it was, it was not that.

Sally's face remained bright and interested. "And Anna doesn't speak of it at all—is that it?"

She was identifying the problem. They all agreed: that was indeed the problem. So Sally summed it up again. "Which means that she doesn't know about it . . . possibly?"

There was a clamor of voices—she *had* to know, it was obvious to everyone.

"Or that she does know, but doesn't want to talk about it?"

Again Sally looked round at them, kind, concerned women, outraged on behalf of the big-hearted, trusting Anna. There was a muttered agreement: that would appear to be the way things were.

Sally smiled triumphantly. "Then that's what we do, then. We don't talk about it," she said.

They didn't like this. They had schemed to get her on her

own, they wanted a leader, they needed advice. They didn't want it to remain forever an unsolved mystery. They couldn't abide a mystery.

"But he's making such a fool of her," Marigold said. "He's humiliating her."

"No, he's not. Just because *he* may be behaving badly doesn't make me think that Anna's a fool or that she has something to be humble about. She's still exactly the same to me."

It was true, and yet it was also not true.

They came up with all kinds of objections and wild plans.

"She will be so furious when she does discover, and she'll know we all knew."

"She won't think we were real friends."

"She should be forewarned."

"It's not fair."

"Could we send her an anonymous letter?"

"Could Sally go and deal with Rita?"

Sally's voice cut straight through. "Every time I come here I wonder why on earth I live in London—you're just a great group of friends, and you can understand that often the hardest thing to do is to do nothing, just to be there. That's what we have to do."

Her hand shaking, she picked up the menu and looked at the choices.

"We can have soup *or* a spring roll, but not both for a starter. Shall we order that to keep body and soul together and Anna can catch up when she comes to join us in about ten minutes?"

By the time Anna came in with her smart new hairdo they were deep into conversation about their children, their jobs, their gardens, their plans for holidays. Anna joined in easily and Sally felt herself breathe more easily. She was surprised at the anger she felt, and the sense of outrage on her friend's behalf.

Oh, yes, she had been able to stop the others from making some stupid, insensitive interventions, she had bossily told them that inaction was the only action. But it didn't sort out her own raging emotion. Sally was almost shaking with anger at the way David had treated the wife who loved him, the wife who sat in an office filing papers to make money for the household. Money that David spent taking this Rita to expensive hotels.

Sally smiled and sort of joined in the conversation, laughing when the others laughed, but she felt that she was on automatic pilot. All the time her brain was working overtime.

Sally and Anna had no secrets. Ever. Was there any kind of a case for telling her about David? Or was it an infatuation that would burn itself out? What would she like in her own case? Suppose her Johnny had a Rita in his life and Sally was the only person not to know—would she not want Anna to tell her? Could she bear the actual news being given? Would it not be better if she found out on her own and then went to cry on her friend's shoulder? Sally was going back to London next day. If she were to talk to Anna it would have to be tonight. She would sit on the plane tomorrow, and wonder had she been right or wrong.

She looked at the lively face of her friend as she persuaded the Chinese waiter to take their picture. Ten women, nine of them with a secret about the woman who sat in the center.

When they got home David was there.

"Well, girls, is it more wine or is it glasses of water and Alka-Seltzer?"

His smile was the usual heartbreaking grin.

Sally wondered where Rita was tonight. Was she alone in the studio flat, hoping that this attractive man would eventually tell his wife what everyone else seemed to know already? She could hardly bear speaking to him. She said nothing at all.

"Oh, wine I think, David," Anna said. "It's Sally's last night—we'll want a chat."

"Two glasses, one bottle, one corkscrew. Now who's good to you?"

He kissed them both lightly on their foreheads.

"I'll leave you to it."

But instead of going up to bed, he moved towards the door.

"Hey, David, you're not going out, you're not going to work at this hour?" Anna was amazed.

"Someone's got to pay for all this wine drinking. I just waited until the drinky ladies came home. Now you two can mind the boys and I'll get back to the office."

Sally spoke sharply. "David, what on earth can you do at ten-thirty at night in the office?"

He looked at her without his glance faltering.

"Now, Sally, I don't know what time you write your column, or do your reporting, but I'd never dream of suggesting that there was one time better than another. And in my case sorting out accounts, and arranging woods, and bringing mailing lists up to date . . . those can be done at any time of the day or night, also."

He was looking at her, smiling, daring her to speak.

"Sure." Sally said in a voice that was barely above a whisper.

"Don't stay too late, love," Anna said, full of concern.

"If it gets too late, I'll sleep there."

He was gone with a wave.

Sally dared not raise her eyes to meet those of her friend. He was going to *sleep* at the office, a workshop not half a mile away. And Anna was going along with this fiction.

They poured the wine and talked about the girls that they had eaten dinner with. They talked about their children, they went up to look at the sleeping boys, and looked forward to the time, three years hence, when they could go to London on their own and Sally would meet them at the station. They talked about Sally's teenagers and what they would study if they got their A levels. They talked about Johnny and his wine bar. And all the time Sally wanted to cry.

She managed to make it to her bedroom before the tears came. She laid a towel on her nice new pillowcase and cried silently into it as the clock struck midnight and every hour until seven. At no stage did she hear the door open or David come up the stairs. He had stayed in the office. She could hardly force down the coffee that Anna had prepared. The taxi came to take her to the airport. She shook hands formally with the two little boys who had already got many items on their list of things to do in London. They were getting ready for school; their mother would lead them there by the hand before she went back to work.

It was so desperately sad. Unfair and sad.

Sally looked out the window for the entire journey. She never unfolded her paper, opened her book. When she got to London she took out her mobile phone and called Johnny. There was a message on the machine.

"Darling, if that's you, I'm coming to meet you. If it's not you, then could you please leave a message."

Sally spoke into the phone softly.

"I don't see why I shouldn't be allowed to leave a message as well. I love you, Johnny—you're a good man."

And she looked out for him.

"I'm so sorry to have to tell you bad news," he began. "It's Anna."

"No, no, Johnny, tell me what happened." She had dropped her case on the ground.

"She rang. It's her husband."

"Oh, God, when did she find out?"

"The hospital rang—apparently it was all over very quickly."

"What was over?"

"He died, Sally, darling. I'm so sorry to have to tell you this. I thought it better to come to the airport."

"He *died*!"

"Yes, in his office, last night, apparently."

"He really was in the office—he died in his office?"

"I don't know, darling. She said he was got to the hospital but it was too late . . . and then the hospital called to tell her . . . it must have been just after you left."

"And who got him to hospital?"

"Sweetheart, how do I know? I only know what happened. Does it matter?"

Sally was very pale and very quiet.

"Yes, Johnny, it does. It matters terribly."

Sally sat very still at home for a while before she made any telephone calls. She could call Marigold, or David's sister, Emily. She could call any of the women she had eaten dinner with last night. But it would be disloyal, somehow. She must not learn from them whether David had begun to die in the arms of Rita.

Had Rita taken him to the hospital and left him there?

Had she crept away and asked the authorities not to mention her involvement?

Sally ached to know, but by asking them she would somehow betray the sense of independence and importance that she had gained for her friend.

There were a million questions that she wanted answered but she must not ask them. She had been so strong yesterday . . . was it only last night they had been in the Chinese restaurant? She must not give in now and weaken the dignity that she had fought so hard to create.

She would have to do it herself. Ring Anna, her friend. She dialed the number and waited to know what she would discover.

Anna was very calm.

"He worked too hard, Sally," Anna said. "He has had no proper life for the past two years—you saw yourself."

"I'm so sorry, dear Anna."

"I know you are, Sally. You are such a friend and I know you loved him too."

"And . . . did he get the attack, the heart attack, in the office? Is that what happened?"

"No, thankfully—it was one of the things I have to hold on to and say that it was like a miracle. All the way to the hospital I couldn't bear to think of him dying alone in the office, maybe struggling to get to a phone."

"So where *did* it happen?" Sally's voice was barely above a whisper.

"The most extraordinary thing. When he was in the office he got a call late there, and he went to deliver an order."

"An order?"

"Yes, there's this photographer, she buys a lot of frames from us, and anyway he went round there to deliver some rushed things she needed for an exhibition, and he had a drink in her house and that's where it happened, and that's where it came on."

"In her house?"

"Yes, and Rita, that's her name, she said there was no pain, he just clutched his chest and he said my name. He said, 'Anna,' and she called the ambulance and they got him to hospital, they did everything they could, but they said he died instantly."

"It must have been a shock for her too," Sally said, not fully able to believe that she was having this conversation.

"Terrible—she was quite distraught this morning. I asked her to come over to us, but she said no."

"Probably wants to be alone." Sally could barely speak.

"Oh, Sally, isn't it dreadful?" Anna said. "How am I going to carry on without him?"

"He would want you to," Sally said. Her mind was racing. She herself had left Anna and David's home at seven-thirty this morning. The hospital had not phoned by then. Anna *must* realize that David had spent the night with Rita. If she thought about the timing for two minutes she would realize that it was very odd for anyone to call to someone's house at 5 a.m. for a drink. She had to be fooling herself. Or arranging a cover story that she would live with for the rest of her life. She could not possibly believe that. Which was it?

"Would you like me to come back? Would I be any good?"

"I'd prefer if you were to come next week, if you can, for the funeral. You'd be a great support to me then. Honestly, Sally, everyone is so broken up here. None of my friends seem to know what to say, my father, he can't get any words together at all—I don't even understand what he's saying. It's almost as if he thinks it was David's fault that he died."

"I suppose it's the age thing; he feels that David was so young to go."

"That must be it." Anna seemed relieved with this explanation. Sally thought about it every hour of every day until she flew back to stand at her friend's side on the day of David's funeral. They all wore black, the women who had been in the Chinese restaurant and the strange pale woman with the long fair hair, who stood alone at the edge of the crowd.

"That's Rita. You know, the woman who got him to the hospital." Anna whispered.

Anna's eyes were red from weeping, but her face was innocent. All around her people stood waiting to hug her and mourn the passing of a hardworking father, a loving husband, a tireless workmate. He was such a good man, they all said, and what a tragedy that he had not lived so that they could have had their older years together.

Sally listened, and watched. She saw Anna invite Rita back to the house, but the pale woman with the long straw-colored hair shook her head and went away alone.

Anna moved in the center of a crowd of sympathizers who would be going back to her house, where sandwiches and wine would be served. On the faces of the women who had gathered so recently in the Chinese restaurant Sally saw some pleasure. It was as if Anna had won a battle that had never been declared. Anna was the tragic heroine, the brave young widow, the loved and honored woman, whose name had been spoken by the dying man. The husband who had gone out working to provide for his wife and children with no care for himself, his health, his own wishes.

That's the way history had been rewritten.

The white-faced woman who had been such a danger had

been banished. And punished, while the wife had been cocooned with crowds of loving sympathizers.

The mistress had left alone. Sally excused herself from the group in the graveyard and followed the woman to the small car. She didn't know what she was going to say, but she felt that something should be said.

Rita turned and looked at her with some surprise.

"I'm Sally," she began.

"Yes, I know . . . the media friend," Rita said.

There was something in the way she said it that was exactly like David's voice. Sally could imagine him being fairly dismissive about her.

"I just wanted to say . . ."

Rita looked at her, waiting.

Sally, who could talk to millions of people in her column and on television, was stuck for words.

"I wanted to say you were terrific," she said.

Rita looked at her for a long time. "He always said you had class," she said eventually.

"Well *you* certainly do," Sally said.

And then there was nothing more to say.

Back in the house Sally looked at her friend Anna as if she had never seen her before, and even though Anna reached out her hand several times and squeezed Sally's in gratitude for the solidarity, it didn't make anything clear. Suddenly she didn't know this woman, Anna, who had been her friend since school uniforms. Was this a giant act? Was Anna playing a role because something had to be salvaged from a life that had been going to sour? Now she was the grieving widow, the brave girl who would somehow carry on with the huge support of family and friends. If she had acknowledged the situation, there would not have been this turnout. People would have shuffled with embarrassment and said that in many ways David had deserved his untimely death. Rita would have been the bereaved.

Anna must have known this and realized that other people knew also. But perhaps she was just doing it for today. And for the children. Later tonight, when everyone had gone home, Anna would talk to her, talk to her properly, as they had done for years. Then all this mask and pretense would drop.

Everyone was so pleased that Sally was there. They went home safe in the knowledge that Anna could have no better company and counsel.

They lit the fire and they sat on the floor beside it, with tea and a tin of biscuits, as they had done so often over the years. And Anna took out albums and talked about what a wonderful husband David had been, and how lucky they were that they had made the right decision, and how she would bring up the children in the memory of the best daddy in the world. Sally listened, open-mouthed.

She wanted to cry out, "This is me, it's Sally, who knows everything as you know everything about me. You don't have to pretend anymore—let's say what a hopeless, hard-to-understand thing it all was, and in the end, didn't she behave well, the tramp that took him away?"

But there was no way that any of this would be introduced. It was clear that Anna was not moving out of the role. And that by now it was possibly no longer a role. By now, she believed every line of it. What was the point of saying anything that would upset it all now?

But it did not seem the action of a friend to sit and look at old pictures and mouth things that weren't true. Yet wasn't this the very attitude that Sally herself had suggested when they were all at the Chinese meal? That had been her policy: don't allow a friend to become just another victim. Someone who has to be told something. Give her instead the gift of dignity. Sally shivered by the fire. She had given Anna that dignity—today's funeral was the very proof of it. But at what cost?

She looked at the woman who had once been her soul mate

and knew that everything was now on a different level. The friendship they had once shared had died in the face of all this pretense. Was it better that they should just go on with this huge thing unspoken between them, or was it impossible?

They *could* have got over this together, as they had got over so many other things. It was going to be an entirely new experience having a friend that you couldn't talk to about the hugely important things in life. Sally didn't know why she wanted Anna to face up to what had happened. But she did.

And she knew that what she had offered, dignity and respect, were not nearly as satisfying as a good cry and a lot of nose blowing and a resolution that things could be solved. That was friendship. And somehow in the middle of all this, friendship had got lost.

THE INVESTMENT

Years ago if you had a daughter who was hopelessly in love with an unsuitable man you sent her on a world cruise to cure her. That's what Shona's father said over and over. But he said it only to his wife because nobody was meant to know about Shona's unsuitable young man.

There were complications.

And Shona's mother said that this was a ridiculous kind of thing to keep harking back to. Only one percent of the population, if that, would have been able to afford a world cruise for anyone. Certainly, no one who lived on Chestnut Street could afford it.

What they really needed was to know somebody miles and miles away who would give a job to a lovesick twenty-two-year-old, a job she couldn't refuse.

And suddenly they looked at each other and remembered Marty.

Marty, who had been in the same lodgings as they had all those years ago when they first met. Marty, the American student, who always kept in touch, even though, like themselves, he was middle-aged now.

Maybe they could write to Arizona to Marty and he might offer a job to Shona.

It didn't sound as if Marty made a big enough living to employ strangers, but they could ask.

They wrote to Marty and told him the truth.

That for nearly two years Shona had been besotted with this Vincent. She had dropped out of college, hadn't taken her degree and just sat waiting for him to get in touch.

She would listen to no reason or argument saying that Vincent couldn't love her or else he would be with her. No suggestions that Vincent might have a wife somewhere.

It was a relief to be able to tell Marty.

To tell someone, without covering up, as they had to do at home.

Marty wrote back.

"Tell me about difficult children," he wrote, and he let them know that his eldest boy was also a child who broke parents' hearts.

But this boy was only seventeen. Shona's parents were sure that he was just a kid, a kid in Arizona, trying to prove himself.

Marty wrote them a separate letter, one they could show to Shona.

A letter saying that he ran a general store and he could do with some help.

He really needed a bright girl in her twenties to talk to the tourists who would be driving past on their way to the Grand Canyon.

There would be plenty of time to sit and think and enjoy the peace of the countryside, he said.

Shona read the letter. Her parents didn't dare to meet her eye.

Vincent hadn't been in touch for some weeks now.

"I'd like to go," she said.

They let their breath out very slowly.

When Vincent called three weeks after she had gone, Shona's

mother said she had the address somewhere, but she couldn't lay her hands on it.

When he called again, Shona's father said he hadn't his glasses. He didn't call a third time.

Shona settled in well with Marty and his wife, Ella, sleeping in her own little room above the store. They worked hard and their little nine-year-old twins helped by carrying goods out to customers' cars.

And then there was Nick.

Nick was seventeen, handsome and brooding. He took no part in anything, he shrugged and sighed so much if asked to help at all, that they had given up on him.

His two little brothers admired him from a distance.

He carried heavy loads for his mother, and every morning lifted a basket of washing out to the clothesline. She smiled at him fondly but with a sadness.

Marty looked at his son with mystification and sorrow.

Maybe a dozen times a week he suggested some activity, a drive, a barbecue, a trip to the movies.

The boy barely answered.

He was a master of shrugs. His shoulders seemed to have a life of their own like a mime artist.

Shona had tried in the beginning. But it was useless; the boy had no interest in her.

Once and only once he asked her a question. "Did you graduate?" he asked.

"No," Shona said simply.

"It means a different thing here and there," Marty began. "Shona did graduate from high school, Nick . . ."

It was useless—he just shrugged.

"I heard the lady," he said.

The skies were blue and there was a lot of space. People talked about the presidential election in America. Would Ronald Reagan, the film star, really have a chance of winning? Would there be a Kennedy against him or would President Carter run again?

They talked about the Olympic Games in Moscow.

The summer was hot. Ireland was far away, but every night Shona wrote to Vinnie. She didn't post the letters—she just told him how much she loved him and how she knew it would all be fine in the end.

As she wrote she watched the handsome Nick playing with a computer.

He seemed to do little else.

And the summer went on. Shona saved her earnings. When she got back she would take Vinnie on a holiday. Maybe they would rent a boat on the Shannon. He always said they would do that someday or maybe they would go to the Galway Oyster Festival. She had plenty of money. She spent hardly anything and Marty had paid her a decent wage for fourteen weeks.

After fifteen weeks Vinnie wrote.

He said that he had finally got her address and he knew now that he loved her and wondered had she thought of him at all?

Shona posted all the love letters she had written him in the Arizona sunsets, and then she said she must buy her ticket home.

She told Marty and Ella that she hoped she wasn't letting them down, but it had worked for her, this wonderful opportunity. She had found peace of mind in this place and now the man she loved was calling her home.

They sighed and waited until she had left them with starry eyes before they called her mother and father with the bad news.

Shona went back to her little room to check for her wallet, or billfold as she now called it.

She smiled to herself, thinking about all the things she would have to tell Vinnie. He had never been to the United States. There had been some stupid problem about getting a visa, something silly from his past. She thought of Vinnie as she hunted for the money. And hunted and hunted.

It was an hour before she accepted the fact that her money was gone. She sat still for a long time. But she had to face it eventually.

And it was so unlikely that a thief would have come into her room and not approach the store itself.

But equally unlikely that Marty and Ella would creep in and steal back the wages they gave her.

Or those innocent twins or the shruggy, distant Nick, who hardly noticed her.

She saw their stricken faces when she told them. "Could you possibly have lost it on the bus the time you went on the tour?" Ella had so much hope in her voice.

But Shona knew she had not taken her money that day. She had not dared to risk spending any of it.

She looked around at them all. Nick's eyes were brighter than usual. Most times he seemed miles away, but now he was very much involved. Too involved.

Shona was about to say that she was positive about not taking her money with her that day. But something made her change her words.

"Suppose I had—do you think they might have found any of it?"

"I hear they often find most of it," Nick said.

Shona said she thought she could have left it on the bus.

She was rewarded by the relief in the two good, open faces of Marty and Ella.

Her heart was full of hate for the hurt that this child was going to cause them in the years ahead.

"Maybe Nick can drive me to the bus station to inquire?" Shona said through gritted teeth. He was silent in the car as they drove through the open countryside.

Shona let the silence lie there between them.

Then he spoke. "What's it like, Ireland?"

"Green, small, full of lakes and rivers and roads that twist and turn. Mountains. Sea all round the edges."

"Is life easy there?" he asked.

"Not particularly. No more than it is here." Her voice was leaden.

He handed her an envelope.

"Most of it's there," he said.

"Okay."

"Only thirty dollars gone. I used it to send for some software."

She didn't reply as she looked out the window of the car at the Arizona scenery that she would never see again.

Had she been right to postpone their discovery of their eldest son as a thief?

Had she just done it so that she could escape from this life and leave them without trailing clouds of unhappiness?

They didn't speak at all on the way home.

Shona made up a story about the bus company. She left Arizona for Ireland and Vinnie in high good form.

Vinnie said they would get married. Now, as soon as possible. Then they could use all her money on a honeymoon. Shona wore a friend's dress for her wedding. They had only a few people there.

She would not let her father pay for a big reception. The photographs of her wedding day would not gladden any heart. You wouldn't need to be a psychologist to see the look of strain on everyone's face except the bride and groom.

Shona's face was pure rapture; Vinnie had his nice relaxed smile.

The years passed more or less the way Shona's father and mother knew they would.

They wrote every year to Marty and Ella about the whole story. Vinnie had long unexplained absences. There were no children.

Sometimes they thought this was a blessing. At other times they thought that perhaps children might have settled Vinnie down, made him stay at home and face up to his responsibilities.

Perhaps if she had been a mother, Shona would have had more anger on their behalf. On her own she had none.

Marty and Ella wrote back.

They said that life was fairly unchanged for them. Nick had left home and he didn't really stay in touch.

They knew little of what he was doing except that he worked in computers.

He wrote a dutiful letter now and then, but they didn't understand his moves from one company to another.

At least he was solvent. And honest . . . or at least not in trouble with the law.

Wasn't it hard that you did so much for children and loved them so deeply and they seemed so indifferent to you in return?

Nick had reached twenty-one and they hadn't even known where to send him a card.

Shona's parents wrote to say that they read in a small paragraph in a newspaper that Vinnie had been in gaol, but their own daughter, now a mature woman in her late twenties, told them nothing of it.

Always they invited each other to Ireland and Arizona but they knew they were settled in their ways and they would never make the journey.

Shona opened a guesthouse, and as the years went by, it won all kinds of awards.

Visitors passed its name on from one to another. It had been written up in the best magazines.

Vinnie came back from time to time.

He was always polite to the guests for the first few days, and then they began to bore him. Shona would have to urge him to take a little trip somewhere in order to get him out of the way so that she could keep earning a living.

It was costing more and more of her money.

First she had not been able to buy the new bed linens and towels she needed to keep the standards.

The following year, she had to abandon her plan to build on

the four extra bedrooms that had been her heart's desire. There just wasn't the money.

She was so disappointed, and it almost began to show in her normally sunny face. She couldn't understand it, she said to the bank manager, who was a kind and reasonable man.

"It's your outgoings," he had said sadly. "Maybe if you took fewer holidays."

Shona had been on no holiday since her honeymoon. She bit her lip and put on the brave smile that had been her trademark.

By 1994 the kind bank manager said this was it. The guesthouse could no longer continue. Glumly Shona read the figures.

"It's the outgoings," the manager said again.

"Yes," said Shona, her heart like ice.

She was thirty-six, and had loved a man who had taken everything and given nothing. Until he had taken her guesthouse, she had forgiven him. But now she would have no home, no life, no people coming through. What a waste of a life.

"I have a buyer," the bank manager was saying. He hated having to do this. Shona knew she made it easy for him.

"Ask the buyer to come and see me," she said in a voice without light or shade.

"He'll be in Ireland next week."

"Well, that's good, isn't it." Her smile was so brave the bank manager wanted to cry.

Nobody had ever told him it would be like this. The buyer came next week. He drove up to the guesthouse. She knew it was the buyer, not a guest.

He was young, early thirties, Shona had expected a man of retirement age.

She came out to the door to meet him. There would be no whining—if the man could buy, she could sell.

It was Nick.

Nick, thirty-one years old.

Same blond hair, same slightly hunched, restless way of standing. As if he might run away.

But this time his eyes met hers.

It was a glance between friends, not the look of someone she hadn't seen for fourteen years, someone who had stolen her money and given it back, apart from thirty dollars.

"Why?" she asked.

"No point in sending you back thirty dollars . . . I always knew that."

"I didn't," she said with spirit. "There were days when I could have done with that thirty dollars."

"To buy another necktie for that man . . . of yours."

"He's not my man anymore."

"How often have you said that?" He seemed to care about the answer.

"Never . . . as it happens."

He smiled at her and laid some papers down on the table.

"You're buying my little guesthouse?" She was not able to take it in.

"I'm buying it, for you. You saved my life once; I'm saving yours."

"You can't do that—the amounts aren't exactly similar."

"No, but the circumstances are. I would have gone under without you, maybe you might without me. I kept an eye on you. I waited."

"Why?"

"You were my first love." He spoke simply, without guile.

"There must have been many since then," Shona said.

"No . . . as it happens," he mimicked the phrase she had used earlier.

"You couldn't have loved me—I was years older than you then."

"You still are, Shona, but I sort of caught up." His smile was very charming.

She caught her breath.

"What do we do now?"

"I return your investment. You invested . . . accidentally, I admit . . . in some of my first software. Now I'm a computer millionaire, whiz kid, whatever . . ."

"There's no need . . ."

"There's every need, and only one string attached—it goes in your name, not in his."

"I tell you he's gone," she said.

"That's very good news," said Nick, who was sitting down with the air of a man who might be going to take very early retirement indeed.

THE LEAP OF FAITH

Molly wanted a room for three nights a week. This way she could work in the big financial center for four full days from Tuesday to Friday and then get a late train back to the peaceful place where she was just managing to get her life back together.

She had no idea how appallingly expensive it was to rent a room these days. How did people manage? And how had she not known? All those years living with Hugh in their big comfortable home must have made her completely unaware of how the rest of the world existed.

But the big house was sold and the money divided, and Molly had bought a country cottage, to everyone's amazement. All she needed now was somewhere to stay for less than half the week—it didn't matter how simple—and yet she was unable to find anything at all suitable. Friends had offered her a bed, but Molly valued friendships. She didn't want to perch in their houses; she wanted her own place. Surely, somewhere in a city this size, there must be a plain, ordinary room with a bed and a chair and an electric kettle. She would install a clothes rail and a small television set. She was happy to share a bathroom. She didn't need to live in any great style.

Molly's job in the financial center was a demanding one, with long hours. There would be little time for entertaining. She would be happy to go back to a room at the end of a long day and sleep. Sleep was becoming increasingly important to her these days.

Otherwise she would think about Hugh, playing it all over in her mind, what had happened here and there and how it could all have been prevented. Round and round in her head these thoughts would go, leaving Molly exhausted and confused as ever. Over the months she had discovered that the solution to all that useless speculation was hard work and sleep.

It was ludicrous spending so much of the money that she earned on a small hotel room. She would try yet again, go to yet another accommodation agency and explain her very simple needs.

The woman behind the desk was sympathetic but doubtful. People really didn't want strangers coming into their homes. Now, if she were to consider sharing with others, there were very nice properties on the market.

"But I don't want to share with young people," Molly pleaded. "I'm forty-one years of age—I can't sit and listen to their music and have their friends coming in at all hours of the night. I just want a place of my own in someone's home where I will be no trouble. Is it such a terrible crime?"

The woman's face softened. "Of course it's not, and if I had a home myself, which I never had, then I'd offer you the room straightaway—nothing I would like better."

"So where do you live?" Molly asked.

"With my brother and his wife. Not entirely satisfactory, I may tell you, but they need the rent and I can't afford a mortgage." She shrugged; that was the way life went. She had a kind face—probably in her mid-forties. Her name, Anita Woods, was on a little brass plaque in front of her.

Molly wondered was it better never to have had a house, like Anita, or to have had one and lost it, as she had done herself.

"And I don't suppose you could get a mortgage with just my rent coming in to help out?" she said lightly.

"Sadly, no," Anita said. "Though you're not the first to suggest it, as it happens."

"Someone else in the same position?" Molly didn't have much hope—Anita was only making conversation.

"Not exactly, but there was a woman in here last week. Looking for a house where she could teach music during the day, so she needed the owner to be out during working hours. Said she would clean and garden as well. Very nice person—some story about wanting to get out of her home. The children were driving her mad. Grown-up children, I mean. I'd love to have helped her but I just couldn't find anyone suitable."

"Is she in your files?" Molly asked.

"Well, yes, but what's the point?"

"What's her name . . . ?"

Anita looked through the files. "It was Jackson, Jane Jackson. Really, she was a very good-natured person, someone you'd remember. I just hate to think of all those ungrateful young people leaving her bags of washing and eating everything out of the fridge."

"Why don't you buy a house, Anita? You must have seen something you like on your books—and let Jane and myself be your lodgers."

"But that's ridiculous," Anita protested.

"Is it really?" Molly was very clear-sighted when she wanted to be; this is why she had succeeded so well at work. "Let's have lunch, the three of us—that won't do any harm," she begged, and she could see a serious flicker of interest in Anita's face. The two women knew that there was distinct possibility that this mad scheme might work.

Anita couldn't take more than forty-five minutes' lunchtime during the week and they would need more than that to sort out their future. Jane couldn't cancel the music lessons she had arranged for this week. Molly couldn't be away from her screen in the financial center. So it was a Saturday lunch meeting, in a small Italian restaurant where the lunch had a set price and they would all pay for themselves.

Jane had a music case with her and locked her bicycle outside the restaurant. She looked tired and said that it would be such an ease to have the pupils to her own place, but two of her children worked at home and couldn't bear the noise and disruption. Anita had a briefcase with details of properties on the market so that they could all look and see what kind of thing they had in mind. Molly had brought nothing except a big pad of paper with columns so that they could write down all the pros and cons.

They knew that they were making a leap of faith, three strangers even discussing the possibility of setting up a home together. But still they talked easily about their lives. There was no awkwardness, no examining one another as future flatmates; there was a sense that they were three women meeting for a normal Saturday lunch.

Anita explained that she had never thought of getting anywhere permanent to live since she had traveled so much in her youth and had not wanted to be tied down anywhere. Now she regretted it. Her sister-in-law was a difficult woman and the household was always very tense. Anita longed to let herself into a place where there was no atmosphere or mood in the air.

Jane said that since her husband had died, the children thought they were doing her a favor by staying at home. She knew they told their friends that they just couldn't leave her alone and struggling, but in fact she made their lives very comfortable and was so exhausted looking after three adults that she had hardly any energy left for giving the music lessons that she loved to teach.

Molly spoke to them about Hugh in a way that she had not spoken to anyone else. How she had found a love letter in a jacket she was taking to the dry cleaner's; how he had denied that it had anything to do with him, that it belonged to someone else at work.

The night a woman rang the house to speak to him, and Hugh had said it was a deranged colleague who had been pestering them all. And then the day her sister had seen Hugh and the woman in a hotel.

Without self-pity she told them that Hugh had said she should have let it pass; it would all have blown over. Molly had bought a country cottage to try to change things. It worked, in a way. Sort of . . .

Then they got down to details, and price ranges and room rates. There was a place on Chestnut Street they all liked with a small garden, three large bedrooms, which could be bed-sitters, large enough to hold Jane's piano, Molly's computer. There were two bathrooms and one big kitchen–sitting room.

They got out a calculator and did their sums. They bought another bottle of wine.

They promised to meet in three weeks.

During that time Anita worried less about her sister-in-law's moods.

Jane did less washing and cleaning for her children.

Molly slept longer and more deeply.

By the time they were to meet again, Anita had made an offer on the property and had the keys, so that was where they met. The previous owners had gone abroad, leaving a lot of furniture behind them, so they wandered freely around, talking about their new lives.

Somehow, a whole afternoon passed happily and they were amazed that they had spent so long and with so few reservations. They each decided what they would bring for their bed-sitting rooms, what kitchen gadgets, garden tools, extra bookshelves they would each contribute.

Then they went home to tell the story.

Anita said that she was sure her sister-in-law would be pleased that she would finally have her spare room back. Now there would be room to leave her sewing machine in place, or to invite friends to stay.

Jane told her children that she could either sell the house and give them all a share or let it to them at a fair rent. They must make the choice.

Molly went home to her cottage and told nobody. Her neighbors in the countryside were charming, helpful people, but they didn't really know or care much about her life in the city. They wouldn't be excited about her change of location.

Molly was sad that she had nobody to tell. But when she met the others a week later she thought that perhaps it might not have been the worst situation.

Anita said that her brother and sister-in-law deeply resented her leaving them, accusing her of being ungrateful for their hospitality. They showed little or no interest in her new home; they only regretted the loss of her rent.

Jane said her children had been so outraged they had talked about the possibility of having her certified as insane. They said it was a delayed reaction to grief over their father. Finally they said they couldn't possibly pay the rent she suggested, so she had said she would sell the house and give them their share.

In comparison to all this drama, Molly felt that somehow she was fairly lucky.

The move, when it came, was almost seamless. It was over in one weekend, and on the Sunday night they had a celebration supper before retiring to their own bed-sitters—which had been part of the original plan. But they stayed on longer and longer and put more wood on the fire. They washed up companionably and knew that this was more than just a rooming-house arrangement.

"I give it two months," Jane's children had said when they first heard the news. But two months after they had all gone to live together, Jane was happily installed, giving her music lessons.

"In three months you'll be at the door wanting your old room back," is what Anita's sister-in-law had prophesied.

Hugh telephoned Molly, just to ask how she was. As a friend. Molly said that as a friend she was fine. And the cottage? That was fine too. And did she still stay in a hotel? he wondered.

No, she said, she now shared a house with two other women.

"I'd say that will last for about six months," Hugh said, annoyed at the calm way she spoke to him.

At the end of the first year, Anita said she was going on a walking tour in Italy. The others were interested and even envious. They had never been on a holiday like that.

On the holiday they made a few decisions and when they returned, fit and sun-tanned, Molly arranged to let her country cottage, since she hardly ever went there at weekends anyway.

Jane sold her house and divided the proceeds with her squawking children.

Anita, who had now been made a partner in the accommodation agency, paid for a holiday for her brother and sister-in-law and was back in their good books again.

They knew that it might not be forever, this life. They would not necessarily grow old in a trio. There could be a different and exciting future ahead for any of them. But for the moment they were luckier and happier than most people just because they had the courage to take a leap of faith.

LILIAN'S HAIR

Lilian was born and grew up at Number 5. Everyone who had lived on Chestnut Street then remembered her as a beautiful child with glorious golden hair. They told her mother that she could be in the movies. Mrs. Harris was never pleased to hear this prediction. It was entirely too fast and too far away for their plans. They wanted Lilian to be around and look after them in their old age, Mrs. Harris said firmly.

Lilian was taken on as an apprentice in Locks, a hair salon up on the main road only five minutes' walk from home. She would come back for lunch most days and have a cup of soup with her mother. The other girls in the salon went out and had a proper lunch, but they weren't saving like Lilian was. Saving to buy a house of her own.

Lilian never wanted smart, elegant clothes like the customers in the salon and the girls she worked with did. They all said she didn't need them anyway; her hair was so attractive with its shiny golden curls, that nobody bothered with what she was wearing. She never went on holidays abroad. Why should she? All she wanted was a house in this very street. A house of her own.

If Lilian had a house she would turn the downstairs into a hairdressing salon and work from home. Upstairs she would have a beautiful flat, which she would paint in bright colors.

And then, when she was a woman of property and style, she would look for a husband when she was about twenty-eight.

It didn't work out like that.

Firstly, Mr. Harris, who had always been a careful man, made a very foolish investment. He mortgaged their house at Number 5 in order to raise money for a crackpot scheme. A colleague who was starting a leisure center needed some carefully chosen mates who would put in several thousand each. All Mr. Harris needed, he wept afterwards, was his stake. It was gone in a few short months and so was a lot more.

Mr. Harris found that his job was gone too, since he had been unable to concentrate at the reception desk in the hospital. And his health had gone since he was now suffering from a serious depression.

Mrs. Harris also suffered by all this change. She had never been strong. Now she no longer had a husband who would do the shopping for her. Lilian's savings were needed to pay the mortgage on Number 5, her parents' home. There would be nothing left to buy her own place. Her free time was needed to clean and shop for the family that was no longer able to function without her. She never complained, and at work she was so unfailingly good-humored as well as being an accomplished hairdresser that Albert, the boss, offered her the post of opening up a new store in the center of town.

"I can't take it," Lilian said sadly. "I have to be on my own doorstep. This place is perfect for me—I can even race home in my coffee break to see they're all right."

Albert shook his head.

"It's no life, Lilian. They'll have to live without you one day; best to let them get used to it sooner rather than later."

"Why will they have to live without me one day?" she asked

him innocently, and he got a sudden intuition that this girl was a dutiful daughter, like someone a hundred years ago. That she would live with them forever and sacrifice any plans of her own. An only child who would spend a lifetime thanking them for the life they had given her, but which would now turn into a very empty life indeed.

She must have been about twenty-three then, the manager thought. He too was an only child, but he would not have given up his life had his parents needed him. He hoped that Lilian would not live to regret it.

And, as the years went on, she did not seem to find this life a burden. They seemed to be warm-hearted people, grateful for her attention, but not surprised at it. They would have done the same. Lilian always said that they had big, generous hearts.

She seemed to have no idea of the size and generosity of her own.

Every year she went away on a package holiday for two weeks, thanks to an organization that provided holiday cover for carers. Kind, responsible women would come in and live in Number 5 for the two weeks, often bringing new ideas with them.

Lilian learned about shops that delivered groceries, about local Boy Scouts who did basic garden jobs, about mail-order catalogs where her mother could order clothes for herself and her husband.

When she was on her vacations, Lilian relaxed in the sun, but she didn't get involved in any holiday romance. There were offers, invitations, suggestions along the way. She had plenty who admired her hair and ready smile. But she kept them at bay.

Until she met Tim. And he was very persistent.

"Do you have a husband at home?" he asked her under the starry Italian sky.

"Good heavens, no. I live with my parents."

"A fiancé? A boyfriend? A steady?"

"No, nobody at all—I haven't time."

By the end of the two weeks he knew the scene.

"I'd love to come and see you sometime," Tim offered.

"Please do, Tim, but you might find us a bit dull, my parents and myself. We sit in a lot and look at television, you see."

"Well, why pay for bricks and mortar if you're going to be spending money running away from it, I always say."

Tim had an endearing habit of thrift. Lilian hadn't been used to that and she found it funny.

He knew that if they got the bus from this place rather than that they would save so many lira, that bread and butter was extra in a lot of the little *ristorantes* so they should always save their breakfast rolls.

He seemed to understand entirely why she lived with her parents. Why run two establishments when one would do? Lilian found this restful after so many people trying to persuade her to get a life of her own.

Tim was very easy to talk to. Very nice indeed. She hoped he would get in touch when the holiday was over. And indeed, he did, so she invited him to supper.

He told Mr. Harris how much he had saved by coming on an off-peak train. He told Mrs. Harris that he had grown the little potted plant he brought her from seed and that's why it was in a yogurt carton. He said he grew dozens like that; they made acceptable gifts and cost nothing. He told Lilian that he had got a refund from the travel agency because he said they had given a wrong description of the hotel.

"But it was a lovely hotel," Lilian had protested.

"Yes, but these refunds are available and it's only sensible to take them," Tim said, as if it were very obvious.

Her parents liked him and seemed to enjoy his visits. In fact, her mother took to going to bed early and taking her husband with her to give the young people a chance to talk together. And then, on the sixth visit, Tim asked Mr. Harris if he could stay overnight.

"You mean sleep here? With Lilian?" Lilian heard her father say, surprised.

"Not *with* Lilian, Mr. Harris. I really meant if I could sleep on the sofa, it would save me a lot of money. I have arranged a few calls in the area and I would get all my expenses for coming here without having to make the whole journey all over again." He smiled around triumphantly at his brilliance and they all smiled too. Tim was neat and tidy, and soon he moved to the spare bedroom upstairs and with the passage of time into Lilian's room, and shortly afterwards he and Lilian went to the registry office and fixed a time and a date.

Tim said that it would be a real waste of money to go on a honeymoon. It would mean paying for carers for the Harris parents; why didn't they do up the house and paint it nice, bright colors, instead?

Albert, the manager at Lilian's salon, thought the whole thing was extraordinary. But he knew better than to make any comment.

They made a collection for her but they wouldn't be coming to the wedding. Tim thought it was also a waste of money to throw a lavish event that nobody would really enjoy. His mother and sister would come and two of his friends from work. Miss Mack, the blind lady from Number 3, would come—she had known Lilian since she was a baby—and Mrs. Ryan from Number 14, who had always been so helpful in the past.

Tim came in two days before the wedding and found a busy scene in the kitchen. Mrs. Harris, Miss Mack and Mrs. Ryan were all having their hair permed. Lilian was moving from one to the other, testing a curl here, putting on a neutralizer there, winding and unwinding, drying with towels and a hand-dryer, serving tea and biscuits. Tim looked on with interest.

"Would you be able to do that for my mother and sister?" he asked.

Lilian was delighted.

"Would they not prefer to go to their own salon for a big event like a wedding?" asked Miss Mack.

"They would never go to a salon," Tim said firmly. "It is much too expensive. How much would these perms cost if you had to pay for them?"

Miss Mack pursed her lips. Mrs. Ryan looked vague. Lilian's mother told him.

He was astounded. "You could have made all that money in one evening at home!" he said.

"No, I'm only saying what a salon would charge—you know, with overheads and a posh place and lots of staff. This is very haphazard." Lilian didn't like him making the ladies feel she was being overgenerous.

"And it's a gift from Lilian," Mrs. Ryan said.

"We are *so* lucky," Miss Mack added. "The salon comes to us."

"And Lilian loves to do it—it's second nature to her," said Lilian's mother.

Tim was sitting down with a calculator. If she were to do just seven perms a week . . . imagine! And how much did a salon charge for color? No! Impossible! Could Lilian do that as well?

All they would have to do was to alter the sitting room slightly, put in a basin, a mirror, a couple of chairs, get half a dozen towels.

"But maybe Lilian wouldn't really like to leave the fun of the salon just yet," Miss Mack began tentatively. It was as if she were striving to give Lilian some bit of life for herself outside the door of Number 5.

"Oh, who said anything about leaving the salon?" Tim cried "Couldn't she do this as well?"

Next day, Lilian permed the thin hair of her future mother-in-law, and put a deep henna tint in the mouse-colored hair of her future sister-in-law.

Both women said they were delighted with the results and that they would come regularly.

"You'll have to pay then, of course." Tim laughed and they laughed with him.

"But Lilian will charge less than a proper salon, *and* we can have our tea here, so we'll be winning," his sister said happily.

Lilian watched them affectionately. They got such huge pleasure from a bargain, from the concept of getting value. She had never been that way. You saved for something, certainly, but then you spent it. Tim and his family just wanted to save for the sake of it. Still, it made them happy, and wasn't it a better little habit to have than, say, heavy drinking or gambling?

Lilian washed out the towels and took out her dress and Tim's shirt to iron. He had said it was a waste getting something new when she looked so lovely in that gray dress.

Together they went over the food and plans for the following day, the chicken casserole and rice followed by a chocolate mousse and a very small wedding cake. Mrs. Ryan from Number 14 would have a camera and so would the best man, who worked with Tim as a salesperson.

The telephone rang. It was Miss Mack. She did apologize about the hour but she wanted to discuss a wedding present with Lilian—could Lilian possibly call up to Number 3 for just ten or fifteen minutes? Lilian said she was on her way.

"Try to get her to give us a present in money or a token if you possibly can," Tim advised.

Miss Mack moved expertly around her house, touching surfaces gently so that she disturbed nothing, and was more graceful in her blindness than many with full sight. She opened a bottle of port and poured them a tiny glass each.

"Here's to your hen night, Lilian Harris," she said with a mocking laugh.

"Thank you, Miss Mack." Lilian sipped the drink.

"Don't marry him, Lilian," Miss Mack implored.

"I love him," Lilian said simply.

"No, you don't. You love the fact that he's not going to make you decide between him and your parents!"

"Truly, we get on very well and yes, of course it's helpful that he gets on well with my folks, but that's not what it's about."

"Of course it's what it's about, Lilian, a roof over his head, an inheritance after their time, a wife who is not only going out to work but who will now work at home too. No wedding, no honeymoon, no life, Lilian. Don't do it. I beg you."

Now Lilian was hurt.

"It *is* a proper wedding, Miss Mack. There's lovely food and wine and we don't want a honeymoon—we want to be here doing the place up. And it would be sensible to work from home, as it happens, and make more money."

There were tears in her voice. But Miss Mack was like steel.

"Make more money for what, Lilian? You haven't even bought new shoes or a new handbag for your wedding day. You are on the brink of doing a very terrible thing, marrying a mean man. And I am the only one with the courage to tell you so."

"Being mean isn't all that bad a thing to be," Lilian said slowly.

"It is, Lilian—believe me."

"How do you know?"

"Because I almost married a mean man. I changed my mind six weeks before the wedding, when he said he only wanted gift cards."

Lilian giggled.

"I suppose Tim said that he would like gift cards too."

"Well, he did," Lilian admitted. "But that doesn't make him a serial killer, Miss Mack."

"It does make him a very mean man, and you'll grow to hate him."

"Did you grow to hate the man you said goodbye to?"

"I grew to fear I'd hate him. You see, generous people can't live with mean people; it doesn't work."

"That's only nonsense," Lilian said with spirit. "It's like horoscopes: Gemini is good with Libra but not with Taurus sort of thing! There's no truth in it. Remember years ago they said you shouldn't marry someone of a different religion or race or class, even—that's all gone now."

"You can't marry an ungenerous man; there's no joy in his soul."

"It's harmless, Miss Mack, honestly. It's like a child being pleased with blowing the top off a dandelion the way he gets pleased with a bargain."

"No, child, it's different."

"Maybe your case was different, but as for Tim, he doesn't even know he's doing it—you couldn't explain it or try to change him."

Miss Mack nodded gravely. "That's just it—they can't change," she said quietly.

"So did your friend know what you were talking about when you refused to marry him?"

"Not even remotely. He thought I was hysterical and mad."

"And was it long ago?"

"Yes, decades ago. Long before I went blind. But I never regretted it, Lilian."

"Did he marry anyone else?"

"Yes, quite soon afterwards. And yes, they stayed together, and I believe they're happy. Possibly she was a mean person too. Someone told me she used to pick up old newspapers in trains and parks instead of buying them. And always hung round supermarkets in case people hadn't brought back their trolley and she could get their refund."

"But it's not a crime, Miss Mack?"

"It's no way to live." The older woman was very definite.

"People live with others who snore or pick their teeth. They marry people who vote differently, who don't want children, who won't wash their feet. They marry people who are in secret societies or drug deals or pornography exchanges. Surely marrying a man who is just a little careful about money isn't really so very bad in the whole scheme of things?"

There was passion in Lilian's voice. Miss Mack was very still.

"Go on, Miss Mack, you started this—tell me what you think."

"I think that I'd like to give you and Tim some cash for your wedding present. It always comes in handy," Miss Mack said.

"Please don't be cold and dismissive to me like that. I've had so little fuss made of me, as you said yourself. Please don't insult me with money."

"*No*, Lilian, that's not true, that's not what I'm trying to do. *I'm* in awe of you and your generous spirit, your willingness to live with difference, to accept that we are not all the same. If only I had been able to do that I would have been a much happier person."

"You're being kind now, patting me down."

"No, that's not true. If I had married that man I wouldn't be alone, relying on neighbors. He would have stayed with me when I lost my sight, maybe we would have had children together, a boy and girl who had loved their blind mother."

"You are so strong, so independent."

"I put that on as an act," Miss Mack said.

"Please stay being my friend, Miss Mack. I need you."

"And I need you, but I am sure I have lost you by this intrusion."

"No, no, I need you because there is something I don't want. I don't really want to take in clients at home. I'll be too tired at the end of the day and I don't want to take business away from Albert, who has been so kind to me . . . but I don't know how to organize it. You see, I don't want to upset Tim."

"I see that," Miss Mack said. "And I'll help you. Willingly."

They sat and talked for a while as Miss Mack stroked Lilian's golden hair, which she could see only as a blur, and she explained to Lilian that the street was zoned as residential and that if there was any complaint that somebody had deliberately gone for change of use and begun a commercial undertaking there, then neighbors would object. There would be no question of a home industry.

And Lilian went home and showed Tim the bank notes and he folded them carefully away for their future, and told her that he loved her. And they would have a wonderful day tomorrow.

Lilian lay awake and thought for a long time about Miss Mack and the man she didn't marry.

Two houses along the terrace, Miss Mack lay awake for a long time and thought about the generous girl with the big heart who was prepared to regard terminal meanness as a little flaw, like snoring.

Normally Miss Mack did not worry about what would happen in the next thirty or forty years, but tonight she felt an ache to be younger. She wanted to be around and see this lovely girl, Lilian, make a success of her marriage. It didn't matter that it proved that she had done the wrong thing herself all those years ago.

That was something that Miss Mack did not allow herself to think.

FLOWERS FROM GRACE

Grace was calm when everyone else was fussing about New Year's Eve. It all had to do with the fact that she was so very organized. The hotel had been booked for over a year; they would all arrive on New Year's Eve during the afternoon.

It would be wonderful to get out of Dublin, where everyone else would be frenetic and in noisy, awful places worrying about taxis home.

Grace and her friends would be in this exquisite little country hotel, with its heated swimming pool, its little wood by a lakeside for healthy walks, its legendary menu for a memorable meal to end the millennium.

Her friends said that Grace was a true wonder, so serene in the face of everything that life threw at her, like working for that difficult Lola in the boutique, like being married to that difficult Martin, an accountant so busy that he hardly stopped to notice her at all.

The other couples speculated about her a lot. Was she happy in a life where she seemed to get little appreciation either in the home or outside it? Sometimes they wanted to kill Martin for being so unobservant, for never praising her cooking, for not admiring her appearance. They also wanted to kill Lola, who took Grace for granted.

And now, when everyone else was dithering about New Year's Eve plans, Grace had come up with the perfect place for them all to go.

Four couples in their twenties and thirties, no children yet, any of them. They could have gone to any of a dozen parties, but this seemed a much better idea, two nights away in a very prestigious place. Good to talk about; other people envied them. And Grace had made it easier for them; every month she would manage to collect some money from them, and now at the end of the year the whole festivities had been paid for very painlessly. They now felt they were having this lavish New Year's outing almost free!

"I'm glad we *did* pay her each month," Anna said to Charles. "We'd find it hard to raise that kind of money just at the moment."

"It's only temporary," Charles said hastily. He didn't like thinking of the gambling losses that had mounted up so frighteningly. This weekend would be a godsend; he couldn't think how else they could have seen the New Year in in any style.

"Poor Grace . . . you know, darling, she does all this fussing and organizing because she literally has nothing else in her life," said Olive to Harry. Olive was wrongly very contented and even smug about her own life, which she felt was full of people but did not realize was also full of Harry's girlfriends.

"Oh, I don't know—fine-looking bird," Harry said ruminatively. Grace had never responded even mildly to his flirtations and he had hopes that the New Year's weekend might yield something.

Sean and Judith had spent the last six weeks debating whether or not they would go on the weekend. In the end it always came down to Grace. She would be so utterly disappointed if her dream were to fall apart. They didn't feel they could let her down, even though they really did need time out together alone. It was absurd, this loyalty to Grace, when they should be trying to work out whether they would separate after four years of marriage.

"How can we even think of her when our whole future is up for discussion?" Sean asked.

"Right, you can be the one to tell Grace, then," said Judith, and they knew that they would go on the weekend, like everyone else.

Lola needed the boutique open for a couple of days between Christmas and New Year's. Lots of business, she said, dizzy women who had nothing to wear for the Punchestown races, they would make a mint of money. Lola couldn't come in herself, but she hoped that Grace could. Martin hardly noticed that she wasn't at home.

A lot of four ball games had been arranged at the club; he could always grab a sandwich and soup.

Grace stood in the shop, sold expensive clothes to rich women and thought back on the well-organized but exhausting Christmas with her mother and Martin's parents and assorted aunts. Why did she do it? she sometimes asked herself. They thought it was easy, that the turkey basted itself, carved itself and created all its own accompaniments. Had Martin enjoyed it all? Hard to know—he said so little these days. They saw each other so little.

Unlike Anna and Charlie . . . they were always off to the races together or going to poker parties. Never apart.

And even Olive and Harry seemed to be more companionable, Harry often with his arm draped around Olive's neck. Martin wouldn't do that in a million years. Everyone knew that Harry had a wandering eye, of course, but Olive didn't appear to notice.

She wondered had Judith and Sean enjoyed their Christmas? They seemed tense recently, something to do with Sean being offered a job in the Gulf States and Judith not wanting to go. Still, it would all sort itself out at New Year's Eve.

As she hung dresses back on hangers and filled the till with credit card slips for Lola, Grace thought of the wonderful oasis she had created for them all on Friday. There would be a light afternoon tea when they had all had their swims and walks, then they would retire to their rooms, all with four-poster beds, and get ready for the feast.

Thinking about beds made Grace wonder whether all the other couples might try out the four-posters before dinner, and make love. It wasn't likely in her own case. Martin was tired a lot and might well sit in an armchair and read the newspaper or a golf magazine. Still, it would all be wonderful, Grace told herself, as she totted up the day's takings and rang Lola just before she turned off the lights and headed for home.

"You were right, Lola—much better than we hoped," she said, reading her boss the figures.

"Thank you, Grace. You're very good." Lola did not seem her usual confident self; in fact, she sounded rather down.

"And a very Happy New Year, Lola, and everything."

"Yes, well . . ."

Grace didn't say any more; she had already told Lola many times about their own magical New Year's plans. She had heard nothing in return. They wished each other well and Grace set all the burglar alarms and went home.

Martin was at the dining table with a lot of papers spread in front of him.

"You're not working, are you?" she said sympathetically. Imagine—when everyone else was taking two weeks off, he had office stuff with him.

"You were too," he said, holding out his hand to her.

She was pleased.

"But surely you don't need to do all this?"

"Well, you're only as good as your last client thinks you are." He smiled at her.

Grace loved him so much she wished she were a better, more entertaining wife. But at least she ran his life smoothly for him, and surely that's what he wanted.

"Oh, there was a message from that hotel we're going to tomorrow. They wanted us to call; I waited to let you do it."

Grace was pleased. She knew what it was about. She had asked them to put a New Year's candle and a half-bottle of Champagne in each room; there was money left over in the kitty for that. They would be ringing to confirm.

She was totally unprepared for the news. Everyone in the hotel had come down with flu—the chef literally could not leave his bed, the waitresses just as bad. The family who ran the place had been advised most sternly by their doctor that it would be both irresponsible and impossible to open. They were so very, very sorry, and of course though naturally every penny would be refunded, they would never be able to apologize . . .

Grace didn't hear the end of the conversation. The phone sat in her hand as she contemplated what lay ahead. Everything was in ruins. It was all her own fault. Why had she set out to be the perfect organizer and the one in charge? She had phoned from the kitchen so that Martin would not hear of her little surprise arrangement.

Grace had no idea how long she had sat there by the phone when Martin came out. He knew that something was very, very wrong. Wrong enough for him to pour her a brandy.

"I'll phone the others," he offered.

"No. I invited them, I'll uninvite them," she said grimly.

"We'll get in somewhere else," he said uselessly.

"Sure, Martin . . . a booking for eight people New Year's Eve, twenty-four hours' notice. No problem."

"So what will we do?" He looked at her. Grace, the unflappable Grace, who had a solution to everything. But not tonight.

"Could we eat at home?" he began.

"I've defrosted the freezer." Her voice was flat.

"There'll be places open tomorrow."

"Sure," she said in this strange voice. "I'll call everyone now."

Martin stood by watching helplessly as she spoke in a listless, beaten voice to Anna, and Olive and Judith. He could only guess at what they were saying at the other end of the line. It seemed to be reassuring. She was suggesting that they all come around to this house the following night at eight o'clock.

"We'll think of something," she said in a doom-laden tone before she hung up.

Martin tried to help. "It's worse for the people with the bad flu," he began.

"Much," said Grace. "I'm going to bed now."

"Don't we have to plan what we'll well . . . um . . . do?" Normally Grace liked to plan things down to the bone.

"No point," said Grace. "Goodnight, Martin."

When she had gone upstairs he rang the couples himself.

"What'll we do, Charlie?"

"Four to one she'll be up in five minutes drawing up lists and rotas," said Charlie, who wondered would they get their money back; it would be very handy.

"What'll we do, Harry?"

"I don't suppose we could leave the women to it and sort of cruise the bars—lots of talent out on a night like that," said Harry hopefully.

"What'll we do, Sean?"

"Should we all just sit in our own homes and discuss the future with each other?" Sean asked. It was what he dearly longed to do himself. This could be the excuse he had been dreaming of.

In three homes that night they discussed the problem.

"We must be owed a fair crack each—that wasn't a cheap hotel," said Charles.

"This is *not* the time to ask for it back," Anna warned. "Poor Grace is almost certain to be in therapy over all this."

They knew a dead cert for the races after the weekend. If they had a couple of thousand it would see them right.

Olive and Harry were talking about it all too. Olive thought it was possibly no harm—they were not going to be in a place with people falling out of their swimsuits into Harry's willing hands.

But she didn't say this. She said that Grace was quite likely to have a nervous breakdown. Organizing was her only skill, after all. If that was gone, what else remained?

Judith and Sean said now they had all the time on earth to talk, there was nothing to say. So they didn't have to pack all their clothes and get ready. They didn't have to face, with what would have been a forced jollity, this group of friends so as not to let Grace down. Now she had been let down by the hotel instead.

"It will be a lonely New Year's for her," Judith said sympathetically.

"It's a lonely one for me if I know that you won't come to the Gulf with me," Sean said simply.

"And for me if I know you don't believe that I can't leave my parents and my job," Judith said.

They had got no further; there was no more to be said.

The women all rang Grace next morning: what could they do, what should they bring?

"I don't know, I don't mind . . . whatever you think," she said in tones so different from her own they were all alarmed. They didn't know where to begin; Grace would have organized them all, *should* have organized them all. She knew where things were, she would have phoned the stores, but Martin said she had gone to bed with a detective story.

Martin was getting Champagne, Harry was getting wine, Sean was getting spirits and Charles went out and sold his stamp album to buy mixers and beers.

Anna got bags full of potatoes because even though they were labor-intensive, they were cheap. She made three different kinds. Olive hit the shops only when everyone was closing and she got kilos of sausages and huge flat mushrooms. Judith got ice cream and three dull, tired-looking apple tarts and shared half a bottle of Calvados among them all.

They telephoned Grace and asked whether they should stay the night with her and Martin.

"I honestly don't mind whether you do or not," Grace said pleasantly.

They put their duvets and pillows in the car. They knew the house—there were plenty of sofa cushions. When they arrived, Grace was still in bed. She greeted them pleasantly but distantly, as if they were people she hadn't really known at all.

The women assembled the food in the kitchen. The men were setting out the glasses and the drink. Grace lay in her bed and turned the pages of her book. For the first time in her life they were all aware of her. She could hear them whispering and wondering when she would join them. Martin, most of all.

On Christmas Day, Grace the Organizer had served a meal to eleven people, unaided, unthanked and unappreciated.

Now, just six days later, she was lying in bed doing nothing and they were all anxious for her even just to acknowledge them. Was there some kind of moral here? Some lesson that she had never learned in her whole life until now?

"Would you like another cup of tea?" Martin pleaded. Casual, distant, uncaring Martin, whom she had been trying so hard to please.

"Shall I run a bath for you?" Anna begged. Wild, bohemian Anna, who was at every race meeting and every card table in Dublin.

"Should I plug in your heated rollers?" asked Olive. Smug, complacent Olive, so sure of her Harry, so confident in everything.

"I could iron a dress for you, if you like," Judith offered. Judith, so happy in her independence, her good job, her freedom to make her own decisions always.

Grace accepted everything, tea, heated rollers, scented bath and dress-ironing. Then she asked for the phone. They heard her dial and speak.

"Lola, I forgot to say there are a few people gathering here tonight in case you're free to join us. . . . No, nothing formal. I've no idea what time we're eating, or even *what* we're eating. Something, anyway. . . . You will? Good—see you later, then."

And Grace, who was no longer sure that it was only her organizational skills that kept her as a functioning member of society, as Martin's wife and as everyone's friend, sat back to enjoy the last night of the year. She didn't care that they never found the matching cutlery, the good napkins, the electric plate warmer or the saltcellars. Instead she sat back and watched and listened and smiled. She couldn't quite see how, but a lot of things seemed to get sorted out, things that might never have been sorted out had they been able to go to the hotel as they had long, long planned.

Sean was not going to the Gulf for another year and only then if Judith had found a job in the area that suited her.

Harry told everyone that he fancied the whole of womankind, he thought all women were gorgeous, but he loved only Olive.

Anna and Charles said that they would like Grace to hold half of their money when the refund came from the hotel; they were a teeny bit into gambling, they admitted.

Lola came and sat on the floor and sang Joan Baez songs. She said that Grace was the hardest worker in the world and said that she, Lola, would like to stay the night here with her new friends since there was nobody in her flat on Chestnut Street. And Grace said that would be fine but didn't rush to get linen and blankets. Lola eventually slept under her fur coat on a sofa.

And best of all, Martin said she was marvelous. He said it six times. Four times in front of people and twice just into her ear.

Beside her bed Grace always kept a notebook so that she could write down ideas; this was part of being organized. Tonight she wrote herself one message:

"Send thank-you flowers to the hotel."

She would know in the morning exactly why she must thank them for being delivered from the tyranny of being organized and for being able to join the human race.

THE BUILDERS

Nan at 14 Chestnut Street heard about the builders from Mr. O'Brien, the fussy man at Number 28.

"It will be terrible, Mrs. Ryan," he warned her. "Dirt and noise and all sorts of horrors."

Mr. O'Brien was a man who found fault with everything, Nan Ryan told herself. She would not get upset. And in many ways it was nice to think that the house next door, which had been empty for two years, since the Whites had disappeared, would soon be a home again.

She wondered who would come to live there. A family, maybe. She might even babysit for them. She would tell the children stories and sit minding the house until the parents got back.

Her daughter Jo laughed at the very idea of a family coming to live in such a small house.

"Mam, there isn't room to swing a cat in it," she said in her very definite, brisk way. When Jo spoke she did so with great confidence. *She* knew what was right.

"I don't know." Nan was daring to disagree. "It's got a nice, safe garden at the back."

"Yes, six foot long and six foot wide," Jo said with a laugh.

Nan said nothing. She didn't mention the fact that the house in which she had reared three children was exactly the same size.

Jo knew everything. How to run a business. How to dress in great style. How to run her elegant home. How to keep her handsome husband, Jerry, from wandering away.

Jo must be right about the house next door. Too small for a family. Perhaps a nice woman of her own age might come. Someone who could be a friend. Or a young couple who both went out to work. Nan might take in parcels for them or let in a man to read the meter?

Bobby, who was Nan's son, said that she had better pray it wouldn't be a young couple. They'd be having parties every night, driving her mad. She would become deaf, Bobby warned. Deaf as a post. Young couples who had spent a lot doing up their house would be terrible. They would have no money. They would want some fun. They would make their own beer and ask noisy friends around to drink it with them.

And Pat, the youngest, was gloomiest of all.

"Mam will be deaf already by the time they arrive, whoever they are. Deaf from all the building noise. The main thing is to make sure they keep the garden fence the height it is and in good shape. Good fences make good neighbors, they say."

Pat worked for a security firm and felt very strongly about these things. Jo and Bobby and Pat were so very sure of themselves. Nan wondered how they had become so confident. They didn't get it from her. She had always been shy. Timid, even.

She didn't go out to work because it was the way everyone wanted it. They needed Nan at home. Their father had been quiet also. Quiet and loving. Very loving. Loving to Nan for a while, and then loving to a lot of other ladies.

One evening long ago, on her thirty-fifth birthday, Nan could take it no longer. She sat in the kitchen and waited until he came home. It was four in the morning.

"You must make your choice," she told him.

He didn't even answer, just went upstairs and packed two suitcases. She changed the locks on the doors. It wasn't necessary. She never saw him again. He went without any speeches. Nan heard from a solicitor that the house had been put in her name. That was all she got, and she didn't ask for any more since she knew it would be in vain.

She was a practical woman. She had a small, terraced house and no income. She had three children, the eldest thirteen, the youngest ten. She went out and got a job fast.

She worked in a supermarket and even took extra hours as an office cleaner to get the children through school and on their way to earning their own living. Nan had worked for nearly twenty years when the doctors said she had a weak heart and must take a great deal more rest.

She thought it was odd that they said her heart was weak. She thought it must be a very strong heart indeed to get over the fact that the husband she loved had walked out on her. She had never loved anyone else.

There hadn't been time, what with working hard to put good meals in front of the children. Not to mention paying for extra classes and better clothes. There had been no family holidays over the years. Sometimes Jo, Bobby and Pat went on the train to see their father. They never said much about the visits. And Nan never asked them any questions.

Jo often brought her jackets or sweaters that she was finished with. Or unwanted Christmas presents. Bobby brought round his washing every week because he lived with Kay, this feminist girl, who said that men should look after their own clothes. Bobby often brought a cake or a packet of biscuits. He would eat these with his mother as she ironed his shirts for him. Pat came round often to fix door and window locks, or to reset the burglar alarm. Mainly to warn her mother of all the evil there was in the world.

Nan Ryan had little to complain about. She never told her

children that since she had given up work she often felt lonely. Nan's family seemed so gloomy about the work that would be done on the house next door that she didn't want to tell them that she was quite looking forward to it. That she was waiting for the builders and looking out for them every day.

The builders came on a sunny morning. Nan watched them from behind her curtain. Three men altogether in a red van. The van had DEREK DOYLE on it in big white letters.

The two younger men let themselves into Number 12 with a key. Nan heard them call out, "Derek! The bad news is that we'll be a week getting rid of all the rubbish that's here. The good news is that there's somewhere to plug in a kettle and it hasn't been turned off."

A big smiling man came out of the red van.

"Well, we're made for life then, for the next couple of months, anyway. Isn't this a lovely road?"

He looked around at the houses and Nan felt a surge of pride. She had always thought that Chestnut Street was a fine place. Nan wished that her children had been there to see this man admiring it all. And he was a builder, a man who knew about roads and houses.

Jo used to say it was poky. Bobby said it was old-fashioned. Pat said the place was an open invitation to burglars, with its long, low garden walls, where they could make their escape. But this man, who had never seen it before, liked it.

Nan hid herself and watched.

She didn't want to go out and be there on top of them from the very start.

She saw fussy Mr. O'Brien from Number 28 coming along to inspect their arrival.

"Time something was done," he said, peering inside, dying to be invited in.

Derek Doyle was firm with him.

"Better not to let you in, sir. Don't want anything to fall on you."

Nan's children had told her not to get too involved. Jo had said that the new owners wouldn't thank her for wasting the builders' time. Bobby had said that his girlfriend, Kay, said that builders preyed on women, getting them to make tea. Pat said that a house next to a building site was fair game for burglars and that she must be very watchful and spend no time talking to the men next door.

But the real reason Nan stayed out of their way was that she didn't want to appear pushy. They would be working beside her for weeks. She didn't want them to think she was nosy. She decided she would wait until they had been there for a few days before she introduced herself. She might even keep a diary of their progress. The new owners might like it as a record of how the house had been done up for them.

Nan moved away from the front window and back to her kitchen. She ironed all Bobby's shirts. She wondered if Kay knew that Bobby brought his laundry bag over to his mother every week. But they seemed to be very happy together, so what was she worrying about?

She cleaned the silver that Jo had dropped in that morning, taking a toothbrush to get at the hard-to-reach places, like handles and legs of little jugs. She wondered why Jo worked so hard trying to impress people. But then of course it had worked, hadn't it? Jerry, who had a very wandering eye, was still with her.

Nan made a big casserole and put some of it in foil containers for the freezer. Pat worked so hard in the security firm. She worried so much, she rarely had time to shop, so she cooked very little. It was good to be able to hand her a ready-made dinner sometimes. Nan wished that Pat would take time off, dress up, go out and meet people, find a fellow.

But then what did Nan know about finding fellows or keeping

them? Hers had disappeared without a word in the middle of the night twenty years ago.

Nan kept quiet on a lot of subjects. So quiet that people didn't expect her to have views anymore.

There was a loud knock on the door, and there stood the builder.

"Mr. Doyle," Nan said with a smile. "You're welcome to Chestnut Street."

He was pleased that she knew his name and seemed so friendly, and hoped that he wasn't disturbing her. But he had a problem. The instructions had been to throw out everything that he found in Number 12, and yet a lot of it must be of sentimental value. He wondered if perhaps, as a neighbor, she might know any relative or friends of the people who had once lived there. It seemed a pity to throw such things away.

"I'm Nan Ryan. Come on in," she said. They sat in the kitchen while she told him about the Whites. They were a very, very quiet couple who had hardly spoken to anyone. Mr. White had a job somewhere that involved his leaving the house at six in the morning. He came back at about three with a shopping bag. His wife never left the house. They put no washing out to dry. They never invited anyone in the door. They would nod and just go about their business.

"And didn't everyone around here think they were odd?"

Derek Doyle was a kindly man, Nan thought. He cared about these people, their strange life and their private papers still in the house. It was nice to meet someone who didn't give out or complain.

Old Mr. O'Brien from Number 28 would have fussed and said the Whites were selfish to have left so many problems behind them.

Her daughter Jo would have shrugged and said the Whites were nothing people. Bobby would have said that his girlfriend, Kay, would call Mrs. White "a professional victim."

Pat would have said that the Whites lived like so many people, in fear of their lives from intruders.

"I didn't think they were odd. I thought they seemed content with each other," said Nan Ryan. She thought she saw Derek Doyle look at her with admiration.

But she was being stupid. She was a woman of nearly sixty. He was a young man in his forties . . .

Nan told herself not to be silly.

Derek Doyle dropped in every day after that. He waited until the other men had gone home before he knocked softly on the door.

At first he used the excuse of bringing her old papers from the Whites' house. Then he just came as if he were an old friend. They called each other Nan and Derek, and indeed he was fast becoming a friend.

They didn't talk much about their families and she didn't know if he had a wife and children. Nan told him little about her son and daughters. And nothing about the husband who had left her.

He might have seen Jo, Bobby or Pat when they came in on their visits. And then again, he might not.

For a big man he was very gentle. He carried with him plastic bags belonging to Mr. and Mrs. White as if they were treasures. Together he and Nan went through the papers. There were lists and recipes and handy hints. There were travel brochures and medical leaflets and instruction booklets on how to work old-fashioned, out-of-date objects.

They turned them over, hoping to find some understanding of a life that had ended so strangely two years ago.

"There's no mention at all of their will," Derek said.

"No, and nothing about what he did all day at work," replied Nan.

"If only they had kept a diary. You'd think a woman on her own might have done that," he said.

Nan flushed a little. She had decided to keep a diary of the building work but so far it had all been about Derek Doyle and his pleasant visits. How he had brought a rich fruitcake in a tin, and cut a slice from it for them both when he came in to tea each evening.

How she had taken the bus to the fish shop and got fresh salmon to make a sandwich for him.

How it all gave a sort of purpose to each day.

"Maybe she was afraid it might be found."

"So she could have hidden it well," he said with a smile.

The builders found the diary a few days later. It was behind a loose brick in the kitchen. Derek carried it in like a trophy.

"What does it say?" Nan was almost trembling.

He put down five exercise books full of small, cramped writing.

"Do you think I'd open it without you?" he asked.

She cleared a space on the table. The scones could wait. Now they might discover something about the strange, secret life of the Whites, who had lived on the other side of a brick wall for twenty-five years.

They read together about the long days a woman had stayed hidden in Chestnut Street, fearful to go out, lest she be discovered. Night and day she worried that the cruel husband she had left would find her and harm her again, as he had done so often during their marriage.

Over and over she praised the kindness and goodness of the man she called Johnny, who must have been Mr. White. How he had given up everything to save her and take her away from all the violence.

How her family thought she was dead because there had been no word from her after the night she had run away with Johnny.

"Imagine all that worry and fear right next door!" Nan's eyes were full of pity.

They ate the scones, and as they turned the pages she made them beans on toast and they had a glass of sherry.

Derek Doyle didn't leave until nearly eleven o'clock. He telephoned nobody and no one called him on his mobile.

That didn't sound like someone with a wife, Nan thought to herself. She knew it was silly but she was glad.

There were still two more books of the diary to read.

Several times during the day, as she heard the sound of drills and hammers, she felt tempted to go back to the table and read them. But somehow it seemed like cheating. She went out and bought lamb chops for their supper. They both felt that there might be something sad and even worrying in the final chapters.

Jo phoned.

"I might call in tonight, Mother. Jerry's got a meeting. I have to drive him there and pick him up so I could sort of kill the time with you."

Nan frowned. This was hardly a warm thing for a daughter to say.

"I'll be out this evening," she said.

"Oh, honestly, Mother, tonight of all nights." Jo was impatient, but there was nothing she could do.

Bobby rang to say he would leave his washing in. And could she have it ready for him early tomorrow. Again Nan felt a wave of anger. She explained that it would not be possible.

"What will I do?" Bobby wailed.

"You'll think of something," Nan said.

Pat rang.

"No, Pat," Nan said.

"What on earth do you mean? I haven't *said* anything yet." Pat was annoyed.

"No to whatever you suggest," Nan said.

"Well, that's charming. I was going to go round and check your smoke alarm, but I'll save myself the journey."

"Don't sulk, Pat. I'm going out, that's all."

"Mam, you don't *go* anywhere," Pat protested.

Nan wondered if this was true. Was she like poor Mrs. White . . . who of course was not Mrs. White at all. Her name was something totally different, but kind, good Johnny White had gone out to work in a warehouse—a job he hated—just to keep her safe from harm.

The hours passed very slowly until it was time to take up the story again with Derek. Nan had changed into her best dress with the lace collar.

"You look very nice," Derek said.

He had brought her a bunch of roses and she blushed as she arranged them in a vase. Then they read on.

When they got to the bit where dear Johnny had been feeling too sick to go to work but was refusing to see a doctor, Nan began to worry.

"I don't like the sound of it," she said.

"Neither do I," replied Derek.

They read on, about how his cancer was terminal, how they knew she couldn't live alone without him. With tears in her eyes Nan read about the plans for the trip to the lakes, and sending their financial details and will to a solicitor.

They wanted their home at 12 Chestnut Street to be sold and the proceeds given to a charity that looked after battered wives.

It had taken some time to sort it out after they had disappeared, presumed drowned in the lakes. The law moves slowly, so that was why the house had been empty for so long.

Nan and Derek sat as the light faded. They thought about the couple and their strange, sad life.

"They must have loved each other very much," Nan said.

"I never loved liked that," Derek said.

"Neither did I," said Nan.

BUCKET MAGUIRE

A lot of his customers called him Mr. Maguire. They would be ladies of that generation which felt that to call a tradesman "Mister" somehow enabled the whole transaction. Raised it from a discussion of water and rags and cleaning windows.

Bucket Maguire himself, however, saw no need to raise it in anyone's eyes. It was a perfectly good, satisfying trade being a window cleaner. He had been doing it since he was sixteen, since the day that Brother Mackey had said there wasn't a chance in hell of young Maguire holding down a job in an office.

His father had been disappointed, but then people were often disappointed, and before he knew where he was, he had his bicycle, his folding ladder and his bucket on the handlebars. Mmmmmm.

It was unlikely that anyone remembered that he had been baptized Brian Joseph Maguire. Everyone called him Bucket. Well, everyone except his son, Eddie, who called him Far. Far was meant to be short for "Father." It had been a joke when Eddie was four, but he still used it whenever he came home, which was not very often.

What had Bucket's wife called him? Nobody in Chestnut

Street could remember. After all it was a long time since Helena had left. And she hadn't really been there very long. Eddie was only a baby, really.

But Helena had told all the neighbors that it was the only thing she could do under the circumstances. The circumstances were that she had met a new man who liked her a lot. The new man was in every way more substantial than Bucket Maguire, but what was more he was willing to adopt Eddie as his own. You couldn't say fairer than that.

Eddie would get a proper school and the example of a man with a real job. Even though Helena said that nobody on God's earth could or would say a word against Bucket, but a role model for a son he could never be.

The neighbors in Chestnut Street listened to Helena then fairly grimly. They said little but managed to imply forcibly that it was small thanks to Bucket Maguire, who had gone out hail, rain and snow to clean people's windows and make a home for his wife and son, if he were to be abandoned because he wasn't much of a role model.

There was very little understanding in the street for Helena before she took her son away to the suburbs; nobody came to say goodbye to wish her well. Many came after she had gone off with young Eddie. They all meant well, but Bucket thought to himself that nobody ever said the right thing.

Either they said that she would come back from that fancy man, which wasn't really likely, or else they said that he was well rid of her, which wasn't at all true. Some of them said he would find another woman, a better woman than Helena, which of course wasn't possible. And there were those who said that it was getting more and more difficult to raise a son in today's world and maybe he was better off not having to rear Eddie, since the boy could have become a handful.

Bucket thanked them all gratefully and said he thought it was all for the best and wouldn't Eddie be coming back regularly to see him.

It wasn't so regular in the beginning because Eddie had to settle in where he was—that was only fair, anyone could see that, Bucket said in defense of Helena.

And later, when Eddie went to school, he had so much homework and so many other things in his life it made sense that the lad would come only now and then.

He always came near his birthday and near Bucket's birthday and near Easter and near Halloween and near Christmas and other times. So that was well over half a dozen times a year.

The neighbors saw Eddie kicking a stone disconsolately around Bucket's garden when he did visit, a restless child who remembered none of them and who didn't seem at all grateful for the treats that Bucket provided.

"Ah, you can't expect a youngster to have fancy manners and be thanking for this and for that like a parrot," Bucket would say.

If people believed that the boy's new father was going to be a role model to the child they wondered how it was showing itself. Helena would drop the child off and wave goodbye before poor Bucket could get out to the car to talk to her.

Bucket used to go to Miss Mack in the library—before she went blind—for suitable books and games that he could share with Eddie on his visits, but he admitted that the boy didn't have huge powers of concentration.

"I'm afraid he inherited that from me—I was never much for the books," Bucket said sadly.

Miss Mack wanted to cry when he spoke like that, and it annoyed her so much that Helena could never warn Bucket about when the visits, few as they were, would take place. That meant that Bucket would have to keep taking out the books or games from the library week after week, just in case.

Kevin Walsh, the taxi driver in 2 Chestnut Street, had driven young Eddie and his new lifestyle, not that the boy ever recognized him. The stepfather had a load of money and took taxis a lot.

"To my mind Bucket's well off without the boy, turning into a right young pup he is, giving cheek right and left of him," Kevin said to anyone who would listen. Bucket was not one of those who would listen.

"The lad had a poor start with a broken home and all," Bucket would say forgivingly. "Isn't it only natural that he'd feel a bit lost?"

And when Miss Ranger from Number 10 happened on the information that young Eddie Maguire had been suspended from school for troublemaking, she didn't tell Bucket. She knew in advance what she would hear: "Ah, that's all a misunderstanding. Some of those teachers are very contrary; they have a down on poor Eddie." Better to say nothing.

On one of his window-cleaning jobs, Bucket found a kitten mewing on a roof. Carefully he rescued it and carried it proudly in his jacket to the front door. The man sighed wearily.

"Hell, I thought I'd got them all—this little devil must have escaped."

The man felt that he had done a good morning's work in drowning the seven kittens that had presented themselves, before the children came home from school and made a scene. The kittens' mother, a wily cat who must have read her owner's mind, had hidden them somewhere until they were about five weeks old and then paraded them back into the house triumphantly.

"You're going to drown this?" Bucket asked in disbelief. He could hear the little heart beating under the bundle of gray fur in his hand.

"Give it to me—it'll be over in seconds," the man said.

Bucket shook his head. "I'll take it home, mind it myself," he mumbled.

"Ah, don't talk nonsense, man—they're like vermin when there's dozens of them at that age."

"There wouldn't be dozens of them—there would only be one, and I'll look after it."

"No, you won't. Little bastard will come crawling back to us—they always do."

"Not from me. I live miles away over in Chestnut Street."

The man looked at Bucket in wonder. "You cycle all that way just to clean windows?"

"Sure, aren't I the lucky man to have my health and strength." Bucket beamed at him with pleasure at the good hand that he had been dealt.

"Yes, well. What are we going to do with the animal?"

Bucket took out the small kitten and examined it.

"Could you put her in a room somewhere out of the way and give her a saucer of milk, a bit of bread in it, maybe, and I'll come for her when I've finished the houses in this street, about four o'clock, and take her off your hands."

"I don't know." The man was doubtful.

"Ah, go on—your children won't be back by then, they won't see her and I'd like her," Bucket pleaded for the tiny life.

"What about them all in your home?" the man asked.

"There's no all at home, there's only me," Bucket said and only then did he release the funny little cat, gray with a white chest, thin, wary and frightened, from its great climb to escape death in the bucket of water.

"There you go, Ruby—this nice man will give you a bit of lunch until I'm back for you," Bucket said.

"Ruby?" the man said.

"I always thought it was a lovely name. If we had had a daughter she would have been Ruby."

"No children? Maybe you're as well off."

"Oh, I do have a son, a great fellow altogether. Eddie is his name."

"So there *is* someone at home?"

"No. Eddie lives with his mam—it was better that way. After all, what could I offer him?"

The man seemed to be annoyed by Bucket's good-natured approach to things.

"Right then, I'll give this little fellow a bowl of something and you'll be back for it by four."

"Give her a box with a bit of earth in it as well, won't you," Bucket requested.

"Anything else? Caviar? A sun-ray lamp?"

"I just wanted her to have a sort of a bathroom and not to annoy you or your family by having to use the floor."

"See you at four, not later," said the bad-tempered man.

Bucket was there on the dot, carrying a tin of food for kittens and a brand-new litter tray. He placed the cat in the front basket where he normally kept his chamois, cleaning rags and squeezy jar of soapy liquid. He had a cardboard box fixed in place and tenderly he lifted Ruby in and eased her head out through a hole in the top.

"To give her a sense of the journey and some fresh air during the ride home," Bucket explained.

"You're a decent person," the bad-tempered man said unexpectedly.

Ruby settled in well in Number 11; she never attempted the long journey to find her mother or to seek her long-dead brothers and sisters or return to the unwelcoming home of the bad-tempered man. Miss Mack, from Number 3, told Bucket that she once read in a book about cats that they forgot their past life very easily and slept nearly 60 percent of the time.

"God, wouldn't that be a great way to be!" Bucket said approvingly, looking at Ruby with new eyes. Ruby had grown plumper and glossy by the time Eddie next came to visit.

Nowadays, when he came to see his father, he brought a friend. Well, Helena said, you couldn't expect a grown boy of twelve to just sit there looking at him. A boy of that age *needed* a pal if he weren't to go mad altogether. His pal was called Nest Nolan. The first time he met the boy he had said, "That's a funny name, Nest."

"From a man named Bucket that's a bleeding funny remark," Nest had said.

So Bucket passed no more remarks. He didn't think the boy was a good friend for Eddie; he was rough somehow, no manner, no warmth about him. He had tried to tell this to Helena but she shrugged. Kids make their own friends, she had said. No point in trying to make things different.

Eddie and Nest looked without pleasure at the gray-and-white cat.

"Full of fleas," Nest said sagely.

"Jesus, Far, why did you get a thing like that?" Eddie complained.

"I thought you'd love the puss cat, Eddie. That's Ruby. She and I are great friends altogether," Bucket said, disappointed. "She'd nearly talk to you. I was thinking of teaching her a few tricks. She's very fond of me, you know."

"They go with anyone who feeds them, cats do," Nest sneered. "They don't have any sense of decency. Not like dogs."

"Ah, but I can't have a dog here, Nest," Bucket explained. "I have to go out to my business every day. I wouldn't be able to exercise a dog or bring a dog with me—it wouldn't be fair."

"And what is your business?" Nest asked, although he knew.

Everyone knew Bucket's business—it was written there on his bicycle, QUALITY WINDOW CLEANING. But Nest liked to ask so that he and Eddie could have a laugh when Bucket told him.

"And do you have any quality window cleaning to do this afternoon?" Nest inquired.

"Well, not now that Eddie's here," Bucket explained. He would cancel the bookings he had made.

"Won't the people be pissed off with you?" Nest continued.

"Well, they'll be disappointed, but then I don't see Eddie that often . . ."

"You could go and do the windows; we'd be here when you got back," Nest said.

Bucket refused.

"Aw, go on, Far," Eddie said. "We're not going to be sitting here looking at you for two hours."

"I have a game," Bucket began.

"It's for babies," Eddie said.

"Listen, Mr. Bucket, wouldn't you go out and deal with your customers—we'll stay here and keep your cat company."

"No, no, I was looking forward to Eddie . . . to you both . . . coming. I don't want to miss it." He looked eagerly from one to the other. There was a silence.

Eventually, Eddie spoke. "We won't stay here if you're here, Far. We'll just go hang out round the place, you know."

"No offense, Mr. Bucket," Nest said with a crooked smile.

"Of course, no offense," Eddie reassured him.

Bucket cycled off despondently. There *was* no other way. And it wasn't Eddie's fault. He had just fallen in with a bad-mannered friend, that was all. He went and cleaned windows and bought the boys a big tub of luxury ice cream. One with lumps of butterscotch and nuts in it. They'd like that.

When he got into Chestnut Street he saw that there was a crowd around the gate of Number 11. Bucket's heart lurched in case there had been an accident. Why else would people be gathered there? He threw his bicycle against the railing and ran to see what was going on. People had their hands over their faces in horror and amazement, watching Ruby staggering along on the road. Something had been attached to her paws, making a strange clicking sound and she was very distressed because she was crying like a baby. She hissed and spat when people tried to pick her up but she recognized Bucket when he arrived and tried to move towards him. He lifted her up and found her four little paws had been stuck into pointed shells, like limpets, ones you found on the beach. They were secured in there with candle wax, still slightly warm. It must have been hot when the little paws were forced into the shells. His stomach felt sick. It was red wax like the candle he had on the table in his sitting room, in case anything festive enough ever occurred when he might reasonably light it.

"Shush now, Ruby, we'll get your shoes off," he said, soothing the terrified little animal in his arms.

He pulled one of the seashells, but it didn't come away.

"I just went for a Stanley knife," said Kevin Walsh, the gruff taxi driver from Number 2.

"I brought her a few cat chocolates to calm her down," said Dolly, the schoolgirl from Number 18, who had a cat of her own.

"I was going to ring the Guards," said fussy Mr. O'Brien from Number 28, who had a pedigree cat called Rupert, "but the others said that what with everything, I should wait until you came back."

Between them, Bucket and Kevin Walsh prized the shells from the soft paws. There were still bits of wax left between the claws, but Ruby could walk again. She did a triumphal walk past everyone to show that she was better, then she attached herself to

Bucket's chest and wouldn't allow him to put her down on the ground again. He told people that her poor little paws must be sore and thanked everyone for being so concerned.

"I can't think what kind of a rotten person would have done this," he said with tears in his eyes.

"Your son and his friend did it, Bucket," said Kevin Walsh straight out.

"No, Kevin, they wouldn't—Eddie loves animals."

"They called me over to look at it, to have a laugh, they said." Kevin was adamant.

Bucket was shocked. "No, I can't believe it."

"Where are they now, then? They're hiding because it wasn't so much of a laugh after all." Kevin's mouth was a hard, unforgiving line.

Bucket was looking back at his house fearfully. "There must be a mistake," he began.

"There's no mistake," Kevin said.

People were beginning to move away from Number 11. The drama was over; now the embarrassing bit was starting, the bit where poor Bucket would realize what kind of a thug he had as a son. "He's only a child," Bucket said to the backs of the people who didn't want to hear him defending, yet again, the boy whom he loved but they had always found troublesome.

It wasn't Eddie's fault. The boy was easily led and people were quick to have a down on him. Eddie and Nest were amazed at all the fuss. Hadn't Bucket himself told them only this very day that he was going to teach the cat tricks? Well, they had tried to teach the stupid cat tap-dancing and now they were the worst in the world. They both looked wounded, upset, about to leave, never more to return. Bucket begged them to realize it had been a mistake.

"You see, I don't think you know how careful you have to be with a dumb animal," he said nervously.

"You'd never think it was a dumb animal with all the screeching when we put the hot wax on its paws. You could hear it twenty miles away," Nest said with a crooked smile.

Bucket looked at his son, hoping for some sign, any sign that the boy was disassociating himself with Nest. He saw no sign. He knew that what he said now was important in some way.

"I suppose poor Ruby didn't know it was all a joke," he said eventually. He looked from one boy to the other, trying to read what he saw. Bucket thought he saw scorn and pity.

That night Helena telephoned him. "Are you all right?" she asked sharply.

"Yes, I think so. Why do you ask?" He could sense her shrug.

"Don't know. Something Eddie said. I think he felt you were going potty or something."

He paused. He could tell her now what their son and his friend had been up to or he could let it pass. He let it pass, and he knew that somehow things with Eddie would never be the same again.

Two years later Eddie was expelled from school. Nest had been expelled too. But there was another place that took them on, a much tougher kind of school.

Helena said she was disappointed but then life was disappointing anyway, wasn't it.

Bucket didn't know; sometimes it was, but mainly it was fine.

"You *would* say that," Helena said.

"Will he still come and see me when he's in the new place?" Bucket asked.

"Well ask him yourself—you see enough of him," Helena snapped.

Bucket paused. He hadn't seen Eddie for more than three months.

"When do I see him, does he say?"

"Every Saturday for the last six weeks, or are you so dopey that you don't even notice your own son in your own house?"

"He doesn't come here, Helena," he said in a beaten voice.

"Shit," said Helena.

"Far?"

"Is that you, Eddie?"

"Unless you've a lot of other children we don't know about." Eddie came in the back door of Number 11.

Ruby left the chair she was sleeping in, quite urgently, and scampered upstairs.

"Only you, Eddie."

"That wasn't much to show for a life's work," Eddie said.

"It was enough for me. I wish things had been different so that I could have seen you all the time but I'm always happy to see you. I wish I was a better person to advise you."

"You're okay, Far—you're better than *he* is."

Bucket knew that *he* meant Helena's second husband. "I thought he was meant to be very nice?"

"Oh, yes, when things go well. When they don't go well he acts as if he has a smell up his nose," Eddie said.

"Well, people are different."

"Why weren't you tougher, Far, stronger, you know?"

"I don't know, Eddie. It wasn't my way."

"It's the only way to get on—we only have one crack at life."

"I know that now. I didn't know it earlier."

"Would you have been different, do you think?"

"No, probably not. No, I think I'd have been just the same. I'm a great one for the easy life, not ruffling people. I didn't want to upset your mother when she had her heart set on bettering herself."

"But she must have seen *something* in you to marry you."

"She must have, but I think it was just that I was safe, had my own trade, my own house. In those days having a business was a great thing."

"But it's not a business, Far—it's only yourself, a bicycle, a ladder and a bucket," Eddie said.

"And a reputation and a list of satisfied customers as long as my two arms," Bucket said proudly.

"I don't like my new school, Far."

"You've only been there five minutes, son."

"No, six months. Nest likes it and Harry and Foxy and all my friends, but I don't."

"So what do we do, Eddie?" Bucket was genuinely perplexed. He had no idea how to advise the boy.

"You couldn't let me live with you and go to the place up the road?" He looked so trusting.

"Ah, Eddie son, they wouldn't take you. That's a place for the sons of gentlemen. Your new father might be able to get you in there but not me. And anyway, Eddie, it costs a fortune in fees."

"I'd pay it back, Far, when I did well."

"No, lad, it just isn't possible. I have only the house, and whatever savings I have go into a policy for you when you get to be twenty and for your grandmother's nursing home bills."

"I don't want money when *I'm* old, like twenty—I want it now, Far!"

"If I could do it I'd give it to you this minute with my own two big hands, but I can't." Bucket nearly wept not to be able to deliver when he was being asked.

"I might have known." The boy slumped in the chair.

Bucket decided to give him all the wisdom he had in his possession. "Maybe if you pretended you liked this school, Eddie. I often do that when I get a big job with very high windows, but lots of them. I tell myself this is just the job I wanted. I don't think of the fall from the fourth floor to the ground, I think of the money at the end of the day. And I tell myself that this is a beautiful home, a gentleman's residence, in fact, and, you know, I start to feel better almost at once. If you were to try it in this new school it might work. Really, you know, it might."

"It's too late, Far. They've thrown me out. Today."

"But *why*, Eddie, why? You've only been there for just over six months. . . ."

"It was a mistake, Far. To do with drugs."

"But you didn't have anything to do with drugs, Eddie? I mean, you're only fifteen."

"Of course I didn't. Can I come to live with you?"

"We'll have to ask your mother."

"She'll say yes, Far."

And Helena did say yes. Very quickly. Bucket told everyone in Chestnut Street. Circumstances had changed; his son had come to live with him full-time.

"He'd better watch that cat of his," old Mr. O'Brien from Number 28 said.

"We'd all better watch everything," said Kevin Walsh from Number 2, who knew a lot about life, what with driving a taxi.

School was over. Finished. Eddie explained. It was the "give a dog a bad name" thing being played everywhere, all over again.

"But there are so many careers you could have, Eddie, so many opportunities."

"They're not going to *take* me at any school, Far. Hasn't that gone into your skull?"

"But how will you earn your living?"

"*You* left school at fifteen and you earned your living," Eddie said.

Bucket looked at him. "Yes, but it was never what you'd describe as a high calling," he began. "I mean, that's why your mother took you away to *him,* to an accountant, someone who would have respect."

"He hasn't any respect for me now, Far."

"It's all down to that fellow Nest—you're not a friend of his still, are you, Eddie?"

"No, I am not, not Nest, nor Foxy nor Harry."

"So you can have a clean start."

"That's what I need, Far, a clean start, a few quid, a respectable job, a base here with you."

Bucket had dreamed for years of hearing these words. He could hardly believe it was happening. "You're sure, Eddie?"

"Oh, I am. I didn't realize all these years this is what I wanted to do, to be."

"I'll get a new bicycle tomorrow," Bucket said, his eyes shining. "And we'll get the names painted, MAGUIRE AND SON QUALITY WINDOW CLEANING. We'll make a killing, my boy—that's what we'll do!"

Eddie looked at him, amazed. "No, I mean I'm not going into window cleaning," he said. "I just asked if I could live here and you said yes, that's all."

Bucket knew that this somehow was another moment, something that could change everything.

"That's fine, lad. I thought you wanted a hand up, that's all."

"It wouldn't be a hand up, Far, honestly," Eddie said.

"Okay, Eddie."

"We'll get on fine, Far, if you don't fuss," Eddie said.

"I'm sure we will," said Bucket.

Bucket Maguire was aware that his neighbors were not overjoyed to see Eddie back in the area, but he never knew how much the residents of Chestnut Street pitied him and hated his son. There was no point in their trying to tell him anything. He always had an excuse for Eddie: the boy was unfortunate, people had a down on him, they gave him a bad name just because he once had bad friends.

Bucket went to great trouble to point out that Eddie had risen above these people. But nobody seemed to believe him entirely. They asked vague questions like what did Eddie do all day? And how exactly did he get his wages? And what time did he get home at night? And suppose he didn't come home? Where did a boy of fifteen and a half, sixteen, spend the night?

But Bucket knew you didn't ask those questions if you wanted to have your son around. Things were a lot different now from when he was a boy.

Bucket worked on and on. He longed for an assistant, a young man who wasn't afraid of heights. But there was no way he could bring anyone else into the business. The day would come when Eddie would want to work with him. Bucket could see him on a new bicycle, cycling beside him. It was just a matter of waiting until the time was right.

Then suddenly Eddie left Number 11.

No explanation, just a note: "Gone on my travels, and if anyone's looking for me, you've no idea where I am. It's for the best, Eddie."

Weeks went by and Bucket worried. He couldn't bear to tell anyone that he had no idea where his eighteen-year-old son was.

One evening, out of the blue, Nest arrived at the door. Two young men were standing behind him.

Bucket did not invite him in. Ruby snaked out to see who it was, and as if she could remember only too well, she went back again very quickly.

"God Almighty, is that the same cat there was all the fuss about? She must be a monstrous age," Nest said.

"Ruby is six. Can I help you?" Bucket was brief.

"Well, yes, you can. It's about your son or grandson—I never worked out which it was." Nest smiled an innocent and crooked smile.

"Son. But he's not here and I'm afraid I don't know where he is." Even to this lout Bucket was courteous.

"Oh, I know he's not here—he won't dare show his face in Dublin for a while, a long while."

Nest looked knowing and menacing. Bucket felt uneasy. Best to try and patch things up, he thought. "I know you and he had your falling-out back at school, but isn't it best that you put all this behind you?"

Nest smiled again. "No, Mr. Bucket, nothing is being put behind us. There's still a lot of ongoing business and so if I could ask you to give him an important message . . ."

"I tell you truthfully, I don't know where he is, nor indeed when he's coming back."

"I'm sure that's true, Mr. Bucket, but one day he will get in touch, and if you could tell him that he knows where to find us. Just that. We're in the same place; he's the one who has gone walkabout."

He looked very threatening indeed, as if he were going to do Eddie an injury.

Bucket spoke quickly and nervously. "If he gets in touch with me I'll tell him, Nest. Certainly I'll tell him. But I didn't want you to think that he was in and out of here regularly or anything . . ."

"It's *Mr.* Nest to you. I have always had the courtesy to call you *Mr.* Bucket. I'd like the same courtesy in return."

"I'm sorry, Mr. Nest," said Bucket, with his head down.

The other boys tittered. They walked away like cowboys across the grass in the middle of Chestnut Street.

It felt very cold suddenly.

Bucket didn't sleep well after that. When he did sleep he woke with the smiling face of Nest only inches from his own and it took him ages to realize that it was a dream or Ruby lying on his bed at night purring heavily and guarding him. He began to make his own plans at that time.

One night Helena called very late.

"Is something wrong?" Bucket asked in a panic.

"*Wrong?* Why on earth would anything be wrong?" She sounded slurred.

"It's just that it's midnight, Helena."

"Is it? And does it matter?"

"No, not if you're all right."

"I'm fine."

"And your husband . . . Hugh, the accountant?"

"He's fine too, wherever he is."

"He's not at home tonight?" Bucket asked.

"Hardly any night. Bucket, have the papers been on to you?"

"About what?"

"About Eddie, you fool, what else?"

"The papers, the newspapers want to know about Eddie?"

"The whole country is looking for him—they don't know where he's hiding. Bucket, don't let him in if he comes."

"But I have to let him in—he's my son. And why are they looking for him?"

"Oh, Jesus, Bucket, you're a worse clown than I thought—it's all there every day in black and white."

"But he didn't *do* anything. Did he?"

"Don't open the door to him, Bucket. Phone the Guards; otherwise they'll kill you too. And for what, tell me, for what?"

"Who would kill Eddie and me, Helena? Be reasonable."

"The people he stole from. Nest, Harry and Foxy and all their pals. Our eejit of a son had to make friends with the greatest drug dealers in Dublin and then tried to double-cross them. They can't let him live. They're looking for him to kill him and the Guards are trying to get to him first. The best we can do for him is to turn him in."

"It would be a long time in gaol. Ah, we can do better than that for him surely, Helena?"

"We could arm-wrestle with these guys, who have guns, Bucket, sawn-off shotguns. Yeah, we could get ourselves killed. Terrific."

"We could help him get away," Bucket said.

"Goodnight, Bucket," Helena said and hung up the phone.

Ruby stiffened in the chair beside him, her hair up in great spikes. There was someone in the house. Bucket's hand flew to his throat. Was Mr. Nest back with a gang to wait for Eddie's return? Then a figure stepped out of the shadows. It was Eddie.

"Did you mean it, Far? That you'd help to get me away?"

"Of course I meant it. Sit down. I'll make us a cup of tea in case they're watching the house. We don't want them to see any unexpected activity at this time of night."

"It's too late for tea, Father. They are watching the house."

Bucket noticed with pleasure that this was the first time his son had called him "Father" rather than the silly send-up name of Far.

"Did they see you, Eddie?"

"No. I got over the back, up beyond Kevin Walsh's at the top and through the gardens . . . they're watching from the other side. From the garden of Twenty-two."

"Yes, Mitzi and Philip are on holidays. That would be why the house is empty." Bucket knew all about his neighbors, their plans and hopes and dreams.

"It's over, you know. You do know that?" Eddie seemed to be trying to beat the last bit of hope out of Bucket.

"Drink your tea, Eddie. Take plenty of sugar—it will give you energy."

"Energy for what? To be shot in the head once I walk out that door?"

"Why will they wait until you walk out—if they know you're here, they could come in for you."

"No, apparently not. Nest said he has respect for you. He talks all this kind of Godfather shit about respect; he said you never behaved badly to him in his years of coming here, and he'll not shoot anyone in your house."

"And is Nest the head of it all?"

"He is, yes."

"Imagine," Bucket said.

"I know," Eddie said.

It was like a real father-son conversation. At last. At the end.

They talked about a lot of things, about Hugh, the accountant; about Helena, who would never be happy anywhere. About how Eddie had no money because he gambled it all and what he had stolen from Nest had all gone to pay off debts in a casino and how it would all be very different if he had it all over again.

"But you will," Bucket said.

In the light that came in from the street lamp he saw the flicker of irritation cross his son's face, as so often before.

"Have a sleep, Eddie," Bucket begged. "We don't start until seven-thirty in the morning." He went to go upstairs.

"Don't leave me, Father," Eddie said.

"I'm only going up to get us pillows and a rug. Of course I won't leave you," said Bucket Maguire.

And he sat all night and watched his son sleeping on the sofa of Number 11, tossing and whimpering as he slept.

It was a gray, overcast dawn and Chestnut Street was waking up, as usual. Lilian would be leaving Number 5 to open the hairdressing salon up in the main street, Kevin Walsh might have an early-morning taxi booking to the airport, the Kennys in Number 4 would be going to Mass somewhere, Dolly from Number 18 would be coming back from her newspaper round.

It was time for Bucket Maguire to get on his bicycle, attach his folding ladder, his basket of chamois rags and soapy liquid, and head off with his teetering wobble towards the main road. Except this morning it would not be Bucket who rode the bike, it would be Eddie.

With a long raincoat and Bucket's old hat shielding his face, nobody would know the difference.

Once he got to the main road he was to chain the bike to a railing, roll up the hat and coat in the basket with the rags and catch a bus to the city center.

Bucket had been withdrawing money every week from the savings account. That had been part of his plan. So he had plenty to give to his son.

He thought he saw tears in the boy's eyes, but he wasn't sure.

"You mustn't look round to say goodbye—that would blow it," he told Eddie. "Don't wave at me but nod and wave at everyone else you pass. I know them all, you see, after living here all these years."

And he stood behind the curtain of his house and watched proudly as his son cycled the company transport past the people who were waiting to kill him and past the neighbors who all saluted him, thinking that it was the window cleaner going about his lawful business.

THE OLDER MAN

Berna hated the sound of him; she feared and distrusted every single thing about this man . . . this Chester, who was going to marry her only daughter. But she would have to be nice—she had never known Helen so adamant about anything in her life.

"If you start wrinkling up your nose at him, Mother, if you start being hoity-toity, I just won't stand for it," Helen had cried, flushed and excited, looking younger than her twenty-three years.

"I have no idea what you mean. What can there be to be hoity-toity about?" she had said.

But Helen was having none of it.

"He's been married already and he's nearly forty. . . . Don't you think I know what you're thinking."

"Have I said anything, Helen? Answer me that."

"You don't need to, Mother, you have what Father used to call your snibby face on."

"Your father often saw snibby looks where none were intended." Berna smiled but her heart was heavy.

She knew that Jack too would have hated the thought of this Chester, with his overconfident, brash American accent, flying in tomorrow, to discuss the wedding plans.

Jack would have given him short shrift. What *would* Jack have done? He would have taken Helen for a long walk, he might have taken her out to a meal in a fancy restaurant, he would have laughed and teased her out of it.

Jack had died when Helen was fifteen. Eight years ago. Everyone said it was the worst time for a girl to lose a father. Not many people had said that for Berna, at thirty-five, it wasn't such a great age to lose a husband. But then Berna had always been very good at looking as if she could manage.

Everyone saw how quickly she had learned to drive, got a job, kept the show on the road. If she shed long tears of loneliness and self-pity, nobody saw. Berna knew that people's problems were not very interesting to others, so she kept hers to herself. Even this heartbreak over the older man that her only child was going to marry. She hadn't told her sisters, friends or colleagues how she felt that life had dealt her another cruel blow.

All she knew was that she must keep up the appearances of friendship, since this marriage was most definitely going to happen. She owed it to Helen and to Jack not to break up the family because Helen was going ahead with the most unsuitable marriage in the world.

He had never been to Ireland before, Chester, who had been everywhere. Helen had met him in New York, and flown home after six months to tell her mother the exciting news. Now Chester was arriving in person. He was going to fly to Shannon and hire a car. He wanted to drive through the country, he said, get the feel of it. He'd be at their home on Chestnut Street in the afternoon.

He had sounded plausible on the phone, pleasant, polite, no fake Oirish accents, but that was probably part of his style. He was in advertising; obviously he knew how to manipulate people.

Still, this was no time for negative thoughts. Not now, when he was expected any moment.

She heard Helen cut short one of her many excited telephone

conversations, and run to the door. His car, parked outside, was a modest one, somewhat like the one that Berna drove herself, but then she remembered he had rented it here in Ireland. Back in the States he probably had a big flashy car.

She came to the top of the stairs and had to turn her head away when she saw the passion in the way they kissed, held each other and then stretched apart to look at each other with delight. How had Helen known about such desire? She hadn't learned it in this house.

He had dark curly hair and dark, dark eyes. His smile was broad and went all over his face. He came towards her with both hands out.

"I'm far too old to call you anything but Berna," he said.

How clever—he was admitting he was old. Knowing Helen was watching her, Berna forced her smile to be as broad as his.

"You are very welcome to our home," she said.

They went into the sitting room, a small room, full of memories, pictures of Jack and Helen all over the place.

It must look very poor and shabby compared to his duplex . . . wasn't that what Helen said he had? A flat with an upstairs in it in Manhattan.

But he seemed to like it. He praised all the right things, the lovely old mirror that had come from her own grandmother's home; the first painting Helen had done, which was framed and hanging in a place of honor; the view of the little garden lovingly cared for. He liked it all, without gush, with apparent sincerity. *Apparent.* She must remember that word. He hadn't got where he was without being able to act the part.

He was easy to talk to; there was no denying that. He didn't keep fondling Helen, he asked questions and he volunteered information about himself. He said he wanted Helen and Berna to decide what style the wedding would be. It was to be their day, their choice.

At times it seemed unreal. Berna felt she was part of a film or a play, that she was talking to a stranger about some distant, strange event instead of her own daughter's marriage. Once or twice she felt herself moving her hand across her forehead, as if she felt faint. He seemed to realize.

"Helen, darling," he said suddenly. "This is only a suggestion, but honestly I think that Berna and I would manage better without you."

Helen looked at him with disbelief.

"No, seriously," he went on. "We are both trying so hard to please you, every word we say is like another shot in tennis . . . and we try not to look at you for your approval."

Berna laughed. He had got it absolutely right.

"Where are you sending me?" Helen looked like a small child.

"You have a hundred friends of your own age—go off and tell some of them about your older man." He laughed.

"Will you still be my older man when I get back? You won't let her talk you out of it?"

"I'll be here."

They sat companionably by the fire. Chester told of his first wife, who had died, how they had been happy for three years but how she had grown remote from him, cold. How he had thought he would never love again until he had met Helen.

"I can't give her youth and all that starting-out-together stuff, but I can take care of her. I think she'll like that. You would have liked it, right?"

How did he know? How could anyone have known?

Chester looked around him, at the photographs, Jack waving from a yacht . . . a lot of their savings had gone on that little pastime. Jack in his three-piece suit; he had always gone to the tailor—Berna was the one who looked through the rails for bargains for herself. Jack talking with a crowd of film stars; he had loved hanging around with the famous.

The American's eyes moved slowly from picture to picture as if he could read the years of neglect and loneliness. His voice was gentle.

"I'll always be there for her. I know it's a kind of father figure she wants . . . but I don't mind. I'll be there." He sounded very dependable.

"More than her own father was a lot of the time," Berna heard herself saying, to her own surprise.

Chester wasn't going to go along that route, he wasn't going to destroy a lifetime of carefully preserved memories.

"He was the man you both loved, wasn't he?"

She reached out and patted the hand of this man who was going to be her son-in-law. She didn't care that he worked in advertising and that he was much too old for her daughter. She knew with great relief that she was not going to have to be the voice of authority anymore. This wise man whom Helen had brought home would make all the decisions from now on.

He could start by planning the wedding.

"Where would you like it?" she asked him.

He had the sense not to say wherever *she* liked.

"I'd like about twenty or thirty people, here in this house. In your home," he said.

And she knew that for the first time in their lives she and Helen would both be in complete agreement about something and put their hearts into it together.

PHILIP AND THE FLOWER ARRANGERS

Philip had always known how to succeed. At school he didn't seem brainy but he got better examination results than anyone else. People had been puzzled, but not Philip; he had always known that you had only one crack at proving that you were well educated. He had studied all the past examination papers carefully and worked out the likely approach. It had been the same about choosing a firm for his first job—he took a lowly post in a high-grade office. It would all look better on the CV eventually. He didn't enjoy golf and he positively disliked bridge but he learned both, as they were considered social skills.

Philip realized that a lot of people judged you on appearances, so he made sure that his own appearance was faultless. He did a lot of research about the right kind of clothes to wear and how to have his hair cut so that it looked smart and modern without being arty-farty. He learned to sponge his suits, he learned German from tapes and he attended symphony concerts and operas regularly until he did in fact begin to enjoy them rather than pretending to appreciate them, as he had done for so long.

It was at one of his visits to the opera that he met Annabel.

Discreet questioning on his part revealed that she was very suitable indeed as an acquaintance, a date, a friend and possibly more.

In Annabel he saw a young woman with a comfortable background, an influential father and a perfectly satisfactory job of her own as a teacher in a girls' school.

Annabel saw in Philip a very steady, hardworking and upright young man, who was such a change from her previous, wildly unsuitable boyfriend that it would be a relief to bring him home to Daddy.

Their wedding some twelve months later was, as you might expect, generous and elegant but not lavish. Philip said it would be so much more sensible to put any available money into a house rather than into a showy display. Their honeymoon was not in a far-flung place where they would rub shoulders with nonentity-type tourists. It was in an elegant hotel much frequented by the Established and the People of Power.

Philip's career record was impressive, and he was only in his early thirties. Each career move had been taken carefully, after a great deal of thought. The present and most demanding post that he had just begun involved time off to study Japanese. Philip had suggested in his interview that anyone taking on such a role would need the company's support in providing a language-laboratory course in a tongue that would be invaluable to the firm. It was the point that clinched his appointment. So now he began each day with two hours' total immersion in a foreign language. It did mean leaving for work at 6 a.m. because one had to do one's full day afterwards.

The day extended at the other end too—there were meetings and little so-called informal chats in clubs—but Philip knew that this was where all the power was centered. Sometimes he didn't get home until nine o'clock at night. And those were the nights that there wasn't anything official on, like a dinner or taking overseas contacts to the opera.

There was foreign travel too, and there was the car phone,

so the hour of driving with music on the stereo as some kind of relaxation between the office and his home in the leafy suburb was constantly interrupted with calls.

At first Annabel cajoled, and then she begged. Later she sulked, and finally she went on a transatlantic business trip with him so that they could have time to talk.

It was no life, she pointed out, trying to keep the catch out of her voice. It was no marriage, she said, fighting down the over-powering sense of being wronged that threatened to take over. She had given up her job and moved to a stockbroker belt miles from anywhere to further his career and their life. But apart from the executive entertaining that they did rarely—Philip's contacts were always too busy to get out to what they described as the wilds—there was no reason for her to be there. She was alone and resentful, and she was becoming increasingly anxious about her husband's health and state of mind.

"You are heading for a breakdown," she said in hushed tones in case anyone else in first class might hear.

Philip said that this was hardly constructive when he was head-ing out to close a very important deal. Not wifely, not supportive. Not even remotely likely, either.

As it happened, Annabel left him six months before the break-down did arrive.

They had parted sadly but reasonably amicably. Philip man-aged to block off four hours in his diary so that they could divide the records, the pictures and the furniture. They sold the house with the big garden full of trees that could have supported sturdy swings, the garden that had a pond that toddlers would have explored as a world of magic. They told each other that it was as well that they did not have children. It meant the break could be cleaner and less fraught. Annabel had looked at him thoughtfully and wondered whether he had ever loved her. Philip had looked thoughtfully back and wondered whether he could end the con-versation and get back to the office without seeming unduly curt.

There was no point in wounding a person like Annabel; her only fault had been not understanding the nature of business life. He consoled himself that she would be happier back in town, living perhaps in some sunny garden flat, taking up another teaching job, possibly marrying again. She was a fine-looking woman and only thirty-three, she had many chances ahead of her and a handsome settlement that everyone had agreed was fair.

When she heard that Philip was in hospital Annabel felt no sense of having been proved right. She asked his doctors whether a visit from her might help or hinder. They said it couldn't do any harm.

Philip was annoyed by his breakdown, but he assured Annabel that it was not going to stand in the way of any further progress up the ladder. People were much more enlightened these days, he said. Mental collapse was now looked at the same way as blowing a fuse. It was a matter of breaking the circuit—you restored it and then went on as before.

Annabel said she thought that when a fuse blew it meant that there were too many appliances working at the same time. It was a kind of a warning not to plug in so much at once. Could it not be the same for Philip? He said that her attitude was not constructive, he thanked her for visiting and he sent his regards to her father and his congratulations on new directorships.

Annabel sighed when she left the hospital. She looked back at her ex-husband and wondered what could anyone suggest to slow down his overactive brain?

Philip prided himself on being a realist. He hadn't got as far as this, he told his doctors, without being able to listen to the professionals in their fields. If they told him categorically that he would not heal his mind unless he kept away from work, then he would obey. For three months he would absent himself from the business world that so drew his attention and his interests. He would follow their instructions to the letter. He would read no financial papers, see no colleagues, review no corporate strategy. Then, as methodically as he had learned his spoken Japanese, he would have conditioned himself like an athlete and be ready to return.

He tried going to concerts but his mind didn't stay with the music.

He tried listening to his records but he began to resent those that had gone to Annabel in the division. He played golf only on courses where he would not meet his former colleagues. He bought a dog and walked it and himself mercilessly. And finally, in order to fill what he still found an achingly empty day, he agreed to go to a flower-arranging class. His doctor had said that there was something deeply satisfying about the constructing of shapes and the textures of petals and foliage. Philip doubted it gravely but felt that it would at least take up an afternoon for him in these endless weeks until he was considered fit to return to the real world.

The ladies in the class were pleased to have a gentleman in their midst. Maud and Ethel made coy little welcoming remarks and issued warnings. They would all have to look to their laurels . . . and, tee-hee, every other kind of greenery . . . now that they had a man amongst them. Men had a terrifying habit of winning prizes when exhibiting at flower shows. Philip didn't feel it necessary to tell Ethel and Maud that he wouldn't be with them long enough to take part in flower shows. He had always known an important rule for getting ahead, which was to let the Establishment think you were there forever. In terms of flower arranging, Maud and Ethel were the Establishment. He smiled a sheepish smile and they twittered appreciatively back at him.

Philip learned that today's flower arrangement had to be a triangle, which was something he had never known, even though he had sat behind many of them at banquets. And you had to have a high central flower and two medium ones on each side, then everything was built within that framework.

All afternoon he worked busily, scrunching up chicken wire and sticking it firmly to the base of containers. Then he was moved to the "oasis" table, where he learned to soak a thing that looked like a mad dry sponge in water, having shaved it first to being the right shape. He heard of the glory of pedestal containers, things that looked to him a little like cake stands. He examined the pros and cons of the pin holder, a thing that looked like a miniature hedgehog crossed with a nailbrush. Maud loved these and thought they ran rings round oasis and chicken wire. Ethel had her reservations. Philip worked out the power base and decided to throw his lot in with Ethel but to give supportive whispers to Maud as well. When the time came to clear everything away he was utterly absorbed and muttering to himself, "Design, scale, balance and harmony," which were the four chief principles of flower arranging.

"You'll be fine if you keep that in mind," said Maud with a twinkle.

"And even finer if you never stir without proper secateurs," added Ethel.

"Properly sharpened, of course," Maud warned.

"Strong enough to cut wire as well as flowers," Ethel reminded him.

By the following week Philip had bought three books on flower arranging and had been to two exhibitions. But none of this did he reveal. Never let the Opposition know the breadth of your research had always been his motto. He looked at the Opposition, twenty-two pleasant women who loved the soft autumnal colors of the yellow-and-orange demonstration they worked on today. They stroked the honeysuckle lightly, and admired the chrysanthemum and golden lilies. They sighed their admiration over the elegant way that the flowers were arranged in an old brass oil lamp and the warm foliage of golden privet and variegated ivy as a background. Philip had read so widely on the subject during the last week that he thought the brass container was a little obvious and that something more original might catch a judge's eye. But he kept this to himself and asked Ethel and Maud companionably about other inspired ideas they might have had. When Ethel mentioned the possibility of using an old casket or brass box, Philip felt a surge of excitement. This indeed is what they should have done to win points. A casket with the autumn flowers tumbling down over it was exactly what would have taken the rosette, the trophy or whatever it was that they were all out to win.

As the weeks went on Philip brought all his attributes into play. He had details of the next exhibitions, potted biographies of the judges who might judge the competitions, their likes and foibles. He was a master of disguise. He knew just how to stick the oasis or the pinwheels to the base of the container so firmly that nothing could ever detach from a mooring. He saw the wisdom of putting his arrangements with a light behind them, how to put a little chlorine or bleach in the water on the rare occasions when water could actually be seen. He knew that you worked the larger flowers and larger leaves into the center of any arrangement and got smaller as you went out to the edges. He began to have little patience for those who couldn't grow their own greenery even in flats with small balconies. He was not adverse to working on dried-flower or even silk-flower arrangements.

"They're not the real thing, of course, but very cheering to greet you back after a holiday," thought Philip.

The doctor said that his anxiety level was not noticeably lower. Philip protested strongly; he had obeyed every single rule to the last letter, he said.

"Have you tried that nice, relaxing flower arranging yet?" the doctor asked.

"Oh, yes, I go every week." Philip was impatient to be away. His mind was exercised by a special Halloween arrangement involving pumpkins, catkins and berberis.

"Do you get involved in it?" the doctor asked.

"Very." Philip was terse. He managed to avoid looking at his watch, and put on instead a smile that he thought signified relaxation. The doctor thought it a grimace of pain, and there were several more questions and answers before he could escape to the garden center for further supplies.

Philip won the club's own Christmas trophy hands down. He did the church Christmas flowers, which was a *huge* honor and brought his own containers rather than use the existing narrow-necked, carafe-type vases presented by guilds and Mother's Unions over the years. Chancel flowers and pedestal groups with tumbling winter jasmine, whole poinsettia plants incorporated rich berried hollies. It was a triumph.

Well, it was a triumph for Philip. Not for the ladies who had done the Christmas flowers for years.

At the big New Year's Winter Flower Competition, Philip carried all before him with his vaguely Oriental arrangement based entirely on the Alder pink-tinged catkins. He was interviewed for specialist journals as well as the national papers about the prize-winning display and spoke long and fluently about how a well-shaped branch could last for weeks, how it was important to choose one with small clusters of black cones and how the best should be kept and dried for winter use. He told a local television news reporter that he had hammered the ends of the stems well and soaked them in warm water overnight. At *no* time did he mention the club to which he belonged; he thanked neither Maud nor Ethel for their training, there were no flattering acknowledgments to the efforts of the runners-up.

Philip had always understood at business that the way to get on was to accept the praise gratefully and give what might be considered interesting insights into how the success had been achieved. It was never considered wise to make one of those Oscar-night speeches thanking everyone in sight. It deflected attention from the success in question, it hinted at a lack of confidence, it took away the limelight. Nobody wanted to hear of the people who had not won the trophies.

He smiled as he placed the silver cup on a table in the small and elegant house on Chestnut Street where he now lived. He might arrange a low white creation beside it later on in the year. When there were sweet pea and little white bud roses, carnations and a background of very pale fern. But no, that was not realistic. By spring he would be back at work. Only a week to go and he could start to think about it again.

He would spend that week arranging his study and getting ready the tools of his trade. Reluctantly he knew that he would have to get rid of the tools of the other trade, and say goodbye to the oasis, the chicken wire, the pin holders and the collections of useful standbys, the ferns, the trailing ivies and the catkins.

Still, that doctor had been right. It *had* been useful—the term of flower arranging. And now he didn't need it anymore. The rather sour Ethel and Maud, who had not congratulated him sufficiently, the colorless ladies who attended the same class every week, who had been so open and friendly at the start.

Philip was pleased that he had gone along with the doctor's instructions even though he had thought them rather foolish at the start. Now that he had learned all about flowers and proved that he could come out on top . . . that must prove conclusively that he was master of everything again and ready for anything that the business world could throw at him next week.

REASONABLE ACCESS

It all started ages ago. Just before my birthday. I was nine on May the seventh and there was a terrible atmosphere. I couldn't think what I had done wrong but it must have been something very bad—Dad was banging doors, all kinds of doors, bathroom doors, car doors, the door of the garden shed.

He nearly took the shed door off its hinges. I went out there to see was he all right and he shouted to me.

"For Christ's sake, leave me alone in the shed, can't you. You've already made the house a no-go area—leave me the shed, at any rate."

And then he saw me.

"Sorry, Dekko," he said. "I thought it was your mother." But that couldn't have been right. He wouldn't have shouted at Mum like that. He absolutely loved Mum, she was *his* sunshine, he said.

He had always said this. She was the only girl for him from the first time he saw her in the National Concert Hall.

Every time we passed the concert hall he used to say that there should be a special flag on the place or a notice to say that was where he and Mum had met.

And Mum used to laugh and say that the only thing in the

world that could have distracted her from Liam O'Flionn's wonderful piping was the smile of the man who turned out to be Dad. And that he was *her* sunshine also.

Those were the nice, safe days.

And then there was my birthday itself, and we had nine boys from school and we went to the cinema and McDonald's.

And it was an awful day, really, because Harry, my friend, kept talking about babes at the cinema and making remarks about girls as they passed by, and Mum got cross, and Dad said it was only natural for young lads to look at girls, and Mum said it wasn't natural for nine-year-olds to shout out in public about babes with boobs.

And Dad said she was always a killjoy and she was just trying to destroy Dekko's last birthday.

I got very frightened then, because I thought maybe I had a disease and was dying. Or they were going to send me away.

"Well, it will be the last one *you'll* be at, anyway," Mum said.

"I'll have reasonable access. And by God I'll get reasonable access," Dad said.

And then they saw me looking at them and put awful, tiny, insincere smiles on their faces.

Two days after the birthday, Dad and Mum both came home from work early.

This was unusual for a Monday; usually Mum went to the gym and Dad had a meeting after work.

They told me that they had arranged for me to go to Harry's house for supper because they had a lot to do.

"Couldn't I do it with you?" I asked, and they both got sort of upset.

I always say the wrong thing.

So I tried to explain.

"You see, we don't do a lot of things together anymore, like a family," I said. "It's ages since we all went out to the Wicklow Gap with sandwiches and found a place to sit where you couldn't see any houses at all, only hills and sheep. And we don't do a jigsaw anymore, or cook a foreign dish. Remember when we made the Indonesian thing, and we ate all the peanut butter when we were making it, so there was none left to add to the sauce."

This seemed to upset them more.

So I stayed quiet.

"Tell him now," Mum said.

"I'd have nothing to tell him if you hadn't been so bloody-minded," Dad said.

"Like turn a blind eye for the next twenty years." Mum was cold.

"Like listen to an explanation." Dad was colder still.

I looked from one to the other.

"Tell me what?" I asked.

There was a long silence.

"What were you going to tell me?" I asked again.

"Your dad and I love you very much, Dekko," Mum said, and my heart sank. There was a "but" coming up somewhere soon.

I couldn't see from where.

Was it Harry and all the talk about babes and boobs?

Was it about the time I unplugged the freezer to play one of my games in the kitchen and everything had to be thrown out?

Was it that I hadn't told them about the extra maths classes at school in case I would have to do them? I just didn't know.

"You are the most important thing in our lives," Dad said, and he began to choke.

So I thought, God, I *must* have some awful disease—what else could be upsetting them so much? Maybe it was nothing I had done.

"Am I going to die?" I asked. And then they both started to cry.

I'd never seen this before. It was awful. Awful. I didn't know what to say.

"I don't mind, really," I said. "Will it hurt much, do you think?"

And then there was all this business of telling me that I wasn't dying, and that I was the best boy in the world and I was their Dekko and none of this was my fault.

"None of what?" I asked. I was going to have to get to the bottom of whatever it was.

They were getting divorced, Mum and Dad. I couldn't believe it.

Selling our home and going to live somewhere else.

Well, two somewhere elses, actually. Mum was going to live on Chestnut Street, in a much smaller place but there would be a room for me—it was already called Dekko's room, and I could help to furnish it.

And Dad would live in a flat somewhere—it had yet to be organized.

"And would there be a room called Dekko in that flat?" I asked.

I shouldn't have asked. It was greedy. I know that now. I was just trying to understand what was happening.

"There might well be one," Dad said.

"Not that he will be sleeping in it," Mum added.

"Except at agreed weekends," Dad said, through his teeth.

"Which will never be agreed, not overnights, never," Mum said.

"We'll see about that when the time comes," Dad answered.

I was very relieved they weren't crying anymore, and I was pleased that I wasn't dying of something awful, but I was very alarmed at the way they spoke to each other, as if they were full of hate.

And to be honest, I was very confused about why they were suddenly going to sell this house. I mean they loved our home. They were always talking about how much the neighborhood had gone up and how they were sitting on a gold mine.

"Couldn't you divide the house in half and I could go from one part of it to the other?" I suggested.

But apparently it wouldn't work.

I wondered why but they both got testy and short-tempered and said it just wouldn't, and that was it.

And would I go off to Harry's now like a good boy and let them "get on with it."

"Get on with what?" I asked.

It turned out that Dad was getting a mover to come in a week's time and put his things into storage, and they had to agree on what he should take and what he should leave.

"I could help you divide things up," I offered. Which I could have. I didn't really want to go to Harry's after all this news.

And I would have known which things they each should have taken.

They got upset about this too, but amazingly they let me stay. They began with the tapes and CDs.

We made three piles, Mum's, Dad's and a joint pile.

There was a doubt about *The Brendan Voyage.* Dad thought it was his, Mum thought it was hers.

So I said I'd go upstairs and make a tape of it so they could have one each.

"I think that's against the law," Dad said. "You know, the musicians might not want us to do that."

"They'd want you both to be happy," I said and then they started blowing their noses heavily again.

They moved on to furniture and books and I sat through it all, offering advice.

And I think I was a help, really, because they told me I was. And they wrote everything down and it was all *so* unreal.

Then we all had supper in the kitchen.

It was very nice.

A big steak-and-kidney pie from the freezer that Mum had been saving for a rainy day.

"And, boy, is this the rainy day?" she said and we all smiled at her.

Dad said he'd open a bottle of wine.

Mum said there wasn't really anything to celebrate.

Dad said there was civilized behavior, so we had the wine—they even gave me a proper glass of it—and we talked about ordinary things.

And from time to time, they both reached out and touched me. Just to tap me on the arm or to stroke my face. It was very odd. But not frightening.

And that night, when they thought I was asleep, Dad came downstairs and slept on the sofa.

I said nothing. I had obviously done enough to annoy them, and I didn't want to do any more. And then it all happened very quickly. I came home from school one day and Dad was gone.

He had left a note with his mobile phone number and his address. It was in a big new block of flats not too far from Chestnut Street.

And he said he loved me, and I could ring him night or day, so I did, just to test it, and the phone was on the answering machine.

So I said, "It's Dekko, Dad, and whatever it was I did, I'm sorry. But I'm fine and if I get a mobile phone for Christmas then *you* can ring me anytime, night or day, on it."

And then I wondered was that like I was asking him for a mobile. But it was too late now.

And Mum was very tired. She had to work very hard in her office and she told me they didn't like people's personal lives being brought into things so she hadn't told them about Dad being gone and all the problems.

She said we would be moving in two weeks' time so as to be settled in by Christmas.

"What will we do for Christmas?" I asked her.

"What would you *like* to do, Dekko?" she asked.

She looked very tired and pale. So I didn't want to add to her personal problems and I said I was cool about it all, and even though it meant nothing, that pleased her a lot.

And every Saturday I met Dad at eleven and we went somewhere nice.

He used to look up the papers and ask other people where was a nice place to bring a nine-year-old and we had good times. And I was always back to Mum at six o'clock on the dot.

But he never took me to his flat so I didn't know if there was a room with Dekko on the door there or not.

I wanted to show him my room but he said that we shouldn't annoy my mother over something small like that.

I thought it was quite big, showing my dad my new room. But I had done enough, so I said nothing.

Just about Christmas, when Dad took me back home, Mum was standing at the door.

"Let's talk Christmas Day," she said in a very hard voice.

"I'm available all day, all night," Dad said.

"Yeah, except when the bimbo wants you to play party games with her teenage friends."

"Dekko comes first," Dad said.

"Oh, sure."

"They said reasonable access," he said.

"They also said holidays by agreement," Mum said.

I couldn't bear it anymore.

"What did I do?" I asked.

"You did nothing," they spoke in unison.

"So why is all this happening?"

They had no answer. It was very cold on the doorstep.

"Come in," Mum said.

"Would it annoy you, Mum, if I show Dad my room?"

"No, Dekko, please take your dad and show him your room."

Dad admired everything. Then we went downstairs.

"Would you like a drink, Dad?" I suggested.

"Beer or sherry?" Mum said.

"A small sherry would be lovely," Dad said. And again it all seemed so natural.

"Could I ask you what happened?" I asked. "I'm old enough to accept that you're separated and going to be divorced—can't you tell me *why*?"

They couldn't, apparently.

"You see, not long ago you told me that you loved each other, and that you were each other's sunshine. You used to sing that song, 'You Are My Sunshine.' And now you don't. And it must be my fault. I was thinking maybe if I went away it would be all right again."

"Why do you think that, Dekko?" my father asked.

"Because you told me I was the result of you loving each other—that's why I came on earth. So if you don't love each other anymore there must be something wrong with me. Mustn't there?"

After a long time, Mum spoke.

"You're right, Dekko, I was indeed your dad's sunshine, but I wasn't his *only* sunshine, which is the next line of the song. That was the problem, you see."

"But didn't he make you happy when skies were gray?" I asked. I knew this song very well.

"Yes he did."

"And your mum *is* my sunshine. I just got involved with someone else who was only star shine, not nearly as bright and warm and necessary. That was the problem, you see," Dad said.

"Is that the bimbo?" I asked.

And they both laughed.

A real laugh.

"She does have a name," Dad said.

Mum said, "About Christmas?"

"Yes?" Dad was full of hope.

"Come anytime you like, stay as long as you like, take Dekko out, let him have an hour's stimulating chat with the bimbo, if you want. The main thing is that Dekko never, ever believes that he was anything except the result of our love for each other. Because that is so true."

Dad raised his glass to Mum, too full of emotion to speak.

Harry says I'm not to hold my breath.

They're not going to get back together; people don't, once they've sold the main home.

Harry is very sharp—he knows these things.

But it's not important. I know now that it wasn't my fault and that, whatever "reasonable access" is going to be, it's going to be okay.

BY THE TIME WE GET TO CLIFDEN

They went on a week's holiday every year.

Not abroad, since Harry Kelly didn't like foreign food and Nessa Kelly was afraid to fly.

But there were plenty of places in Ireland if you looked around you. One year they had been to Lisdoonvarna and another to Youghal. They had found nice bed-and-breakfast places and always kept the card in case they went back again. But they never did.

In twenty-four years of summer vacations they never once went back to anywhere, no matter how wonderful they said it was at the time.

This year the research had come up with Clifden. They would drive there from Chestnut Street on a Tuesday, starting early, leaving plenty of time. They would pack sandwiches and a flask of coffee, because you never knew. They began to pack the suitcases on the Friday before they left. Better to pack early, Nessa said, because you never knew what you might forget. Harry liked to pack from a list. Wiser to write it out and tick each item off as it went into the case, he said; otherwise you could easily think that things were packed when they weren't.

Nessa brought their five pieces of silver to the bank, each one wrapped in a piece of cotton and then all zipped into a little yellow bag.

For the rest of the year they lived in the bottom of a cupboard. No point at all in tempting burglars by displaying them on shelves or anything. Harry went round all the window locks and tested the alarm system several times. Better be sure than sorry, he always said. They wished they had a reliable neighbor who might water their little garden but sadly it was only a wild, unkempt girl with red hair and a boyfriend who stayed over nights in Number 26. No point in asking *her* to do anything for you.

They nodded at her courteously—always better to make friends of these kind of people rather than enemies. She used to shout, "Howaya, Nessa? Harry?" which was very forward of her, since she must have been less than half their age.

The evening before the Kellys set out for Clifden they had everything ready for the off. Sandwiches in the fridge, two eggs to boil and just enough bread to toast for breakfast. The house would be left neat and tidy to welcome them back a week later. Then Harry would have five full days to recover before he went back to work. It was a long, long journey—they knew that. They would both be very tired.

There was a ring at the door. They looked at each other in alarm. Eight o'clock at night! Nobody would call at that hour.

"Who is it?" Harry asked fearfully.

"Melly," the voice said. "Can I come in, please, Harry?"

They didn't know anyone called Melly.

"From next door," the voice said. "It's urgent!"

They let her in. Her red hair was wild, she wore a horrid purple top that exposed her middle bits and jeans with patches on them. Her face was very pale.

"I just don't want to be alone just now. Could I stay for an hour, please? I won't be any trouble. Please, Nessa? Harry?"

She looked from one to the other.

"Are you unwell?" Nessa asked. "Should you go to a doctor? The hospital?"

"No, I'm frightened. Mike, my fellow, he's been smoking bad stuff—God knows what he might do to me. I don't want him to find me at home."

"Won't he come looking for you here?" Harry was very alarmed at inviting such trouble under his roof.

"No, he'd never think I'd come here," she said.

"Well . . ." They were doubtful.

"Oh, go on, Harry, Nessa, you can keep your eye on me. I'm not going to go off with your silver or anything. Just an hour or two or whatever."

"I don't know," Harry said.

"Harry, you're a decent man. How would you feel if I were beaten to death and you could have saved me?"

They found themselves nodding.

"But we can't stay up late because we're going to the west tomorrow, and by the time we get to Clifden we could be very tired."

"I'll just get my bag," Melly said and hopped back home for a giant lime-green sack.

"I've everything here," she said, as an explanation, when she turned.

"But . . . um . . . Melly, we told you we're going to Clifden tomorrow!"

"I'll come with you!" Melly said, overjoyed. "He'll *never* think of looking for me in Clifden—it's perfect." She smiled from one to the other.

She slept on the sofa with her things strewn over the floor. During the night they heard him shouting and looking for her.

"Do you think we should *do* anything?" Harry whispered to Nessa in bed.

"We *are* doing something—we're driving her to the other side of the country," Nessa said, trying to put the man's raised voice out of her mind.

Next morning Melly took all the hot water for her shower and used the nice new towels they had prepared ready for their return. She made them breakfast, however, saying that since there were only two eggs she had made an omelet and divided it into three.

Harry and Nessa looked at each other, aghast. Their whole plans had been thrown totally out of order by this ridiculous girl whom they hardly knew. By now they should have been in their car and beyond Lucan. Instead they were still at home, plotting how to get Melly into the car.

"He could be looking out the window so we'd better take no risks," Melly warned.

"You could lay a rug over me and I could crawl very slowly into the backseat."

Then there was her lime-green sack—he would certainly recognize that. So Harry had to hide it in a black plastic bag.

"By the time we get to Clifden we'll be ready to go to a mental hospital," Nessa said into Harry's ear.

"If we'd ever get there," Harry whispered. "She's talking of doing things en route." That was something Harry and Nessa never did, visit anything en route. They just got their heads down and drove there, wherever there was. It didn't look as if it was going to be like that this time.

When they finally got away and Melly emerged from the rug it was nearly time to put on their audiocassette and listen to an improving book. By the time they got to Clifden this year they would have heard the three-and-a-half-hour version of Thackeray's *Vanity Fair*. But they had reckoned without Melly. She didn't like it at all. She did, on the other hand, like the scenery and the places they passed. She chattered nonstop about the housing estates, the road signs, the huge walled demesnes, the factories and the traffic, so that Harry and Nessa lost completely the story of Becky Sharp and were forced to turn it off.

"That's better," Melly said. "Now we can chat properly."

She phoned ahead on her mobile to friends in Mullingar and said she wanted them to prepare lunch, that she was bringing two pals called Harry and Nessa.

They protested vigorously. By the time they got to Clifden it would be very late. And they did have sandwiches.

But Melly would have none of it. And in Mullingar the two hippies who lived in a squat had made a magnificent lentil-and-tomato dish with lots of crusty bread. The hippies were perfectly at ease with Harry and Nessa and asked them to deliver some honey to Shay in Athlone because he had a bad throat.

"But we might not stop in Athlone," poor Harry began.

"Normally you wouldn't," they agreed with him. "But because of Shay's sore throat you will this time, won't you?"

Shay was very welcoming, and he made tea and toasted scones. He said that Harry and Nessa were everyday angels—that was the only phrase for it—rescuing Melly from that monster.

"If she hadn't met two everyday angels like you he'd have trashed her, you know. He'll probably have trashed her house and yours as well when you get back," Shay said cheerfully.

Nessa and Harry looked at each other. Their glance asked the question: Should they go home? Now, this minute? There was no time. Melly was on the mobile phone to Athenry. And then they were waving goodbye to Shay and back in the car heading west.

They were expected in this pub in Athenry, you see—there would be chicken in a basket for them when they got there and a great gig.

"By the time we get to Clifden they'll have given away our room," said Harry in a voice that sounded like a great wail.

"Nonsense, Harry, we can give them a ring," Melly said.

Nessa took out her little sheet called "Emergency Numbers and Contacts for the Journey" and found the number of the B&B.

"Could you ring them, Melly?" Nessa asked. "You seem to know our plans better."

Melly saw nothing wrong with that.

"Hiya, you've got a couple called Nessa and Harry coming to stay with you. . . . Yeah, Mr. and Mrs. Kelly, that's it. It's just that we keep getting held up on the way—you know how it is."

The voice seemed to know the way it was and sounded sympathetic.

"Oh, no idea at all when. Could you leave out a key and a note—you see, we're not even in Galway, only on the way to Athenry, as it happens. . . . Thank you, yes, thank you for being so understanding—see you when we see you, then. Oh, and could I sleep in a chair or something for one night just till I get myself settled?"

That seemed to be agreed too.

"Who am I? I'm Melly, I'm their great friend and neighbor and they sort of rescued me. No, not fussy people at all, dead easygoing—you must be thinking of other people. No, real cool. We're going to a gig in Athenry, maybe a drink in Galway just to be sociable, and then we're going to get out of the car in Maam Cross and look at the goats and the sheep and smell the Atlantic. We wouldn't be with you before one or two a.m. anyway, but haven't they the week to get over it?"

She leaned in between them from the backseat of the car. "There, now, that's sorted," she said proudly.

Nessa and Harry smiled at each other, absurdly flattered to have been called "dead easygoing" and "real cool."

Melly genuinely didn't think they were fussy people.

And by the time they got to Clifden perhaps they wouldn't be fussy people anymore.

THE WOMEN WHO RIGHTED WRONGS

When Wendy and Rita were friends at school they used to plan that one day they would run a company together. Possibly a detective agency. Or maybe a restaurant. Or a health studio.

But things don't always turn out like you think they will when you are fifteen, and so it didn't work out like that.

Wendy went to university in London and studied art history. It was all she had dreamed of and more: she got the First Year Prize and the Second Year Medal. Halfway through her course she met and fell in love with Mac, a dark, handsome, fiery lecturer in political science, who loved her too. So Wendy didn't work so hard after that—there were so many things that needed to be done for Mac, not just cooking, cleaning, typing and all those normal matters, but also helping him set up lectures outside the university.

She spent so many hours helping create the perfect CV for him that there was little time to spend on her own studies. But what did that matter? Mac loved her; he was so grateful for all she did.

But perhaps he didn't love her all that much. Certainly not enough to be anyway enthusiastic when Wendy became pregnant.

Wendy had thought it would be simple. They could share a

flat, she would continue to look after him and the baby, of course, when it arrived, she would keep up her art-history studies when she could and eventually be able to get a proper job and bring in real money.

It had turned out to be far from simple.

Mac had not been ready to settle down; surely Wendy had known this. There had been a term full of tears, and Mac had used his new CV to get him a job far, far away. He had said he was sorry but there had been no question of their having children. Wendy must look after all this business entirely on her own.

Not only did Wendy not win a prize at her third-year examinations, she did not even sit them.

He was the image of Wendy, all freckles and red curly hair so she didn't have to think of the handsome, dark Mac every time she looked at her son.

She still kept in touch with Rita. In fact, it was often easier to talk to Rita by phone, or letter or e-mail, than to people nearby.

Rita hadn't been on the spot to warn her against Mac, as so many others had. Rita's own career news had not been great either. She had gone directly from school, with her long dark hair and huge brown eyes, to work in a boutique called Madame Frances in a town more than a hundred miles from her home. She thought it would give her independence and teach her to stand on her own two feet. In fact, it brought her a lot of loneliness and empty nights. And because she was on her own she thought a great deal about work and came up with some very good ideas for the dress shop where she worked.

It was in a busy market town, where quite a lot of their customers were middle-aged, larger women who were constantly having to leave without making a purchase, since there was nothing in their size. Rita had suggested to Frances, who ran the place, that if they stocked larger clothes they would make a great deal more money.

"But it must be elegant," wailed Frances, who was always a perfect size eight and always would be.

"We could stock elegant larger clothes," Rita had pleaded.

And it had worked. Magnificently. They had moved to new and better premises, Madame Frances had been interviewed by television crews and fashion columnists. Nowhere did she give any credit to Rita.

But Rita struggled on, coming up with ever-new ideas.

What they often needed was someone to do alterations on the premises. Madame Frances would not consider hiring more staff so Rita went to classes. She learned how to move zip fasteners, loosen waistbands, lower hems.

Madame Frances did not have to pay Rita any more money for this skill so it was included in the price of the garment.

The number of customers increased again.

Again no gratitude was shown to Rita.

"Why do you stay?" Wendy wrote to her.

"Because I like the customers that come in. I know them and because I built the place up, I don't want to hand it over to her."

"But you *have* handed it over to her," Wendy said.

"Why didn't you go to the courts and get child support from Mac, then, if we are talking like that?" Rita wrote with spirit.

"I didn't want to let him think he'd won, that I ended up squabbling about money," Wendy said, defending herself.

"But he *has* won; he is going from strength to strength in his career while yours is on hold as you are raising his son for free."

They had one of their rare phone calls after that. Usually they kept to e-mail; it was much cheaper. But they seemed to have a need to speak.

"I'd love to kill Madame Frances for you, Rita," Wendy said suddenly to her friend.

"And I'd love to kill Mac for *you*, Wendy—believe me, I would," said Rita in return.

There was a silence.

"I think there was a movie about this once," Wendy said.

Rita remembered. *"Strangers on a Train."*

"It ended badly, I think," Wendy said.

"Well, murder usually does," Rita said. "Maybe we could just wound them. Quite badly."

"I hate blood," Wendy said.

They decided to meet and have a planning session. Which bed-sitter should they choose?

"Imagine, we once thought we would be company directors and tycoons at this stage," Rita said with a laugh as she agreed to come to London to see Wendy; at least the baby might be less disturbed in his own surroundings.

"We could still set something up, you know. 'Wrongs Righted,' that sort of thing. Avenging-angels type of business. It's even got our initials, WR . . . Wendy and Rita, for heaven's sake!"

"I'll think of woundings without too much blood in them all the way up in the bus," promised Rita.

It was as if they were back at school again, the conversation between red-haired Wendy and dark-haired Rita was so easy.

Rita envied Wendy the bouncy little Joe, who smiled and gurgled and did not bellow at all. Wendy envied Rita's skill, the way she had made herself such an elegant skirt from a remnant of material and was able to mend the curtains and put a trim on the cushion covers as they chatted. By the time they had finished the second bottle of wine they had the plan sorted. The wounding was not going to be physical. This way there would be no blood but a great deal of satisfaction.

They decided it would take a month, so in thirty days' time

they would meet again and discuss how their wrongs had been righted. It would need a bit of homework. So each would give the other a dossier as background. The very bad Mac and the very bad Frances were not going to sail any longer unpunished through life. Not now that Wrongs Righted was on the case.

It had not been difficult for Wendy to find out Mac's movements from the university office. All she had to do was to pretend that she was organizing a conference and to wonder when he might be free to attend. It could not be in the next three weeks, since his department was hosting a series of lectures on politics with some very well-known public figures attending. But afterwards, maybe . . . ?

Wendy expressed huge interest in the series of lectures. Who would attend? Just students of politics or the general public? Would the press be there? She got all the information she needed and typed it out for Rita.

Meanwhile, back at the Madame Frances Boutique, Rita had begun her own research and activity. She left out in a prominent position several brochures for a wholesale fashion fair in London. Eventually Frances was tempted. She thought she owed it to the boutique to attend.

"Could I go instead, Frances? It might give me some of that polish you say I need?" Rita knew that she could ask, as it was totally out of the question.

"Certainly not, Rita, but I think I will take three days there— you'll manage for three days, surely?"

"I can't do it on my own, Frances. Suppose I have to do alterations? Who'll look after the boutique? You'll have to get someone to cover for you."

Frances bit her lip. She didn't want to get a stranger in, some-one who might realize just how much she owed to Rita, just how truly this shop was Rita's creation.

So exactly as Rita had suspected she would, Frances decided to keep it in the family. She would ask her sister, Ronnie Ranger, to come over from Dublin to step in for three days. Ronnie would know how to keep that young Rita in her place and not allow her to become too familiar with the customers.

Frances booked her hotel in London.

"Will you be making appointments with the press?" Rita asked innocently.

"I hadn't thought of it—why?"

"No harm in telling them about your success story here." Rita's eyes showed no guile. "It would get the boutique a lot of atten-tion, you know."

"Well, I might," Frances said and settled down at the com-puter to write a glowing account of herself, which she would cir-culate to the press.

Later Rita read it all on the machine with a grim smile and copied it, with her own notes and details of the wholesale fashion conference, to Wendy.

Mac was pleased with the coverage that his lecture series was get-ting, and in particular with his own publicity.

He had been described as the handsome young firebrand lec-turer. That couldn't hurt him. It was the kind of thing that Wendy used to get said about him way back.

Wendy.

It was a pity it had all turned out the way it had. But then she couldn't have expected him to settle down. He missed her from time to time. No one else had been able to get him such publicity, media attention and write such a dazzling CV for him. But then again look at all the fuss that was being made of this lecture series; it was almost as if Wendy had been there at his side.

What was creating most interest was that Mac had thrown it open to all young people, not only the registered students. He had said that if the young were to become interested in politics it must not be confined to the privileged few who got the benefit of university education.

Mac didn't actually remember having said that, but he must have, and anyway it had resulted in live television coverage on Sunday, so he was very glad that he must have said it. All he had to do now was to look brooding and firebrandish at the same time. He would buy a new black leather jacket.

Frances was disappointed with the response from the fashion magazines. There was no reply from some, while others had said that since this meeting was for trade buyers only it wasn't of any interest to their readers. One woman telephoned, however, saying that Frances's letter had been passed on to her and she was most interested in doing an exclusive on it all. The boutique from a market town that could lead the way and show its London competitors how it was done! A story of personal triumph.

Frances flushed with pleasure. This was what she wanted. She wanted to do the interview in London, far away from Rita and her giddy, eager ways. But the journalist wanted to come to the boutique.

"Perhaps we could meet socially first in London while I'm there," Frances begged.

The woman journalist said fine, and suggested a very elegant bar. She was a handsome young woman, red curly hair and freckles, wearing an emerald-green outfit that Frances knew cost a fortune; they had one back in the boutique and so far no one had been able to afford it.

The journalist seemed very familiar with the Madame Frances Boutique and the fact that it was a one-woman operation.

"With a seamstress," of course Frances had explained.

"A what?"

"You know, a person who does alterations, helps here and there, makes coffee."

She didn't want to talk up Rita's role but she couldn't pretend that she worked single-handed.

"Not important to the operation, then."

"Oh, no, they grow on trees, these sort of people," Frances had said with a tinkling laugh. She thought she saw the journalist's face harden momentarily, but she must have imagined it.

Mac thought he looked rather well in the new jacket on the Sunday morning, and certainly he had no trouble in getting any girl to return his glance at the brunch that the university hosted for his guests. There was a particularly bright little number with jet-black hair straight down her back, short skirt and high boots, a real looker, but she was more than just a pretty face.

She had read every single thing he had ever written. She said she had followed his career and couldn't believe that she had actually got to meet him at last.

"Could I sit near you on the stage when the debate is being televised?" she pleaded.

"Well, yes, but you'd have to be able to contribute." Mac didn't want to seem like a pushover.

"I can contribute. . . . I'd like to say how you alone are able to make young people enthusiastic about politics. For years they have been so indifferent. You should have your own political party."

"Oh, I say," Mac said.

"But perhaps you don't want to do that—maybe you're a family man with a child, children of your own, you don't want to give the time . . . ?"

He wished he could remember her name.

"No, I've no family, no ties," he said. Did he imagine it or did a shadow of anger cross her face? He must have imagined it.

Wendy had the emerald-green outfit immaculately dry-cleaned and returned to the Madame Frances Boutique. Then she telephoned a national newspaper and said she had a very good story to offer. It would be something they would love, she assured them, a real feel-good account of how the underdog might eventually triumph. The newspaper loved that sort of thing, and said it was very interested indeed.

Rita had made friends with a lot of people, including men in the television crew. She had told them she would be sitting beside the great Mac on the platform.

"Will you be speaking?" they asked.

"If anything happens that I have to respond to, then I will," Rita said and she smiled a mischievous smile.

Wendy asked Madame Frances if she could invite some of her best clients in to the boutique for the photo shoot. Why not give her a list of ten or so and Wendy would choose. She chose the people that Rita had suggested.

Rita had managed to circulate a large number of typewritten questions before the lecture and debate began. They all had to do with "responsibility." The fact that we all had to take responsibility for our own actions just as the state had to feel collectively responsible. She told people she had been asked to pass them on. They were all slightly different but on the same theme. People read them thoughtfully; they looked like good topics. They were questions that would be asked.

Wendy suggested that Madame Frances might invite her ladies round on a Sunday morning and offer them shortbread and coffee to entertain them. Frances noted to herself that since it was a Sunday, the dreaded Rita wouldn't be there being overfamiliar, and said it was a splendid idea. Frances said nothing to Rita about it all—let her hear later.

Rita had other things on her mind that particular Sunday. She had to make sure that she was well within everyone's vision once the row began. As it would begin.

Mac was looking more and more confident and arrogant; he had no idea that the whole hall was busy debating arguments about "personal responsibility."

Wendy and the photographer from a big national newspaper were poised and ready. The well-dressed, well-coiffed ladies nibbled their shortbread and dusted their mouths in readiness for the pictures that would be taken. They were anxious to speak as well as possible of the Madame Frances Boutique and the charming girl, Rita, who looked after them. Odd that she wasn't here today. She was the very center of the whole operation.

The television broadcast began and Mac seemed bewildered that none of the questions he had expected were turning up. Instead there was a very heavy emphasis on personal responsibility, and although he could and did manage to turn it against several well-known politicians who had been notably lacking in that area, he had an uncomfortable feeling that some of it seemed to be directed personally against himself.

But he must be paranoid. Nobody here knew anything about Wendy and the child that she had so irresponsibly conceived.

Madame Frances was incensed.

All these women, egged on by the horrible journalist and photographer, seemed to be talking about Rita nonstop and her brilliance in knowing what suited them and adjusting clothes at no extra cost.

"Why haven't you mentioned her at all?" the horrible journalist asked, and the photographer took more and more pictures of an angry, blustering Frances.

The piece was going to be called "The Hunt for Rita . . . Mystery Woman Who Had Not Been Informed of Her Day of Triumph."

It was going to be a big story, they told Frances over and over. The Cinderella whom all the customers loved, a Cinderella whom the proprietor couldn't find, no matter how many times she phoned.

The television camera team was getting very excited. Normally they didn't have such audience response. The guy in the black jacket was being practically howled off the stage because he wouldn't say whether or not there were areas of his own life where he felt that personal responsibility didn't count.

And then to crown it all, a pretty girl on the platform leaped to her feet and asked him to keep his hands to himself.

"I didn't touch you," blustered Mac in his leather jacket. "But if I had, you would only have had yourself to blame, in your short skirt and with your long hair . . ."

The television crew knew that they would get a huge commendation and maybe even an award for such amazing live documentary work.

Wendy and Rita treated themselves to a rather smart dinner out. They ran over all the events as if it were a movie script. They laughed a lot and drank endless toasts to each other. The waiter was a kind old man.

"You ladies seem very happy. That's nice to see," he said.

"We run a company together," Wendy explained.

"It's called WR, which stands for Wrongs Righted," Rita added.

"Sounds as if there should be a lot of call for things like that," said the elderly waiter and gave them a small port each on the house because they looked so cheerful, unlike a lot of the rest of the clientele.

THE SIGHTING

Not everyone on Chestnut Street owned a car, which was just as well. There were thirty small houses all in a semicircle, but room for only eighteen cars. Of course, some people like Kevin Walsh at Number 2 took up a lot of space with his big taxi. But that didn't really matter, since Bucket Maguire from Number 11 cycled everywhere, as he had done for years.

Mitzi and Philip lived in Number 22, and they had two sons who worked in New York. The boys, Sean and Brian, came home once a year in July with their families to see the old folk, even though technically Mitzi and Philip were not all that old, having married when they were twenty. They were only in their forties now, parents of two grown-up sons and grandparents to four little Americans. But of course to Sean and Brian they were very old indeed.

Mitzi would make a Fourth of July picnic for her grandchildren to have under the chestnut trees opposite their home, and it became a regular event.

Sean and Brian and their American wives seemed to love the week's vacation, Mitzi thought. And so they should enjoy it. Such preparation had gone into the six nights that they would all be there.

She herself would take a week off from the shop where she worked. She spent the time cooking and freezing meals, and cleaning the house from top to bottom. It was no use telling her that the boys and their families might be more comfortable in—and could easily afford—a hotel.

This was their home and this is where they would stay. Philip was also very pleased that they came back, but in a less excited way.

He would ask the lads into the pub on a Friday evening to meet a few of his workmates. He liked to show off his two strong sons and boast how well they had done over in America. He liked Sean and Brian to see that he still had friends and was well thought of in the factory.

One year they showed up at the pub too early and saw their father in a booth with his face very close to a young woman. She was much, much younger than their mother. She had a short red skirt and bare midriff, and she had long curly hair and a small, cheeky face. She made their own young wives seem middle-aged in comparison.

They were shocked to the core. Their own father! Playing away from home with a woman half his age, while poor Mother had no idea.

They were outraged but couldn't find the words to accuse their father, and they watched from the shadows while the girl kissed him on the cheek and scuttled away. They were short and abrupt with his friends but he didn't seem to notice.

That night their mother said that she thought her sons looked tired.

"You're very good to go out with your dad. He does love showing you off to his friends," she said affectionately. "He doesn't have much else in his life to look forward to, you see."

They looked at her, stricken. No good would come from telling her that he had plenty to look forward to and to look back on, if their eyes hadn't deceived them.

They talked about it together long and often during that visit.

They wished the sighting had never taken place. That they had not seen their father's little bit on the side. It gave a new slant to everything he said.

When their father said that he'd love to travel while he still had the energy for it, Sean and Brian exchanged glum looks. Of course he would.

They felt sick as they heard Mitzi say that she was a real stick-in-the-mud; she had been to Spain and Italy and the U.S.A. and that was it. If *she* won the lottery, she'd build a beautiful big conservatory at the back of Number 22. A glass room with a beautiful wooden floor and window seats. She could almost see it already.

Their father shook his head in disbelief at her nonsense and Brian and Sean felt very brought down. This had been the year they were going to present their parents with an all-paid holiday to the States, a visit to one of the great national parks and a tour of Arizona or New Mexico.

But now, after the sighting, what was the point?

If Dad wanted to travel, it was with Miss Bare Midriff, and Mother had said she didn't want to travel at all.

"Will we just give them the money for the conservatory?" Brian wondered aloud.

"But then what happens when they have to sell the house if Dad goes off with the little tart in the pub?" Sean said. "It would break poor Mother's heart even more if she were to lose the conservatory as well."

They found it increasingly difficult to be civil to their father. His words about family life seemed hollow, his toasts to a wonderful wife and sons seemed shallow. And his plans for the future so unlikely and false. Like his saying to his grandchildren that one day he'd teach them to fish. That was a ludicrous thing to promise. He wouldn't be around here if he had his way. He and Miss Short Red Skirt would be somewhere else, far from doing something aging like teaching a grandson to catch a fish.

Before they left, Sean and Brian moved tentatively around the topic by talking about how hard their mother worked.

"If I were to work twenty-four hours a day I couldn't repay your father for how good he's been to me," she would say, shaking her head at the enormity of his kindness. "And this way I can get us little treats like take him to the cinema and to a Chinese supper, or maybe a nice new shirt."

Her sons were enraged, but yet they couldn't bring themselves to say anything about the young woman they had seen.

When it was nearly time for them to go back to the States, would they say anything to their father or not? Sean wanted to say something, but Brian thought it might make matters worse. And suppose they were to say something? Neither of them knew how they would phrase it.

On the last night, their father was out. He wouldn't be home until after 9 p.m.—he had got extra hours at the factory.

"What does he do with all his money?" Brian asked.

"Oh, I've no idea. He's saving for something—that's why he takes all the overtime that's on offer." Their mother's face was affectionate, indulgent about men and their little ways.

Sean could bear it no longer. "You know how people are, Ma. He's probably having a pint with the lads—and the lassies too, by the way. The place is full of them."

"I don't think there are many lassies up in your father's pub, only that girl Rona. You know the niece of Liam Kenny over at Number Four?"

"I don't think I know her." Brian was cold.

"Well, if you saw Rona you wouldn't forget her. Skirt up to her knickers, hair all the colors of the rainbow."

That was her, all right.

"What's she doing hanging round Dad's pub?"

"She works there. Her father—Liam's brother—owns the place and sometimes young Rona helps out, but mainly she's a salesperson for conservatories. I used to talk to her about them in the days when we thought we might be getting one." Their mother sighed, then busied herself getting the supper ready. Their father would be tired when he got in, tired after a very long day.

That night, Sean approached his father in the little garden.

"By God, the week went quickly, son," Philip said.

"I'm not going to make small talk, Dad. I want to talk to you about Rona Kenny."

"She's never been round here, has she? She promised she wouldn't."

"No, she hasn't, but . . ."

"I *told* her your mother would be out at the airport tomorrow; she could come then and I'd let her in."

"Why are you telling me this, Dad?" Sean's face was full of grief.

It was bad enough that his father was unfaithful to his own wife, but to glory in it in front of his own sons. That was grotesque.

"Why weren't you and Mam happy enough for each other?" Sean asked.

"I don't know." His father sat down on the garden seat. "I'll never know, son, but what's past is past. You boys were never to know—we said it would be private between us and forgotten. It's strange that your mother should tell you now."

"Mother told us nothing."

"So how do you know?" He was bewildered.

"Know what?"

"About your mother and I having, well . . . those problems in the past."

"Not only in the past, I'd say," Sean said. He never saw anything as sad as his father's face.

"Oh, Sean, lad. I don't believe you—it can't be true. She'd never have met him again, she'd never fancy him still."

"What are you talking about?" Sean was totally confused.

"She promised me, and we were getting on so well. No, it can't be true she's seeing him again."

"Mother seeing a man?" The world was tilting over for Sean.

"But that's what happens. She fell in love, you see, because I was too dull for her. He wanted her to go away with him but she gave him up to keep the family together." He spoke admiringly of her. There was no grudge. This was a great and noble thing to do.

"When was all this, Dad?"

"Years back. You and Brian were in short pants then. I can't believe she met up with him again."

"Dad, aren't you seeing Rona Kenny?"

"Of course I am. To arrange the conservatory. She's coming in tomorrow to measure it all up. . . . But now you tell me your mum's seeing *him* again, then she won't care about the new room."

"No, Dad." Sean spoke very gently. "I got it all wrong. I saw you and Rona whispering in the pub the day we went in, and I thought, I thought . . . I thought the wrong thing, you see."

"As if that little girl would fancy a silly old man like me."

"No, Dad. It happens. I'm sorry."

"But does this mean that your mother *isn't* seeing him again?" The relief in his father's voice and the look on his face were almost too much to bear.

They heard people calling from the house.

Number 22 was all lit up and welcoming, with a table for ten. And next time they came back there would be a conservatory.

He had his arm around his father as they came in, and he saw Brian look at him in surprise. Sean shook his head very slightly.

He watched his mother, flushed and excited from bending over the oven, wisps of hair clinging to her face. His own mother had had an affair with another man. Met him secretly, adulterously, passionately.

It was too hard to take onboard.

He didn't think he would tell Brian. Only that they had been misled about the sighting.

THE LOTTERY OF THE BIRDS

He was a peacock. She knew that the moment she met him. He was looking at his own reflection, not at the picture behind the glass in the frame. He stroked the lapels of his very expensive jacket softly and with pleasure. She knew exactly what she was letting herself in for.

"I'm Ella," she said simply. "That is *the* most beautiful jacket. Is it wool?"

He seemed pleased, but not surprised. He talked about the jacket briefly, with unaffected enthusiasm. He had bought it in Italy three weeks ago—but his manners wouldn't let him go on too long.

"I'm Harry," he said. "And shouldn't we be talking about your clothes, really?"

"Not tonight," Ella said. "Tonight I just came straight from the office."

His smile could have lit the fire that was set in the grate of the art gallery. A fire that was pure decoration.

"It must be a very elegant office, then," Harry said, and Ella was lost.

She always told herself afterwards that it had been as deliberate an act as she had ever known. She had walked in, eyes wide open, into the situation she had spent most of her adult life trying to rescue her friends from. She had fallen in love with a man who was going to break her heart over and over; she would lose the sympathy, the patience and eventually the company of her friends. Ella, who was known for her self-control and her calm, practical way of looking at things, had fallen for a peacock full of charm. Not even the silliest of them would have thought there was even half a chance with Harry.

But Ella didn't mind. She knew the odds; and then promptly forgot them. She did all the things that the women's magazines used to advise in her mother's day: she was a good listener, she drew him out about himself, she discovered his interests and pretended that they were hers too. She didn't press to meet his family on Chestnut Street; she didn't impose hers on him.

In fact, it was all so successful that Ella began to wonder whether those old-fashioned ideas about pleasing a man might not be far more helpful than all this modern advice about being yourself, and being equal from the word go. At any rate, she was very shortly Harry's constant companion: she was on his arm at every public event, and in his bed when the night drew to a close.

It was hard work, of course; but then Ella told herself that you don't keep a peacock by your side without a great deal of effort. Anyone could attract a sparrow, she thought, looking without much pleasure at some of the men her friends were going out with. Some of them were indeed like old crows. Only Ella had the peacock, the glorious Harry, who turned every head; and she didn't mind when he looked at other women and smiled. They thought he was smiling at them; but he was thinking as much of the actual act of smiling. He knew it made people feel good. He did it a lot. Sometimes he smiled in his sleep, as Ella sat and watched him, his facial muscles stretched into a pleasing, warm half-grin.

She was often awake at night as she learned the plots of operas. *La Traviata:* that's the one about Alfredo and Violetta, and a series of misunderstandings. *Rigoletto* was the one about the court jester and *Norma* was the Druid high priestess who did a Romeo and Juliet number with the Romans.

Ella worked for a publisher. She ran it down to Harry: terribly dull people, frightfully boring authors, very tedious and not worth taking up his time. But Harry's job—now that was different: he was in wine importing—*there* was an interesting career for you. Ella made it sound like a magical world. It had involved a lot of studying, more than the opera, even: types of grape, *Appellation Contrôllée,* this vineyard, that importer, this warehouse, that family firm . . . Harry accepted her interest. She was right—it *was* a fascinating business. His previous girlfriends hadn't understood that nearly so well.

He introduced her to his colleagues; her admiration of the business was so obvious she could do him nothing but credit.

The boss and his wife were a cynical, weary couple who had seen it all, done it all.

"You have a far better chance of nailing him down than the others," said the boss's wife as she dabbed her nose viciously in the powder room after dinner.

"Oh, heavens, there's no question of that," Ella protested with a little laugh.

"Keep that kind of line for Pretty Boy," said the older woman.

Ella felt sorry for her. All she had drawn in the lottery of the birds was a bad-tempered, bald and molting eagle, not a glorious, multi-colored peacock.

She went back to the table, where Harry sat, his chin on his hand, in that way that made total strangers stop their conversations and look at him with admiration. The light fell on his fair hair, making it shine. Ella's heart soared to think that she had captured this wonderful man.

It pleased her to think that she had "a better chance of nailing him" than anyone who had gone before—and there were many who had. Sometimes they passed through town.

"An old friend of mine wants me to have a drink in a wine bar," he would say from time to time.

"Oh, but you must!" Ella was insistent. It would give her time to catch up on some new looming opera. *Fidelio*. This one was by Beethoven, about Leonorea, who pretends to be Fidelio. Another three hours of cross-dressing and misunderstanding.

Or on the housework. She hadn't actually moved into his flat, but as near as made no difference. He hated seeing her cleaning, yet he wouldn't employ anyone else to do it. She did it in secretive, hurried darts when he wasn't around. She wanted Harry to think that fresh peaches for breakfast, clean towels in the bathroom and big vases of colorful flowers in clean water sort of happened by themselves when Ella was around.

And, because peacocks don't think for too long about the world in general, that's exactly what he thought. He would put his arm around her and say that everything was much *nicer* when she was there.

She took seven shirts of his, every Monday morning, to a very good place just beside her work. No, honestly, darling, she reassured him, I'll be taking my own stuff anyway. He never noticed that everything Ella wore was drip-dry. He thought it was a miracle that his wardrobe was always full of gleaming shirts; he savored choosing them, holding the ties up against them.

"It used to be very disorganized," he said with a puzzled frown, shaking his head at the mystery of it all. Ella shook her head too, as if she couldn't believe that things had not always run this smoothly.

She never complained about him at work, or sought advice, so her friends just worried about her to one another and not to her face.

It did not become public until the day she refused to go to

the sales conference. For personal reasons. There were no reasons, personal or even global, that allowed you to miss the sales conference. Ella's friends took her aside.

"Come on, what's he doing, what mammoth task has he agreed to do that he needs you to hold his hand?" Clare had been a friend and colleague long enough to speak in that tone. But only just.

"You couldn't be more wrong. Harry didn't ask me not to go; he doesn't even know it's on."

They looked at one another, shocked. What kind of relationship could he have with someone in publishing and not know about sales conferences?

"You'll be passed over, Ella. The boys upstairs will never stand for this. No matter what lies you tell them."

"I won't tell them any lies. I'll just say that it doesn't suit me."

"Not only are you completely cracked, but you're letting us all down. They'll say women can't cope, that you're premenstrual or having the vapors or that you're pregnant. Lord, you're not, are you?" Clare was aghast.

"No, certainly not." Ella spoke in a voice too calm, too normal for the crisis she was bringing down on all of them.

Clare waved the others away majestically. "Let's have a glass of the emergency tequila," she suggested. The emergency tequila was a ludicrous bottle stashed away at the back of an office drawer for an occasion just like this.

"No, honestly, it's too early, I couldn't swallow it," Ella protested.

"You *are* pregnant," Clare said.

Ella looked at her friend with a great but almost distant affection. Clare was married to an owl, a wise old owl peering over his spectacles with an indulgent look at Clare. In a million years she wouldn't know what it took to hold a man like Harry.

"I can't tell you—you'd feel honor-bound to try to talk me out of it," Ella said.

Clare looked relieved. At least there was a hint of a smile on

Ella's face again; they hadn't seen that for a long time, only a look of grim concentration.

"It's his parents. They're coming up for this *Fidelio;* he's got tickets for all of us."

"Ella, *Fidelio* will come back again—it's not some new, experimental work that might sink without trace."

"No, but it's . . ."

"Even his parents will come back again. They're not like Halley's Comet, coming round once every seventy-four years. You *can't* miss the conference. What about your authors? You can't let them down."

"Someone else can present their books. Come on, we spend our time telling each other not to believe that we are indispensable. . . ."

Clare looked at her in exasperation. It was one thing to realize that you could be replaced; it was another to walk out on your authors. They *expected* you to be at the sales conference, to talk up their books to the reps, who then had to go out and sell them into bookshops. Apart altogether from what the boys upstairs would say.

"I'm sick of the boys upstairs," Ella said; and all on her own, Clare opened the emergency tequila and drank most of it out of a coffee mug.

Back in the office, Ella faced the silent reproach of Kathy, her assistant.

"I wish you'd change your mind," Kathy said eventually.

"No, you don't." Ella was cheerful and brisk. "This is your big break. It's like the understudy hoping that the decrepit old bat of a leading lady won't be able to go on. Suddenly, a star will be born."

"It's not remotely like that." Kathy was cross. "For one thing, you are not a decrepit old bat, no matter how oddly you are behaving. You are only three years older than me, if I remember correctly. And anyway, this is not becoming a star, it's taking over all your work as well as my own."

"You're well able for it," Ella encouraged her.

"It's not fair, Ella, even if there was a good reason. And how am I going to deal with that madman from Australia?"

"Oh, God," said Ella. "I'd forgotten the Jackaroo."

"Well, he hasn't forgotten you." Kathy was triumphant. "He has an appointment to see you at five o'clock."

"Not *this* evening. I can't meet him this evening!"

Kathy lost her temper. "I think you should play fair with everyone, hand in your resignation, sit at home and plan your hope chest and let the rest of us get on with trying to publish books."

When Ella was very young, her father had always told her that it was a great virtue to be able to see the other point of view. She used to be able to do that; in fact, it was one of her great strengths. She could imagine what it was like to be an author, or a bookseller, a rival editor or an office junior. Perhaps of late she had been very preoccupied. She had been seeing another point of view, certainly, but only Harry's. She had been trying to out-guess him, solve the problem before it occurred, wipe away the frown before it started to pucker on his forehead. She looked Kathy straight in the eye.

"You are absolutely right," she said. And for the first time since she had met Harry, she picked up the phone to tell him that she wouldn't be meeting him.

Harry was astonished. "Who do you have to meet?" he asked in disbelief.

"This Australian—he's an author. I won't be going to the sales conference, you see, so I have to talk to him about his book and what plans we have for it."

"But he's an *author*," Harry said. "I mean, you're his editor; he should be pretty bloody grateful that you take any interest in it at all!"

"He is." Ella's voice was firm.

Harry sounded aggrieved. "I'd have made other plans, if I'd known. Now I'll be hanging about."

"Come and join us, then. You and I weren't going to meet until six anyway. Come to the bar beside my office; that's where we'll be, at the back."

He grumbled a bit. But he said he'd be there.

Ella took her notes on the Jackaroo's book. It was a zany first novel—it was very different from anything else. It was quirky, not in the mainstream. She did regret that she wouldn't be there to explain at the conference how it should be approached. But she had made up her mind. She had not spent all this time taming her beautiful, strutting peacock—making him adapt to a domestic lifestyle and like the idea of her being permanent in his life—just to throw it away. There would be other Jackaroos, other zany first novels, there were sales conferences every six months; but there might never be another shot like this at Harry.

She had never met the man she called the Jackaroo. His manuscript had been very neat, and she had imagined him as a small, fussy sort of person—like a penguin, possibly. He had assured her, on the telephone, that he was hopelessly disorganized, but that he happened to be in love with his word processor. He said it had tidied up his mind. Now he wished he could find a machine that would tidy up his house.

"What about a wife?" she had asked him.

"Oh, I have one of those," he had said.

Or maybe he had said that he *had* had one of those—she couldn't remember. It didn't matter, anyway; all that mattered was that she explain to him that even though *she* wouldn't be there, Kathy would do everything to ensure that the book was appreciated before it set out on its journey with all the other books.

She looked around the bar. Nobody looked remotely like a penguin.

A huge, shaggy man with long hair and a long, droopy coat stood by the bar, sipping white wine.

"I'm looking for a middle-aged trout called Ella," he said to the barman.

"One middle-aged trout reporting," she said with a laugh.

"God, you're different to what I thought!"

"You too." She wanted to be brisk, get as much of it over as possible, perhaps even all of it, before Harry came in. He looked a reasonable kind of fellow. About as far from a penguin as she could imagine. They sat down together.

"Is it worth my getting a bottle of wine?" he asked. "I'm timid with publishers—I don't want to assume or presume."

"You're not timid with publishers—you call them 'old trouts.' "

"Ah, but I was wrong. Is the bottle going too far?"

"No, but I'm the editor, I'll get it. Anyway, I've a friend joining us later."

"You get the second one, then." He had a wonderful laugh, short, sudden and unexpected but very infectious. She found herself laughing too.

They talked a little about the book. He said it was like a dream, to have made it all the way from the outback to a really smart bar in London and to find that the old trout he had thought was patting him on the head like a good little colonial was a gorgeous bird.

"You're like a lorikeet, in those lovely blues and oranges," he said.

"A lorikeet?"

"You've never seen a rainbow lorikeet?" He wondered at the strangeness of it. He told her about the rosellas and the fig parrots and the noisy pittas.

"You're making them up!" she pleaded.

Somehow, they hadn't got round to talking about the book by the time that Harry arrived.

Harry, in his soft sweater that was exactly the color of his eyes. But *exactly*. It had taken a lot of choosing and selecting and bringing it out of the shop to the daylight.

Harry said that the bar was a collector's item; he couldn't imagine how they had found somewhere so scruffy.

"I thought it was a smart bar," said Greg. She had stopped thinking of him as the Jackaroo.

"Oh, well," Harry said. It didn't mean anything. It could have meant that if you didn't know better, it was a smart bar; or it might have meant that if you came all the way from Australia, it could possibly look like a smart place. It might have meant, "Oh, well, it doesn't matter—the main thing is that we're all here having a drink."

Ella realized that Harry rarely explained himself. Beautiful people didn't have to explain themselves or tell stories. A peacock didn't have to explain itself or tell stories. A peacock didn't have to do anything except be a peacock: everyone else did things around it.

She realized what bird Greg reminded her of: an emu, a big, scrappy emu . . .

"Tell me what emus are like?" she said, and he told her that they were big, flightless things always looking as if they needed to be put through a car wash—or indeed as if they *were* a car wash. They were innocent and interested in everything, he said. You only had to sit and wave a handkerchief out of the car and a great big mob of them would come meandering through the scrub to investigate.

Ella found that both endearing and funny. She threw her head back and laughed. They sat opposite her, Greg and Harry, both looking at her with admiration. But Ella realized that Harry was looking just past her. There was an old mirror behind her. He could see himself nicely.

"Tell me about this sales conference," Greg asked.

Ella looked straight at him.

"It's next week," she said. "I'll be there to hold your hand."

MADAME MAGIC

If you're telling fortunes for a charity, you have to do your home-work just like everywhere else.

Melly, who lived in Number 26, was very popular in the street, which was unexpected since she was a real old-fashioned hippie with a long floral skirt, long hair and long amber beads.

She even had a lovely smile, which meant that even the diffi-cult and fussy Mr. O'Brien, next door, liked her. She was kind to her fellow men and women, which meant that the very religious Kennys, who lived in Number 4, approved of her, whereas nor-mally they might have had words to say about hippie culture.

Her neighbors, the dull Nessa and Barry, had become less dull since they knew her. Melly would always feed a cat or dog if any-one was away and had even been known to take a pair of some-one's canaries for a walk in their cage in case they felt it was too dark for them indoors.

Melly had held the ladder for Bucket Maguire, window cleaner from Number 11, when he looked as if he would fall down in the next gust of wind. She went regularly to read for Miss Mack, the blind woman in Number 3. It was wonderful that Miss Mack liked all the stuff about the court of King Arthur.

So when the neighbors decided to have a fete in the central piece of grass that made Chestnut Street into a kind of a horse-shoe, they asked Melly to be the fortune-teller. They knew she would say yes because it was in aid of a Kosovan orphanage and she was so good-natured and she would look the part too, with a scarf around her head with little coins attached to it. Melly would see something good ahead for everyone, and money would be raised for children without much hope ahead of them.

But they had forgotten about the Glastonbury Festival.

Melly went to that every year of her life. She was desperately sorry. She would try to donate something to the Kosovan children but not her time.

This festival was the center of her year.

"Do you think you could possibly find anyone else, Melly?" Nan Ryan in Number 14 begged. "You see, we don't know any other artistic people like you."

Melly was pleased to be called artistic. She did know a girl who read palms but she took it quite seriously. She would be insulted to do something just for fun.

It was not going to be as easy as people thought.

And she needed to let her house for the week she would be in Glastonbury. So many things to worry about.

Then it came, the phone call from Agnes!

Agnes had been living in a commune in New Mexico. It had all gone very wrong as everything Agnes attempted would go very wrong. That would be too harsh but she always happened to be at the heart of it, all the same.

This time she was looking for a bed, a place to crash for two or three weeks until she got her head together again. Agnes said that sadly she didn't have any real money or anything because communes worked out much more expensive than they led you to believe, but of course she would *do* anything, weed gardens, make bread, mind children, dogs. *Anything.*

"Can you tell fortunes?" Melly asked her. And Agnes said she'd give it a bash.

Agnes arrived a week before the fete.

She settled happily into Number 26.

"Bricks and mortar," she said, stroking the walls sensuously. "What wonderful things they are, Melly. You must never underestimate them."

"Whatever happened to 'property is theft'?" Melly remarked.

As a slogan it had been misunderstood, Agnes thought. She said she loved Chestnut Street and asked all about the neighbors.

She didn't want to go out and meet them or anything. She had this unexplained bruise on her face. She would wait until she looked more presentable.

Melly hesitated before telling Agnes about the square, middle-of-the-road people who lived in the thirty houses of the horseshoe.

It was all so different from the "alternative lifestyle" that Agnes and Melly had lived. Surely Agnes would be very scornful of such a settled area.

But no, it appeared that she was interested and asked a lot of questions about people's lives.

Melly chatted on about Mrs. Ryan in Number 14, who had fallen in love with the builder who came to do up the house next door and how they were married to each other. She heard about Kevin, who took care of his wife, Phyllis; about Lilian, the hairdresser in Number 5, who looked after her mother and father and was married to a frugal man; about Liam and Brigid Kenny, who had their house papered with holy pictures and statues of every known saint on every available surface; about Mitzi and Philip in Number 22, who worshipped their new conservatory as if it were a religious altar; about Dolly in Number 18, who was a really nice kid but with such an unusual mother.

Agnes nodded and sympathized. She had got much easier to

live with, Melly decided, calmer, certainly, and noticeably less frantic and mad.

She said she would manage fine on lentil soup, she'd make her own bread and Melly was not to leave any food for her, but if there *was* a book about the stars or birth signs or something, that would be great.

Melly was now ready to go off to Glastonbury, happy and contented her house would be looked after. There would be a fortune-teller at the fete. Agnes was going to call herself Madame Magic and turn up at 3 p.m.

"You won't frighten them or anything, will you?" Melly said just before she left.

"Go, Melly," Agnes begged, and studied that people born under the sign of Libra were meant to be balanced and level-headed.

Glastonbury was wonderful, as usual. Such great music, such marvelous people.

Once or twice Melly wondered was there a possibility she might just be getting slightly too old for the festival?

It was just that everyone else looked younger somehow, but was it just that the rain was wetter, the fields more muddy, the lines waiting for fast food or slow toilets longer?

Once or twice Melly half wished that she was back in staid old Chestnut Street going to the fete.

Then she began to worry about Agnes.

Had she done something totally madcap, like the old days?

It seemed a long time before she would be back there to find out how it all went.

She noticed that her house was still standing at Number 26. So far, so good.

Melly let herself in. There was a wonderful smell of curry and a note on the table.

Welcome home, Melly.

Dinner's on me. That wonderful Mr. O'Brien in Number 28 gave me a basket full of vegetables—he really is such a sweetie. Dolly will be in later, I'm teaching her to make bread. I'm across the road reading psychic tales to Miss Mack just now. Back at seven. Oh, by the way, I decided to tell people that we didn't know each other—it seemed wiser somehow.

Love, Agnes

Melly felt her heart sink.

Why was it wiser somehow that she should not be known to be a friend of Agnes?

What did she mean Mr. O'Brien was a sweetie? He was a nightmare.

Dolly coming to learn how to make bread? In *this* house?

Had Agnes gone totally mad?

She must stay calm and find out what the situation was.

There would be no flying off the handle.

No matter how insane and confused Agnes might turn out to be, Melly would stay calm.

Agnes came back carrying shortbread. "Miss Mack insisted you have some—you see, she thinks we don't know each other and wants me to make a good impression on you."

"And what does she think you're doing living in my house if we do not know each other?" Melly spoke each word like a very short burst of gunfire.

"She thinks we met through an ad. Everyone sort of thinks that."

"Why do they think that?" Melly was keeping calm but her voice sounded like a robot, a Dalek.

"Well, because the Madame Magic thing went so well, really. Honestly, Melly, you wouldn't believe this but they were coming round again and again for more details. And, you see, I didn't want to tell them that I was a bit of a fraud . . . that *you* told me all their secrets."

"But I didn't tell you all their secrets. I don't know their secrets," poor Melly said, horrified.

"But you did, Melly. You told me all about Kevin and Phyllis, and all about Dolly's mother and the Kennys' being religious maniacs . . ."

Melly's face was red and angry. "I told you these things as a friend in confidence. I didn't expect you to go blabbing them everywhere." Her voice sounded very far away in her own head.

"But I didn't blab. I was much more diplomatic than you were—I was much more sensitive."

"Oh, really."

"*Yes* really. They loved it all, Melly, honestly they did, and I bet I did them a lot of good pointing things out, you know, where they needed to be pointed out."

"Agnes! *You* point things out to people?"

"Well I tell you this: Dolly's mother is being a bit more careful about things since I told her I saw a great shadowy figure approaching her door. Came back to me three times, she did."

"I don't believe this." Melly felt faint.

"And that Mitzi woman from Number Twenty-two, she's going to stop worshipping her conservatory from now on. I told her about flesh and blood being more important than status, and that she should send an e-mail to her sons every week. She was mad about me."

"I'm sure!"

"No she *was*, Melly, and Mr. O'Brien thinks that his cat, Rupert, believes that he is too gossipy, so he is going to be more discreet. And as for Lilian! Remember all you told me about how people walked on her. I don't think they will anymore."

"You told her to get up off the ground and stop being a doormat?"

"No, I told all the others in that household that she might

walk out unless she was properly cherished. I said I saw a figure with long red hair leaving the house silently by cover of darkness. They all thought it was Lilian and that softened their cough, let me tell you."

Melly listened, stunned.

"And did you make any money for Kosovo, Agnes?" she asked eventually.

"Loads. I was by far the most popular draw on Sunday. Some people came by three times. And, by the way, I've been seeing people on a proper fee-paying basis here since. I hope you don't mind."

This was it.

All pretense at calm was now over.

"*No*, Agnes, *no*. This time someone has to speak to you before things go wrong. I will *not* have you pretending to know the future to a lot of decent people, taking money under false pretenses from *my* house. When the law comes, as come it will, I will not stand up for you and say we met through some advertisement. You will not deceive people in this way."

Agnes was calm. "I'm not pretending anything; I'm very interested in them and I want to help them."

"By taking their money and feeding them lies."

"There are no lies. I'm only feeding them the truth. They loved it—they keep coming back for more. I'm good at this. I've never been good at anything before."

Before anyone could say anything else there was a knock on the door.

It was Dolly and her mother.

"I told Mam I was learning to make bread and she wondered if she could come and watch?" Dolly asked.

"Well, it's really up to Melly—this is her house," Agnes said politely.

"Do you two get on together now you've met?" Dolly asked, interested.

"Um, yes," they both said at the same time.

"Please stay," Melly agreed.

"She's a genius," Dolly's mother whispered to Melly. "She told me some of the most important things I've ever heard in my life. It was Fate that brought her here, Melly, believe me."

"Yes, yes."

"You *do* like her, don't you, Melly? It would be great to have someone as wise as that living in the street."

"Living?" Melly gulped.

"Well, staying, working, whatever."

"Oh, yes, certainly."

And as she heard them all slapping the dough, an oddly comforting sound, Melly sat and thought about it. It would be nice to have half the rent, of course, and the company.

And Agnes *did* seem much more normal than before.

But she must be practical.

It wouldn't work out well in the end; nothing ever did for Agnes.

But then they were growing a little older, possibly even mature.

And there was something settling about Chestnut Street.

Melly felt her shoulders relax.

It was much nicer coming home from Glastonbury to this house of bread-making and a nice curry made from Mr. O'Brien's vegetables than it had been coming back to an empty house last year.

Madame Magic could easily begin to live up to her name.

SAY NOTHING

Nuala did not like her daughter's fiancé, Tom. He was always talking about the fast lane and anxious to live in it. But Nuala's friends said that whatever she said . . . she was to say nothing.

It was hard to say nothing. Very hard. But when she was young, some friend of her mother's had said that it was nearly always the wisest course.

Nuala had wanted the very best for Katie, her only child. Katie, who had been ten when her father had left their home on Chestnut Street.

"Why doesn't he love us anymore?" Katie had asked her mother over and over.

Nuala had gritted her teeth and said over and over that of course Daddy loved them both greatly; it was just better for him to leave.

There had been the weekly visit when Michael would take his daughter to the zoo, to the ice rink or to a theater matinee. Over the ten years he introduced Katie to three different "special friends."

Each of them ladies who, at the time, were significant in his life.

At first Katie would prattle on about Daddy's new friend.

Nuala wondered would her teeth wear down since she was gritting them so hard.

But by the time Katie was sixteen she had stopped talking about them; possibly something in her mother's fixed, polite smile of assumed interest rang false.

"How was Dad?"

"Oh he's okay," Katie would say with a shrug.

No information, no detail and slightly less interest.

It wasn't long before Katie had other things to do with her time on Saturdays. Better things.

Like going out with her own friends. There were apologetic phone calls or texts to her father.

Always some very vague excuse or even "Sorry, Dad, tied up tomorrow," which made him realize that she no longer cared about meeting him.

He visited Nuala at work.

Nuala was a nurse in a nearby hospital. It didn't suit her to have visitors while she was on duty.

"Five minutes," he begged.

"I'll take a break," she said wearily.

She took him to the end of the corridor, where there were some chairs.

"I see you've managed to turn her against me," he said bitterly.

"No, Michael, I said nothing to her," Nuala said quietly.

"Why else would she refuse to meet me? Don't fool me, Nuala—I know the way you go on."

"I don't go on, actually, Michael. I agree I did when you left first, but now . . ."

"Now what?"

"Now it doesn't matter what you do, honestly. It used to matter, but now I just wish you well and I don't think about you at all."

She spoke calmly; he seemed to believe her.

"So why then does she want to go off with her friends instead of meeting her father?" He was genuinely bewildered.

"Because she's seventeen," Nuala said.

"And you're happy with this?" He had a concerned-parent face that annoyed Nuala greatly but she managed not to show any sign of it.

"I'm happy she has friends, yes."

"I asked Katie to meet me on some other day in the week and she said she was busy with homework." He was most aggrieved.

"Yes, she does study a lot during the week, which is why she appreciates the freedom of her weekends." Nuala sounded mild and accepting.

"Do you have another partner, Nuala?" he asked suddenly.

"Why do you ask?"

"Because you're different somehow—you don't cluck cluck cluck like a hen."

"Oh, that's good. Sorry, Michael, I have to go back to the ward."

"What am I to do?" he asked.

She remembered that little-boy-lost look too.

"Lord, I have no idea," she said and walked down the corridor.

"I saw your dad today," Nuala said that evening.

"Oh, yeah?" Katie didn't even look up from the magazine she was reading.

"He thinks I'm stopping you from seeing him."

"Typical," Katie said.

Nuala said nothing.

"I suppose you're going to be on my case now, asking me to see him."

"No, indeed. You're seventeen—you decide what to do and who to see." Nuala sounded bright and cheerful.

Suddenly Katie got up from her chair and embraced her.

"You are the best mother in the world. Sit down and I'll make the supper."

Nuala smiled to herself. Whoever had advised her somewhere along the line to say nothing had been so right.

Katie studied hard and was accepted in a teacher's training college. She had a life crowded with friends and more study and practice-teaching.

She saw her father one weekend in four for ever-shorter times. She still lived at home with Nuala.

On the night of Katie's graduation, she met Tom, and everything changed.

Tom was very charming: Nuala would admit that much.

He was good-looking too, and good company.

But her own husband, Michael, had been all these things once.

Katie was very taken with him. Soon after she met him, she explained that she would be getting her own flat. All this was said without any reference to Tom being on the scene. But it was as clear as day that Katie was in love, and that this was her chosen man.

Nuala knew that Katie had to leave home sometime but she didn't want it to be with Tom.

She wondered why exactly she didn't like him, didn't entirely trust him. He seemed to be deeply smitten by Katie. He didn't seem to flirt with other girls, and they had been together for months and they had never had a quarrel. He might well be a faithful husband or partner. Why did she think that he was not good enough for her daughter?

The night that Katie and Tom came in to tell her they were engaged was the night Nuala realized why she didn't think he was the right man for Katie to marry. He was a man possessed by money and success and being in the fast lane. This was a dangerous road for her only daughter to go down.

Katie would spend a lifetime worrying and being anxious, waking up at night to wonder if this investment was safe or if that project was doomed.

Nuala had seen people like this over the years, people worried sick by money at risk, anxious about overinvesting, buying second homes.

It *did* seem the right thing to do; property would never lose its value. A lot of the nurses had bought very expensive homes and were paying huge mortgages. It would be well worth it in the end, they said; they would have something to leave their children.

Sometimes they tried to persuade Nuala to get herself a bigger place in a smarter part of town. It was so easy these days to get a loan from the banks; they were leaping over the counter trying to get you to take their money.

But Nuala had refused. She saved something every week but it was in a nice, safe deposit account.

She had little time for Tom's schemes, all of which involved borrowing money to set up his own consultancy. There were so many people these days who *needed* advice, he said, and it would be a runaway success. Katie would leave her teaching job and help him in the office; it would be much more tax-efficient. They were putting a deposit on a really nice place—it was the bargain of a lifetime.

They were dying to show it to her. It was rather far away but then distances were nothing these days in a fast car. And they had a fast car.

The only thing, the only little thing, was that they needed a little help with the deposit on the house. All the money they had borrowed from the bank was geared for the consultancy. Tom explained it ruefully. He simply could not ask his own parents for any more help. They had already given so much.

He held his head slightly on one side.

Nuala had savings.

Every week she put a little money into her building society savings account. Over the years it had mounted up. It was for a rainy day. Nuala looked at all the hope and longing in Katie's face.

The rainy day was obviously here.

"I can help you both with the deposit," she heard herself say.

Tom bounded across the room.

"What a mother-in-law-to-be," he said.

"It's only a loan, Mum," Katie said, her eyes shining.

"It's a beautiful house, Nuala—you'll love it—and only an hour's drive away," Tom promised.

It was indeed a beautiful house; it had three bathrooms if you called the shower room downstairs a bathroom. It had a patio with a barbecue, a kitchen that would not be out of place in a gourmet restaurant, a turning circle in the front, room to park five cars, at least.

It was a very smart address, and one hour and forty-five minutes away from Nuala's house, whatever kind of car you were driving.

Nuala wanted to say a lot of things.

Like that they would be crippled by the mortgage.

Like it was too far away for her to visit or for them to come to her very often.

Like a young couple didn't *need* such a home.

Like the price of houses might fall. What then? They would be left paying for a house that could never realize the amount of money they had paid for it.

But Nula said nothing like that.

She saw the way they stroked the house as if it were a big family cat, she saw the hope and the future in their eyes.

"It's beautiful," she said, and they hugged her tight.

So they moved in, and it was all too soon to plan the wedding because they were so busy and exhausted setting up the consultancy, entertaining possible clients, going to first nights and gallery openings and networking with the right type of people.

Nuala wondered when they would fix a date but she said nothing. She came to lunch in the big new house occasionally and her own house was always open to them.

Katie sometimes dropped in to Chestnut Street.

They would have a big bowl of soup, which Katie said was very comforting. She and Tom seemed to live on sushi and canapés these days.

Katie sounded tired. She missed teaching, but the business was everything; it had to be built up and they were getting top-scale clients now.

She began to talk about a big Christmas housewarming party they would have two weeks before the day itself. The invitations would go out early—it was going to be a hot ticket.

They would have a theme of black and lime green, all the candles and the linen and the ornaments on the Christmas tree in these colors.

"What on earth will I wear to the party, I wonder?" Nuala asked.

"Oh, Mum, you won't come. You'd absolutely *hate* it, all kinds of awful people braying and shouting, and Tom and I will be so busy flitting around we won't be able to . . . no, you'd really and truly be wiser to avoid it."

Nula said nothing.

She did not say that since all her savings had gone into that house the least she could expect was to see the house being warmed.

She did not say she was disappointed, insulted or upset.

She clung to the notion that it was wiser to say nothing at all.

Her silence upset Katie.

"I mean you don't *want* to come or anything, Mum, do you? Better come on a day when we can talk and everything?" Katie's face was anxious.

Part of saying nothing was to avoid looking like a martyr, so Nuala put on her happy face.

"No, sweetheart, it's a relief, actually. I'd much prefer to go for a nice relaxed meal with just the two of you," she said.

"Oh, Mum, I *knew* you'd feel like that—it's just Dad that's being a real pain about it all."

"Dad?"

"Yes, he actually heard about the party from someone and says that he is insulted that he wasn't asked. So of course we had to send him an invite. I *told* him like I told you what it was going to be like, but nothing will stop him—he's coming and he will be *so* out of place."

Michael telephoned Nuala at work.

"One cup of coffee on your way home?" he begged.

"One cup," she agreed.

"When are those two getting married?" he asked when she sat down. His face looked tight and angry.

"Katie and Tom? Oh, when they can afford to have a big wedding, I imagine."

"Is the house in her name?"

"I'm sure if you asked Katie she would tell you all this."

"I never see her—she's become impossible to find. Then there's this party . . . you're not going to it, I gather."

"It's not really my sort of thing."

"What *is* your sort of thing? I've never known." His face was red, as it always was when he was picking a fight.

But these days she didn't try to placate him.

"You never tried to find out," she said mildly, without accusation. Just as if it were a fact.

"So tell me now."

"I suppose I want a peaceful life and I want our only child to be happy and make the right choices."

"So you lend them money to buy that white elephant of a house?" he said with a sneer.

"It's what they want." She was still calm, unfussed.

"We all want things we can't have or shouldn't have. That house is an unexploded bomb. Property is beginning to get shaky, houses aren't getting their prices."

"Did you invite me to have coffee with you to discuss the economy, Michael?"

"And that fellow's job prospects are way out of line. There's a recession coming; he'll lose everything. I just want to know if Katie's safe or if she's tied into it all with him."

"Well, ask *her*, Michael—please don't ask me. I don't know anything."

"Are you sure you don't have a partner or something? I have never known you so . . . I don't know . . . so confident, so sure that you're right about everything."

"I'm off now," Nuala said.

She thought about it on the way home. Saying nothing had certainly been the right way to go with Michael. In the bad old days she had ranted at him, begged him to change his ways; now she was cool and vague and said very little. It was working amazingly well. He would have come home with her had she shown the slightest encouragement.

But then she didn't want that at all now.

But was it right to say nothing to Tom and Katie? That was the question.

There was a message on the machine at home.

Tom's parents were popping in unexpectedly and there was nothing in the freezer, nothing they could offer them. They couldn't get away from the office. Could Mum ever send round one of her marvelous supper dishes in a taxi?

It would be *so* marvelous.

Nuala found a beef casserole in the freezer and some spiced red cabbage. She put twelve small potatoes into a bag and called the taxi firm that Tom and Katie used.

There was an embarrassed pause.

"I'm afraid they no longer have an account with us," the voice said.

"But they didn't tell me?" Nuala was astounded. "I'm Katie's mother. I know they are great customers of yours—can you check again?"

"I have checked—they're on stop."

"What does that mean?"

"Just that there's no account," the voice said sympathetically.

"Like they haven't paid the bill?"

"I have no idea," the voice said.

Nuala found a local taxi man and paid him a small fortune to take the food across the city.

"This must be an important meal," he said as he carried it into the back of the car.

"I think it's deadly important," Nuala agreed.

She sat by the fire and wondered.

Was this dinner a bid to get Tom's parents to invest more?

Was Michael right about the price of property being on the slide?

Was Tom flying much too high?

Was it time to say something, and, if so, what would it be?

Nuala managed to wait until lunchtime next day before she rang her daughter.

She knew at once from the sound of Katie's voice.

"I just hoped that the beef casserole was all right?" Nuala asked brightly.

"It was terrific, Mum, as usual," Katie said in a flat voice. "And I'm so very sorry you had to send your own taxi. There was some kind of mixup or confusion in our firm—we're changing them anyway."

"How did the dinner go? Tom's parents in good form?"

"Not really, Mum. They're not like you, they're like Dad. Difficult and they're full of views and what people should do and what they should have done."

"Oh, and what was their main problem?" Nuala asked.

"They want us to cancel this party, Mum. We've been working on it for months. They say it's ludicrous and that everyone knows we are broke. Everyone's broke, Mum, it's only by putting on a big show that you get them to have confidence in you. Tom's mum and dad don't get that. They say we should quit now. Imagine the humiliation of it. We haven't an intention of doing that."

"And did it end all right?"

"Not really—they're not like you, Mum."

Two weeks after the party, which had not been the huge success that they had hoped for, Katie and Tom faced reality.

Nuala listened as they told the story.

They would sell the house quickly, as quickly as possible.

They could get out of the office premises easily, since the man who owned the building was getting out of the country.

Katie could get a job teaching. Tom would find something. Anything.

Great Christmas ahead.

"And where will you live?" Nuala asked.

They would rent somewhere. A room, maybe. They were in very deep with the mortgage; even when they sold the house there would be more to pay. No room now for fancy living.

Nuala took a deep breath.

Years of saying nothing had paid off but now it was time to say something.

"I'd love it if you were to stay here," she said. "Eventually we could divide the house—you know, make one flat upstairs, one down. But for the moment would you come and spend Christmas here?"

There was a silence.

Tom shook his head.

"I can't, Nuala. I already owe you for the deposit, *and* I don't know what kind of a job I can get and where and as what . . ."

She paused.

"They are looking for people to push trolleys in the hospital," she said. "Maybe it's not what *you* were looking for . . ."

They both looked frightened and lost. She hoped she had not insulted him in a way that would put her on the side of the enemy, like his parents were already and Katie's father too.

Then she saw the hope in their eyes. "Oh, Mum, that would be great," Katie said.

At the same time Tom came towards her, tears in his eyes. No practiced charm anymore, just gratitude and love.

"You were always so wise, Nuala, since the very start—I said it to Katie. 'Your mother has all the wisdom in the world,' I said. I'll go to the hospital tomorrow and see if I can get the job and we would be honored to stay here. Honored, lucky and proud."

Christmas had often been hard since Michael left; now it looked a lot easier.

She would go back to saying nothing—people seemed to regard it as wisdom.

How wonderful.

EAGER TO PLEASE

❧

The first time I met her was when she had arranged to go on holidays to three separate places with three separate people all at the same time. She couldn't say no to any of them. Not to Eve, who had just been jilted three days before her wedding and really needed a holiday companion; nor to her sister, who was considered too young to go abroad alone; nor to the crowd at work who needed one more to make up the number in order to get the reduction.

She went nowhere that year, but stayed at home on Chestnut Street. The group went off without her, each paying a grudging two pounds extra; her sister sulked at an Irish seaside resort and said that the world was out there waiting if only she had been able to get to it; and Eve said loudly and often that this life was peopled only by other humans who let you down when you needed them.

I think that Ruth hardly ever did anything in her life without trying to please someone, and with the strange justice of the world, she ended up pleasing very few people and making herself miserable. She is in hospital now, and that's because she tried to please someone too, but a lot happened before she was admitted to the ward last week.

Ruth was very, very funny about her job in the civil service; she always said that you were sacked automatically if you thought. Thinking was the one crime. If she saw how the work could be made easier for everyone she daren't say it for fear of disapproval from seniors, who said the younger generation of service people were beyond talking about. If she saw how it could be done quicker they were all afraid that someone might be sacked; if she saw injustices and unfair promotions of people being passed over it was better to say nothing—you were branded a troublemaker and could be sent somewhere awful yourself.

But Ruth was not able to sit forever saying nothing, and in an effort to help a much older man get the promotion he deserved, she did everything in her power and attempted a lot beyond it. She went around to his house and convinced his wife and himself that he was being humiliated, she told her own immediate boss, she threatened to tell the papers about it, and she begged people to sign a petition. With nine brave signatures on the piece of paper she was called in to the supervisor's office and was told that the man was a hopeless alcoholic; worse, because he was a secret drinker, it was a choice between leaving him where he was doing little harm or getting rid of him. Now she had filled everyone's heads with dreams of power and nightmares of corruption and nepotism. Reluctantly she listened to proof. It was too late: the man now felt it a matter of principle and resigned over it all; he died two years later.

"He was nearly sixty," we all told her hopelessly. "He would have had to die sometime from all that drink—his liver was very bad."

Sometimes her impulsiveness was less dramatic and worrying but equally misplaced. She went to see the headmistress of a school where I taught, saying that I would like Saturday mornings off and I looked tired and she wondered could the timetable be arranged to suit me. That was a beautiful one to try to explain away for a few terms afterwards. She kept ringing the ex-boyfriend of someone we all knew, saying that she suspected this girl was going to become a nun as a result of the breakup. Words will never describe the confusion and embarrassment caused by all this, but Ruth came out the loser anyway. She bought two tickets for a package holiday for her parents and cried for a week when they wouldn't go on it at two days' notice, and she lost her deposit to the travel agency, which made her parents feel terrible about it too.

She took on the position of treasurer for a voluntary committee, was always late for meetings, kept losing the subscription book and saying, "Well, I'm sure you paid anyway," and filling in the gaps with her own money. They took the treasury away from her and gave her publicity, and she would swear that posters would be up in pubs and shops but would get involved talking to someone with a problem in the first port of call and the rest of the propaganda never saw a wall at all.

She was very reassuring, though. "Of course you should bring that dress back to the cleaner's—I'll come with you. You have to be firm; it's better for everyone in the end." But she wouldn't come or couldn't come, and you would be left looking foolish saying, Yes, yes of course chemicals could only do so much, yes indeed, sorry.

She was the one who would volunteer to give a party for some returned emigrant, but he would be well back in the new land again before she ever thought of him, and yet all the time she meant well from the bottom of her big generous heart.

There's no point in saying I like her; everyone likes her. You couldn't dislike someone as full of goodwill as that. She never talked much about herself, which is another rotten reason why you like people. She just said the job was beyond belief, but she got a lot of reading done, and was even thinking of doing a postal course in something during working hours. You never thought of saying that she should better herself, because she seemed just fine where and how she was.

She was never boring about her men either, just exuberant. "Yes, it's Geoff—remember I told you I met him in Killarney. He's got the most dreadful friends who all call each other by their surnames, but that's not the worst thing in the world, I suppose. They play a lot of squash. I'm terribly fond of him, and he gets on very well with my family . . . but you never know, do you?" And you don't, because six months later it was, "Michael, a guy who was on this hike thing I told you about: well, he's not what you'd call very responsible but he's so kind and good and loves animals, and he is thinking of setting up a sort of dogs' hospital in his area, if he could get a vet to work part-time for nothing. Do you know any vets, by any chance?"

I was very surprised indeed when she asked two of us for a loan. She couldn't say what it was for, but she would pay us back. Whoever said you shouldn't lend money unless you can afford not to get it back was right, because we got some, and then we never saw Ruth anymore. She was too embarrassed to come anywhere we might be, and though it wasn't the margin between survival and death, it was enough of a barrier to make us think, "What on earth can she have needed it for? And why can't she pay it back?" And, you see, society being as it is, you can't ring someone and say just that. They think, reasonably, you are pressing them for the money. So we never asked, and felt a bit cross, and a little bit anxious. But to be honest, I think more cross than anxious.

She married the most unexpected man in the world. Oh, all right, doesn't everybody, but Ruth's marriage was out of sight. He was twenty years older than her, separated (or divorced or something vague enough to be mysterious), very wealthy and fairly well known in his own field. They got married in London and had a huge cocktail party afterwards where I hardly knew anyone, least of all Ruth, who was fawning and impressing and telling the most unbelievable things to people: "Yes, I used to work in administration, very interesting, very challenging, but of course I'll have so much entertaining to do now I won't be working anymore." She gave me the money in an envelope quietly and furtively and said she was desperately sorry and that after two years there should be interest on it, but to thank Mary and give her the money and she hoped we hadn't been starving.

"Dennis knows lots of people," she said, with her usual impulsiveness. "You must come around lots and lots, and have dinner and things and meet loads of people. Some of them are single too," she added darkly, commenting on my unmarried, manless state with disapproval. "You'd never know."

And indeed, you never would, because it was for once one of the promises Ruth kept. I was deluged with invitations to meet Dublin's most eligible men, until it became a joke between us all and I would say when we were introduced, "Could you ever marry me immediately and get it all over with?" Which I thought was funny and they usually thought was uneasily funny and Ruth thought was a scream. Dennis didn't think much of it. But then I didn't think much of Dennis either, so that evened itself out.

Ruth went on being disorganized and inviting all the wrong sort of people for dinner, and saying that the dessert was going to be fabulous, and it would be raw or burned, and Dennis's displeasure was greater and greater, and anyway I went off somewhere on holidays and they forgot about me, or at least maybe they forgot or maybe they struck me "off the list." But I heard that Ruth was still trying urgently to please him, and to please her parents, whom he didn't like, and to please all her old friends, who would have understood anyway. She made a few classics during those years, like telling a woman who had been trying to have a baby for seven years with no luck that she should "stop this selfish life and settle down and have three children one after the other." She also gave a surprise party for Dennis on a night when he had a board meeting and didn't turn up until midnight, when all the guests were drunk and all the food was gone. She alienated her younger sister forever by telling her that she "ought to know" that her fiancé had had a child by someone else, something we'll never know or care whether it was true or not. But her sister and fiancé cared to the extent of breaking off their engagement, and Ruth's sister went to America, from where nobody hears much about her.

Dennis was getting more and more irritated, and Ruth more frightened. There was a son by his previous marriage, a nice, shy, nervy sort of boy of about seventeen at the time, I think. Ruth would write him ten-page letters telling him that she would not try to replace his mother, but she did want to be friends. He worked on a farm, which his father thought was idiotic and Ruth thought was lovely. She drove a hundred miles to see him, and they had a conversation that must have been staggering, knowing Ruth and not knowing the shy boy, who hadn't a clue about this strange, eager woman with her flood of words, and must have thought her part of his father's smart set, and even smarter than most because she had managed to get a wedding ring.

He wouldn't come and stay, but Ruth had done up a room for him and bought prints of horses and country landscapes for it, and kept sending him cards asking would he like a red or blue carpet. And this wasn't great for the son because they were postcards, and his employer kept asking him was he going to leave or wasn't he—could he make up his mind?

I was going to say nothing happened for a few years, but of course that's ridiculous—something must have happened every hour of every day. I just didn't know what it was. People said Ruth and Dennis were very suited and lived a very dull life. You'd always see his photograph in the paper signing things; you'd never see anything of Ruth. Andy, her stepson, never came to live in his room, though it was always called "Andy's Room." Ruth's parents visited the house less and less. Ruth tried to join the Samaritans but was told that they were very grateful for her offer but she wasn't the stuff they needed. She was apparently philosophical and forgiving about this too and said that of course they needed balanced, reliable people. She never complained—she kept promising and planning and interfering.

The Mary who had lent her the money ages back met her and had a lunch where Ruth kept promising to use her influence to get Mary's husband promoted, and Mary had seven sleepless nights until she felt free to think that Ruth had forgotten it.

I saw her recently and she said she knew someone who was a great friend of a prize-winning writer and she would write to him to get me an introduction, and to this day I am afraid she might have.

She sent someone a bottle of wine by post that broke; she bought rose bushes for a cousin with no garden; she sent me money for a woman I had told her about and I had to tell her that the woman wouldn't accept charity and I would have to give it anonymously through the proper organization, and she was sad because she wanted to become a friend of that woman.

She apparently had only one row with Dennis, or one she speaks about: he got a presentation of a watch and he said he didn't know what to do with it since he already had one. Beaming with happiness, she reminded him it was one she had given him for his birthday, shortly before they were married, and he laughed and said that that was only a trinket—he had exchanged it for one that looked a bit similar but would work. The trinket that Ruth had paid so much for was the reason for her borrowing from us all those years ago.

Sadly, she realized that the whole thing had been a bit misty; she wasn't much good at anything. Perhaps this was just the one moment she allowed herself a bit of self-pity. But she told me that if she hadn't done much for Dennis she was going to rectify it and that's why she had driven off to find Andy last week; and he said for God's sake to leave him alone, he wished her no harm but he was over twenty-one and he found that her "your-father-really-wants-you-deep-down" remarks were amateur psychology and professional meddling. And he said to her the kind of thing she was always saying to others: "Why don't you have children yourself and leave me out of it?"

And her eyes had been a bit blurred with tears and she swerved the car to avoid a dog and hit a cyclist instead, and he had two broken ribs and she had a lot of bruising only, and a broken wrist. Which is how she ended up in the hospital.

But she was busy pleasing people still. She asked me to put the flowers in a mug, not to disturb the nurse, and I did, and it was some sterilized thing that the nurse wanted and there was aggro about that, and she said she had arranged for a restaurant to send in meals for Dennis while she was in hospital and they were all going bad because he kept eating out, and she didn't bother telling the doctor about the dreadful headaches she had, because, really, the man had so much to do with looking at her wrist, and anyway, headaches were just headaches, weren't they. And please, why wouldn't they let her go and see the poor cyclist and tell him it was all her fault and she would pay for everything for him to get better? And did I have So-and-so's address because her husband had just died and she wanted to tell her that there was a very nice widower, a friend of Dennis's, who was just aching to get married again. . . .

SEEING THINGS CLEARLY

It was very easy to bore Will. He bored very quickly and had what could be called a short fuse for topics that didn't interest him. Nostalgia was one of these topics, and families and other people's problems. So Gina reminded herself of this several times a day. No point in telling him about the way the autumn leaves fell in Chestnut Street, making a golden carpet that rustled and sighed as you walked. Will would shrug. Golden leaves—who needed them? But she loved him so much it didn't matter what he thought about leaves.

"You left the place," he would say. And Gina loved him so much she would snuggle up and agree. And of course she *had* left five years ago to live with him in London. She had said goodbye to kind, decent but introverted Matthew, the local vet, who admired her but never declared himself. He had seemed disappointed that Gina was leaving but said nothing to persuade her to stay.

She had left her life as a schoolteacher living a quiet life in the basement of her parents' house, which they called the "self-contained flat." In fact, Mother and Father came through her self-contained flat six or eight times a day as they went to the garden.

Once she had suggested having a door on the stairs for privacy. "What on earth do you want privacy for?" her mother had asked. And Gina never had the heart to tell her.

It had not been difficult for Gina to get a teaching job in London, and children were great no matter where they were. She missed not knowing their families, as she had in Dublin, but that was a small price to pay.

Will made her very much part of his life, which was a researcher on a television talk show. It was his job to find new exciting people as guests and book them on. It was very stressful dealing with agents and managers and PR people. Gina did a lot of message-taking and e-mailing when she wasn't at school or marking papers. He wished she could do more. He particularly disliked her habit of going back home once a month.

"It's ludicrous, Gee—you're just getting them into the habit of expecting you," he begged. "I don't go round annoying *my* mother all the time."

Will's mother was forty-eight and a glamour puss, Gina's mother was seventy-three and becoming very forgetful. Gina's father was a frail seventy-eight who walked unsteadily. There was a great difference in their situations.

Will didn't know how much they looked forward to her visits, kept things behind the clock on the mantelpiece to show her, listed their problems so that she could solve them in the hours she was there.

Her brothers didn't come back to Chestnut Street—well, not more than once or twice a year.

David was a financial consultant in Edinburgh, married to the beautiful and wealthy Laura. They had an elegant home in Morningside, where they entertained a lot. A life too full to involve trips down south.

James had an Internet business in London. He lived with terrier-like Kate, who encouraged him to work a fifteen-hour day. So there was very little time to go home and no time whatsoever to meet his sister. Gina had been lonely in London when she went there five years ago and wrongly hoped that they might welcome her to their home.

But Will was too busy to take all that into account; he was under huge pressure at the moment. There had been a tiny rumor that the talk show where he worked might be axed next year—it just wasn't getting the right ratings. Will wanted to jump ship before that happened, and even well before it was even known. He had his eye on a Hollywood talk show; he even knew the man who might be able to hire him. His eyes shone with excitement when he talked about the whole thing.

And Gina, with a lump of lead in her heart, nodded and agreed that it would be a huge step up and that Will deserved it. At the same time she wondered exactly what love meant to him. He thought she would drop everything and come with him. It was simple: they loved each other. And Gina had already dropped almost everything to come to London. So what was there to get heavy about? Could he not understand that since it was impossible for her to come back from California to keep an eye on her parents, she just couldn't go with him? It wasn't lack of courage, it was gratitude. They had married late in life and been good to their three children. They must not be abandoned now, when they needed someone around.

Gina sighed heavily as she got off the bus on the High Street. She would do a little shopping before going home. Father liked those currant buns, which she would toast for him. Mother loved fingers of shortbread. They could have bought these things themselves or asked Mrs. Cloud to do so, but years of denying themselves things had got them out of the habit of buying little treats.

In the supermarket she met Matthew Kane. He always had a smile for her.

"What was the best thing that happened to you at work this week?" he asked her unexpectedly.

"Let me think. The most disruptive, anti-social kid I ever

taught said she was going to enter a poetry competition. That really cheered me. And you?"

"A lovely ginger cat with a big smile and a big lump that turned out to be benign in the lab report and I was able to tell that to the children who own him."

"So, it's not been a bad week, all in all," Gina said cheerfully.

They didn't talk about private lives so she didn't tell him that actually it was a very worrying week indeed. Mother had sounded more distracted than ever on the phone. Father less able to cope than usual. Mrs. Cloud was never there when Gina had called.

Will was up to high doh because his American contact was in town and Gina *must* be back to cook a pie in their flat—Americans went crazy over a home-cooked pie. *And* she was to glam up for the night as well.

It would have been great to have someone to tell. But Matthew Kane was not the person and this was not the time.

She let herself into 30 Chestnut Street and smelled sour milk and bad food. Her heart skipped a beat until she heard their voices calling out a greeting to her. It turned out that they had sacked Mrs. Cloud since she was much too expensive, and that they were managing fine on their own.

The kitchen table was covered in half-opened, half-eaten food, the door of the refrigerator open, no washing had been done and the sink was full of dirty dishes. Gina looked around in disbelief.

A huge wave of self-pity came over her. She was a woman of twenty-nine, she had been a reasonably good daughter and sister, she had loved one man since she was twenty-four and been faithful and good to him, she taught children conscientiously all day. Why was she being punished as if she were an evil-doer? It was so very, very unfair.

The wave of self-pity washed backwards and forwards over her for about two minutes and then it went away and she got down to work. She toasted the currant buns and then suggested they go into the sitting room while she did a little tidying up. They accepted this as if she were just someone a little overfussy.

For two hours she cleaned the kitchen and gathered all the rotting food into several black sacks with disinfectant. She filled the washing machine, scraped the burned food off the cooker. She made them scrambled eggs on toast and called them in to supper.

"This is very nice," Mother said.

"Nice to have hot food in the evening," her father said approvingly.

Mother talked endlessly of people who were coming in later this evening. The "girls," she called them. She listed names that Gina had never heard before. And then went to get her nice stole so that she would look well when they came.

"Who are they, Father?" Gina asked fearfully when she left.

"They're the girls she worked with in the bank fifty years ago; she thinks that's where she is now, you see. She can't quite place *me* at times," he said and he looked like a bloodhound, his face was so sad.

They went to bed and Gina sat alone in the kitchen. She made the list of foods she would buy and stock for Mrs. Cloud, of what arguments to present to Mrs. Cloud so that she would agree to ignore her dismissal and come back and hold the fort. She would have to persuade David and James to take a more active part. And they hadn't forgotten Mother and Father in their hearts, surely? The beautiful, elegant Laura in Scotland would not prevent David from helping. Surely? The eager, hardworking Kate in London wouldn't stop James from coming to help in the decision. Surely?

Her mother came into the kitchen.

"Are we having a midnight feast?" she asked in a girlish tone.

"Sure, Mother."

Gina got them some milk and shortbread. They ate companionably.

"I hope I get married," her mother said.

"We all hope to get married sometime," Gina agreed, knowing that her mother's mind had wiped out three decades of a happy marriage.

"You know the way I feel about it," her mother confided. "You can have all the fun and all the infatuations you like, but when it comes to it, you know. You can see clearly that it's wrong for you, like a big, clear light."

"And did you see things clearly?" Gina asked.

"Well, I think that I did." Her mother spoke as if she were talking to an equal, not to her own daughter. There was a girlish sense of confiding about it all.

"I used to love the assistant manager, you know, but you were right, all of you, my friends—he didn't really love me at all."

"Did he love someone else?" Gina asked gently.

"No, I don't think he did." Her mother was matter-of-fact. "It was just that all of a sudden I realized that I was no part of his life."

"So what will you do now? Now that you know this?" Gina whispered.

"I won't rush into anything, that's for sure."

"No, no," Gina agreed.

"It's very feeble to think that you only exist if you have some slavish relationship with a man."

"No, I agree entirely." Gina had never had a conversation with her mother like this before in her whole life.

"So I'm going to consider myself free from now on. I'm going to regard the end of this obsession as a liberation, and if I do see other people I might like, I'm free to look at them."

"And is there anyone out there that you might like . . . do you think?"

"There *is* a nice man—I don't think you've met him. He's called George, very quiet, doesn't push himself forward like the assistant manager, but he's very interesting to talk to. Now that I see things more clearly I'll have time to talk to him properly, you see."

Gina smiled with tears in her eyes as her mother's seventy-three-year-old face smiled coquettishly. But mainly Gina smiled because Father's name was George.

Gina was up early in the morning. She begged Mrs. Cloud to hold the fort.

"I'll be back then—I'll get things sorted," she said. Then she went to the supermarket to buy what was needed for her parents. She also bought a very expensive pie. It was lamb and apricot—it would take forty minutes to heat.

Matthew Kane was there. "Do you *live* here?" they asked each other at the same time and laughed. They examined each other's trolleys.

"An awful lot of creamed rice," she said, mystified.

"Four very weak little puppy dogs turned up at my door. They can't eat anything else just now," he explained.

"I see. Good luck with them," she said.

"Very up-market pie," he observed, looking into her trolley.

"I'm going to pretend to some American hotshot and his druggy girlfriend that I made it myself."

"I see—good luck with them," Matthew said.

Somehow she got back to London and placed roses on the dining table. She was showered and ready when Will brought them home after many cocktails in a trendy new club.

"It was so great, we just didn't want to leave," Bret said.

Bret's girlfriend, Amy, looked either drunk or stoned and very uncoordinated.

"Can I see your bathroom?" she asked as a greeting.

Gina was about to show her when Bret interrupted.

"Not here, honey, no need. We're with family here," he said.

Gina left them and went to the kitchen. She looked back and saw Bret and Amy leaning over the coffee table in the sitting room. There were two lines of white powder there. People were doing drugs here in their apartment. Will was beside her.

"Please, Gee, don't be all heavy now, not now, of all times, I beg you."

"Who's heavy?" she asked.

He gave her that smile that always worked.

She carried the dish in.

"Here we are, lovely homemade lamb-and-apricot pie."

"You don't think for a moment that just because you made it that I'm actually going to eat that pastry, do you?" Amy asked.

"No, I didn't expect you would," Gina said pleasantly.

They all looked at her with surprise.

"No, I see from your lovely, slim figure you probably never ate pastry in your life." Gina looked at her admiringly. "Still, the others might like it. Will here can eat anything and he never puts on an ounce—I'm sure it's the same with you, Bret?"

Will looked at her, delighted. Gina realized for the first time in five years that it was actually very easy to keep people like Will happy. All you did was tell lies and flatter them all the time and pretend that there was nothing else in your life.

Amy didn't form a major part of the night's conversation but Gina did. She talked on and on about how talented Will was, how good with people, how much he was loved by the talent, how celebrities always asked for him when they went back on the talk show. Bret wondered if it would all cross the Atlantic.

"If Will wants it to, then it will," she said confidently.

Bret was impressed. Will came back into the kitchen, triumphant.

"It went really great—he likes me," he said.

"What's not to like?" she said gently.

"I'm meeting him tomorrow morning; imagine—a Saturday!" Will crowed with pleasure.

"Good. I have to go back home—will you call me and tell me how you get on?"

"Not again?" He was annoyed.

"Yes, but you have your meeting—you might go to a club or something afterwards."

This weekend there would be a lot to do, brothers to ring, hospitals to contact, day centers to inspect. She might ask an architect to come in and see about altering the house in Chestnut Street, she might inquire at her old school if there were any vacancies. There were puppies to be visited, poor little puppies who ate only creamed rice. She would sit at the kitchen table and would make decisions. Big decisions. And because she could see things clearly now, none of them had anything to do with going to California.

FAIR EXCHANGE

Ivy wished that people would write letters as they did in the old days. It used to be lovely hearing envelopes fall through the letter box. Nowadays there was nothing but bills and free offers and people telling you that you had won a cruise when it turned out you hadn't won anything of the sort.

For a while Ivy wrote her own letters to nephews and nieces. She wrote to people she used to work with when she had been in the flower shop. But it was always the same. They wrote guilty notes scribbled on the back of Christmas cards; they were so sorry, they should have replied, of course, but, really, life was so rushed, and what a pity that Ivy didn't text or use e-mail.

Ivy thought she might as well try to fly to the moon as learn anything like that.

So she sighed and said that it had all been a turn for the worse. She wasn't lonely or anything; she had had many offers in her time but she had never really concentrated on them. Somehow she had made a mess of relationships. It was just that she liked to keep in touch with people, to know what was going on in their lives.

She would like to tell them that she had won a prize in a

pastry-cooking competition, or how her small dog could now go to the newsagent to pick up the paper all on his own. Or maybe a bit about the holiday she had taken in the Scottish Highlands, or the art-history lectures in the local museum. She could have written about how she ran an informal book club, which met in her house every week; they had snacks and wine and sometimes they had even read the book!

Not earthshaking stuff, but it was comforting to people to know that a woman of nearly sixty still had a good lifestyle. She had even taken to entering competitions where they asked you to write slogans, and it turned out that Ivy was quite good at this. She had already won a set of suitcases, a garden shed and a year's supply of breakfast cereal. And now today she had heard she had won a major prize in another competition.

She would know this afternoon what it was. It was being given by a store down in the shopping mall. Ivy hoped it might be a voucher. She would buy some new cookware and a very up-market food processor. . . . She dressed up smartly to receive the gift in case there might be a photographer from the local press.

Everyone except Ivy gasped at the generosity of the prize. It was the last word in laptop computers, plus a mobile phone, which was so magical, apparently, that it accepted and sent e-mails, whatever exactly they were.

Ivy, who had been brought up to be very polite, thanked everyone and said it was a wonderful gift that she would treasure.

"Maybe you could exchange it," one of her friends said helpfully. But Ivy thought that might look very rude, as if she hadn't liked it.

"Maybe you could raffle it later?" another friend suggested.

"But suppose they heard about it?" Ivy was such a kindly person she couldn't take the risk.

So she brought the package home and looked at it glumly. Ivy was not technical.

She couldn't set the video. She had great trouble in getting money out of the hole in the wall. She didn't have a telephone answering mechanism. There was no way she could get to grips with this machine.

It was a pity because if only she could, then she could contact her favorite nephew, who was in South America; she could keep in touch with some of those nice women she had once worked with who now seemed to have turned into semi-machines and couldn't communicate without technology.

Ivy told herself that she wasn't stupid. Suppose she did learn how to use it? But twenty minutes at the manual showed her that it was another planet.

Suppose she got lessons?

Everyone said that classes were hit or miss. Either they all streaked ahead of you or they were so slow you fell asleep. What you needed was one-to-one tutoring. But that was expensive and Ivy didn't have money to throw away.

If only there were a way.

Next week at the local supermarket she studied their community notice board. People were offering babysitting, removal of garden rubbish, shiatsu massage or newspaper deliveries. Nobody was offering cut-price one-to-one lessons in making you computer-literate.

Other people were seeking help with ironing, someone to do home hairdressing or anyone who would like to take an unexpected litter of beautiful kittens. It didn't look promising.

But then Ivy got an idea.

And very soon her advertisement was on the board.

I NEED ABOUT FIVE LESSONS IN HOW TO SET UP MY COMPUTER, GET ON THE INTERNET, AND SEND TEXT MESSAGES. I WILL OFFER, IN RETURN, FIVE LESSONS IN COOKERY.

She waited with interest. And then there were three replies. Two people were entirely unsuitable. One of them said there was nothing to computing—you just plugged in and away you go. The second said she was only interested in cooking with yeast, and unless that was on offer, she would not share her computer skills.

The third was from a twelve-year-old boy called Sandy.

He said he had just come to live with his grandfather on Chestnut Street and neither of them could cook. Could she come to their house and teach them five simple meals and then he would come to her house five times and get her on the Net and the Web and whatever she wanted?

He was by far the best on offer.

They made the arrangements on the phone: they would have one trial lesson in each place and then they would see. She decided to go to his house first.

Sandy had sticky-up hair and a lot of freckles. He was welcoming and apologetic.

"The place is a little disorganized," he said, waving vaguely at an extraordinarily messy kitchen. "It's just that we're not really used to it, running a house and everything, if you know what I mean."

Ivy was much too polite to ask why he was now living with his grandfather. It would emerge or it would not. It was as simple as that.

"Yes, I know what you mean. Do you think we should sort of tidy up a bit to give us some space?"

"Would this have to count as one of the five lessons?" Sandy asked anxiously.

"No, not really. Perhaps you could spend the first day helping to tidy up my electronics for me when you come," Ivy suggested.

That seemed satisfactory.

Cheerfully, they set about cleaning the place up. Saucepans were scrubbed, dishes washed and dried, and a list was made of the provisions they might need to buy before the next visit. Ivy noted what kind of food Sandy and his grandfather wanted to cook; she said she would teach him to do one fish dish, one chicken, one meat, one vegetarian and a series of starters and desserts.

"Will your grandfather be taking part in the lessons, do you think?" Ivy asked.

"No, I think he's sort of leaving it to me," Sandy said. Ivy had always had this great ability to leave things as they were, so she said no more and they arranged to meet the next day at her house.

Sandy came on time with three pages of notes and told her that the main thing was not to be frightened by it all. It just took a little time and then you knew it forever and ever. She loved the way he thought there was a forever and ever stretching out ahead of her.

Sandy had brought a screwdriver, and he changed some of her plugs to make things easier; he found her a good, firm cushion for her chair and showed her how to use the best light possible. By the time he left she could look up Websites and spend a happy few hours checking out things that interested her, like holidays on canal barges, or how to find the people you were at school with, how to identify common garden birds. . . .

He would teach her how to contact people by e-mail in two days' time, and, meanwhile, she was to telephone people and find out their e-mail addresses.

Ivy sat up late trying to work out a suitable easy dish to teach this boy and his grandfather. She settled for cod cooked in foil, with vegetables and herbs. She also brought very simple notes that he would understand, with very specific advice.

Ivy had not understood it when it said to "boot up your computer" so why should Sandy understand instructions like "cook till ready" or "reduce by half."

Sandy was a quick learner.

"You're so bright," Ivy said wistfully. "Your young mind is like a sponge—you take everything in. . . ."

"Yours isn't bad either," he said. "It's a bit deeper than mine, actually." And he got all her friends and relations into a list called

Contacts on the machine and suddenly they were all in touch with her regularly. Sometimes only three or four lines but she knew more about their lives than she had ever known before.

And she taught him how to make a basic beef stew, a chicken with lemon and olives, a vegetable casserole, plus a Moroccan salad of grated carrots, orange juice, raisins and pine nuts.

Several times he said that his grandfather had liked the food so far. And that he was going to join the last lesson himself.

Ivy found herself a little annoyed at this. She had grown to enjoy her conversations with Sandy. What was he like, this poor old man who worked mending jewelry? He must be way too old to be still at work. How could his old eyes see the work, anyway?

She must remember to speak clearly and distinctly to him. Sandy had said that he was very nice but that he didn't understand much of the world.

A pleasant-looking man in early middle-age was sitting in the kitchen when she arrived. He must be an uncle or something. Sandy was always fairly vague about family.

"I'm Ivy—Sandy and I have an exchange system going," she began.

He stood up to shake hands, tall, handsome, with a lovely smile.

"Don't I know all about it? We have never eaten so well in our lives!"

"Oh do *you* eat here too?" Sandy had been vaguer than she had realized.

"I'm Mike, his grandfather."

She looked at him, dumbfounded. This young man as the poor, witless grandfather? He seemed to read her thoughts.

"He didn't describe you well either, Ivy," Mike said. "I thought you'd barely make it in the door. And look at you!" He was full of admiration.

It hadn't happened for a long time.

This time she wasn't going to make a mess of it.

THE WINDOW BOX

Gwendoline was often at her window. She knew it was a bit old lady–ish for a woman of thirty-seven but . . . well . . . you had to know who was coming and going in the street, didn't you?

She sat a little back from the curtains but she could still see.

She had seen a small van take away what was left of poor Miss Hardy's things. A recluse, the woman had been; nobody had even known she was dead until the Pakistani man in the corner shop had asked about her. And then she was found. No relations, apparently, nobody at her funeral, Gwendoline heard. And then, of course, the landlords had the whole place cleaned and fumigated and now it was ready to let again.

It was of interest to Gwendoline because her window looked straight across the street at the flat on the first floor of the house opposite. Not that there had ever been anything to see except for a pair of curtains always fastened with a big safety pin. Perhaps the new people might have something a little less depressing to look out on. A nice blind, maybe. Good drapes with a pelmet?

This street was coming up a bit, and once the last of the poor Miss Hardys and her kind were gone, it would be really quite an acceptable place to live.

Gwendoline got home from work around six-thirty each evening. She walked from the tube station through a market and
often got very good value in what they were selling off at the end
of the day. This evening she had got some haddock at half price,
and some tired-looking tomatoes and green beans for a fraction
of what they had cost to others earlier on. She could have got a
bunch of flowers for ten cents if she had wanted to but it seemed
silly, so she left them. She came home well satisfied; her supper
had cost her so little. She worked in the accounts department of
a big company. She knew only too well, from the repossession
orders and legal hassle, the trouble people got themselves into by
falling into debt. It wasn't something that Gwendoline was ever
likely to do.

She came into her flat, and looked around her.

It would have been nice to have had a dog to welcome her, but
you couldn't keep a dog cooped up all day in a flat. A cat would
have been nice—she *had* thought about getting one once. But
someone at work pointed out that they tore your good furniture
to shreds. And of course a husband would have been nice, but
that hadn't happened and Gwendoline was damned if she was
going to make all the sacrifices that her friends had made just in
order to have the title Mrs. in front of her name.

And it wasn't as if she were *lonely* or anything. Of course not.

She had her television and her books and from her first-floor
window she could see all that was going on in the street outside.

She saw the van draw up at the house opposite and a woman
get out of the front seat. She looked about the same age as Gwendoline, but maybe she was younger. She had long, dark curly hair,
wore jeans and a floppy red sweater and there were four much
younger people with her.

As if they were unpacking a summer picnic, they carried all
her boxes and crates upstairs. They laughed as they ran up and
back and eventually they went round the corner for bags of fish
and chips.

Gwendoline could see them sitting around the table, which they had carried up earlier. She could see them perfectly because the new person who had come to live there hadn't put up any curtains or blinds. Nothing at all. The room was wide open to look into. Extraordinary.

When the fish and chips were finished, the young people left. From down below they called up to her.

"Happy days, Carla. Good luck, Carla." And they were gone.

Her name was Carla.

Who were these people who had moved her in and shared fish and chips with her? Nieces, nephews, cousins, friends, colleagues?

For some reason Gwendoline found herself drawn to look in the open window. Carla washed the dishes and made herself a mug of tea. Then she began what looked like some kind of carpentry at the table. In about twenty minutes she had assembled a window box and placed it out on a windowsill. Then she carefully filled it with earth and compost from two big bags. And finally put in half a dozen bedding plants, which she took lovingly from transparent bags. She watered it with a little watering can and then stood looking at it with great approval.

Gwendoline had her half-price haddock, and her tired vegetables and for once the sheer value of it all didn't give her a warm glow of satisfaction. She felt a bit colorless compared to the woman across the street, the woman who had spent her first night in her new home treating her movers to fish and chips and planting a window box.

Gwendoline ironed her blouse and scarf for next morning and tried to concentrate on her book but somehow she found herself looking across the street most of the time. Carla had filled a bookcase. Imagine having all that number of paperbacks instead of borrowing them from the library, where they were free.

Gwendoline watched as the woman across the street admired the bookshelves and then sat down to watch television. Gwendoline could just see her face lit up by the screen. Carla was laughing at something she was watching. Gwendoline scanned the channels. There was nothing remotely funny on. Maybe this woman had got herself a video.

She seemed curiously self-sufficient in an annoying sort of way.

Next morning Gwendoline was looking from behind her curtain.

Carla was up and squeezing orange juice. Then she examined the contents of her window box, picking some minuscule weed that could have grown in the night and spraying the plants lightly.

She put on her coat and so did Gwendoline. She would see which way the woman went to work. But Carla stopped at the corner shop.

"Hallo, I'm Carla. I've come to live round the corner, and I'll be a *great* customer," she said.

"Good, good. I am Javed."

"Is that Mr. Javed or is Javed your first name?" she asked.

Gwendoline was stunned. She had lived here for seven years and had never known the man's name.

"It is my first name. My family name is Patel," he said.

"Well, it seems a very friendly neighborhood. I am going to like it here, I know," she said.

"It is fairly friendly, yes," Mr. Patel said.

Gwendoline had her opportunity. She *could* have said, "You are welcome to the neighborhood. Yes, it is a nice place. My name is Gwendoline. Why don't you come for a cup of coffee tonight?" But you just didn't *say* things like that. Not to strangers. So she just bought a newspaper and left.

At work one of her young colleagues commented.

"You actually *bought* a newspaper today, Gwendoline!"

Gwendoline flushed with annoyance. Yes, she *had* said that it was ludicrous the way people spent a fortune on newspapers on their way to work and then wondered where their money went. But that was just common sense; it didn't make her into a Scrooge, an eccentric. She found herself wondering where this

Carla worked. She looked a bit bohemian, you know, slightly untidy. Maybe she was something in arts and crafts.

The day went slowly. Gwendoline found a magazine that someone had abandoned. She sat in the canteen and read an article about doing up a patio, which was pretty pointless since she didn't have a patio. She noticed how expensive the potted plants were. Imagine that woman across the road putting six of them in a window box up one floor.

Someone in the office was leaving, a guy called Harold—they were making a collection. Gwendoline said truthfully that she didn't know him.

"So you don't want to sign his card, then?" the girl asked.

"No, I think not. As I say, I don't know the man," Gwendoline said.

She probably imagined it but she thought she saw the others exchange glances and shrug their shoulders. But if they did, so what? She would be broke if she were to contribute every time someone came rattling a box. And, anyway, she had other things to think of—she was meeting her brother, Ken, tonight. They had to decide about a nursing home for their mother.

Ken had suggested a ludicrously expensive café to meet, but Gwendoline had put a stop to that very quickly. He could come to her flat, she said, and bring a bottle of wine. She would cook him a meal.

To her great annoyance, she had to work late. And to her greater annoyance, the market had closed up when she went through looking for bargains, so she had to go to Mr. Patel's convenience store and pay far too much for her liking.

Mr. Patel was talking about her neighbor. The new lady called Carla. She was a very good, kind person. She was a nurse, apparently, and she had bandaged Mr. Patel's finger where he had cut himself. She had a very happy mind and she bought lots and lots of packets of flower seeds.

Gwendoline listened impatiently. She couldn't care less what this woman had bought. She made several calls to Ken's mobile and left messages saying she had been delayed, but always got the answering service. If people went to the trouble and expense of having a mobile, why didn't they leave it turned on?

Very bad-tempered by now, she let herself in and on the hall floor was a note from Ken. "I guess you've been delayed. I left my cellphone at the office, but I'll hang about and come back again about seven-thirty." She checked to see what was happening across the road and, to her total shock, saw through the open window in the flat opposite that her brother was having a glass of wine with Carla across the road.

Some hanging-about that had been!

Just making straight for the nearest female who would give him a drink. That figured.

Gwendoline was unreasonably annoyed. She knew it was unreasonable. Why shouldn't Ken go in somewhere else? Better than hanging about in the street. It was just that it was too fast somehow, too casual, too easygoing, as if they were all students or something. Not grown-ups with responsibilities.

Ken rang her doorbell at a quarter to eight.

She buzzed him in and began to prepare his supper.

Expensive lamb chops she had bought from Javed Patel, frozen peas, two small ice cream desserts, but he stopped her. He had eaten a mushroom omelet across the road. Carla was just making her supper, so he had shared it with her. He was afraid that he had opened the bottle of wine while he was there.

"Thanks a lot," Gwendoline said sourly.

"No, I mean, she did give me my supper—it just seemed right," Ken said apologetically.

"Sure." Gwendoline wrapped the lamb chops in foil and rammed them into the small freezer compartment of her fridge.

"You're not going to eat?" he asked, surprised.

"No point now. Let's talk about Mother."

"It's simple, I'm afraid. She won't go into a home, Gwenny."

"I hate you calling me that. And you're right. It *is* simple. She'll have to go into a home. She's not safe on her own."

"But she's not going. She's adamant."

"So you suggest that you and I should spend our whole lives going round to her house, picking up after her and cleaning and fetching and carrying . . ."

"No, I don't suggest that. I suggest that Millie and I go and live with her," Ken said.

"She won't accept that. You and Millie aren't married."

"I think she'll find it better than a home, which is the only alternative."

"It's not the *only* alternative. I'm in the picture too. I expect you think she'll leave you her house."

Ken shook his head. "No, I don't expect that or want that, but we will have to take in a tenant to help meet the costs."

"What costs? Won't you and Millie be living there rent-free?"

"We have to get the house adapted. Ramps for Mother, a bedroom downstairs, a bathroom adapted to what she can manage. And we have to pay something towards an extra carer. Millie and I will be out all day working."

"And where do I come in? I suppose you expect me to give up my weekends."

"No, Gwenny . . . I mean, Gwendoline . . . I don't expect that; neither does Mother."

"Oh, she does—wait until she's on the phone about it."

"Does she ever ring you, as things are?" Ken asked.

"No, but that's only because she's afraid that I'm going to mention the home to her."

Ken was silent.

"So, why are you here then, Ken, if it's all arranged?"

"Because I don't want to start making changes in Mother's house without letting you know."

"Or *your* house, as we will soon learn to call it." Gwendoline's mouth was a hard, thin line.

"Mother is making her will tomorrow; she is leaving the house on Chestnut Street to be divided equally between us, at my request. It was quite hard to persuade her, but I wouldn't agree to the arrangement otherwise. She said that you were cold, hard and unforgiving and mean of spirit. I said that you were just lonely, and eventually she agreed."

"She said all that about me?"

"Only because she gets frightened when you threaten her with an old people's home. That's how she sees it—a threat."

"But it's *not* a threat! It's for her own good," Gwendoline said.

"This might be for her better good."

Ken stood up to leave. There was no more to say. Gwendoline didn't offer him tea, coffee or wine. She was standing by her window looking over at the flat across the road. Carla was watering the window box again. Really, the woman was obsessive. Ken watched his sister.

"She's nice. She'd be a good friend for you, Gwenny."

"I don't *need* a friend. How dare you say I'm lonely—I most certainly am not."

"No," he said, and left.

Gwendoline watched him look up at her window but she made no sign that she saw him. She watched him wave up at Carla and the woman waved back with her little watering can.

The night felt very long to Gwendoline but she would not allow herself to brood about what her mother had said. It was true she and her mother did not get on well together, but then most mothers and daughters didn't. Mothers always preferred their sons. It was a known fact.

She wasn't hungry. That food would do another evening.

But when it came to bedtime she was wide-awake. They often said that a breath of air was good. She would walk around the block.

At the far end of the street, to her amazement, she saw Carla with a trowel and a paper bag digging at a big, neglected-looking flower tub.

"What on earth are you doing?" Gwendoline said, before she could stop herself.

Carla looked up and smiled a big broad smile. "Oh, hallo. You live opposite me. I've seen you going in and out."

"But this isn't your flower pot."

"No, I know—isn't it terrible? It's crying out for someone to look after it, poor old thing." She patted the pot affectionately.

"And why are *you* planting things in it?" Gwendoline was suspicious.

"Why not? I always put seeds in people's tubs or window boxes. It's a little hobby of mine. You'd be amazed how many of them flower. Some of them die, of course, but a good percentage come up. It's like magic looking at the street begin to bloom."

"But people mightn't *want* you to put flowers in their property," Gwendoline said. And even as she spoke she realized how ridiculous it sounded.

"Most people are pleased when they see the flowers, surprised but pleased," Carla said. Then she reached out and took Gwendoline by the arm.

"I've finished here. Why don't you come back and have a cup of coffee with me, Gwendoline?"

"How do you know my name?"

"Your brother told me. He was upset because you weren't home when he called. He was nervous about breaking the bad news to you."

"He talked to you about me? I don't believe it."

"Come back with me. We'll have a chat about everything. Old people can be so difficult, you know. Tell me about it—I work with them all the time. Your mother doesn't *hate* you—it's only from fear that she lashes out like this."

He had told her all their private business.

Gwendoline had a choice: she could have gone back to the flat with the window box and talked to this obviously well-meaning woman. Or she could go back home.

"Thank you—it's kind of you, but coffee would keep me awake," she said and left.

As she heard the sound of her own feet walking up the street Gwendoline wondered if there were flowers around every house, if these packets of seeds worked, would the property value improve? Would the street go up, after all?

FINN'S FUTURE

The whole problem was Finn's future.

Finn was only seven, so by anyone's standards he had a lot of future left. I had met the child only a few times because it seemed better to stay out of it all. But I talked about Finn a lot—boy, did I talk about him and his future—Dan could think of little else.

Dan and Molly had separated when Finn was three. Oh, I don't know what it was all about, really. Some fellow Molly had at work; she was a receptionist at a leisure center. Dan being away too much on business; he was a salesman. Molly wanting to be near her family and not near Dan's family.

Basically they just fell out of love. That was all. But it wasn't like going off someone when we were all young and single. There was Finn to consider, and his future. And unlike normal separated couples, Dan and Molly were quite unable to come to a satisfactory arrangement about the boy they both loved, even though they didn't love each other anymore.

Dan didn't want to be a Saturday father, taking his son to the zoo or for a hamburger and making awkward conversation. Molly didn't want her only child to go and sleep in a strange house with the Lord-knew-who-else who might be around, and no proper heating and maybe a bed that wasn't aired.

They discussed leaving Finn with his grandparents on either side for Dan to visit his son there. But that didn't work either. Molly's parents thought that Dan was worthless and the less contact that the beloved Finn had with him the better. Dan's parents thought that Molly was a tramp and that if Dan had any guts he would sue for full custody. So this was a nonstarter.

And then I met Dan, adding yet a new element to the problem. I had my own house on Chestnut Street. It wasn't in a fashionable part of town but at least it was a house with three little bedrooms and a garden. And we were getting married so it wouldn't be a house of ill fame or anything. And I had a job as a nurse in the local hospital so I wouldn't be a wild, irresponsible bit of fluff who would ignore Finn and let him die of malnutrition.

But Molly didn't like this at all. She was more adamant than ever that Finn didn't come and stay.

"We have to think of his future," she would say. "He doesn't want to grow up confused, not knowing where he lives, where he belongs."

And then Dan would say that he *was* thinking of Finn's future, and he didn't want the boy to think he had abandoned him, which he hadn't.

So do you wonder that I stayed as far out of it as I could? I used to fantasize sometimes that Molly would get a job as an exotic dancer on a cruise ship and she would leave Finn with us for three months and when she returned he would say he was so happy in our house that this is where he would stay.

And I got one of the rooms ready for him. Put in a little desk, where he could do his homework, and bought a dictionary for him and a book of facts, and an atlas. I even got nice, bright orange curtains and a duvet cover because I heard he liked bright colors.

But still Molly persisted: she didn't want Finn getting sucked into another life; his father was perfectly welcome to come and visit him in her home at weekends. And she added that any court in the land would say that she had been generous about this.

And poor Dan would come home from these visits glum and upset. Finn apparently would ask him at the end of each visit why did he have to go.

"*This* is your home, Daddy. Don't go," he would say and Dan would stumble and bluster and say it used to be but now he had his own place, and Molly would just shrug as if none of it were her doing.

So Dan and I got married, and my family, who loved him from the start, wondered would little Finn be coming to the ceremony. But apparently not.

Molly said that it would make Finn anxious about his future if he were to be part of anything like that.

And then, when he was seven, Finn started at a new school, which by chance was not too far from where we lived. So Dan tried again. Could he collect the boy a couple of days a week and bring him back to our house? He would give him milk and whatever Molly suggested. But all Molly said was that we would wait and see.

And this particular morning I looked at Danny's sad face across the breakfast table, a nice, round table looking out on the garden, where Finn would probably never play because it was going to be unsettling for his future. And I got a surge of rage against Molly. How dare she deny that child all the love and welcome that was waiting for him in this house? How *dare* she make Finn's father so wretched and inadequate about his lack of parenting since he was only dying to do it?

But I would not, under any circumstances, heap fuel on the fire by telling Dan that his ex was the most selfish woman to walk the earth. Nothing could be gained from that. I would smile and tell him that since I had a day off I would go shopping today and make him a steak-and-kidney pie. And his sad face brightened up and he said he was a lucky man.

But I was still a restless and annoyed woman. And as I set out to go to the shops I decided to go past Finn's school. The children would be in the playground about 10:30. I could just have a sneaky close-up look at this boy whose future was actually wrecking our present and our future as well.

I saw him immediately. He was practicing juggling with another boy. They managed to keep the little clubs in the air with great skill. Soon a small crowd had gathered around them.

Dan loved juggling too. Had he ever been able to teach this to his son or had the boy picked it up by himself? I would probably never know.

A few other people stood watching the children through the big fence. There was no access to the yard—you would have to go in through the school. How times had changed, I thought. Children have to be protected from strangers looking at them through the bars of a playground. Then I realized, of course, that I was the kind of person they would want to keep out. The second wife of the father of one of the pupils. Bound to be trouble there. Thank God nobody saw me here. It would look very suspicious. Then I glanced over at a woman who was looking at me intently.

It was Molly and she had recognized me.

I decided to speak immediately.

"Isn't your son a wonderful juggler," I said.

"Yes, that's just what he is. *My* son. Just so long as you remember this." She was small, blond and very angry with me.

I could have kicked myself for having come along here and even more so for being spotted. "Yes, of course he is. And you must be very proud of him."

"I am. Very. And you can be proud of *your* sons when you have them. Rather than coming down here, spying on my son." Molly's face looked peevish when she snapped like that, not pretty and doll-like as she looked when she smiled.

I don't know what made me say it. I never tell anyone.

"I won't be having any sons, or daughters. I can't have children," I said.

I hadn't even told my mother and my sisters, who all kept annoying me, wondering was there any news?

"I don't believe that for a moment," Molly said.

"Well, it's true. Sad, but very true." I shrugged.

"And what does Dan think?"

"He's sad too, but he knew this when we got married, and he already has one son whom he loves very much." I gestured with my head towards the playground.

"And whose life will not be turned around and whose future will not be destroyed just because you couldn't have children," Molly said.

"I know," I agreed.

"So what are you doing here?" Molly was still suspicious.

"I don't know," I said and maybe she saw from my face that I was telling the truth. "I really don't know, Molly, what I am doing here. It had something to do with Dan's face this morning."

"Did he send you? I *told* him he wasn't to come hanging about—I didn't think he'd ask *you* to come."

"No, no, he has no idea I'm here." Again I think she believed me.

The school bell rang and the children went inside. Molly and I looked on proudly as other boys were clapping Finn on the back over his juggling. He hadn't seen either of us.

"Well," I said, "I'd better be on my way. I have a day off."

"So have I," Molly volunteered. "What are you going to do now?"

"I'm going to buy some meat and make Dan a steak-and-kidney pie."

"Well, he lucked out with you then—I couldn't cook. Still can't."

"I'm not very good," I admitted. "I have to keep reading the recipe. But he lucked out with you much more—you had a son for him."

She stood and looked at me for a moment as if weighing up what she was going to say.

Then she said it.

"Why don't we go shopping together?" she suggested.

I didn't pause. Not for a second. "That would be great, and you could help me know what to get. The recipe is for four, so I suppose I'll just have to order half of everything." I knew I was beginning to burble but it didn't matter.

She had made a huge step. I had met her halfway.

Could I take another step or would that ruin it?

Oh, what the hell—I'd say it.

"Or maybe we could *keep* it as a recipe for four and you and Finn could come and eat it too. Like a sort of act of faith, if you know what I mean."

She paused. Maybe I had gone too far? I often do. Perhaps this woman was just sorry for me not being able to have children, which was why she had suggested going shopping. Bringing the much-loved child to the enemy's house was different. Maybe this might make her nervous of Dan and me. Maybe, on the other hand, this might make her feel less nervous. No fear now of Dan having further children, which might make him forget the first-born. I might never know what thoughts were going through her mind.

Then she said, "Everything we do is some kind of act of faith, isn't it? We'd be delighted to share the steak-and-kidney pie tonight."

And I didn't imagine it—the sun started to shine through the autumn trees and left lovely morning shadows all over the playground.

ONE NIGHT A YEAR

It's only one night of the year, but people do go on about it. Where are you seeing it in? Are you going to a New Year's party? There's as much pressure on you as if it were some kind of contest. People don't like you saying that you are doing nothing. It makes them feel guilty, as if they should invite you to whatever they are doing.

That's what they felt about Cissy in the staff room. Cissy had one hell of a year in 1997. During the summer vacation her husband, Frank, had run away with a trampish girl from fifth year. It had been the school scandal, all over the papers, and it had broken Cissy's heart. It was widely suspected but never confirmed that he had taken Cissy's life savings as well.

The other teachers knew that at least she was all right for Christmas. She was going to her sister's house—there would be children there, which would distract her. But New Year's Eve? They chewed their lips; maybe someone should ask her. It was the one night of the year you didn't want to be alone. Cissy saw it coming and told them she was having friends round.

Friends?

Cissy never talked about friends. But they didn't feel so guilty anymore.

So the night came and Cissy sat alone in her flat on Chestnut Street. It was just an ordinary night, she told herself over and over. But it wasn't. There had been five New Year's Eves with Frank.

On the first one he had proposed to her and the other four they had gone to the same noisy restaurant and told everyone it was the anniversary of their engagement. And now he was living in England with this jail-bait girl, Lola, who was considering a career in modeling and Frank was going to be her manager.

By ten o'clock, Cissy could bear it no longer. The remorseless cheer on television. The sounds of revelry coming from outside. It all seemed to mock her. She put on her coat and wooly scarf and went out. She went to Gianni's.

Martin had planned a New Year's Eve dinner with Geoff. He was going to cook a pheasant and had ordered it from the butcher. Geoff would be home from Christmas with his family. Geoff's parents still thought he might marry and give them a spring wedding and several grandchildren. They knew nothing of his happy life with Martin in the big city. They were old and set in their ways, Geoff said; no point in trying to make them understand something they never would.

That was fine for Christmas. Martin always helped out at a Christmas charity, and before he knew it Geoff would be back again, full of stories and plans. But this year Geoff had telephoned. His parents were giving a big New Year's party and he simply had to stay. At first Martin thought that he was being invited to join the party, and when it became clear that he was not, he fought hard to hide the bitterness and disappointment from his tone. He wished Geoff well at the party and warned him to steer clear of prospective brides.

Martin canceled the pheasant and stayed at home listening to music. And eventually he became so restless that he thought his head was going to burst. And around ten o'clock he went out. He didn't know where he was going, nor did he care. He couldn't spend one more moment in the home he had made for Geoff. And he walked for nearly an hour, hardly noticing his surroundings. He passed a chip shop called Gianni's; it didn't look very full. He had to eat somewhere, so he went in.

Josie and her sister Rosemary ran an organic vegetable shop. Well, Josie ran it; Rosemary dressed up and stood in the shop giving people recipes and talking about the celebrities who ate nothing but organic food. Rosemary was willowy and lithe and much admired. When anyone did interviews about the little store, which they often did, Rosemary was pictured at the door or beside the big juicing machine. Well, Josie didn't really look the part. Big, honorable Josie, in her cardigan, not the image you wanted for healthy living. Even if she did go to the market and visit the suppliers and even if she was the one who put in ten-hour days while Rosemary went to lunch and talked to the right people.

They lived in the same house. Rosemary had all of upstairs, two floors, and Josie had the basement, but tonight the whole house was needed because Rosemary was having a party. Her fellow was free because his ghastly wife had gone skiing with the awful children, so he and Rosemary would have a great New Year's bash. This had been signaled to Josie several times. It had not been said out straight but it had been very heavily implied that Josie should not be there for the party.

They would need the basement for the caterers and Josie didn't really like crowds of strangers, did she? Josie had never been so hurt in her entire life. She told her sister that she was going out to friends anyway and staying the night. Rosemary didn't ask what friends. It didn't occur to her that Josie, who worked all the hours God sent, might not *have* any friends. Josie booked herself into a bed-and-breakfast place on the other side of Dublin. She paid in advance but could not stay in the cold, forbidding room. Downstairs the landlady and her extended family were getting into the spirit of things. Josie put on her coat and went out. There had to be a better place to spend the last hours of the year. She saw a cheerful-looking fish-and-chip shop. It would do as well as anywhere else.

Louis was tired. Back in New York this would have been a normal day—he could have got his business done, find what he was looking for. But this crazy country seemed to have closed down for two whole weeks. It was no way to run an economy. He was here to do a job that should have been simple on the face of it, but every complication under the sun had turned up. His client would never understand these delays. Perhaps the place might return to some kind of normal working function in two days' time. He sure hoped so. He had rented a service apartment for himself for his time in Dublin. It was clean and efficient but without any soul. No way to come back to the city of his birth. But, anyway, coming back as a sort of hired gun, a spy, wasn't great either.

Louis went into the neat little kitchen. There was nothing to eat. He didn't fancy going to a big noisy place. On his way back here he had passed a fish-and-chip place. Maybe he could get a takeaway. It was only half a block away. Gianni's—that's what it was called.

Gianni's father asked how business was. Gianni lied, as always.

"Very good, Papa. Many, many people," he said.

"I don't think so, Gianni."

"Why do you not think so, Papa?"

The old man moved between chair and bed and never came downstairs anymore.

"Because if there were many, many people, you would have had your shoes mended, my son."

"We have enough business, Papa. We live, we live well."

"You can't be free, get married, have a life of your own!"

"I don't *want* to get married and have a life of my own. I like to live here with you."

"Well, go downstairs and serve all these customers, then."

"I will, Papa."

Gianni ran down to his café, which had been empty before, but now there were four people looking around in some confusion.

"I'm very sorry—I was up with my father. He's old and he fusses a bit. Now, who was first?"

None of them seemed in any hurry; they were polite people. Not like the drunks who often came in, but then it wasn't closing time yet.

"Well, then sit down, won't you, and I'll take your orders."

"Can you eat here?" the big woman with the funny knitted hat asked.

"Indeed, but perhaps it's not very festive for New Year's Eve?" Gianni looked around his drab little premises without much pleasure.

"I'm happy to eat here," said the woman with the knitted hat.

"Me too," said the well-dressed young man in the well-cut coat. Gianni would have loved a coat like that and some new shoes. Someday, perhaps.

"And I would like to sit down as well. Too much festivity out there." The woman in the dark coat with the scarlet scarf was attractive. She didn't look like someone who would be eating alone in a greasy-spoon place on New Year's Eve. Then neither did the rich American businessman. He was entirely too classy for this place.

But he had a license only for a takeaway. Not a proper restaurant, with people sitting down. The little table was just for people waiting to collect their packages from the fryer.

But Gianni didn't turn away good money. He ran around assembling tomato sauce and vinegar and paper napkins, and then got four plates from the back of the shop.

They had settled at the table as if they had always intended to have supper here.

"Please," Gianni warned. "Please, if other people come in and want to sit down, will you tell them you are my friends? There are some people who might want to come in here and not go home, if you understand?"

They looked as if they understood.

"So you just say you are friends of Gianni? Okay?"

They seemed to get that too.

As he went to fry the fish Gianni heard them introducing themselves to one another. They all actually seemed pleased to meet three strangers and sit down at the plastic-topped table. Weren't people extraordinary.

They had no small talk, the people at the table; they plunged straight into what they felt about the year that was just about to end in under two hours.

Martin said that he was lonely because his great friend Geoff had gone to his parents' instead of eating roast pheasant with Martin. He had been so looking forward to the evening, when they would make their plans for the next year.

"Well, at least he went to his parents'," Cissy said. "My husband ran away with one of my pupils. Now that's way worse than your scene."

Cissy stopped speaking, as if amazed at herself. Normally she froze anyone out who asked about the situation, and here she was, blurting it all out to complete strangers.

"That's very bad, certainly," Martin agreed. "At least Geoff is coming back the day after tomorrow. Would you take your husband back if he came and asked you?"

"I don't know. I really don't. I'd like to think not but you are never sure what you might do if the time was right."

They looked expectantly at the other two, waiting for something to be divulged.

Josie had taken off her knitted hat.

She spoke seriously.

"My sister and I run this vegetable shop, and we were there till seven o'clock tonight with last-minute shoppers. Well, I was there. My sister was at the hairdresser's. She's having a big party at our house tonight and my face won't fit—well, any of me won't fit. So I said I was going out with friends." She looked very sad.

Louis, the man with the American accent, patted her on the hand. "And in a way you *are* going out with friends. We are all having dinner with you."

If Louis had mentioned nothing about his own situation, the others didn't seem to notice it.

The cod and chips were served and Gianni was pleased to see them all brightening up. From time to time customers came in. Occasionally they looked at the little table of diners.

"I didn't know you were going upmarket, Gianni," one of them said.

"These are my friends," Gianni said proudly.

"*Ciao ciao,*" Louis said cheerfully, and they all said it. Gianni was so pleased he brought them all a plastic mug of vermouth each. It tasted like a horrific cough medicine but they all struggled with it.

"I could really do with a glass of decent wine now," Louis said. "But of course I have nothing in that apartment I rented."

Martin said that he had plenty of wine at his home but it was a long way away.

Josie said that she had no access to anything either.

They didn't want to break away from the comfortable intimacy of their little table but they couldn't face another glass of the medicinal vermouth.

Cissy said, "I only live round the corner, on Chestnut Street—come back to my place."

And that was how it all began.

Ten years ago tonight.

They all trooped up to Cissy's flat.

She got out the white wine and Christmas cake and they talked like old friends. They sorted out one another's problems. Martin should not try to force Geoff to come out if it would break the parents' hearts. If you loved someone you wanted their happiness. Cissy should start separation and get an immediate order against Frank for the savings that he stole. This was not the time for decency and rising above it. Cissy needed the money. She must go on a luxurious long holiday. They agreed that Josie must hire a business manager to assess the contribution of each sister. Louis unbent enough to tell them that he had fought with his family many years back and had gone to the U.S.A., where he had done well in one kind of thing after another. He worked hard, he made money, but it wasn't actually the life he had wanted. They suggested he get in touch with his Irish family. Louis said that Hell would have to freeze over before he would even consider doing that. Then it was midnight and they all raised a glass, and said it was a pity to have to go home.

When they said the word *home,* they each said it with varying degrees of scorn. For Martin, home was a house without Geoff; for Josie it was a cold bed-and-breakfast place; for Louis it was a service apartment without a soul. And if they all left, then Cissy would be left in a home that was no longer a home without Frank.

"Why don't you all stay here?" Cissy said.

She and Josie would share the bedroom, the men could sleep in the sitting room. It was all so much better than the places they had left. Nobody had to be asked twice. Next morning Cissy made everyone an omelet and the good mood of the night before was still there.

No addresses were exchanged. No plans were made, but they agreed that if chance were to bring them in this direction next New Year's Eve, they might resume the friends-of-Gianni role.

The new year had begun well for them. Something they had never expected.

A year went by and none of them had done what they had half agreed to do. Cissy had not started proceedings against her wandering husband.

Martin still hoped that Geoff would come out to his parents and take Martin home with him.

Josie had done nothing about the unfair workload between her and Rosemary. She now worked eleven hours a day.

Louis had finished his work in Dublin without contacting his family. He had gone back to the stress-filled job in New York.

New Year's Eve was approaching and, just like last year, Cissy assured her family and colleagues at work that she was going to be with friends; Josie told her sister that she was going out with friends and, as before, Rosemary showed no interest. This year it didn't matter because her fellow's wife wasn't going skiing so there would be no party. Martin wished he could have been more generous about Geoff going to yet another desperate attempt from his parents to marry him off. But he knew that he sounded resentful and sulky and that Geoff was growing away from him. Louis felt like he had missed out on something in life. He had told many people in New York that he was going to Dublin for New Year's Eve and, as far as he could see, nobody cared.

Louis was the first in the door of Gianni's. He had brought a couple of bottles of wine, which he handed over the counter.

"From the friends of Gianni," he said.

"Are the other people coming?" Gianni asked.

"I sincerely hope so, Gianni; otherwise you and I will have to drink these together."

The door opened and Josie came in; Cissy and Martin arrived minutes later. The year since they had last met had disappeared; it was like a family reunion. And this time, they had brought nightwear and clean clothes, and the men had brought extra rugs.

It was better than before, and this time they learned that Louis was some kind of investigative spy. He checked people out for big companies, made sure their CVs were accurate. He was good at his job but it was beginning to get to him the number of times he had exposed eager young people trying to get on. He had brought their dreams crashing down.

Josie said that Rosemary was now worse than ever, as her fellow was being kept on a much tighter leash than before.

They were disappointed that the others hadn't changed their lives as had been hoped, but they were all defensive about themselves.

This year they felt that they knew one another well enough to give their full names and addresses.

And so it went on, year after year. Including the year when Gianni had a black armband on because his father had died during the year. They had all cried with Gianni, even though they had never met the old man. Gianni said if only he could have his life over again he would have taken his papa back to Italy while he still had the strength to enjoy it.

And Frank had tried to come back but Cissy had said no way. Cissy was now the vice principal, and she was going on occasional outings with a new man. She wasn't forty yet, she had got courage from her New Year's Eve friends, she didn't think her life was over.

Josie had been afraid to face them all after ten years of promising to deal with Rosemary. So now she had actually done something. She had also moved out of her sister's house and left the whole building to her in exchange for running the vegetable shop solo. She had a little flat upstairs and a hardworking assistant.

She had joined a bridge club and next year she was going to lose eighteen pounds' weight.

Louis said he had been so touched by Gianni's devotion to his father that he had made contact with his family. They had all forgotten whatever the hard feelings were, and though he remembered, he thought it more politic to forget it all also.

They brought their overnight bags back to Cissy's place and saw in the New Year cheerfully. For the tenth time together.

"Imagine that we only see one another one night a year," Josie said.

She looked different these days, no more silly knitted hats and much more confidence in her manner.

"There's nothing in the rules to say we couldn't meet more often," Louis said.

Louis was going to be spending much more time in Ireland anyway and would welcome the congenial company of a friend of ten years' standing.

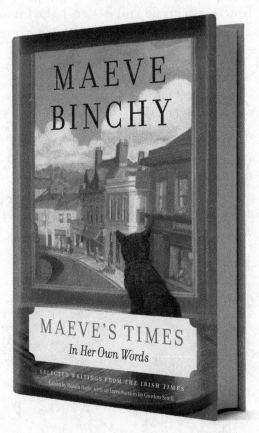